To Nancy

From Rod / Josh. 24:15

5/10/03

Comments about

BEAR HOLLOW

"Very good writing...impressive research, strong characterizations."
– *Hilary Hemingway, Director, Hemingway First Novel Contest*

"Bear Hollow makes terrific reading and it'll look great on the big screen – or even a lot of little ones."
– *Hy Cohen, Hy Cohen Literary Agency*

"Rod Cochran has created a rich, evocative novel here, with some wonderful hunting sequences that are really quite compelling."
– *Leslie Schnurr, Editor In Chief, Delacorte Press*

"There is some great writing in this novel and both the concept and execution are solid."
– *Paul D. McCarthy, Senior Editor, Simon & Schuster*

"Rod Cochran, into timber and writing, represents Pennsylvania well."
– *Napoleon St. Cyr, Small Pond Magazine*

"The story is certainly a dramatic one...Cochran gives us a sense of place."
– *Jonathan Galassi, Editor In Chief, Farrar, Staus & Giroux*

"I am very familiar with this area of the country, having grown up in western Pennsylvania, and I thought the geographical context of the book was excellent."
– *Harry Helm, Editor, Bantam/Doubleday/Dell*

"Bear Hollow does have some polish."
– *Joseph M. Fox, Senior Editor, Random House*

"I read the book with much interest."
— *Thomas Dunne, Publisher, Thomas Dunne Books,*
St. Martin's Press

"...a touching, old-fashioned sort of story."
— *Meaghan Dowling, Assistant Editor, Harper Collins*

Recognition for

BEAR HOLLOW

Finalist, Hemingway First Novel Contest

Winner, Willamette Writers Kay Snow Writing Award

Winner, West Branch Christian Writers Fiction Prize

Excerpt, "The Cherry Tree," published in the New England
Literary Journal *Small Pond*

Excerpt, "Farm Girls," published in the *Willamette Writer*

Bear Hollow

By

Rod Cochran

Copyright © 2003 by Vincent Rod Cochran

ISBN 0-7414-1457-0

Published by:

PUBLISHING.COM

519 West Lancaster Avenue
Haverford, PA 19041-1413
Info@buybooksontheweb.com
www.buybooksontheweb.com
Toll-free (877) BUY BOOK
Local Phone (610) 520-2500
Fax (610) 519-0261

Printed in the United States of America

Printed on Recycled Paper

Published April 2003

For Jean Cochran (1931-1998) and Ann Colliver (1926-1992), my mother and mother-in-law and my first fans. Mom and Annie, I miss you.

Choose this day whom you will serve.
But for me and my house,
We will serve the Lord.

Joshua, Son of Nun
Joshua 24:15

To accomplish great things
We must not only act but also dream,
Not only plan but also believe.

Anatole France

Neither a scrooge nor a patsy be.

C.L. Franke

The following contributed in some way to the development of Bear Hollow. My heartfelt thanks to Cindy Cochran, Katie Gehman, Jason Gehman, Matt Cochran, Bob Cochran, Dick Colliver, Chuck Peffer, Randy Morgan, Brian Edgcomb, Gary Cochran, Gary Parker, Chuck Broughton, Barney Custer, Wilma Johnson, Pat Young, Elizabeth Hollenbaugh, Holly Lawrenson, Beth Hurler, Brenda Baker, Paula Potter, Kasey Dunham, Harold Plank, Mike Wagner, Earl Bliss, Howard Fry, Rich Wilkinson, Kerry Gyekis, Mike Hale, Bob Cunningham, C.L. Franke, Dorothy Price, Francis Mitstifer, Bill Connolly, Ollie Litzelman, Luke Pierce, Mike Bollinger, C.J. Houghtaling, Mary Carter Ginn, Gayle Morrow, Michael Seidman, Hy Cohen, Napoleon St. Cyr, Hilary Hemingway, John Harnish and the Staff of Infinity Publishing.

Contents

Prologue – Jacob's Landing

Steam Valley, PA – February 1851

Jacob Miller watched the last log slide with an icy splash into swollen Blockhouse Creek. It bobbed in the swift current, its brand, a King's Arrow, showing clean against the mudcaked ends of the log. Soon the mud dissolved and the brand blended into the butter-yellow surface of the sawed end. But the brand was there, denoting its owner, hammered deep into the pine wood by a strong hand. Jacob Miller's hand. His log. His brand, registered with the Commonwealth of Pennsylvania, the stamp of the King's Arrow Timber Company. His company.

Jacob Miller was a timber-maker and log-driver with a reputation for only shipping the best. The King's Arrow stood for quality timber. Since the 1600's scouts for the King had explored the vast pine forests of the Northern Alleghenies, seeking spar timbers for the arrogant British Navy. Only the best trees were selected, those deeply notched with a King's Arrow. It was forbidden for anyone other than a representative of the King to cut one of those trees. American colonists, especially the rebellious Scotch-Irish, took a symbolic delight in falling one of the high and mighty. After the Revolution the colonists appropriated the King's trees and Jacob's grandfather appropriated the standard. The King's Arrow had served the Miller family well for three generations.

The log bumped against the groaning mass of seven thousand more logs that lay like a crust over a ten-acre manmade dam. This was a timber landing, Jacob's landing, purchased for the present and future use of Jacob's company. Three days before the crust that choked the dam had been snow-covered and quiet, supported by a placid iced-over pond. Then an unseasonable rain brought in by a warm south wind melted everything and the pond was growing uneasy.

i

It had been a dry summer, a rainy fall and a snowy winter. The ground was saturated. The thaw had unlocked the water which was now rushing off the mountainsides in a gathering fury. The Susquehanna and its tributaries would rage this spring.

It was time to break the dam and go with the flood.

Jacob Miller had not made the decision to float his timber to market, the early thaw had made it for him. This year's product, a million board feet of saw logs and a raft of two-dozen ships' spars, would be delivered two months early.

The saw logs would be driven south down Blockhouse, Little Pine, and Big Pine creeks, entering the West Branch of the Susquehanna at Jersey Shore. There the logs, along with thousands of other logs, would follow the river east to the huge timber cribs of the Susquehanna Boom Company at Williamsport. The seventy-five mile drive would take two weeks.

At the Boom the logs would be sorted by brand and diverted to the log pond of the sawmill contracted to buy them. Cochran-Wolverton had agreed to a premium price of seven dollars per thousand board feet of timber delivered to the mill. King's Arrow logs would bring seven thousand dollars this year.

But Jacob's trip didn't end at Williamsport. The timber raft would pass by the Boom and travel the length of the river, two hundred more miles, to the Chesapeake Bay, where it would be met and towed by steam tug to the Baltimore shipyards. There Jacob's squared timbers would be converted to masts and sold to the very particular owners of clipper ships who prized King's Arrow timbers above all others. For prime No.1 Susquehanna white pine not less than ninety-two feet long, the H.H. Harman Spar Company agreed to pay twenty-five cents per cubic foot. None of Jacob's timbers were under one hundred feet in length, several were more than one-fifty. There was eight thousand cubic feet in that raft and it would bring two thousand dollars.

Nine thousand dollars was a lot of money, but it wasn't enough, for Jacob Miller was broke. One half of his product and all of his profit still lay in the woods. Jacob Miller was stuck in the mud and would have to borrow money to pull himself out.

It had taken six thousand dollars to buy the land and outfit the ten-man crew for the eight-month job, three thousand of his own money and a three-thousand advance from Cochran-Wolverton. The men split a third of the gross and the mill got their advance back, which left him with his original three thousand. But that was how much he owed Hermann Longsdorf for the trees they cut. The agreement with the landowner required a payment of a dollar-fifty per thousand feet and they had cut two million. That final payment would just about wipe him out.

Louisa said her father would take his share for the logs delivered this year and wait for the balance to be paid after next year's drive. That was good news. It meant her father wanted another drive. It also gave Jacob fifteen hundred to work with. That, along with the three hundred he had left, and another advance from Cochran, would finance next year's operation.

That Hermann Longsdorf trusted him counted for something. The stiff former Mennonite trusted few and was especially suspicious of strangers. But Jacob had broken through his reserve and earned the landowner's respect and admiration.

The respect came from Jacob's honest dealings with him. Their timber contract specified a select cut of mature trees over two feet in diameter at waist height and limited clearcuts to slides and landings. As he did with every promise, Jacob adhered to the contract by the letter, for Jacob Miller was an honest man.

The admiration came when Jacob and his crew helped the community build the covered bridge over Blockhouse. The King's Arrow men simply showed up, unasked, with two ox carts laden with squared timbers and went to work. In one day they set the supports and deck and raised the timbered frame, with Jacob and his carpenter Orlando supervising. Jacob trimmed and matched the bridge timbers himself, for Jacob Miller was also a talented man. It was during the bridge raising that he met Louisa.

The bridge project endeared the King's Arrow men to the locals, and when Orlando was killed by the panther, the stern Protestants gave the loyal Papist a proper funeral.

That winter spent in the dark valley between Blackwolf and Bear had been brutal. Jacob would have to replace six oxen and four horses...and one man. Jacob felt fear and anger at once when he recalled the killing of Orlando. Around what was left of the body were the largest cat tracks he had ever seen. Seagreaves, a former shipwright who had sailed up the Amazon, said they were the size of a tigre.

Jacob had a plan. First he would eliminate the predators. Next he would remove the downed timber on Blackwolf. Then he would cut Bear.

He looked west. Over the top of Blackwolf rose the formidable top of Bear, partly hidden by Steam Valley's peculiar silver mist. Within that mist grew the grandest stand of Black Forest evergreens Jacob had ever seen. It served as a coverlet and a shroud, that mist, concealing both beauty and danger.

His thoughts were interrupted by Ike McFee, his woods foreman, who hailed him from the breastwork of the dam. His work done at the slide, Jacob slogged down the muddy bank to meet McFee.

The rugged Scot was dressed like Jacob; fur cap, red checkered wool shirt open at the neck with red woolen underwear showing underneath, and corduroy pants tucked into high-topped leather work shoes. Because of the mud at the landing Jacob had pulled knee-high rubber galoshes over his.

"Two men to see you, Jacob," said McFee, nodding toward the opposite bank. "They say they're the hunters you sent for." McFee didn't elaborate but his sharp eyes said *be careful.*

Anxious to get this business over with and be on his way, Jacob hurried across the logs. Preoccupied, he didn't hear McFee's warning to remove his boots.

A deep-rutted wagon road paralleled the east bank of Blockhouse above the landing. Two wagons were parked there, loaded with provisions, women, and children. The men met Jacob on the road just out of earshot of their families.

Immediately Jacob was on guard. The two were clad in greasy buckskins and wore black wide-brim hats. Heavy Bowie's slanted across their waists, encased in fringed sheaths. They were tall, a shaggy head taller than Jacob's stocky five-ten, and lean, like hungry wolves. The two were indistinguishable except for their knife handles, one was ivory, the other polished walnut. Neither offered to shake hands.

The one with the bone-handled knife spoke first. "We be the Poorbaugh's," he said, "down from Kinzua. I'm Saul. That's Jesse. Our families are yonder."

Jacob acknowledged the greeting and glanced over. There were four Indian women and at least a dozen restless children. Two of the women were obviously pregnant. He felt a twinge of revulsion which he suppressed. Prejudice was a dangerous attitude to display on the frontier. These were squawmen, starting a tribe of their own.

Jacob decided to establish some authority. "Where you been?" he challenged. "I advertised for hunters four months ago."

Saul's response put them on equal terms. This was a shrewd man. "Didn't hear about the fix you was in 'til early January," he said. "'Sides, we couldn't leave our wives in winter. It ain't fatherly."

Jesse grinned a lewd, knowing grin. Through his wiry, rust-tinted beard Jacob could see jagged tobacco-stained teeth. He hadn't spoken yet but he and his brother shared an unspoken language. Saul and Jesse were twins with the same pale, cold eyes.

Jacob evened his tone. "I'll need one of you to provide camp meat for the drive. The other can stay here and hunt for the family."

The pair went back toward the wagons and conferred in private.

For the moment Jacob had presented them with a domestic dilemma. They were working out who would get to stay a fortnight with the two unpregnant wives. Jacob observed ruefully that the one that got the warm blankets also had the most mouths to feed.

The twins returned. Saul said, "I'll go," then added, "You want me to kill Algierines?"

"No. Just chase them off," replied Jacob emphatically. Algierines, absurdly named after the pirates of Algiers, were log thieves who cut off the ends of the branded logs then sold them to dishonest drivers with registered brands who rebranded them. The willingness to kill a man for the theft of a log told Jacob a lot about Saul Poorbaugh.

"What's the pay?" asked Saul.

"One hundred a month for camp meat and a bonus for panthers and wolves."

"How much of a bonus?"

"Five dollars each."

Saul shook his head. "Ain't enough. We get eight dollars for each catamount, six a wolf, and five a bear. That's a bargain considerin' there's reports of some mean critters in these parts."

Saul was establishing his authority. By "we get" he meant the bounty hunters knew what they were doing. "Mean critters" was his signal they knew about the panther attacks on the livestock and Orlando.

Still, Jacob tried to bargain a little. "The bears haven't bothered," he said.

But Saul Poorbaugh was adamant. They had their standards too. "No matter," he said. "Price stays the same. And we keep the hides."

Jacob gave in. He didn't have time to dicker or send for other hunters. After they killed the predators he would send the Poorbaugh's away. "Done," he said firmly, adding, "But I get the scalps and ears."

"Where the varmints comin' from?" Jesse had finally spoke up. His voice was raspy and captivating, like the hiss of a copperhead.

Jacob pointed west to the highest mountain. It still lay in its steamy, silver mist. "Up there," he said. "Bear Mountain. They come from there and the big swamp behind it."

Jesse studied the mountain. Saul spoke again. "There's one thing more, Jacob Miller."

"What's that?"

"We get our pay a month in advance."

Jacob paused. The cash he had left was in his pack at the Longsdorf house. At first he considered sending them to Louisa for it, then changed his mind. He didn't want to subject her to men like these. "I'll bring it to you before the day's out," he said, then turned and left.

Jacob Miller was an ambitious man facing failure. He could accept that. What he couldn't accept was not trying. He believed he could accomplish anything with ingenuity, industry, and strength. Capital helped. But if that ran out he still had the other three. And for next year's effort he had something new to spur him on. Louisa. When he returned he would ask for her hand, finish the harvest of the Longsdorf lands, and build a mill. He would build it here, on the east bank of his landing. A King's Arrow would be stamped on the end of each board.

After two decades of wandering he had decided to settle down and raise another generation of timbermen. Jacob Miller was forty-one. Louisa Longsdorf was nineteen.

He slogged back across the crust of logs looking for McFee. The log carpet rolled underfoot. Contained too long by the jam, angry Blockhouse rattled its cage.

McFee and Seagreaves worked along the breastwork of the dam, trying to undo what they had done. The breastwork was a compressed tangle of logs; several stuck straight up, like totem poles. The timberjacks were prying with bars and pikes, seeking the key log that would unravel the jam. Getting closer, Jacob heard Seagreaves shout that he had found the key.

The main channel of the creek ran deep and hard here, exerting terrific force. Water spewed up between the logs in high spouts. Jacob leaned against one of the upright logs. It moved.

"Get those boots off, Jacob!" yelled McFee. Immediately after came Seagreaves' shout the key was loose.

Both warnings came too late for Jacob Miller as the logs underneath him were sucked into a violent whirlpool. The key had opened a hole in the bottom of the dam and the creek rushed to freedom through a log funnel. Jacob's boots filled and he went with it.

It was cold in that whirling maelstrom of logs and ice and deep water. For a few seconds he could see diffused light above him. That was up, the way out. But he was being pulled down, down, away from the light. Then it grew black as the following logs were pulled into the pool and blocked the light. Then there was no distinction between up and down. Then the realization there was no way out. In the blackness there came a crushing weight as the breastwork suddenly collapsed and squeezed toward the center, grinding him into the gravel of the streambed. There was a desperate minute of resistance and suffocation and pain before Jacob Miller succumbed to the force of the creek and his logs. Then there was the blankness following the loss of all earthly senses.

Then there was warmth and a beacon of light.

Chapter 1 – Steam Valley

Lycoming County, PA – August 1954

The sun was setting on the hot August day. The gliding shadow crossed over the rim of Bear Hollow, dipped down the steep side, then circled back. On the rim, dry leaves rustled under the snake as it worked its way to the warmest exposed rock on the ledge. The sluggish female, with a dozen squirming kin inside, was near term, and careless.

There was another rustle of leaves followed by a rush of wind with weight upon it. Vicelike grips squeezed behind the snake's head and around her belly. Pain coursed through her as talons pierced flesh and backbone. Then a final rustle of leaves as powerful wings beat the ground and the snake was taken aloft, writhing and buzzing an angry, futile protest.

The shadow continued its silent glide. Starting above the heavily timbered sag beyond the mountain rim and the dense laurel thicket surrounding it, the shadow passed the rim again, dipped down the steep, rocky side of Bear Hollow, then up the more gradual opposite slope to the top of Blackwolf Mountain. Going east across the mountain the shadow skimmed the treetops the length of Longstar Hollow to Blackwolf Swamp, then flanked the swamp to Jacob's Landing, the gravel bar formed at the junction of Packhorse Run and Blockhouse Creek.

The shadow had reached the bottom of the mountain, a journey of five miles in twice as many minutes, its passage only frequently breaking through the vast green canopy of trees to the ground below. From the Landing the shadow skirted the lower edge of the village of Buttonwood, meeting U.S. Rt. 15 at the Big Curve, then banked southeast directly over the road, into the middle of the valley of steam.

The shadow passed over the pickup as it rounded Big Curve. When it got to the straighter, safer stretch that cut through the forested valley the pickup slowed, its driver peering upward for a glimpse of the bird. The sun casts a long shadow at the end of the day. It took a while for the bird itself to appear.

When it did Tom Donachy was startled, and he was used to woods things.

It was low, so close to his open side window he could reach out and almost touch it. It was big, five feet at least from wingtip to wingtip. It was powerful, a struggling four-foot snake as thick as Tom's forearm was no hindrance. Instinctively, he drew his own arm inside. And the bird was determined – a great horned owl beating a steady course down the valley to his perch tree for supper.

Tom guessed where the big owl was headed – the huge dead chestnut that towered over the roadside parking area and water tank at Steam Valley Spring. The FFA boys had cleaned up that two-acres for the township before school started a year ago and Tom had noticed owl pellets under that tree. High and hollow, still sturdy after thirty years, the chestnut left a lingering impact, like the portrait of a dead president. Once a forest monarch, its bare gray branches still stuck way above the other treetops at the fringe of the parking area. To Tom, who reflected on such things, the tree was the sentinel of the valley. When the valley cooled and the fog rolled in, like steam, the last object covered was the great chestnut.

Below the chestnut, at the north end of the parking area, was the water trough called the Tank. Hip deep, skillfully built of laid-up stone, the remnant of an 1870's gristmill, the tank was fed by pipe from an artesian spring flowing out of the base of Laurel Mountain. The overflow created a small marsh of ferns, cattails, and swampgrass between the flat packed-dirt parking area and the woods. The marsh was a haven for wildlife. Rusty cans and buckets scattered around the tank littered an otherwise pretty spot. The Tank was a natural attraction – visited regularly by the highway travelers of the day and the hunters and scavengers of the night.

It wasn't night yet, just getting that way, so the owl was early. It had rained hard the night before, canceling the Grays-Pioneers ballgame in Williamsport for Tom and his

2

friends, and last night's meal for the owl. He hadn't eaten in forty-eight hours. He was hungry and went hunting early.

Tom followed the owl, fascinated by the grace and ease of its flight. By its thickness he figured the snake to be a rattler and wondered how the owl was going to control its live catch in that perch tree.

It wasn't.

As they neared the Tank, the owl suddenly soared higher and Tom lost it. His attention turned to an approaching car. Coming too fast, he mused, especially for going into the sun and Big Curve. Must be a stranger. Nice car, he noticed, as it drew closer. Late model, cream color, must be a... Just then the snake landed on the car hood with a heavy metallic crunch, split open and spread herself and her babies over the windshield and top of that hot, new, cream-colored car.

The driver, a woman, braked, pulled over and stopped near the tank. She screamed when she realized the commotion outside was a snake flopping on her windshield. Tom turned around, pulled alongside, and yelled at her to stay in the car. He got out, grabbed the broom kept in the back of his pickup, and removed the convulsing rattler, flinging it into the ferns. He swept the baby snakes that remained on the car to the ground, stomping on the their heads with the heels of his workshoes. He didn't get them all. He could see bloody trails in the parking area dust where the surviving babies wriggled frantically toward a life somewhere.

He didn't pay any more attention to them. The lady, she seemed young, had her face in her hands but had stopped screaming. Tom noticed she had pretty, strawberry-red hair. He dipped the broom in the tank, swept water over her car, a Ford Convertible, then wiped it off with the towel he used as a seat cover. He made a bad job of it. Tom worked for his brother in the woods, the towel was more dirt and oil than fabric, and left dirty streaks. But when he finished all evidence of the snake was gone, except for the dent in the hood.

"There," he said. "Good thing the top was up." The awkward attempt at conversation made her laugh. You never are very smart around girls, he scolded himself, throwing the wet towel into the box of the pickup. But the laughter calmed her down and she thanked him.

"My name's Tom," he said, trying again. She noticed him then for the first time; a tall, big-boned, homely boy with unruly black hair and mischief in his hazel eyes. An intelligent, sensitive youth who needed to shave every day.

"Mine is Abigail," she replied and reached through her open car window to shake his hand.

As his big calloused hand enveloped hers he noticed she was trembling. "You look a little peaked," he said. "You want to go back to the Turkey Ranch for a Coke? You just passed it."

"That would be nice," she answered. Then, pointing to the ferns where Tom had tossed the snake, she asked, "Do things like this happen often up here?"

The "up here" told Tom that Abigail was not used to the mountains. "This is a bit out of the ordinary Ma'am," he said. "But unexpected things do happen...up here."

"Oh," she said, and drove off toward the Turkey Ranch.

Tom threw the broom in the back of his pickup. As he did the shadow returned, passing over the parking area. Tom paused, located the owl, watched it light in the chestnut, settle, and look down.

"You're supposed to hit the road with that trick," he admonished, expecting the shy bird to fly at the sound of his voice. The owl just sat there, regal and magnificent, ignoring Tom, an insignificant peasant in his realm, waiting for the big pest to leave so he could eat his dinner.

Then there was a shot, a puff of feathers and a screech of woe, and the owl fell fluttering to the ground.

Out of the woods stalked the shooter; a stoop-shouldered, wary, malevolent man, carrying a twenty-two pistol and a canvas pack. From his pistol belt hung a sheathed bone-handled Bowie. Damn, Tom thought, Spike Poorbaugh!

The hunter clubbed the wounded owl to death with a stick. He then found every baby snake, tracking the live ones in the dust, and holding each one down with the stick,

4

sliced the rattler bud off the end of the baby's tail. He pocketed each bud and let the maimed snake go.

He wants it to live and grow a new tail, thought Tom with disgust. He has a meanness in him, Spike Poorbaugh.

The hunter turned to Tom. His gaze leveled with Tom's, the only man in the valley tall enough to do that. His eyes were a pale color, almost yellow, like a cat. "Where's the mother?" he asked. His voice was low, and raspy.

He knew where she was. The question was his way of making sure Tom wasn't claiming the snake for himself. Tom pointed to the ferns beyond the tank.

Spike Poorbaugh brought the dead snake out draped over his stick, spread it lengthwise on the ledge of the tank, severed and discarded its head, dipped the body in the clear water, then held it up. The bright yellow and black markings rippled and glistened in the lowering sunlight. "Nice skin," he said. "Bring a good price. These kind come from the Big Woods."

Big deal, thought Tom.

Poorbaugh gathered his harvest, stuffing the owl and snake together in his pack. "Been a good day," he said. "'Sides the skins, another eighteen dollars from the Governor."

Tom agreed it had been a good day, got in his pickup and left.

Spike was talking about the bounty paid on certain undesirable predators in 1954 – one dollar for a rattlesnake and five dollars for a horned owl. But it wasn't the state of Pennsylvania that paid the bounty, it was the county. Spike was illiterate and wouldn't know that.

As Tom drove toward the Turkey Ranch, twilight now, the sun finally setting behind Bear Mountain ten miles back, it seemed an injustice to him that of the three predators meeting at the spring, the one that didn't have a bounty on it was the one that required it the most...the man.

Chapter 2 – The Turkey Ranch

The Saturday evening crowd and smoke had cleared by the time Tom entered the Turkey Ranch. He found Abigail in one of the booths along the restaurant's row of front windows. Her head was down. She had found out that she wasn't so brave when she got out of her car. She was pale and unsteady as she tried to erase the image of the flopping, birthing, dying snake from her mind.

Tom went behind the counter, drew a large Coke from the fountain, added ice and a straw and brought it to Abigail. On the way he got the attention of a waitress and nodded for her to follow.

"Something wrong, Tom?" she asked.

"Horned owl just dropped a snake on her car."

"Oh dear."

She sat down beside Abigail, who felt a reassuring presence. "Tom, why don't you clean up? I'll sit with her for a while."

"Okay," said Tom. As he left he yelled back, "Her name's Abigail," not caring that he had also told everyone else in the restaurant the upset girl's name. The waitress smiled knowingly.

"I think Tom's taken me under his wing," said Abigail, weakly. She took a sip of her drink and looked up. She saw a taller girl with large brown eyes and a beautiful smile.

"He does that," replied Julie Spencer, and the two young women appraised each other for the first time.

Julie Spencer saw a trim, attractive, blue-eyed young woman with red hair, wearing the right clothes and perfume.

Abigail Whalen saw a slender, full-bosomed girl with a tawny ponytail, in a waitress outfit, smelling of onions and french fries.

Both women noticed that neither wore a ring.

Tom returned and sat across from the women, his gangly six-foot-six frame taking up most of his side of the booth. He brought his own Coke with him. "I used to work here," he explained. Then, in his direct way, he made sure they all knew each other.

"How far is it to Fallbrook?" asked Abigail, feeling better. "The Sheafer's were expecting me around eight but I got a late start."

"About ten miles," said Tom. "Are you the new teacher? Fred said they had rented their apartment."

"Fifth grade," replied Abigail, taking another sip of her Coke. Turning to Julie she asked, "Can I use your phone?"

"You sit," said Julie, rising. "I'll call them for you. Tom, you want some supper? The blueberry pie is fresh today. What about your brother?"

"I'll take the turkey special and two pieces of the pie, Julie. Mac should be along soon. I had to deliver a load of firewood for Evie. Mac was still cutting when I left."

"You men will die of overwork," said Julie. "You both were in here for breakfast at five."

"Sunup to sundown and some on both ends," countered Tom, observing wryly to himself that Julie had worked the same hours.

Abigail felt a little guilty. She hadn't gotten up until eight-thirty. She had spent a leisurely morning packing and visiting with her mother, not leaving Harrisburg until mid-afternoon. Her schedule would change soon, she knew.

"Abigail, your color is back. Do you feel like eating something now?" Julie's tone was comforting and friendly.

"No thanks," replied Abigail. "I'll just nurse this Coke."

As Julie headed for the kitchen a truck turned noisily into the parking lot, its headlights scanning the dining room before going out.

"There's Mac," said Tom.

Julie looked back before entering the kitchen.

The door opened, the bell attached to the door frame announced the presence of another customer, and the man walked in. Abigail was attentive, curious to see this Mac they were talking about.

She was surprised. He stood in the doorway a moment, looking for Tom who wasn't at his usual place at the counter.

Abigail could feel his presence. The kind of man that receives attention even when he doesn't want it. In college the girls would call him an "interesting" man; the kind you tell your roommate, but not your mother, about.

He was almost as tall as Tom, without his brother's youthful rough edges, wearing similar clothing, army-green T-shirt and blue jeans, stained with the sweat and grime of that day's work. His shoulders were unusually heavy and broad, his arms and back corded with muscle. He's built like an Olympic athlete, thought Abigail.

He spied them, strode over and stood before the booth looking down and smiling mildly at Tom and Abigail. Abigail just looked.

He had thick wavy black hair, a day's growth of blue-black beard, and deep, deep green eyes. "I can see why you didn't sit at the counter, Tom," he said. His voice was low and gentle as he appraised Abigail.

She squirmed in her seat.

"This is Abigail Whalen, Mac."

"Jonathan MacEwen," returned Mac formally and sat down beside Tom. There wasn't any room left in the booth. Abigail thought he might be more comfortable sitting beside her.

"We call him Mac," said Tom, obviously proud of his older brother.

Mac gave Tom a questioning look. His brother didn't usually attract pretty girls. Tom described the events of the past hour. Mac listened attentively, saying nothing, frowning when Spike Poorbaugh was mentioned.

Abigail remained quiet, a hard thing for her to do. She noticed the firm set of Mac's jaw, the heavy beard, the slight cleft in the chin, and specks of gray in the black hair. There was a streak of white grown over a scar above his right ear. This man is older than he looks, she thought.

Julie came over with Tom's order and a cup of coffee for Mac. She spoke first to Abigail. "I called the Sheafer's for you. They're waiting up."

I'm in no hurry, thought Abigail.

8

"What can I get you, Mac?"

"Just a cold beef sandwich and another cup of coffee to go, Julie. I'm in a hurry."

You're always in a hurry, Mac," she scolded. She ran her forefinger through the hair curling at the back of his thick, tanned neck.

That's cheeky, thought Abigail.

Julie continued: "You two better get to a barber. They won't let Tom back in school with hair like that." Her point made, Julie left to get Mac's coffee and sandwich.

Mac watched her go and Abigail watched Mac watch her go. She noted ruefully that Julie really did have a stunning figure.

He turned to Tom. "I broke the chain on the big McCulloch. I've got to get to Frank's before he closes. No hardware stores are open on Sunday."

"So, we're working tomorrow?" returned Tom, obviously hoping they weren't.

"There's work for those that want it," said Mac, his intent clear.

But Tom was persistent. "I thought Abigail might want to be shown around. She's new here and only has a week to get ready for school."

Abigail, seeing Mac's hesitation, interrupted. "That's sweet of you, Tom," she said. "But I really wouldn't want to interfere with your work."

Tom's gaze was a direct appeal to his brother. The big, upfront, sometimes awkward boy made friends easily. Mac could tell Tom liked the attractive teacher and knew he had earned some time off, but time was also the resource that Mac was most reluctant to waste, particularly now. Yet his answer was typical of the quality that endeared his brother and his men to him the most. He thought of them.

"I have been pushing all of you pretty hard," he said. "Especially you, Tom. I'm going to lose you when school starts and you will be hard to replace. Knock off tomorrow at noon."

Tom beamed at the compliment and the prospects of an afternoon off.

Julie returned with Mac's sandwich and coffee. Mac rose and thanked her, adding, "Put everything on my slip will you Julie?"

On impulse Abigail touched his wrist. "Why don't you take the evening off and come along too?"

Julie stiffened at the invitation.

Mac, caught off guard and unaware of Julie's reaction, smiled an I-surrender smile and answered, "We'll pick you up at six."

Abigail, feeling much better, smiled sweetly and said, "Fine."

Julie walked quietly back to the kitchen.

The doorbell jingled as Mac went out the front door.

"What do you and your brother do, Tom?" asked Abigail.

"We're loggers," was the reply.

"Oh," said Abigail. She winced and bit her lip at the way it came out. Several images, all negative, had combined to create an involuntary and insensitive reply. Through her mind swept the scene of two wool-shirted lumberjacks bumping chests, spilling beer on each other. Only two letters and one second long, it was still too late to hide her disappointment.

Tom heard the "oh" and hung his head. He had caught the meaning. All at once he was embarrassed, resentful, and didn't know how to continue the conversation, so he pretended to enjoy his supper.

Abigail was uncomfortable too. A bias had surfaced which offended this boy. Her teacher instincts told her he was confused right now and was shutting her out. It was time to go. She finished her Coke, patted his right hand to get his attention, noticing at the same time that he ate with his left.

He looked at her. The exuberance displayed during the past hour was gone, replaced by a hard watchfulness. Tom's first impression had changed. She gave him an affirmative smile. "I'll see you tomorrow," she said, hoping it didn't sound like a question.

"At six," he said.

Chapter 3 – Half Brothers

The tires of the sturdy one-ton slapped the cracks in the pavement as Mac drove north on 15 to Fallbrook.

Saturday night in Steam Valley. He should be taking Julie to the late show at the Rialto. Tom should be with Squeaky and Joe, at the same movie maybe, or at a ball game, or cruising the town looking for girls. They should stay out late, sleep late, eat a late breakfast, and go to late church. Instead, they were working late.

He hadn't asked Julie out yet and he had been home since June. The transformation to civilian life had been harder this time. Flashing black and white images of battle in Korea still plagued him, resurrecting memories of older battles in France and Germany. Tom's father had died in Germany, in the Battle of the Bulge. His stepson hadn't been far away.

There were the damnedest ironies in war. The young infantry officer fighting at the front escapes without a scratch. The middle-aged sergeant with the support troops at the rear runs over a mine.

Mac had been fond of his stepdad. His own father had died in a train wreck in 1932. Mac was ten. His family loved hard and it was said his mother would never get over Terrance MacEwen. She never did. Then the pretty seamstress met Michael Donachy, it was the middle of the Depression, and a family needed a man.

Big Mike was not the dashing Black-Irish train engineer Terrance MacEwen had been, but he was a steady man with a wry sense of humor. A skilled mechanic, he always had work. Betty and her son grew to love him.

In 1937 Tom was born and it was his father who first noticed the streak of pixie in him, saying the boy was born with a light heart. The Donachy household bustled after the arrival of Tom.

When World War II came the two men were sent overseas. The older didn't come back, the younger rarely did.

Delia Connolly's Dear Mac letter received just before D-Day had a lot to do with that.

The breakup with Delia set a reckless fire under Mac. He earned a battlefield commission, leading dangerous paratrooper and commando raids behind enemy lines. The end of the war found him a captain, one of the Army's most decorated soldiers.

He stayed in the service after the war, assigned as a foreign advisor training commando and special force units. Tiring of that, he wrangled a transfer to the Army Corps of Engineers, working on Forest Service and dam projects out West, in the process earning two degrees under the GI Bill. Then Korea heated up, bringing the career soldiers back to the front.

In the midst of the Korean conflict their mother died suddenly of a stroke. He had suffered a bad head wound and was recuperating slowly in a military hospital in Japan. Tom, a tall, gangly teenager, fended for himself. By the time Mac returned to assume the role of big brother and parent Tom had acquired a streak of independence impossible for the older brother to overcome. He regained some control over the headstrong boy but kept the reins loose. Having lost his mother and two fathers, he wasn't about to lose his brother.

From Mac's viewpoint as a soldier it appeared that Tom had unwittingly seized control of the community. He was like the friendly stray no one could resist feeding. He didn't play up the orphan bit though. Tom worked hard, giving more than a day's work for a day's pay. He paid his bills and saved and bought his own truck and supported himself, all the while staying at the top of his class and being Fallbrook High's most dependable athlete. He had inherited Big Mike's steadiness, but the streak of pixie was still there, even after the loss of his parents, and surfaced on a regular basis. Tom Donachy was one of Steam Valley's main sources of action drama.

Normally gentle, the rugged boy had unbelievable strength when riled. The locals were still talking about the

13

flap that occurred when some county do-gooders decided Tom belonged in their orphanage. The sheriff sent two impatient deputies to escort him there. They got rough with Tom, who sent both to the doctor and spent a night in jail until Squire Hayes bailed him out.

The law had penned the wrong stray. Indignant locals, led by a stalwart Aunt K and the influential Republican Ladies' Auxiliary, raised a fuss. The elected officials made sure the county bureaucrats forgot about Tom.

Now he was a high school senior. The boy whose spirit spiced up the life of the town would only be here another year. He was almost, but not quite, a man. College or the service beckoned. His older friends viewed this last year with sadness and anticipation. A personality like Tom only showed up every generation of so. In his own amiable, roguish way Tom blundered into people's hearts and stayed there. In a few short years he had made himself as well-known and popular as Bud Cole.

Bud Cole. The kingpin. Fallbrook's number one citizen. Delia's husband.

Fallbrook was a company town. Bud Cole owned the company. Bud Cole owned the town, or thought he did. For half a century Cole Industries had viewed itself as an enlightened monarchy. It was more like a benevolent dictatorship with Bud Cole developing this dichotomy differently than his father and grandfather. The nature he displayed was benevolence. The nature he repressed was that of a dictator. Occasionally the blacker, truer nature came out.

Mac wondered how Bud would react when he heard the news. His bid for the Longsdorf land had exceeded the Company's by five thousand dollars. More than anything Bud Cole hated to lose.

It was obvious Bud Cole had not expected competition when Squire Hayes auctioned off Louisa Longsdorf's estate. He didn't attend the bid opening, sending the company treasurer instead. The treasurer expressed his boss's regrets, explaining that he had flown to New Jersey to return Delia and Amanda from their cottage at the shore. Mac noticed the mention of Delia's name didn't wrench at him like it used to.

When the bids were opened the treasurer appeared shocked. He demanded a look at Mac's ten percent security deposit. Instead, Squire Hayes showed him Mac's cashier's check for the full amount of his bid. At this Jonas Pemberton slumped in his chair, mumbling that he had told Cole not to go low with his bid. Two other businessmen, dairy farmer Harry Raker and junkman Mort Fessler, both with property adjoining the Longsdorf's, had bid almost as much as Bud Cole. The bids indicated the company's dominance was being tested. Other economic forces were showing some muscle.

In Mac's case his muscle was borrowed money. Harry's and Mort's was not.

Already busy tongues were wagging. Harry Raker was on a party line and gave his wife the results from the phone near the loafer's bench at Sawyer's Hardware. That was Thursday morning. By nightfall every beauty shop, diner, and garage in Steam Valley knew that MacEwen had beat out Bud Cole.

Two of his logging crew had bet on how long it would take for the news to get out. Luke Ballard, the crew's sawyer, said twenty-four hours. Charley Bower, their crusty teamster, said twelve. Charley won. Gossip, said Charley, pocketing Luke's two dollars, bounced like an echo, only faster.

The rumor mill had a field day. What would those two want with four thousand acres of rock and quicksand? Mort and Harry were neighbor to the Longsdorf property, they had a reason for buying it. But Mac and Bud Cole? Did they know something the rest of them didn't? What was it if they did? What will Delia think? Did she still carry a torch for Mac? What will Bud Cole do? Cole and MacEwen never did like each other. Wasn't Mac involved with that vixen Julie? Betty Donachy must be turning over in her grave! And where did Mac get fifty thousand dollars anyway?

Mac wanted it for what was on top of the rock and quicksand. He suspected Bud Cole wanted it for what was underneath. Cole Industries had bought a worn-out strip mine on Bloss Mountain a year ago. It was a bad buy. The local tycoon was looking for a cheap source of fuel for his tannery and milk plant, as well as shipping to other coal-burning factories that were building up in New York and Pennsylvania. He sat right in the middle, in a vast undeveloped area rich in natural resources. He was an ambitious man, Bud Cole.

Mac wanted the trees. Behind the forbidding countenance of the slopes that fronted Steam Valley – a junkyard, a cliff, an overgrown farm, a swamp – lay a land of rugged beauty, growing the finest hardwood timber he had ever seen.

The locals assumed the Longsdorf woodland was cutover acreage from the 1880's when the timber barons scalped the mountains, but a one-day examination of the estate's records and three-day backpack revealed otherwise.

Louisa Longsdorf had been a meticulous bookkeeper and diarist and had carefully preserved everything written in Jacob Miller's hand. The timber-maker's journal detailed a select cut on Blackwolf, which meant he left most of the trees. There were no results posted from the more remote Bear. Louisa Longsdorf never married, never sold another tree.

On a map the Longsdorf land lay in two counties, Lycoming and Tioga. It ran northwest, on paper a neat, flat rectangle scaling out to two miles wide and three miles long. The height and varied contour of the two mountains easily doubled that. Mac only had time to hike the perimeter and cruise the timber on the flanks of Blackwolf before the bids were due. Even so, his cruise estimate was astounding. The tally on that mountain alone was worth twice the minimum bid of forty thousand set by Squire Hayes for the entire property.

The locals were unaware of the timber on Blackwolf and Bear because none of them went there. *Ever.* In fact, they purposely avoided the area. The reasons were simple. The going was hard, and the mountains were the domain of the Poorbaugh's. Mac would be the first to challenge the Poorbaugh's.

The lane to the farmhouse and buildings, gated and locked since Louisa Longsdorf's death twenty-five years earlier, dead-ended below Three Oak's Spring. The spring burst out of the base of a high cliff called Caleb's Rock and ran through thornapple-choked bottomland to Blockhouse Creek.

Caleb Skinner had been the first white settler in Steam Valley. The township history said he sold his four 1,000-acre warrants to Brenner Longsdorf in 1807 and went west looking for an easier place to live. He left behind a bark shanty, a hand-dug well, and a provision in the deed – no one was ever to harm the three giant white oaks that grew over the spring.

Skinner himself was part of an Indian legend about the spring. He was friendly with the Seneca's who sent hunting parties yearly to Steam Valley and camped under the three oaks. One bright fall day in 1799 he was visited by a party whose leader, a chief, had brought his son along on his first hunt. Skinner sent the boy to the top of his "rock" to gather honey from a bee tree near the edge. Something happened up there and the boy fell. The grief-stricken chief buried his son under the triangle of trees and cut one notch in each oak. Every year when the leaves changed the chief returned, henceforth hunting his son's killer, and left after cutting another notch in the trees. After eight notches Caleb Skinner left, protecting the oaks forever with his deed. The notches stopped at sixteen. After that Brenner Longsdorf, a practical Pennsylvania Dutchman if there ever was one, claimed to hear a sound like a voice from Caleb's Rock on windy fall nights. It was the wind, he said. It bounced funny off those high rocks. It was the son, the legend said, calling for his father. After notch sixteen it called for another avenger.

The cliff made up most of Blackwolf's east slope and circled north, shouldering into Potash mountain high above Mort Fessler's junkyard. The south slopes of Blackwolf and Bear and the west slope of Bear were flanked by the adjoining wetlands of Blackwolf Swamp and Great Marsh. Draft teams, tractors, bulldozers and their drivers had sunk out of sight in Blackwolf. The more distant Great Marsh remained a greater mystery. And beyond the wetlands were more thousands of acres; cutover wilderness that timber companies let revert to the State for back taxes in the 1920's.

The only vehicular access was a deep-rutted wagon road up Longstar Hollow, the pass between Blackwolf, Bear, and Potash mountains. Longstar was the English translation of Longsdorf, many German place names being changed after World War One. This trail passed by the Poorbaugh homestead on the backside of Potash and ended at Great Marsh. Jacob Miller had built it, widening an Indian path for his oxcarts.

The Poorbaugh homestead was not on Longsdorf land. It was just over the line. Nor was it owned by the clan. They were squatters on land now owned by Mort Fessler. In spite of holding no title Spike Poorbaugh acted like he owned it, claiming an inheritance from Saul and Jesse. He did not welcome visitors.

Louisa Longsdorf alluded to fear of the family in her diary. They "shiver me" she wrote. A century later a Poorbaugh was still shivering people.

Jacob Miller's journal referred to a southern fork in the oxcart trail leading to a ponded basin between Blackwolf and Bear called the Bear Wallow. Here he had built a log camp and was attacked by predators. The journal made vague references to points on Bear Mountain named the Panther Patch and Bear Hollow but specific detail describing the westernmost mountain was missing.

Mac yearned to explore this area but resisted the impulse. His immediate concern was to get the accessible timber on Blackwolf to market and pay off the bank loan.

The fifty thousand came from Merchant's and Farmer's Bank in Fallbrook. The volume estimate from Mac's cruise, Fred Sheafer's guarantee of a steady market, Squire Hayes' personal recommendation, and the army officer's reputation influenced the new bank manager to recommend the loan. Of course, the amount was over his authority and the timetable was sort, he would have to take it before the directors for approval. The Bank Board accepted Steve Heffner's recommendation without question; it was great to have the celebrated soldier back home for good.

It also helped that Fred and The Squire sat on the board. Bud Cole did too, but he had gone to the beach and wouldn't be back until Sunday.

The loan terms were strict. The principal was due in six months, the rate was seven percent, and interest payments were required monthly. Fred Sheafer had objected to the shortness of the term, advising Mac after the board meeting to make it a year. Damp weather blotches the ink on timber deals, he said. Heffner readily agreed to this change, saying he would add a six-month extension clause. Mac accepted his word on that.

The note could be paid off in six months, with any luck at all he could do it in five. The timber resources were there. He had a good crew. If managed properly the timber would pay off any debt and provide the brothers with a good living for years to come. If he got in a bind he could extend the note further or sell the valley farm. Mort and Harry had expressed their interest in that by bidding.

Mac viewed his projects from a military perspective. This timber job was very much like a mission. There was an objective and there was risk. He was trained to simplify his objective, to minimize his risk. But there was always risk. Life was risk.

His objective was to cut two million board feet of timber, skid it out of the woods, and haul it across the steel bridge at Buttonwood and down Blockhouse Creek Road to Sheafer's Mill six miles away. Defining the risk was simpler–achieve his objective in less then twelve months or lose all. Minimizing the risk was simpler still – work every daylight hour. Mac had never missed achieving an objective.

Mac put up all they owned as security for the loan; the Longsdorf property, his vehicles and equipment, the Donachy house and repair garage. The deed to the Longsdorf land was written in the name of both brothers as tenants in common but the loan was only in MacEwen's. He owned all the liability and one-half of the asset. When reminded of this by Squire Hayes, who noted that Tom was a minor and only a half-brother, Mac held firm. That's right he said, we're half-brothers. That means half of all that's mine is his. Tom was there and said he felt the same way. That's how assets were shared between the brothers MacEwen and Donachy.

It took all his service savings to buy the one-ton Willys he used as an equipment vehicle, the modified Army six-by-six truck to haul his logs, and the Caterpillar dozer for skidding and building his roads and landings. The five-thousand-dollar advance Fred paid to bind their timber contract would serve as working capital until the money for the delivered logs started coming in.

On Friday he and his crew had cleared a two-acre landing in the woods above Blockhouse. By late Saturday ten thousand board feet of logs was piled on the landing. It was a good start. Without any breakdowns he could load and deliver two shipments to the mill by himself tomorrow. It was a plus the mill was so close.

Fred and Aunt K would frown on his missing church, especially while delivering logs to their mill. Fred would be more understanding than the strong-minded Aunt K. Right now that loan controlled his destiny. He could go back to church in six months She had a forgiving nature, Aunt K.

He scowled at the timing. He could deliver three loads if Tom hadn't roped him into a date with the new teacher. Then he recalled that she was the one who invited him. She *was* pretty, and already more forward than Julie. With Tom along Julie wouldn't get the wrong idea. At this point he wasn't sure Julie cared.

He couldn't seem to get anywhere with her. She motherhenned them when they were all together, especially Tom. Alone with Mac she was friendly, but cautious. Julie's was a wholesome, soft, distant beauty. There was an attraction, a chemistry, they both felt. Both were confused by it. Yet neither would commit to the other. Each had committed once before and been hurt. Too cautious, they built up a barricade of reserve which seemed to grow higher instead of wearing down.

The one-ton's tires changed their tune, droning steady on the smoother pavement recently laid just south of town. It was after closing, the stores, with the exception of their window displays, were dark. The one store still open was Frank's.

They both worked too hard. Julie supported her mother, teenage sister, and five-year-old-son. Julie never married, never dated after Danny was born, and never revealed the name of the boy's father. Her motherhood bothered Mac and contributed to his reserve, yet in another way it made him want her more. She was a mysterious woman, Julie Spencer.

Chapter 4 – Farm Girls

Harry Raker didn't like it. The only time he had ever seen more skin was during the hootchy-kootch show at the Bloomsburg Fair. That show had cost him five dollars.

A thrifty man, Harry had sneaked in through the tent's open side flap when a little carney kid spotted him. This kid would either be in prison or president some day. He said he'd yell like hell if Harry didn't fork over five dollars. Harry looked around, saw several faces he knew, thanked God they were all looking stageward, and forked over the five dollars. He was supposed to be at the tractor exhibit but he didn't need a new tractor. If he had paid at the gate he would only be out a dollar. A forgiving, sometimes forgetful man, Harry had the recall of an elephant when it came to wasting money.

So here he was, on his open front porch, checking his Sunday paper for the deed transfers, getting treated to a skin show for free. His wife Becky sat calmly beside him, snapping green beans. Their only child, Carol, lay sunbathing on a blanket in their front yard. Why didn't she go out back? He wished she'd put more on. *It* wasn't decent.

It was called a bikini. Carol had bought a black one with her egg money. Ever since she had seen that dark-haired actress Joan Collins model the "petite" two-piece in New Star magazine, Carol had wanted one. Carol had dark hair too and was what the other ruddy-faced farmers termed a "right pert" eighteen, meaning she was perty in the right places.

Those places were barely covered right now. Harry was uncomfortable about it and said so. What if someone drove by and saw her?

Becky, the practical farmwife whose own pert had blossomed into plump over their twenty-five years of marriage, wasn't concerned. Their's was a back country road, they lived in the middle of seven hundred acres that they owned and was all paid for, and their nearest neighbor was more than a mile away. Read your paper Harry and don't fuss. Had Squire Hayes transferred the Longsdorf deed yet?

No, he hadn't. Probably tied up in court on Friday. Mac moved in though. Saw him cross the steel bridge with his equipment from our field behind the schoolhouse. I'm going to pasture some young stock over there. Think Bud Cole will quit taking our milk for bidding against him?

Becky didn't think he would. If he did shut them out, so what? They made a good product, someone else would buy it. She was tired of him riding herd on everybody. If Louisa Longsdorf hadn't staked his grandfather he'd be nothing.

Harry looked down the road. Good, no dust. No company. That hardpan dried out fast after a rain. In cold weather it sure didn't. It had been a wet year so far. He had gotten three cuttings of hay and every barn he owned or could rent was filled. He could have used the Longsdorf place, hopefully Mac would entertain an offer later. There was money to be made this year. Still, if this wet keeps up, he may not be able to get on his fields next spring.

Harry looked down at Carol. She lay on her stomach, napping, or pretending to. She was shrewd, like Becky. She knew a lot more than she let on. Except for the white edges revealed by the scant two-piece, her body was deeply tanned. She helped Harry with the fieldwork, on hot days wearing a tied-up cotton shirt and cutoff jeans, but that was different.

He noticed a slight flicker of movement in the small of her back. A sweat bee languished in the delicate silken hairs that fanned out above the bikini bottom's elastic band. In the midst of all that tanning oil and beaded perspiration that little fellow probably thinks he's died and gone to heaven. Harry decided not to say anything to his daughter about the bee. That was the chance she took, exposing herself thataway.

Carol yawned and rolled over on her back. The sweat bee took his leave. Maybe she was asleep. The girl's firm, full breasts glistened like half-hidden cantaloupes in a truck farmer's field. Here was fruit soon ripe for the plucking and it was August, almost harvest time.

Harry Raker was a dairy farmer, a good one, who measured his life in cow terms. He observed that every frisky heifer gets found by an eager bull eventually. This offended Becky who tartly told him he wasn't funny. Lowering her voice she reminded him they had no sons but their daughter loved the farm. It was time her dad saw her as a desirable woman as well as a good farmhand. If they wanted a son to carry on the family farm it was up to Carol to get him.

Harry was about to argue that his bull and heifer analogy was saying the same thing, then noticed the fire in his wife's eyes and wisely held his tongue. Sometimes cow talk didn't work and this appeared to be one of them.

The stiff silence that follows a healthy argument in a good marriage was interrupted by the engine whine of an approaching vehicle. Everyone's ears picked up at the recognizable clatter of that flathead six.

Tom Donachy's cherry red pickup careened toward the farmhouse, jauntily kicking up a cloud of yellow clay dust.

Husband and wife exchanged glances. Without saying a word each made their point. Harry's look said – see I told you a young bull would show up. Becky's look said – don't you chase him back over the fence, Harry Raker.

Carol stood on the blanket in her bare feet and not much else, waving toward the pickup and hoping that husky Joe Ballard was with Tom. He was, and waved back from out the passenger side window. The smaller Squeaky Fabel sat in the middle. Carol felt some disappointment; from the speed of the pickup it was obvious the boys weren't going to stop for a visit.

"Come on, Tom," begged Joe. "Just one minute."

"Nope," replied the determined Tom. "Your minutes last an hour and I'm late now. What's that she's wearin' anyway?"

"She said she bought a new swimsuit yesterday. Your windshield's smeared, darn it. Slow down so I can see. Why it's a…"

"Goddess," interrupted Squeaky, who had read the classics and could see better.

24

The Raker's witnessed the sight of three youthful male faces taking up all the space of the driver's open side window, and heard Joe's plaintive "I'll be back, Carol!" just before disaster struck.

That week the township supervisors had widened the west side of the road, which brought the farm buildings opposite from the house five feet closer to the berm. Harry had approved this change because it made it easier for the milk truck to maneuver around the barn. He had hoped the grader would tip over their chicken coop, which now set dangerously close to the road. Unfortunately, the grader operator was experienced and missed the coop by six inches. Now Harry had to pay to move it himself.

Joe forgot to tell Tom about the change in the road.

The boys' first indication of misfortune was the rushing wave of choking black dust that invaded the cab through its open side windows, convincing Squeaky, who'd gone to Sunday School that morning but skipped the service and a church picnic to go fishing with Tom, that darkness could overrule the day. The next indication was the crack of wood giving way to metal and the unanimous squawk of two dozen rudely-evicted, airborne chickens, the survivors of the holocaust finally persuaded the sky was falling.

Tom braked the pickup, whose box had become enveloped by the roof and two sides of the coop, and stopped in the barnyard remarkably close to where Harry had intended to relocate the coop in the first place. Dust and feathers started to settle over the land.

The Raker's reacted in different ways. Carol was exasperated, a natural response for a girl concerned about the relationship between her boyfriend and her father. Becky thought it was the funniest thing she had ever seen and went laughing to the kitchen for her butcher knife and heavy shears to finish off some flopping chickens. Harry thought it was funny, too, but decided not to show it. He had an advantage over those boys now. Someone else would have to pay for a roost for Carol's chickens.

Carol's friendly cowdog Rusty was the first on the scene, plopping his big front paws over the ledge of the passenger side window, licking Joe Ballard's dirty face. It was fun when Joe was around.

Carol was next, in sandals and wrapped in her blanket, pointing an emphatic forefinger in Tom's equally dirty face. "Tom Donachy," she cried, "you're always getting my Joe in trouble!"

That was when Harry Raker, next on the scene, knew for certain a plan *was* in effect to perpetuate the family farm.

Abigail spent Sunday with the Sheafer's. They went to church and a picnic lunch. After a short nap Aunt K came up and helped her unpack and set up her apartment.

It was a cozy, furnished walk-up situated on the second story of the Sheafer's large Victorian home. It had its own downstairs entrance from the deep open porch that wrapped around three sides of the house. A wainscoted hallway ran to the Sheafer's living quarters on the first floor. A wide staircase of matching polished dark oak led up to the hallway on the second level.

Abigail's suite contained a living room with a sofa-bed, an eat-in kitchen with gleaming porcelain-white appliances, a small bath with a modern tub and shower combination, a large bedroom with a four-post double bed, and two walk-in closets. Abigail would need both closets. Here also was a wood office desk set against one wall with bookshelves expertly installed overhead. Fred and Aunt K obviously hoped their new tenant's stay would be a long one. Abigail felt a little guilty about that.

The living room and bedroom had new carpet with sections cut around the original grated floor registers to allow heat to escape upstairs. Aunt K explained that this apartment set directly over theirs; although it had its own hot water radiators she and Fred couldn't see any reason to waste good heat. What rose from their quarters was free, what ran through those copper pipes they had to pay for.

The materials and workmanship bespoke quality and simplicity. Her landlords had high standards. Well past middle age, Fred and Kathryn Sheafer were prosperous and conservative, set in their ways. They reminded Abigail of her own parents.

Aunt K's thick eyebrows raised when she heard Mac and Tom were taking Abigail for a Sunday drive. She mentioned their connection with the younger brother first.

"That Tom's a rascal," she said, smiling affectionately. "Betty used to say his right ear was bigger than the other from all of us tugging it. Now he's so tall we can't reach it, but he still needs it pulled once in a while."

Then she grew somber. "He's lost a lot. His parents are gone. The only family he has left is Mac. A boy his age would normally be wallowing in self-pity. Somehow Tom slogs forward. He absorbs life's terrible blows and says life is still good. Very few of us have his strength. He stayed with us for a while after his mother died. We hadn't had a boy in our house in five years."

Aunt K paused, took a breath, then elaborated. "Our own son David was killed while in the service. When Tom came he put the spunk back in our lives."

Aunt K bent over and picked up Abigail's heavy trunk. With the ease of a stevedore the sturdy lady put it on the bed. Abigail, hanging up dresses folded in a suitcase, saw the opportunity to ask about Mac, her real interest.

"Frankly," answered Aunt K, "I'm surprised Mac took time off for a date. He has a timber deal cooking that Fred says will keep him in the woods for a year. You accomplished in ten minutes what every single girl in Steam Valley's been trying for months." Aunt K probed curiously. "How did you manage it?"

"Well," admitted Abigail, "it wasn't his idea. We were all together in a booth. Tom invited me and I invited Mac."

"That was a neat little trap. You don't waste time do you?"

Aunt K didn't wait for an answer. She already knew it. "Understand that Jonathan MacEwen is a driven man, always proving himself. He would have squirmed out of that date if he could." Reconsidering that statement Aunt K appraised Abigail carefully. "Then again you're a very pretty girl and he's still a man. Handsome devil, isn't he?"

Abigail sighed, said yes, and asked his age.

Aunt K thought a moment. "Thirty-two or thirty-three. I had him in the town school in sixth grade. He hasn't been around much because of the service. Betty told me she thought Delia hurt him."

Damn, whispered Abigail to herself, another woman. This is getting complicated. That Julie's interested in him too. "Delia?" she asked, trying to sound casual.

"Delia Cole. Ravishing creature. Black hair, Irish, like Mac. From Tannerytown too. Delia Connolly before she threw Mac over and married Bud Cole. Delia liked money and Mac didn't have any. To my mind she made a bad bargain. There's talk she may want to renegotiate."

A *real* other woman, thought Abigail. Married too. Let's find out more about this. "Do you think he's still in love with her?" she asked, still trying to sound casual.

"He never talks about her. I don't think you can hurt Mac and get him back."

That's better, thought Abigail. Good-bye Delia. Let's change the subject. "What did Mac do in the service?"

"He never said exactly. I think Fred and Charley Bower know, but the old veterans don't talk, except among themselves. Fred did say it wasn't nice. Paratrooper, scout stuff. He was in the Rangers, led highly trained search and destroy teams. We got that from the newsreels. Came out of World War II a captain. Then he spent a year in Israel training commandoes. That was hush-hush too. Stateside he worked for the Army Corps of Engineers on Forest Service projects out west. Mac did write us about that. Built roads in the national parks. In Korea he commanded a special forces unit and was wounded. LIFE did an article on the army officers involved on Heartbreak Ridge. Our "Major Mac" was mentioned. But when we picked him up at the train station his trunks were stamped Colonel MacEwen."

A Colonel? This logger *was* more that he looked. Still trying to contain her enthusiasm Abigail made an observation: "That explains his speech, he talks like an educated man."

"By now he should," responded Aunt K. "He holds degrees in forestry and engineering from Penn State."

This time it was Abigail's eyebrows that were raised.

She was incredulous. "He's an engineer? He's a colonel?" She almost shouted her surprise. This was the 1950's.

A man with those qualifications could write his own ticket. There were airports and roads and schools to build. Russia had rockets and the H-bomb. The nation's defenses needed shoring. And Mac was here? In the middle of nowhere?

"Why is a man like that cutting trees down for a living?" she asked disbelievingly.

The offended look that drew over Aunt K's face told Abigail she had blown it again. But Aunt K wouldn't let her get away with it like Tom had done. She liked this perky redhead but wasn't at all reluctant to put her in her place.

"Trees have provided us with a good living for forty years, young lady," lectured Aunt K sternly. "Fred let me teach school. I didn't have to."

Abigail didn't like the idea of a husband "letting" a wife do anything but held her tongue.

Aunt K continued. "A man should do what he does best. Mac's at his best in the woods. He's done plenty for his country. He wouldn't be happy behind a desk. In that way he's like my Fred. Fred's pushing sixty and logging is hard dangerous work, but his most satisfying days are those spent cutting with Luke Ballard in the woods."

Abigail was a city girl with city priorities. She was ignorant of country ways. That was part of the reason she was here. She also had a stubborn streak and hated to back down. She correctly sensed that Aunt K was not really angry with her, she was taking a stand. Abigail had a stand too, and so far was not convinced she should change it. A skilled college debater, Abigail attempted to break down Aunt K's defense with a leading question.

"Military officers and engineers make good money, a lot more money than us teachers," she said seriously, intending to involve Aunt K in her point of view. "Don't you think Mac is wasting his talents here?"

Aunt K snorted. She had learned long ago that sophistication was no match for direct talk. "Last year Luke Ballard made more than a teacher, a colonel, and an engineer put together. I know because I helped him with his income tax. Mac will too, you mark my words."

With that statement she snapped Abigail's emptied trunk shut and slid it under the bed. It was time to fix supper, she said, leaving the bedroom. See you at six.

Meekly, Abigail replied she would be down at six.

Abigail hung the last dress and shut the closet door. The full-length mirror affixed to the outside panel threw a shaft of reflected sunlight across the room, drawing her attention to the glass. The girl in the mirror with the strawberry hair and long soft eyelashes was trim and healthy... and twenty-five.

That girl wanted to marry and have a family. Someday. Not today. That girl could be the wife of an engineer, or an army officer, someday, as long as she could have her career too. That girl could never be the wife of a logger. She looked away from the glass.

What was she doing thinking of marriage now? She came to teach school and do research for her master's. She didn't come here to find a husband. She had never even been alone with this man, this Jonathan MacEwen.

She looked in the mirror again. The girl in the glass seemed as excited about that prospect as the girl in the room. Even her image resisted her ambition and urged her to mate. To her image it didn't seem to matter if the man was a logger. All the man had to be was a man.

———

Mac called for Abigail promptly at six. Aunt K met him at the downstairs door.

"Where's Tom?" she asked.

"He's not here?" responded Mac, genuinely puzzled. Tom was always on time.

Seeing some concern pass Aunt K's face, Mac made light of his brother's absence. "He went fishing with Squeaky and Joe. He's probably asleep under a shade tree with his ball cap pulled over his head."

Aunt K was mollified. "Come in and sit," she ordered. "You're having supper with us. By the way, you need a haircut."

Mac dutifully followed her thickset frame down the hallway, through the kitchen and into the dining room. Fred and Abigail were already seated at the table. Before Mac could greet them Aunt K gave him a scolding.

"By the way Mr. Big Brother, I don't like you skipping church. If you skip, Tom skips. You're not setting a good example."

Mac winked at Fred, leaned over and kissed her broad forehead. He had always liked the scent from the cameo sachet she wore. It was the scent of a flower, a flower called mother.

Aunt K grumbled and beamed.

Mac teased her. "Is it Tom's wayward soul you're anxious to save, or do you need his voice in the choir?"

Aunt K grumbled some more. "You're right," she finally admitted. "When Tom skips, Harold Fabel skips, and my whole male section goes to pot. Now you sit down and behave yourself. Tom's missing my noodles and roast beef. That's his penance."

While their hostess was in the kitchen Fred explained to Abigail that Aunt K's noodles and roast beef was legendary. Once a year she prepared a community supper as a fund-raiser for the Lutheran Church. Last year, while Tom was living with them, she assigned him the task of sketching the posters and distributing them around town. She gave him a pattern to copy with the heading AUNT K'S PIT ROAST BEEF. Tom did as he was told, sort of, substituting the word BEAST for beef and pasting a magazine photo of a buffalo alongside. Orders doubled and the unprepared and flustered Lady Lutherans ran out of food. Only substantial profit and a good hiding place saved Tom from sharing the roasting pit with Harry Raker's donated steer that weekend.

Mac grinned broadly at Fred's story. Abigail noticed he had a dazzling smile, very even, very white teeth. He was obviously adept at handling older women. She wondered how he did with the younger ones.

Providence, she thought, must have gotten in Tom's way. Too bad.

Supper lasted a pleasant hour. Abigail was fresh and lovely in a bright red cotton blouse and white slacks. Her nails and lipstick were an expensive new red called Cute Tomata. She was the center of attention. Abigail became animated whenever the conversation involved her two favorite subjects, teaching and herself.

She was a '52 graduate of Temple with a bachelor's in education. She was working on her master's which she expected to finish next year. She didn't give anyone time to question her about her thesis. If that came up she had decided ahead of time to lie and say she was undecided.

She had taught one year at an elementary school in Harrisburg and lived with her parents. She found that to be too constraining after being away from home five years. She wanted to teach in a rural area, she saw the Fallbrook position advertised in a trade journal, she applied, was granted an interview and was hired.

The trade journal part was a little fib. Her mother knew Mr. Bates, the school superintendent. She didn't mention that.

Her parents held different opinions of the move. Her father, a stiff-backed college professor, liked having his intellectual daughter at home. Her mother, a high-ranking official in the Department of Education, a competent and practical woman who was not above changing politics to keep her job, felt her daughter should strike out on her own. She had also added "finding a man," but Abigail didn't mention that either.

Abigail and Aunt K did the bulk of the talking, teacher stuff mostly, while Fred and Mac listened politely. When Aunt K left to get their dessert, which Abigail declined because she was stuffed, there was a lull in the conversation. Abigail scanned the tastefully furnished dining room.

On the papered wall above the mahogany-veneered credenza were photos of David arranged in life order – a baby in a cradle, a toddler hugging a dog, a child in elementary school, a graduate in cap and gown, an airman in uniform. The most striking was the colored portrait of the school child–a beautiful boy with compelling blue eyes and shiny hair the color of white gold. The boy could have posed as the perfect German. Abigail said as much.

Fred's response was warm and proud. "We're descendants of a Hessian soldier who changed sides during the Revolution," he said. "Pure American, though, was what David was. We lost him in a freak accident six years ago."

Abigail found it difficult to comprehend the vibrant boy in the photo was dead. He seemed so…alive.

Aunt K came in with the dessert and the men's attention shifted to her warm apple pie sided by a smaller wedge of sharp cheese. Abigail sipped her coffee and quietly regarded the photo, the room her hosts, and Mac. He *was* an interesting man. She decided she would not tell her mother about him. Not yet.

After dessert Mac suggested they all join him for a drive. He had brought his mother's four-door, there was plenty of room. He mentioned showing Abigail the new high school and Sheafer's mill. He had set aside a twelve-foot maple log in Fred's timber yard this morning. It had a rare curly grain. He wanted Fred to see it.

Abigail gave Aunt K an appealing gaze, who understood immediately, and shooed the young couple out of the dining room. Fred can see that log tomorrow, she said. They would be on the front porch later, after she and Fred did the dishes.

"Let me drive," suggested Abigail, as they strode down the walk together. "That way I won't get lost when I go on my own."

Without answering Mac walked her to her convertible. The top was already down, prepared in advance for a warm evening's drive. He opened the driver's side door for her, then got in on the passenger side. He knew he was being maneuvered. His green eyes held a glint of amusement.

It was the closest he had been to her all evening. He was freshly shaved. She could smell faintly the clean aroma of soap and lather. A mass of thick black hair tumbled out of the open neck of his polo shirt. Her female instincts told her she had attracted this man; her reason cautioned her that this was no pink-cheeked, fumbly college boy. This was a man, an experienced man. Abigail had never been serious with a man, a prospect that both excited and frightened her.

Hurriedly, she started her car.

Fallbrook, in tandem with the rest of the nation, was in the middle of a baby and building boom. The soldiers returned home to their wives and the reunited couples made up for lost time. The fruit of their labor was everywhere, buzzing around like a swarm of worker bees, whose main task was to get out of the hive and enjoy the waning hours of the pleasant day, and return in time for a bath before it ended.

All kinds of pedaled apparatus clattered along the sidewalks; kids on bikes and trikes weaved aggressively around slower moving strollers and carriages guided by new moms and grandmoms. In the background there was urgency; the rapid pounding of hammer on nail, the grainy peal of a power saw ripping plywood, as dad's and granddad's hurried to finish do-it-yourself projects before nightfall. There was also an occasional high-pitched male curse if the hammer bent the nail or the saw bit too deep into the expensive plywood, generally followed by a higher-pitched female rebuke to watch your language, there's children.

The children didn't notice the attractive couple in the convertible, but the adults did. There were about seven hundred homes in Fallbrook; by bedtime half of those households would hear that Mac had a girlfriend, they think she's the new teacher.

Fallbrook lay at the northern mouth of Steam Valley, a wide undulating plain flanked by foothills which were in turn contained by steep timbered mountains blue in the distance. The community was bisected east and west by Blockhouse Creek, which fell over a ten-foot rock ledge near the town's center, hence the name Fallbrook. U.S. Route 15 paralleled the stream on the east side. The two combined to form a north-south corridor that divided the town.

Governmentally both sides of the corridor were incorporated as the Borough of Fallbrook. Historically, however, they were two entities.

To the west of 15 was Main Street, the public schools, the Protestant churches, and four hundred New England homes. This was Original Fallbrook, established between 1820 and 1880. To the east of 15 were the factories, the railroad yard, the Catholic churches, and three hundred company homes. This was Tannerytown, established between 1880 and 1920. There was a lively mix between the two sections and some crossovers, each depended on the other, but strong differences remained.

Main Street extended west, perpendicular to Fifteen, three long blocks of two and three-story brick mercantiles with ornamented cornices and painted key blocks. Business signs hung from posts over widened sidewalks, the sign in front partially blocking the others behind, like dogeared corners of known cards, and the trimmed plate glass fronts underneath hawked a back-to-school theme.

At Jone's Five and Dime a Hopalong Cassidy lunchbox went for $2.89. Bob's Corner Red and White was sponsoring a drawing – first prize was a delivered box of groceries, second was a pair of adjustable rollerskates. Roup's National Brands Store was selling Dickies and Blue Bell clothing for twenty percent off. Sawyer's Hardware was touting a "hooky-players" special; twenty-two shells for a quarter a box. And Bailey and Bailcy Jewelers were willing to finance an engagement ring for that Certain Senior Girl for two dollars a week.

Being Sunday, the only establishments open were Brown's Cigar Store and Newsstand, the Fallbrook Hotel, and the Rialto Theater.

A nervous sailor sat the bench in front of Brown's, chain-smoking. If the bus didn't arrive soon he'd be listed AWOL in Philadelphia Monday. Brown's was the Greyhound Bus Stop, sharing that responsibility with Evie's Creekside Store in Buttonwood and the Turkey Ranch at the southern extreme of Steam Valley.

At the air-conditioned Rialto a handholding couple bickered over whether to go in late to the seven p.m. showing of *The River of No Return* starring M. Monroe or wait for the nine. Soon they decided, disappearing inside the swinging doors of the movie house. There were better things to do after nine.

Around and beyond the business section lay a grid of residential side streets named after shade trees. The Sheafer's lived on Elm although the trees were either oak or maple. After several residential blocks Main Street turned into School Street at the foot of Jew Hill, which was as aptly named as Elm. Fallbrook raised Protestants and Catholics and freethinkers, but no Jews. Here also School and Main intersected with Williamson Road, a country-two lane that ran south to Buttonwood along the western side of Block-house Creek. Abigail took the incline up School Street.

On a flat spot gouged out of the slope by the WPA, tilting on unstable soil, set the soon-to-be-replaced Town School. Before the war this structure housed grades one through twelve. This year grades one through six would fill it.

Abigail's second story classroom fronted the street, behind five tall colorless windows with grimy frames set in bricks of a drab yellow. Her room looked cold and it had been a warm day. I'll have to make some bright hang-ups for those windows thought Abigail, shuddering as she drove by.

Overlooking the town sprawled Fallbrook's commitment to its children; the gleaming new high school, a rectangular mass of steel and glass and concrete, flat roofed, boasting a thousand seat auditorium and a high-domed gymnasium containing a basketball court built college-size. Across the street was the freshly excavated and staked site of the new elementary. Abigail pulled in the dirt lot now occupied by construction trailers. This is where I could be next year she thought, then pushed that misgiving from her mind.

She was relaxed now. The aggressive male she half-feared, half-desired had not materialized. Mac was polite, easy-going, a good listener. Other than telling her about the town he hadn't said much. Obviously, to him, this wasn't a date, it was a drive. If she wanted a date it would be up to her to turn it into one.

"Show me where you live," she said brightly.

Mac pointed to the opposite hill to the east. The steep-pitched roofs of Tannerytown poked through a briny evening haze.

He directed Abigail back down School and Main to the traffic light at the Main Street bridge. The sailor still waited in front of Brown's. When the light turned green, and she crossed the wide concrete bridge over Blockhouse, the complexion of Fallbrook changed.

At the bridge Main Street was renamed Cole Avenue, which ran between the gray frame tannery buildings on the north and the orange-tiled condensary buildings on the south. Also on the milk plant side was the power plant, its transmission lines weaving a high net of cable over the factories they fed.

The Tannery, condensary, and power plant all had high smokestacks, fuming even on Sunday, their stringy sulfur clouds bent by the prevailing west wind toward the Company houses tightly packed on the hill to the east.

On the flat past the factories stretched the cindered railroad yard and depot. Abigail had to stop at the crossing, the freight locomotive Edward T. Johnson had the right of way. Mac observed casually that business always came first in Tannerytown.

The crossing bell applauded the Edward T., which had just delivered twenty carloads of soft coal and was making its swing to pick up eight carloads of powdered milk and a dozen carloads of sole leather. The freight's destination was back north, the only way to go, as this was the southernmost extension of the New York Central's Fall Brook Line.

Dark smoke from the Edward T. rolled skyward with force, puncturing the more dissipated pollution above it, creating the effect of an impressionist painting, a study of black against a background of mustard and gray.

The crossing bell fell silent, the barricade lifted, and Abigail entered the residential section of Tannerytown. On this side of the tracks Cole Avenue narrowed into Tannery Hill Road.

Built by Zebulon Cole around the turn of the century to provide housing for an immigrant labor force, the Company homes were uniformly built houses arranged in rows above streets that switchbacked up Tannery Hill. Over the years about half had been sold to tannery employees. The remaining half were still owned by Cole Enterprises, the rent deducted from the worker's paycheck. If that worker lost his job, he lost his home.

Mike Donachy's father had been one of the buyers. The house was a neat two-story with a steep-pitched roof, enclosed front porch, drives along both sides, and a postage stamp yard in the back. Flowerboxes lined the width of the porch, overflowing with yellow mums and red geraniums. Mac explained that the boxes had been built by Tom, who tended them faithfully and transplanted the flowers to his mother's grave.

Abigail noticed that flowers grew in abundance in Tannerytown, splashes of color in fabric close-knit, in seeming defiance of the sulfuric pall that hung overhead. And those that tended their flowers in the cool of the evening, amidst the clamor of their own thriving families, noticed her.

Abigail turned around in Mac's drive and headed back the way she came, a little red-faced. She had wanted to see what the house was like inside but Mac said no. She learned it was improper for a single man to invite a single woman into his home on their first outing, especially in the Irish-Italian-Polish community of Tannerytown, where members of the first generation still lived and imposed their standards on the second and third.

The signpost at the end of Mac's street said Highland Avenue, elevation 1504. A stray evening breeze swept down from the mountains towering in the northwest, and, for a moment, lifted the haze. Even so there was a trace of brimstone in the air.

Fallbrook was actually split by the smokestacks and the prevailing west wind. West of the smokestacks, under cleaner air, dwelt the storekeepers, the managers, the professionals, and the lucky, in their Colonials and Georgians and

Victorians, amidst the smell of success and grass, fresh-mowed. To the east of the stacks, under bitter air, dwelt the factorymen, the railroaders, the pensioner's widows, and the unlucky, in their look-alike Company homes, their fragrant flower boxes contending with the smell of brine and coal, fresh-burned.

Chapter 7 – Sunday Drive

At the traffic light Abigail had to wait for the Greyhound bus to make its wide turn south on 15. The sailor sat in a window seat looking down at the redhead in the convertible. He gave a tentative wave. Abigail waved back. The sailor grinned and waved again, this time with more confidence. Then, in the rattle and flash of diesel and metal, he was gone.

Mac chuckled. "I know how low he feels. It always lifted my spirits when the girl waved back. Especially if she was a pretty girl like you."

The compliment was genuine and Abigail flushed. With all her maneuvering, an automatic, natural reaction on her part had generated the warmest response. *Now* we're getting somewhere, she thought. "Which way to Sheafer's Mill?" she asked.

"Back way or Rt. 15 way?"

"Back way. I've been on 15 this time of day and it's dangerous." She nodded toward the dent in her hood.

Mac laughed again, passed the snake incident off as an aberration, and told her to take Main to School then turn left.

Williamson Road was a pleasant country two-lane, winding between the wooded foothills of Potash and Blackwolf Mountains and the west bank of Blockhouse Creek. Mac explained that this was the original road financed by land developers in the 1790's to provide a northern passage through the mountains to the fertile tableland of western New York. The developer's agent was a determined Scot named Williamson who got a difficult job done. Most of the pioneers that stopped here never intended to stay, added Mac.

That's me, thought Abigail.

Like the other primary routes through town, this too was freshly paved, yet the area was unsettled. It seemed odd to Abigail that this pretty but untravelled route should deserve such treatment and she said so.

"Just keep driving and you'll see why," Mac said grimly. Noticing Abigail's frown of consternation at his vague answer, he elaborated: "Bud Cole owns all this. He won't allow any development close to *his* house."

At the county line, where Fallbrook Township, Tioga County, ended and Jackson Township, Lycoming County began, Abigail came to the fenced-in part of the Cole country estate. The white plank fence rushed by for about a mile, ending where the new pavement made a tee.

The right branch meandered up a tree-lined lane to a stately colonial mansion. The grounds between the house and road were a combination of woods and lawn but even the woods were manicured. In front of the mansion a couple was unloading luggage from a station wagon while their black-haired child, a girl about twelve, chased an excited collie dog.

Abigail, trying not to look obvious, strained for a look at the mother, the woman who jilted Mac for this mansion in the woods, but the trees obstructed her view. She glanced next at Mac. If he still felt anything for Delia, he didn't show it.

The left fork of the tee crossed Blockhouse through a rugged and weathered covered bridge, meeting Route 15 flanking the other side. The loyal township supervisors; part-time roadmasters, smalltime politicians, and fulltime tannerymen, had agreed that Bud Cole needed not one paved route to his estate but two.

Beyond the tee Williamson Road continued as hardpan and gravel, well oiled to keep down the dust, just in case the wind blew the other way.

Another mile brought Abigail to a second private lane leading northwest into the foothills of Potash. This lane was as wide as the township road and as well-maintained. A large billboard capable of being seen across-creek from Route 15 marked the entrance:

MORT FESSLER
JUNK AND PARTS MISC.
CASH PAID FOR GOOD JUNK

Mac described Mort with affection. The cigar-smoking junkman was part of the local color that kept life interesting in Steam Valley.

Past the junkyard the road seemed to narrow. This was an illusion created by tall groves of thornapple and choke-cherry that had grown over abandoned farm fields right to the sides of the road. Springing from fertile soil, the tangle grew faster than the roadmasters could clear it. It was a moist and buggy channel. They had to shield their faces when Abigail sped through a swarm of flying grasshoppers. They were getting close to the creek, said Mac, and another bridge leading into Buttonwood.

At the end of the tangle Williamson road made a sharp ninety-degree bend east toward the creek. Abigail slowed and noticed another lane that led southwest into the com-pressed foothills of Blackwolf Fountain. This lane split about two hundred feet from the township road. The west fork was a rutted wagon trail crowned with waist-high weeds that led into the timber on Blackwolf. The other fork was a wide farm lane, also crowned with weeds, whose entrance was guarded by two pillars of mortared fieldstone. The pillars were wrapped in vine, evidence of wealth gone to ruin after a score of years.

A rusty iron gate ornamented with a gothic letter L leaned against the blade of the big bulldozer that had pulled it down. The bald and shiny surface of a fresh-cut drainage ditch ran alongside the lane towards the boarded-up farm buildings. A huge Army six by six was parked near the dozer.

This was the Longsdorf Farm. Mac did not mention that he owned it but Abigail knew he did. She had overheard Fred and Aunt K discussing the deal in their kitchen while Aunt K prepared supper. Fred feared repercussions from Bud Cole and Spike Poorbaugh and prayed to God it didn't rain. Abigail didn't know what their fears meant but they sounded serious.

Her landlord's had left their heat register open. Abigail heard Mac's name mentioned and knelt over the grate to hear more. She could have closed the register from her side but she didn't.

Abigail glanced over at the thick wrist and veined bicep of Mac's left arm. Only a man of immense physical strength could prop that iron grate against the dozer blade. Only a man with tremendous confidence in himself would attempt it. This man employed muscle and brain in his occupation and enjoyed it. Aunt K was probably right, he wouldn't be happy stuck behind a desk. But Abigail convinced herself the right woman could keep him content if he was.

They entered the hamlet of Buttonwood from the steel bridge built high over a faster and deeper Blockhouse, the bridge linking Route 15 with its predecessor once again.

At this junction Abigail stopped for gas at Evie's, a mom and pop store that teetered above the creek, between the bridge and intersection. Besides selling gas and groceries, Evie's served as Buttonwood's post office and bus station. Evie's was the only grocery store open on Sunday in Steam Valley and prospered for that reason.

Across 15 from Evie's sat the Buttonwood school, surrounded by a farm field, its grounds outlined on two sides by a fence of woven wire. How quaint, thought Abigail, drumming her fingertips on the steering wheel while Mac pumped the gas, a one-room school. She wondered idly if the fence was to keep the livestock out or the kids in and decided the answer was both.

Seeing Mac, and taking note of the new girl, Evie stepped out and introduced herself. Her face was seamed with the experience of eighty-five years, but she had the alert gray eyes of a canny Scot, which is exactly what Evie McFee Todd was.

Abigail's scrutiny of the schoolhouse interested Evie. Mr. Bates had been by, she said. Told her the school board had decided to retire the old school next year. She thought

45

that was a funny way to put it – retire a school. With the valley kids going to Fallbrook, well, she guessed she'd retire too. She and the schoolhouse were about the same age. Her mother and Louisa Longsdorf had made her father build it.

Her eyes sparkled with a favorite memory as she went back in time. Prodded by a resolute young wife and a firm boss, the Longdorf Farm foreman had cut and shaped the timbers, dug the well, and organized the work bee that raised the school. Ike McFee even hung the bell. His rope still rang it. Evie swore she could still smell her father's pipe tobacco in the fibers of that rope.

A place grows on you, she said wistfully. She liked the noise the bell and kids made. She and Burt Todd never had any kids of their own, so they adopted the school kids, sort of. Now Burt was gone. In another year the kids would be gone. Why, without the kids around she'd be as empty as the old school. Think they'd let her have the rope?

The gas pump numbers quit rolling at $3.90. When Abigail reached in her purse to pay, Evie shook her head. No, she'd put it on Mac's bill. It wasn't right for the lady to pay. When Abigail protested Evie dismissed her with a wave and walked away.

Behind the enclosed cashier's counter of her store, at a roll-top desk pigeonholed with stock orders and sorted mail, Evie posted the purchase to Mac's account. She would bill him at the end of the month. The MacEwen's and Donachy's had always been good pay. Mac hadn't acted smitten by the redheaded girl. She was one of those modern, career girls. Imagine, wanting to pay! She wondered if Julie Spencer knew.

Turning south on 15, Abigail felt for the first time the magnitude of the region. Here, at it's middle, Steam Valley narrowed, pinched into a notch by four high mountains shouldering each other. They made her feel small and insignificant.

Buttonwood was an inhabited speck beneath a quadrangle of uninhabited mountains. All were heavily forested. North and west rose the steep, practically inaccessible slopes

46

of Potash and Blackwolf. South and east reared the blunter, more agreeable slopes of Laurel and Steam.

Mac pointed out the overlook built by the state on Steam Mountain. He then pointed to the higher cliff fronting Blackwolf and Potash called Caleb's Rock. Far off, shimmering in the distance, protruded the region's highest peak, Bear. If you want the tourist view, he said, you drive up Steam. If you want a real view, you climb Blackwolf or Potash and sit on Caleb's Rock.

"What's the view like from there?" asked Abigail, looking beyond Blackwolf to Bear.

"No one knows."

"You mean there are places no one has been?"

"I think so. It's wild country back in there. And it doesn't end at Bear."

Abigail decided the tourist view would do. At least the overlook would have a bathroom. She wasn't interested in climbing Blackwolf, or any mountain, for that matter. They were beautiful, imposing, and forbidding. Not for her.

She noticed that Mac didn't seem daunted by these mountains, if anything he seemed challenged by them. It would take nerves of steel to drive equipment up and down those slopes. A wife would worry about that.

At Buttonwood, Steam Valley curved east for several miles and Route 15 curved with it. Blockhouse Creek, however, stayed south, entering a deeper, lower notch cut between Steam Mountain and Blackwolf called Packhorse Run. A potholed macadam road followed the old freight trail along the creek to the village of English Center twelve miles away. Midway down Packhorse, where Black's and Texas creeks joined with Blockhouse to form the Little Pine River, on a high gravel bar overlooking this turkey track of streams, there Fred Sheafer had built his mill.

In contrast to the sooty factory complex at Fallbrook, the sawmill gleamed. The three primary structures; the mill, truck garage, and equipment shed, were long, airy, metal-clad Quonsets sporting fresh aluminum paint.

The only frame building was the office, ranch-style with board and batten siding of weathered rough-cut hemlock, paneled inside with the finest cherry veneer. The office reflected Fred's character; rough and splintery on one side, warm and genuine on the other.

Fred's inventory of finished lumber was spread over several acres, piled in high stacks according to type and size, ready for shipment. Most of the stacks were tagged with a destination slip. There was such demand for lumber the stacks were already sold.

Fred's inventory of logs, about five thousand this time of year, was piled according to species and quality as close to the mill as efficiently possible. Abigail noticed that some of the log piles themselves had destination slips on them. Did a lumber mill resell its logs?

Mac, in his element now, answered with enthusiasm. Those were "fancy" or special purpose logs to be retailed to other manufacturers, he said. They could be identified by the scaled volume in board feet neatly painted on the ends of each log.

One pile of prime red oak was destined for a flooring mill in Ontario. Another pile of black cherry was to be hauled to the Port of Philadelphia, then put on a boat for a furniture maker in England. A pile of white ash was sched-uled to be sent to the ballbat factory in Galeton, there to be sawed into four-foot blanks, then trucked to Kentucky where a lathe operator would turn each blank into a Louisville Slugger. And one grand black walnut, sixteen feet long and three feet in diameter with no rot, from a tree almost buried by the contractor building the elementary school, was to be loaded on a flatcar at the Fallbrook Depot on Tuesday, des-tined for western New York. Ithaca Gun Company had bid $1.00 per board foot for that log. The number 998 was emblazoned in red enamel against the dark sawed end. Mac hoped the big curly maple he had cut on Saturday would qualify for the same shipment…and the same money.

Abigail did not share Mac's fascination with these prod-ucts from the forest. What did impress her were shifting aromas of cut wood: pungent pine, tart cherry, sweet maple, bitter oak, a sawmill potpourri. She could smell a newly constructed house in the suburbs; split level, framed with pine, floored in maple, paneled in oak and cherry, and, if this relationship clicked, occupied by a happy teacher and her engineer husband.

Growing impatient, Abigail cut Mac short, hugged herself, and said she was cold. Twilight *was* invading Pack-horse Run, it *was* growing cooler. This time it was Mac who was embarrassed. He had opened up and talked too much and hadn't realized his guest was uncomfortable. When they got back in the car Abigail put the top up and turned the heat on high. But she had been more bored than cold.

In Buttonwood she had to wait for traffic to get by before entering 15. She turned to Mac who hadn't said much since leaving the mill. She realized then she had gotten him talking about what was important in his life and thought-lessly shut him off. *You've got to learn to listen, Abigail, or you'll die an old maid.* That was another comment from her mother, made just before she left Harrisburg.

I've got to get him talking again, she thought, and pre-tend I'm interested. "I'm hungry," she said decisively. "How about a hot cup of coffee and a piece of that blueberry pie?"

Route 15 was clear. Without waiting for Mac's reply Abigail turned in the direction of the Turkey Ranch.

Julie didn't see them walk in. She had heard the bell but hadn't bothered to look up. It had jingled continuously since noon when the churches let out. The parking lot was stub-bornly full and she had Posey's books to do yet. Her eyes watered from lingering smoke and fatigue. She was short a waitress this weekend and had worked her second double. The overtime helped moneywise but she felt guilty. She needed to spend some time with Danny before he started school.

She directed a busboy to clear table four. The three picky old biddies she had just served there, widows with money wearing little black hats affixed with pearl stickpins, had tipped her a dime. God, you could tell none of them had ever been a waitress!

A couple had just been seated at table four. She brushed a stray wisp of blond hair off her brow with the back of her wrist and started over, grabbing a pitcher of ice water and two glasses. Along the way she engaged in some friendly banter with two of her regular customers. One was a cowboy-booted hidehauler on his weekly run from Chicago. The other was game warden Jim Morningstar. Supper at the Turkey Ranch was a weekend ritual for Jim and Missy and their pigtailed twins with different colored ribbons in their hair. Missy had whispered earlier that she was expecting again in March.

When Julie got to table four she was caught off guard. Mac sat there with the pretty new teacher. Just the two of them, fresh and clean, enjoying the end of their Sunday drive. Julie forgot to pour their water.

"Where, where's Tom?" she stammered.

Chapter 8 – The Tycoon

Benjamin "Bud" Cole seethed with anger. Disappointment dove like a lead weight to the pit of his stomach. He felt sick, and mean. Pemberton's report of the Longsdorf bid had an I-told-you-so ring to it. Someday he'd fire that prickly old bastard!

He propped his elbows on his office desk, rubbing his beefy face with beefy hands, trying to regain some control. He failed.

Damn Delia and that crap about their need for a vacation! If he hadn't gone he would have gotten wind of MacEwen's interest in the Longsdorf lands. For sure that jellyfish banker would have told him. They could have estimated Mac's bid from the amount he was borrowing and the project statements he filed with the bank.

The money to beat him came from his own bank. And he didn't know about it! He was chairman of the board for chrissakes!

He would have to stop that loan, make the jellyfish sting. Pemberton's report said the estate was paid in full by a cashier's check for fifty thousand, but Squire Hayes hadn't cashed it yet or recorded the deed. It was early. The lawyer didn't come in until nine. There might still be time.

Why had he bid so low? Because he wanted to steal it, that's why. Same as Mort Fessler and Harry Raker. Harry wanted the farmland and a place to put his cheerleader daughter after graduation. Mort needed to spend some of that black market money he'd stashed during World War II. Those two were the reason Cole Enterprises had bid five thousand more than the minimum. Just in case another greedy capitalist tried to walk away with it. It would have worked, too, except for MacEwen.

Why had he bid so low? He should have bid eighty thousand. Pemberton's memo recommended a like offer to MacEwen. Buy the competition off, it said. Pemberton's mind dwelt in the world of sound business logic, he was not

51

affected by the personal. Bud Cole would never give Mac-Ewen a profit. Never!

Hell, he could have bid a hundred-and-eighty and made money. Real money. Maybe a million. Maybe more. God!

He had bid low because he didn't want to borrow while negotiating a discreet million-dollar line of credit with Dauphin Deposit in Harrisburg. It didn't look good to have to borrow a little bit of money while attempting to borrow a whole lot more. Damn, what timing!

Bud Cole was short of cash. He had dipped heavy into his capital to buy the milk plant and strip mine. The milk plant was breaking even, the coal mine was breaking his back. He had bid low to preserve funds needed to cover operations when business slowed over the winter. He knew that was coming. There were unknowns to contend with too.

The state had sent an inspector to measure the pollution in Blockhouse Creek. What would it cost to treat his sludge? Where the hell else could he put it?

The New York Central was considering the abandonment of the Fall Brook Line. What would it cost to operate a railroad spur? Should he buy a fleet of trucks instead?

Shoe manufacturers were making shoes with cheaper synthetic soles. Sole leather orders were down. What other business should he get into? Another mine? Plastics?

Worst of all, the AFL had held a meeting at the Grange Hall. Few came but that didn't mean they wouldn't try again. A union? In his plant? What the hell!

Yes, damnit, he should have bid twenty dollars per acre as Pemberton suggested. To turn land into money you got to have the land, his treasurer said. Twice in the past year he had defied Pemberton and his stubbornness cost him. Pemberton was strongly against the Bloss mine – another man's leavings, a wornout woman, he'd said. He was strongly for the Longsdorf purchase – a healthy maiden, worth a good dowry. He always thought the youngest Cole to be a good judge of women, up to now.

Bald, bookish, and old, Pemberton had the ability to foresee trends and had guided three generations of Cole's.

The other two regarded their offspring from their portraits now. Zebulon and Reuben looked stern. What's ailing you, Benjamin?

He knew what they were thinking: Pemberton's Declining Generation Theory was true. The first generation builds it, the second sustains it, and the third loses it. Somehow they kept Pemberton alive to keep that from happening. They were harsh masters, two out of three ruling from the grave. He'd prove them wrong, damnit!

Agitated, he rummaged through the Longsdorf file, looking for evidence to convince himself it was a bad buy, to thank God he lost, to breathe a sigh of relief, and walk away. He didn't find it.

There *was* timber. Lots of it. The aerial photographs, a military technique being adapted to business and recommended by Pemberton, showed dense concentrations of trees, particularly on the remote western slope of Bear Mountain. But trees were incidental to the subsurface wealth on Bear; he would level and burn them.

According to the geologists the veins of Bear Mountain ran black with coal. For some as yet undetermined reason the strata had a steep tilt and ran contrary to the neighboring mountains. Bear Mountain was different.

It occurred to Bud Cole that a man was continually tested by the contrary. Bear Mountain was contrary. MacEwen was contrary. The union was contrary. Spike Poorbaugh was contrary.

He held a sample of soft coal taken from an exposed seam at the bottom of Bear's steep southern slope. That was as far as the geologists got. The three-man team, sent in secret in May, were stopped, menaced by a pack of hounds. The fools had ventured into that unknown region unarmed. Luckily, Spike Poorbaugh called off his dogs. The survey team got the message and left, convinced he would have killed them if they hadn't. The township supervisors were worried. The mountain man had gotten more aggressive lately. He had even been seen on the Cole property.

Bud Cole clenched a hamlike fist and crumbled the coal. He had expected trouble from the trapper. But he had been blindsided by MacEwen. He relaxed his grip. The grains of coal sifted out from his palm and darkened his clean desk pad. Angrily he brushed them off. That's what you did with the contrary. You crush them and sweep them away.

That it was Mac particularly galled him. All his life he had come in second to MacEwen. When Mac was in tenth grade and he was a senior, they had fought. There was no resolution, Big Mike broke them up, but Mac had marked him by breaking his nose. Then Mac broke all his high school athletic records. Then Mac went to war and became a hero while he stayed home. He wasn't afraid! He wanted to go! But Reuben Cole died and his son was required to stay home and manage a plant important to the national interest. Making soldier boots. Mac came back an officer, went to college, became an engineer. His higher education came from Pemberton, smoke-filled rooms, trade journals and the market place. Mac had been around the world. He couldn't go to New Jersey without a crisis happening like this.

Why didn't Mac stay away? He knew what they were saying – he really came back for Delia. The weight in Bud Cole's stomach twisted into a knot and tightened. He used milk with his morning coffee, the mixture was curdling now. He had won with Delia. But he sometimes wondered if he didn't come in second there too.

Who the hell were "they" anyway? "They" had a profound influence on life in Steam Valley. People's actions were determined by what "they" thought or said. "They" had an evaporating credibility. Whenever "they" said something and the attempt was made to find out who "they" were, "they" were nowhere to be found. "They" would rarely betray a source but if "they" did, the source was sacrificed mercilessly. "They" remained unfound. "They" had as much influence as he did, maybe more.

Regardless of what "they" thought, Steam Valley was his. Fallbrook was his. "They" were his. All followed the

Golden Rule. As defined by Pemberton: He who had the gold made the rules.

He, Bud Cole, had the gold. It wasn't money. It was those smoking plants out there that transformed raw material into something useful and kept hundreds of people busy. The gold was the willingness, his willingness, to keep making a product and not scrap the plants and park the money. Because of him, and his gold, "they" survived.

He, Bud Cole, gave them their jobs, fed their families, furnished their homes, bought their cars. He knew their names, their wive's names, their kid's names. He thought they looked up to him. They acted like they did. If they didn't like him, they could at least be loyal. You didn't have to be good to work for Bud Cole, just loyal.

Bud Cole had been raised a tanner. Two thousand cowhides a day were shipped to his plant to be converted into leather, good leather. He expected the processed equivalent to be shipped out daily too. If not, every employee heard about it. Sometimes he had to get rough to get their attention. Pemberton said his methods were crude. Someday he would have to change. Someday somebody was going to knock him down a peg or two. Bud Cole scoffed at that.

Now there were rumblings of a union. Hell, he paid a fair wage. A new hand got a dollar an hour, some of the pieceworkers were making two. And he had closed the company store and wrote off the bad debts and kept the rents low in Tannerytown. There were widows up there who hadn't paid a cent in rent in years. And those ingrates want a union?

Pemberton said let it happen, you can't stop a rising flood. Bud Cole saw it as losing absolute control. That meant overtime and sick leave and health insurance and higher pensions. He was already required to pay worker's comp and social security. If the tannery organized, the milk plant and strip mine would too.

Pemberton said the only way to fight it was to pay better than union scale. Why waste money? The union costs were predictable and could be passed on to their customers. The

55

other tanneries were doing it. The union wasn't as big a threat as his own bullheadedness. That goddamn Pemberton could be contrary, too.

Pemberton had not approved of his most recent solution to the union problem. Just made it worse, he said.

Bud Cole had goaded the fiery organizer O'Conner into a tanyard fight, then beat the hell out of him. O'Conner was a big man, a former marine, and new on the job. He worked in the beam house, one of the hardest jobs, and was strong.

But his boss was big and strong too, and faster and better coordinated than O'Conner. Bud Cole was a fleshy man with an engaging smile and a friendly backslapping manner. He didn't look like a fighter. But underneath that soft-looking exterior lurked a powerful brute, a brute that smiled as he beat O'Conner. The men that watched were reminded of what he really was – a heavy, steak-fed bull capable of trampling anything that dared threaten his territory.

They should have warned O'Conner, but he was a troublemaker and some thought he had it coming. Reuben Cole had forced his son to learn every job in the plant, including the strenuous tanyard and beam house work. On a regular basis Bud Cole would don his coveralls and work a day with his men, and keep up with the best of them. There was more than the chief executive way to show who was boss. He couldn't do that if the union came. He was not a lazy man, Bud Cole.

Although raised in a mansion, Bud Cole spent his boyhood in the rough and tumble world of the factory and Tannerytown. It was in Tannerytown's back lots and dirt playground that his inborn athletic skills were tested and developed. It was there he first saw Delia. And it was there he and MacEwen fought to an exhausted draw.

They never quite finished it.

Chapter 9 – The Lawyer

His sign read Clarence L. Hayes, Esquire, Attorney at Law, but the town had taken the formality out long ago and renamed him The Squire.

The office lights were on so he pocketed his keys, opened the door of 23 Main, and walked in.

His receptionist Jane looked up from reading his morning paper and gave him an impish smile. He had taught her well. The smile was the most basic ingredient of a good business, of a good life, and Jane had a good one. She kept his paper too. He'd have to buy another one at Brown's.

They had a ritual, he and Jane. Whoever got to work first got the paper. The ritual began ten years before when Jane went to work after her son Ted started school. She was married to Pete Jones, a steady man who owned the five and dime one block down.

"Good morning, Dad," she said.

"Morning, honey. What's the news?"

"It's Monday, August 21st. It's supposed to be sunny and breezy with a high about 80. That's as far as I've got. The phone's been ringing off the hook."

"From?"

"Steve Heffner and Bud Cole. I think they're having a bad week."

The Squire smiled back at that. "So, the fox has caught the goose, eh?"

"Yep, and is wringing it's neck slowly. Steve's voice has been higher with every call."

"The Longsdorf documents are all done aren't they?"

"They're on your desk, ready for your appointment with the Judge and Recorder this afternoon."

Many times Squire Hayes thought his daughter should be the lawyer, she was that good. She was content to be his assistant; she wanted Ted to be the lawyer. But Ted liked his dad's store. It was a problem families had.

"How about the money?"

"I transferred all the funds to the estate's checking account in Williamsport Saturday morning. I deposited Mac's check there too. With the exception of the bank stock, which is still in Louisa's safe deposit box by the way, it's all cash now. Big bucks."

There was that smile again.

She continued breezily. "Then I bought a new dress at the Carroll House, compared prices for Pete at Woolworth's and Kresge's, and had lunch with sister Amy at the hotel. You bought our lunch. The receipt's in the cash drawer."

She was a crafty one, Jane. She knew her men didn't approve when she shopped out of town but they couldn't say much when she ran errands for them. He liked it when his daughters got together. Amy was married to a young engineer who worked for Piper Aircraft in Lock Haven. He told himself, you're a lucky man, Clarence Hayes.

"I'm going for the mail. I'll write the heirs' checks when I get back. Give me the safe deposit box key, will you?"

As Jane handed him the key she looked to see if there was any concern on his broad face. This was shaping up to be a tense day and her dad was 68 years old. He appeared calm but he was a great actor. He wore glasses with wire frames that emphasized his eyes. He had piercing brown eyes, and an intense gaze like a falcon, a gaze that could change from soft to hard in an instant. You didn't play games with Squire Hayes. His gaze was soft now.

"Dad," she said, "I think they're trying to block the sale."

The softness turned to stone. "They won't do it," he said firmly, and quietly pulled the office door shut behind him.

After a few seconds she looked out the office window to see which route he had taken. This too was part of their morning ritual but only Jane knew. He was going his usual way. He didn't walk across the street to the bank. The fox and the goose would have to wait.

58

Her father was a man of medium height with wide square shoulders and wide powerful hands. A hearty handshake from him was a bonecrusher. Pete said the Squire did not know his own strength. He took short steps, his gait had a bit of a shuffle. He didn't hurry. He didn't have to.

The Squire had a routine that only a court hearing could interrupt. Rain or shine, every day at the same time he would go for the mail. Starting at nine he walked the three blocks east to the post office, picked up his mail, crossed over to the North side of Main, walked the three blocks west to the bank, then recrossed Main to his office. The bank was always his last stop on his route. Today would be no exception.

As long as Jane could remember Fallbrook's mornings began with two clocks – the tannery's steam whistle at seven and her dad's journey to the post office at nine.

Squire's morning walk was the time he sorted his thoughts and planned his day. It was also the time he said hello. Some days it took two hours to get the mail.

The first stop was the dimestore, where he'd complain to Pete about that brassy wife of his stealing the paper and, when Ted was working, find out what was happening with the teenagers. Next he'd stop at Woody's Diner for a half-cup of warmed-over coffee with Frank Sawyer and get the news from the Saturday night crew that occupied the nail kegs along the center aisle of the hardware store. Next was the post office where he'd pick up his mail and share another half-cup of lukewarm thermos coffee in the sorting room with Jerome Ives, Steam Valley's rural mail carrier. Crossing Main, he'd buy another Agitator from Brownie and get the weekend bar and VFW news from its one-armed proprietor. Last was the bank, where he'd grab the previous day's edition of the Wall Street Journal and chat with secretary Helen Kuhl.

Along the way he returned the greetings of others, always inquiring how *they* were, giving *them* his attention. He made you feet at home, Squire Hayes.

The lawyer was in a reflective mood as he walked downtown, arranging his day, recalling his long association with Louisa Longsdorf. He had buried her once in 1929. Today he was burying her again. Twenty-five years ago he buried her physically; today he would bury her legally. He wondered, idly, if an influential person ever really died.

Louisa Longsdorf had never gotten over Jacob Miller. She never married, content to love a dead man for eighty years. She inherited one-third of the estate from her father and bought the other two-thirds from her wastrel younger brother. Hermann, Jr. was the prodigal that never returned and died penniless and young, but not before fathering four children who had children who were all supported by their rich Aunt Louisa. Today, with the issuance of seventeen checks, that support ended.

Today, too, The Squire's own modest means increased. Today he became the largest stockholder in Merchant's and Farmer's bank.

Louisa's will stipulated that twenty-five years after her death the residual of her estate was to be divided among her remaining heirs; all the residual, that is, except the bank stock. That went to the executor or his heirs as payment for services rendered. Not one of the Longsdorf heirs had ever complained about the administration of Louisa's estate. The executor was Clarence L. Hayes.

That stock didn't amount to much when the market crashed two months after Louisa's death. Although the heirs' proxies gave him voting power, he didn't have the income or the full ownership benefits derived from owning the stock. Consequently, he kept his profile low on the bank board even though he was the bank's solicitor. Only he and the heirs knew who the ultimate owner of the stock would be. Voting control didn't matter during the Depression when the directors were united in the common goal of making sure the bank didn't fail. The bank didn't start making money until forty-two and hadn't paid a dividend until forty-six. Actually, voting control wasn't a factor until Bud Cole was made a director in forty-three.

It was a small bank. There were only ten thousand shares, all closely held. After he met with the judge he would own thirty-three hundred; three hundred acquired on his own and three thousand inherited from Louisa. Bud Cole came next with twenty-five hundred inherited from Reuben. Jonas Pemberton held seventeen hundred, all acquired for next to nothing from anxious shareholders who wrongly predicted the bank would fail after the crash. Fred Shaefer owned a thousand shares, all inherited from his father, and Romolo Barbano, an Italian shoemaker in Tannerytown, held five hundred. Rom acquired his shares the same way as Pemberton.

The five of them, representing ninety percent of the shares, made up the Bank Board. The bank's charter required that the top three shareholders be represented on the board. Traditionally the major shareholder was elected chairman. Each director had one vote, the shares being voted only at the bank's annual meeting or on special shareholder meetings authorized by the Board. The remaining one thousand share were held in one-hundred share blocks by Elwyn Bates, Evie Todd, Pete Jones, Mort Fessler, Harry Raker, Becky Raker, Helen Kuhl, Delia Cole, Posey Alexander and Frank Sawyer.

At par the shares were valued at five dollars each, current market had them at eighteen, the bank was earning six dollars a share and paying an annual dividend of one. Louisa had left a substantial nest egg that would allow he and Lola a comfortable retirement income. He doubted he would retire though. He had no hobbies, except being a lawyer.

Main Street was slow on Monday. It was kind of a recovery day, an adjustment he thought, to the most recent God-given phenomena to America called the Weekend.

His grandson was sweeping the sidewalk in front of the dimestore. Ted greeted the Squire with the same impish grin his mother had, and pointed out Tom Donachy's battered pickup parked in front of Sawyer's Hardware. It was loaded with lumber and rolled roofing for Harry Raker's chicken coop. Tom, as honest as Abe Lincoln and as homely, had told Ted the whole story before entering Squeaky's dad's barbershop for a badly needed haircut and another razzing. Squire laughed heartily with his grandson. Ted idolized Tom, who had taken time to teach the slightly built, introverted younger boy how to shoot a basketball. It had made a difference.

The news from Frank Sawyer at Woody's was sad. Ernie Rollins passed away Sunday. Hadn't Ernie been in the Squire's outfit in France?

Jerome Ive's information at the post office was serious too. Jim Morningstar had asked him to report any sightings of Spike Poorbaugh. The State Police and County Sheriff had made similar requests. It was obvious the trapper's recent sojourns into the valley were making folks nervous. Jerome thought the Squire should know.

After buying a paper at Brown's, the Squire sat on the bus stop bench and read the obituary of Ernest Rollins. Ernest had died at age fifty-seven of lung complications from being gassed in World War One. The VFW and Masonic Lodge would honor him at the viewing. The funeral would be at the Brick Church Tuesday.

Ernie had struggled physically after being gassed. The Squire had been in the same trench when it happened, along with Samuel Poorbaugh, the rest of their unit, and three German POW's. Ernie's gas mask malfunctioned and he collapsed. Poorbaugh bayoneted one of the prisoners and gave the dying German's mask to Ernie. Samuel Poorbaugh held the lowest rank, was the least of the least except in a scout or a fight, and was too much trouble to ever earn a promotion. He, Captain Hayes, was the unit's leader and there was a lieutenant, a sergeant, and several corporals in between; but Private Poorbaugh was the only one capable of an immediate battlefield reaction like that.

He saved Ernie's life but he had taken many others. But that was war and several times his kind of savagery was necessary, even requested. But he had assaulted civilians, too, and displayed an unnatural attraction toward very young women. Of that only he and Ernie knew. There was a peculiar twist in the uncivilized mind of Samuel "Spike" Poorbaugh.

On Armistice Day the Squire would advise Samuel to stay in the mountains where he belonged.

———

When he got to the bank Friday's Journal wasn't in its usual place. Bud Cole had it, filling a chair in the bank president's office, impatiently checking the price of cowhides in the futures section. From the scowl on his face even the news there was bad.

The bank president was at Helen Kuhl's desk reviewing a document with her. The goose had managed to slip away. Seeing The Squire approach, he quickly slid the document into Helen's work pile.

Helen's greeting smile was genuine. Steve Heffner's was fake. Helen was much better trained. Squire Hayes acknowledged her first.

"Helen, could I get you away from all that important looking stuff for a while?" He handed her a key. "I need the Longsdorf box."

She left immediately for the vault. The Squire turned his attention to the college-boy wonder that was her boss. "And how are you, young man?" he asked.

The bank president didn't look at The Squire directly or return the greeting. He just motioned for the lawyer to follow him to his office and mumbled the need for a "private conference."

The door glass gleamed with fresh goldleaf lettering - Steven P. Heffner, President. Squire Hayes had lobbied for it to read Helen H. Kuhl but had been outvoted. The majority of the bank Board favored the fresh-faced young outsider with the Masters in Business Administration to the plain, efficient, mature insider with a high school diploma and Experience in Business Administration. From the pile of work on her desk it was becoming obvious that Helen had ended up with two jobs – the one she didn't get and the one she already had.

Jonas Pemberton had disagreed with Bud Cole over the selection, saying he slept better when someone he knew managed his money. The vote was supposed to have been kept secret but Bud Cole wasted no time telling Steve Heffner who his supporters were.

The glass rattled within its frame when the door was opened. Bud Cole put down the Journal. The glass rattled again when the door was closed. The Squire noticed Steve Heffner's hands were shaking. He was a blond-haired, well-dressed young man in his late twenties. He was fit and trim and appeared sure of himself. But in a tense situation he became rattled and shook like the glass in his door.

"Squire," he began nervously, "we're having some second thoughts about the MacEwen loan."

"Who are the *we*?"

"Well, Bud here, and Jonas, and Rom." He paused, then added "and me."

Cole Enterprises was lining up against Mac. Romolo's son Lundy was a new clerk at the Tannery. Lundy would be on the street by noon if Rom failed to support Bud Cole.

"You didn't have any misgivings on Thursday when you recommended the loan. The board backed you unanimously."

"I know, but I didn't have enough information then."

"What new information do you have?"

There was another pause. The banker glanced at Bud Cole for his input. The brooding brute kept silent. The lawyer decided to go on the offensive.

"You mean you didn't know Cole Enterprises was putting in a bid for the Longsdorf land. None of us did. But the company's interest does nothing to reduce the quality of the MacEwen loan. The bank is well secured."

The eye contact between Steve Heffner and Bud Cole told him this ground had already been covered and Bud Cole simply didn't care. He wanted MacEwen's loan stopped regardless of the ethics, regardless of the legal consequences.

The lawyer directed his next question at Bud Cole who had the sullen look of a restrained bull. "Why didn't Jonas attend the meeting?"

"He was covering for me at the plant, damnit!"

Bud Cole was on the verge of losing control. The lawyer kept up the pressure. A temperamental man is a reckless man. He'll blurt his guts any minute, he thought. "So, we didn't know you wanted it, and you didn't know Mac wanted it. Sounds like the perfect setup for an honest bid to me." He let that sink in.

Bud Cole ignored the inference. "MacEwen's bid is invalid if we stop his loan. You haven't recorded any documents so the property hasn't been legally transferred."

"That will be done this afternoon."

"Save yourself the trip. Steve here is instructed to tell MacEwen the bank has changed its mind."

Squire Hayes directed his hard gaze upon Steve Heffner. "Since when did the bank formally change its mind?"

The goose, in the conspiratorial clutch of the fox, obviously worried about the stronger legal grip of the falcon. "Since this morning," he answered feebly. "The majority of the directors agree with Bud."

The falcon swooped in for the kill. "The Bank Board may have changed its mind, but the Bank hasn't. You can't go back on a done deal."

"Why not?" Bud Cole's remark was more a smug answer than a question.

"The bank entered into a binding contract when it granted Mac the loan. It tendered to him its guaranteed check which the estate publicly accepted as payment in full for the land. That check was cashed on Saturday and I'm mailing the heirs their money today."

Steve Heffner groaned. He thought Squire Hayes still had the check. He had hoped to get the check back and placate MacEwen with the promise of another loan on a less sensitive property. Now another bank had the check and it would have to be honored. He said resignedly, "It's beyond our control Bud. I can't bounce our own check."

Bud Cole tried another approach.

"You voted for the loan," he said accusingly. "That's a conflict of interest. You voted for money to go to the estate you control. You should give the money back to the bank and rebid."

Squire recognized the keen mind of Pemberton at work and glanced at the banker.

Steve Heffner straightened Bud Cole out. "He recommended MacEwen, but he didn't vote. He abstained."

But Cole bit his lower lip and brooded some more. Squire Hayes decided to probe further. "What you two have been proposing is illegal. Why are you putting yourselves and the bank at risk?"

"Because of the coal! It could make us all rich!" Bud Cole may have been angry, but he had enough control to remember the best way to get allies is to appeal to their greed.

Steve Heffner offered a more sophisticated explanation: "There's coal on Bear Mountain. It would mean more industry, more jobs, more wealth for the valley. For the greater good Cole Enterprises should have it."

More wealth for Bud Cole, you mean, thought The Squire. Sometimes "greater good" was used as a legal justification for thievery and this was one of those times. "Since when did the government grant the bank and Cole Enterprises the power of eminent domain?" he asked.

He didn't wait for the answer, firing another question at Bud Cole. "If you were so concerned about the greater good why did you bid so low? The plain truth is, you blew it. You had more information, more time, more money, and a better chance than the competition, and you blew it. I will not allow this bank to become involved in this scheme. If you want that coal, buy it from MacEwen."

The suggestion that he deal with his rival brought out the mean spirit in Bud Cole. "Pemberton told me you'd be difficult. Tell him the rest of our plan, Steve."

The banker cleared his throat. He hoped it wouldn't go this far. "If you refuse to cooperate, Squire, the Bank Board will appoint a new solicitor and remove you as a director."

The Squire had been expecting this. This tactic was typical of Bud Cole. He would bet his bank stock Pemberton hadn't been appraised of this approach. "You're acting like you have a vote in this young man, which you don't. Have the other directors been advised of this action?"

The banker answered, offended at being talked down to by The Squire. "Not yet. We know Fred won't go along, but we're confident Jonas and Rom will. That's all we need. Will you reconsider?"

"I'm recording that deed and mortgage this afternoon. Judge Elliott is serving as my witness. You can come along and describe your concept of the 'greater good' to him if you like."

The lawyer made his point. The words "fraud" and conspiracy" invaded Steve Heffner's quick brain. So did "jail" and "ruined career." Bud Cole would still have his job, but what would he have? "We won't be there," he said.

Bud Cole's next comment was thick with sarcasm. "It was nice having you on the board, Squire."

The lawyer rose to leave. "Don't be so sure of yourself, Bud. That's a decision to be made by the entire board. The major shareholder might want to be involved in this, too."

"She's dead."

"No, she's not dead. Not really." Then he explained why.

He had the Wall Street Journal with him when he closed the office door.

Chapter 10 – The Banker

Steven Heffner rummaged for the pack of cigarettes buried on his disorderly desk, found it, shook it once to force a half-dozen tips to show at the open corner of the pack, selected one, and lit up. The effort was a practiced one, appearing sophisticated was important to the young banker. Remembering his manners, he offered one to Bud Cole, who shook his head. He had forgotten. Bud Cole didn't smoke. Delia - lush, alluring, sophisticated Delia - did.   In the banker's discreet, Ivy League opinion Bud Cole lacked class. Bud Cole, he decided, wouldn't fit in anywhere but here.

Fitting in was also important to Steve Heffner. His ambition was to be at the top of the corporate pyramid, supported and admired by those beneath, to be declared the best of them, but still *one* of *them*. He needed the strength of the crowd. The thought of going it alone was frightening to him. He distrusted and envied the loner types.

The banker was a single man of twenty-nine, still on the lookout for the "right" girl. So far the only one that met his criteria was married to the brute across his desk.

What attracted classy women to these caveman types? He looked like the hulking center of the Cornell football team. But he possessed a natural charm, Bud Cole. When he wasn't angry he had a roguish personality, a naughty-but-nice, one-of-the-boys appeal. He was a difficult man to resist. So far only Jonas Pemberton and Squire Hayes had bucked him.

Steve Heffner pondered that. The smoke from his ciga-rette drifted in lazy bands between him and Bud Cole. The factoryman sat there strangely quiet; thinking, scheming, he was sure. The banker wondered if they each shared the same private, low opinion of the other and decided they probably did.

In Fallbrook the pyramid apexed at Bud Cole. That could not change. Toppling Bud Cole would topple them all. In Fallbrook the banker was one of the more important ele-ments of the pyramid. Being near the top had to suffice. Sophistication didn't count for much. You needed courage to reach the peak and stay there and he just didn't have it. Bud Cole – arrogant, brutal, charming, paradoxical Bud Cole–had courage. Most people, including himself, were afraid of Bud Cole.

Pemberton and Hayes now. Members of the Old School. They were not afraid. Right was right. Wrong was wrong. There was a clear distinction between black and white. There were no in-between shades of gray. But they were established and he wasn't. They could afford integrity. Maybe, when they were younger, they compromised their principles because they had to. Maybe, when they were younger, they were weak. He hoped so. It meant he had a chance. He'd rather be like them than himself. There were times Steve Heffner did not like himself.

It was the factoryman who broke the silence. His voice was controlled, purposeful. "I want to go over this again. What's the term of the MacEwen loan?"

"Six months."

"And the security?"

"The Longsdorf property, everything else I could attach, including the house on Tannery Hill."

"Good. If he hasn't repaid the fifty thousand by the end of February, we can foreclose, right?"

"Not exactly."

"Why not?"

"I agreed to a six-month extension."

"You did *what*?"

"Hold on, I haven't filed it yet. It's still on Helen's desk. She was about to give it to The Squire to record but I put it aside."

"You mean the extension is not part of the mortgage that's being recorded today?"

"Not yet. It's all signed and approved but…"

"Destroy it."

"It's signed, Bud."

"Destroy it. It'll be your word against his."

"And Helen's. She typed it…and witnessed my signature."

69

"Don't make a big deal of it. Don't talk about it. Just destroy it. Maybe she'll forget."

"You know better than that. Helen never forgets." Under his breath he muttered, "*I* forget, but not Helen." Sometimes he wished he could be like her, too.

Bud Cole heard. "She'll forget if she wants to keep her job. I may have to kowtow some to The Squire, but I still have three votes on the board. That's all I need. If the contract doesn't exist all MacEwen has is an argument, which will sound like sour grapes because we foreclosed. He doesn't have a copy, does he?"

"He doesn't have any paper proof at all. All he has is my word and a handshake. Nothing legal. Nothing substantial. He's not a detail man. He's left that to us."

Bud Cole grinned maliciously. "He'll regret that if he doesn't perform. Did he provide us with any insurance policies on the Longsdorf farm?"

"Not yet. I'll remind him though."

"Don't."

"That diminishes the bank's security, Bud. If there's a fire, I'll look bad."

"I'll cover your hind end. Every young businessman is entitled to one mistake." The malicious grin was still there.

Steve Heffner took a final drag on his cigarette. It tasted stale and didn't provide the relaxation he sought. This Mac-Ewen deal, last week lily-white, was turning very, very gray.

He had gone into banking because it was a safe and secure business and a steady paycheck. He needed that kind of environment. He was not a risk-taker, didn't have the instincts of the entrepreneur. His roommate in college, the son of a lucky wildcat oilman, scoffed at banking, claiming it was a business for thumbsuckers. That may be, but banking in league with Bud Cole was risky business.

He told himself it was smarter to risk the bank's assets on MacEwen than to risk his future on Bud Cole. He should get out, now. But he didn't possess the courage to stand up to the stronger man. He wasn't a Jonas Pemberton or a Squire Hayes. He wondered if he ever would be. "What you're contemplating Bud," he said finally, giving in to his weakness, "is breaking a man."

The factoryman rose leave. "Wouldn't hurt my feeling any," he replied.

Steve Heffner followed him out. He needed to retrieve the extension agreement from Helen's desk. He felt diminutive behind the powerful bulk of Bud Cole and wished he was bigger. A very pretty woman, a stranger, had just finished an interview with Helen Kuhl. "Hel-lo," he said, directing the factoryman's attention toward Helen's desk.

He noticed her too. "Don't get your hope's up, Big Boy," he chided. "She drove by my place yesterday...with MacEwen."

That bit of information strengthened Steve Heffner's resolve.

Helen was walking with the young woman to the front door. Bud Cole joined them. The banker watched as Helen made the introductions and noticed the ease with which the big man captured the girl's attention. He had no smooth, polished moves. He was simply Bud Cole, the big, genial factory owner with the winning smile. In the few seconds it took to open the door for her and follow her out he had made a favorable impression. He acted the country gentleman, but gentle he was not. Sometimes Steve Heffner even wished he could be like Bud Cole.

The banker moved to Helen's desk and read the account card of Abigail Whalen. She was twenty-five, single, a teacher, and she had money. She had opened an account with a thousand-dollar deposit. And she was pretty. On paper, in looks, she met his criteria. He *must* get to know her. Then, remembering his purpose and that she had already been located by MacEwen, he rifled through Helen's pile of work, seeking the extension agreement.

It wasn't there.

Chapter 11 – The Superintendent

"What do you mean, I'm being reassigned?" Abigail's question was one of panic and exasperation. After doing her banking she had breezed in to school management's office to announce her presence and touch base with her boss Mr. Bates, her mother's old friend. He had an announcement of his own.

"I repeat, Miss Whalen. Mrs. Brown has retired unexpectedly and I've had to reshuffle my staff. Mr. Rumsey has agreed to leave his junior high position to teach fifth grade for one year. You will take Mrs. Brown's position. I can't very well have a man teaching first-graders. The PTA wouldn't hear of it."

"But I have a contract to teach fifth grade," she argued.

Mr. Bates peered over his bifocals at Abigail. He was a wiry little man, balding, with eyes of authoritarian blue. "You have a contract to teach elementary school, Miss Whalen. As Superintendent I can assign you where you're needed. Since you have no seniority you must take the least desirable assignment. I have no choice and neither have you."

I can quit, thought Abigail. But she had signed that contract and other school districts frowned on hiring applicants who had broken their pledges elsewhere. She tried a different tactic, one that had worked with her previous school district. "I wonder what my mother will say."

She was hoping Mr. Bates would be intimidated by involvement from the bureaucratic higher-up.

He wasn't. Elwyn Bates ran his own show and the Department of Education left him alone. He put out a good product in Fallbrook and the Department, particularly Martha Whalen, was curious how he did it. He knew her mother wouldn't interfere. Not with him anyway. He knew Abigail could be saucy too. He was prepared.

"I called her this morning," he replied mildly. "She sends her best wishes. She was concerned how this assignment would affect your research. Since your thesis involves comparing rural and urban school children, I told her this assignment was actually better for you. You would see rural education in its simplest form."

"But it's a one-room school...with six grades!" Abigail's response was more a plea than a protest. She was comfortable in a self-contained one-grade room. That's what she intended to compare – the one she had in the city with the new one in the country. Both nice and cozy and disciplined and well-organized. The prospect of thirty-five primary and intermediate kids combined into one disheveled lot made her definitely uncomfortable, even fearful. "You know I have no experience teaching primary," she added, vainly seeking a way out of this. "I don't even like primary. I'll spend half my times wiping noses and tying shoes."

Mr. Bates stifled a smile. Martha had warned him her daughter could be a spitfire. He liked that. The spunky ones made the best teachers. Taught with energy and enthusiasm. Her mother was spunky, too. So was he, thank God. His response to Abigail was a bit wistful. "The Jackson Township School is one of the last of the one-room schools and I, for one, am sad to see it go. My first job was in one...teaching eight grades. You get the older kids to wipe the noses and tie the shoes."

He went on. This time he was more emphatic. "Next year our modern elementary school will be finished and all the outlying schools closed. If you choose to stay, and we both know that is improbable, you can have your choice of self-contained rooms. The trendsetters are saying that bigger is better. We're in an age of consolidation and change. The wave of the future. But waves sometimes break on rocky shores. I question whether we're doing the right thing, but I've been given the assignment and I intend to carry it out. I expect you to carry out yours as well."

His manner softened. He became almost friendly. "Enjoy your year, Abigail. It could very well be the most memorable year of your teaching career."

I'll remember it alright, thought Abigail.

He handed Abigail a sheet of tablet paper written by a nearly perfect hand. "Mrs. Brown's list for getting ready for school," he explained.

Abigail scanned the list: "Clean the stove, oil the floors, and lime the latrines?"

Mr. Bates stifled another smile. "I have instructed Principal Anderson to give you every cooperation," he said.

Chapter 12 – The Last One-Room School

The scene was postcard pastoral as a resentful Abigail entered Buttonwood and pulled into the gravel drive of the Jackson Township School. The building set in the middle of a square lot; framed by a cornfield, a pasture, a country lane and the main road. It didn't look frightening until Abigail reminded herself she wasn't just teaching here, she was managing the place. The items starred on Mrs. Brown's list convinced her of that.

The task ahead was perhaps exemplified by the traffic sign designating the school bus stop on 15. SLOW, it read, CHILDERN CROSSING.

If it had been someone else's school she would have laughed. Slow Childern? Childern? What kind of rubes was Bates assigning her to teach? Her mother said these country kids were good students. Childern? Taking a second look the new teacher was disappointed to learn she couldn't blame the locals for the misspelling. It was a state sign.

She drove slowly up the washed-out drive, grading it was on the list, and parked in front of her one-room school. Until today her experience with this kind of educational facility, if it could be called that, was limited to discussions in History of Ed. class and a field trip to one that had been converted to a museum in Lancaster. "Congratulations Abigail, you are now part of a museum. Won't that look good on a resume?" She spoke aloud, her voice thick with sarcasm.

With increasing reluctance she stepped out of her convertible.

The structure was a wood Federal Colonial painted white. All white. The only trim was the year of construction painted in black on the face of the building. 1870. A bell tower rose above the front center of the roofline and a brick chimney jutted above the upper sidewall. Tall double-frame windows provided light and airflow, augmented by a rickety front storm door that was new in September and worn out by

June. Another door was on the list. A covered porch ran the width of the front and in its far corner stood a high hand-pump well. A dented metal dipper hung on a nail close by. A new dipper was also on the list.

Abigail groaned when the significance of the well pump dawned on her. Oh God, no indoor plumbing? She hadn't been without that since Girl Scout Camp in the Pocono's. Surely there was an indoor bathroom for the teacher, and hot water. She had a right to expect that much, didn't she? Didn't she?

Beyond the schoolhouse were three outbuildings, the biggest one directly behind the school, the smaller two at the opposite far corners of the one-acre lot. The bigger shed was unpainted, with a sliding barn door and two chutes where windows had been. Coal sifted out one, stove wood stuck out the other. She could cross those two items off her list. That cheap Mr. Bates must have ordered her winter fuel in the summer when prices were lower.

The two smaller sheds were painted the same white as the school, had vents for windows, and differed only in ornamentation which was also black lettering. The shed at the far right was lettered BOYS. The shed at the far left was GIRLS.

Abigail walked the fieldstone path to the "girls," opened the door a crack, and peered in. How nice; a state of the art fourholer. She wrinkled her nose. She hoped there was lime in the woodshed.

The "girls" side of the schoolyard was the genteel side. Here were the standard elementary playground items – metal swing set, teeter-totter and slide. Two rope swings also hung from the sturdy lower branches of old beech trees that grew near the vine-covered woven-wire fence that separated the farm fields from the school grounds. Rugged wooden benches were built around the tree trunks and eighty-four years of romances were recorded in the bark.

It was cool and pleasant in the shade of the patient beeches. Abigail studied the names and initials inscribed there, the permanent roster of the Jackson Township School.

People she didn't know or care about. There was Jim and Missy, and Luke and Hattie, and Harry and Becky. Odd, that one showed recent work. The faintest, found by one of the swings, was E. Mc. & B.T. Evie maybe? And Burt Todd? She did know someone here! Not well, but she knew of them. And one was dead. Probably many were dead, their names etched here and on their gravestones, and nowhere else. Abigail realized then that a person doesn't get many chances to make a mark in this world. At this little school some at least got two.

Caught up in her reverie and out of her mad, Abigail sat in one swing and imagined her own initials underneath the big branch. A.W. and J.M. She swung, a pretty red-headed girl in a blue cotton dress and brown penny loafers. This was one opportunity she never had in the city.

She was brought out of her daydreams by the rumble of a heavy truck laboring through its turn from Williamson Road onto Route 15. It was Mac. On his way to the mill with a load of logs.

She jumped off the swing and hurried down the drive to stop him and explain her predicament, but he had already made his turn and hadn't seen her. She felt abandoned right then and alone. The truth was she didn't know how to accomplish many of the tasks on Mrs. Brown's list. Discouraged, once again resentful, she kicked some loose stones on her walk back up the drive. Damn that bully Mr. Bates and his contract and his one-room school, and for putting her here where she didn't belong! And damn that Jonathan MacEwen for not looking when he should!

The "boys" side of the school yard was not genteel. A stone path started for the privy but sank out of sight between third and home and didn't reappear until deep right field. A tall sapling had been trimmed into a pole and wired to the right corner of the privy. It was painted cherry red. Affixed to the pole was a board hand-painted the same red with an arrow pointing left and lettering that said FAIR. A confiscated section of PennDot snowfence was strung between the outhouse and woodshed and another red-lettered board in the center said HOMER. The school's white flag-pole had been removed from its dignified setting on the genteel side and wired to the schoolhouse's back right corner. Red letters running vertically down the flagpole spelled FOUL. Narrow passages had been cut in the fence to allow the necessary access to the privy and woodshed. And on the front wall of the shed, directly above the sliding door, hung a basketball hoop. It too was painted cherry red.

I've seen that color somewhere before, mused Abigail.

Climbing the porch steps to go inside, Abigail could see the schoolhouse was the center of action. Paths sprung from it like spokes of a wheel; the fieldstones running to the ball diamond, the "boys," the woodshed, the "girls," the playground, the shade trees, and the bus stop across from Evie's store. The fieldstones were driven deep, trampled down by the annual herds of schoolchildren. This was the last year the herd would come and for that, right now, Abigail was glad.

Chapter 13 – The Buttonwood PTA

Abigail reached for the key in her dress pocket. "Well, let's see this stove that needs cleaned," she said resignedly. With mounting apprehension she unlocked and opened the front door.

A blast of hot, dusty air dirtied her face and blew grit in her hair. Within that breeze was the telltale ammonia of something dead. Abigail wiped her eyes with her hanky, and, keeping it over her nose, walked in.

Immediately the dry floorboards creaked under her weight. So that's what the oil is for. She hadn't known. All the window shades were drawn. She couldn't see well and the rotten smell lingered. Several flies buzzed past her, making their escape out the open door. Maybe she should too. She steeled herself though and released one of the shades... and recoiled. The window sill was buried under dried flies...from a semi-dried bird.

Birds. Birds had taken residence here. A flock of very dirty, very poopy, very desperate birds had found their way in and couldn't get back out. Their wormy, dessicated bodies littered the room and the flies they created littered them.

This was too much for Abigail who gagged and looked for the bathroom. There wasn't any. She fought for control, held her breath, steadied, and talked herself out of being sick. Abigail had a strong stomach, a basic requirement for an elementary teacher, but right then she decided to relock the door, return the key to Mr. Bates stuck in the beak of a dried bird, pack her bags and take her chances in Harrisburg.

Then the floorboards squeaked a second time. The slight figure of Evie Todd stood in the doorway.

"Looks like we have our work cut out for us, don't we?" she said.

"We?"

"Yes, we," she answered, emphazing the we. "You, me, and the mothers. They'll be here shortly."

Evie circled the room lifting the seven remaining shades, allowing she hadn't expected a mess like this. She was tougher than Abigail, who decided not to say anything about quitting and resolved if a little old lady could stand it in here, she could.

"Help me open these windows," said Evie, straining at a stubborn latch. "Let's get some air in here."

As they worked together Evie pointed to the firebox of the ornate potbellied stove. The heavy cast iron door hung open.

"They came down the chimney," she explained. "Probably to get out of a storm. Starlings like to gather round chimneys. They're not smart like jays. A jay would have remembered his way out. Those starlings just followed a dumb leader and now they're dead. Like some people I've known."

The windows opened they sat out on the porch steps and got to know each other. Abigail was drawn to this spirited woman. "How did you know I was coming?" she asked.

"Mr. Bates called. He thought the Buttonwood PTA could lend a hand. We always have."

"I have a PTA?"

"*We* have a PTA." Again Evie emphasized the we. "I guess we've always had one. We just never knew what we were called. Mr. Bates started the first one in Fallbrook and named us the Buttonwood branch when the schools were joined. Delia Cole is President."

Abigail's lined eyebrows raised. "I met Mr. Cole at the bank this morning. His daughter attends here?"

"Amanda will be in the sixth grade," Evie answered, smiling. "She can be a help, and a handful."

Abigail let that hint pass. "Why don't they send her to the town school? They have more to offer there."

"Mr. Bates wouldn't allow it. Bud Cole tried to buck him but Mr. Bates made it stick. Said the little school would be good for Amanda." Evie paused to make a point. "He was right, too."

"He told me the same thing."

"There might be more to offer here than you think."

Abigail doubted it but didn't argue for fear of offending Evie. Instead she changed the subject. "Did you close your store?" she asked.

"It's never busy on Monday. What customers come will leave a note telling me what they got."

"Does the school have an account with you?"

"Mr. Bates and I wheel and deal," she said with a chuckle. "We both enjoy haggling. Besides supplies, I contract for the wood and coal and the mowing and plowing. I pay for the labor but Burt and I used to do it all. Tom Donachy helps me now."

The mention of Tom's name reminded Abigail she had some fences to mend with him. That association made her recall the color of his pickup – cherry red.

A vehicle turned into the drive and Evie rose to her feet. The help was here. It was time to get to work. "One more thing, Abigail," she said seriously. "We can't ever tell Hazel Brown her school got like this. It would shame her. Her husband was the janitor. He's in Fallbrook Hospital you know, dying of cancer."

"I didn't know," replied Abigail.

———

The first parent member of the Buttonwood PTA to arrive was Ruby Broadwater, a chunky pinkcheeked woman driving a battered cattle truck loaded with six chunky pink-cheeked boys. Theirs was a rough and tumble world, the Broadwater's.

The boys lined up dutifully behind their mom as Evie introduced their new teacher, Miss Whalen. They were a healthy patched-pants lot exuding restless energy. Abigail, who was good at seizing opportunity and directing kids, thought fast.

"Mr. Bates is offering a reward of ten cents for every dead bird removed from school property," she announced authoritatively.

81

In less than three minutes Harry Raker's cornfield was sprinkled with new fertilizer and Abigail was out $2.90. Evie was impressed. Ruby Broadwater became Abigail's friend for life.

The boys didn't wait for new instructions. Led by Hank, the oldest, they had the smelly stove ashes taken out and the floor swept before the other PTA members arrived.

Delia Cole drove in next, the back of her new Country Squire crammed with cleaning tools and supplies. "I couldn't get here any sooner," she called, dropping the tailgate. "I ran up to the tannery for a few things."

Her dark hair was tied back with a red bandanna. She wore jeans and a short sleeve gingham blouse both filled out by a great figure. But to Abigail, who was checking her out minutely, the most striking aspect of Delia Cole was her flashing white smile.

She had help unloading the station wagon. These Evie identified as her daughter Amanda and her housekeeper Nadia. "That Amanda's a tomboy," whispered Evie. "Nadia is a Lithuanian refugee and doesn't speak much English, but I think she knows more than she lets on."

Face to face, Abigail found Delia to be direct, friendly, and, Aunt K was right, ravishing. This lady made a presence even wearing work clothes. Her complexion was clear ivory, offset by thick auburn hair, intelligent hazel eyes, and beautiful teeth, large perfect white teeth. No wonder Mac and Bud Cole wanted this woman.

Surprisingly, Fallbrook's Chief Society lady was excited about this country get-together and not at all daunted by the dirty job. She and Nadia joined Ruby scraping the bird-bedecked desks. Amanda, a plump budding picture of her mother, joined the Broadwater boys stacking stovewood and rearranging the coal pile.

Soon several other family groups arrived and Abigail and her schoolhouse were overrun with eager, efficient workers.

She met Hattie Ballard and her pretty elementary-age daughters Rachel and Sylvie. Like Delia, Hattie also drove a big late-model station wagon. There were two older boys, she explained, and they needed the extra room. Luke, her husband, worked in the woods. For Mac, Evie added.

Next she met Mary Spencer, a tall worn-looking woman, her skinny teenage daughter Nan, and her grandson Danny. His mother worked, she said, so they came in her place. Danny was going in the first grade and was shy around his teacher. He wore a Yankee ballcap that was too large and had the bluest eyes. Amanda grabbed his hat and took off and Danny tore off after her, his tousled white-gold hair flying.

She'll let him catch her, said Mrs. Spencer smiling. They go back a ways, Amanda and Danny. She took in washin' and sewin' and lived right here in Buttonwood. Would Miss Whalen be interested in her services? Abigail, who hated those chores, engaged her on the spot and made another friend in Naomi Spencer.

Last came her farm neighbors Becky and Carol Raker. Becky, in a checkered cotton dress and plain kitchen apron, had been canning peaches and brought a jar for everyone. Carol came in from raking hay and was still in her field clothes. The earthy Ruby suggested the tanned farmgirl stay inside and work before she caused another wreck. This brought snickers from the group, especially Carol's mother and Hattie Ballard.

Abigail spent the afternoon working alongside the members of the Buttonwood PTA. In later years she would describe that day fondly, as one of the highlights of her teaching career.

By suppertime the schoolhouse was clean. The sickening odor was gone, replaced by the spice of cleansers applied briskly to wood and metal. The oiled floorboards could be stepped on without complaining and the nickel-plated room stove gleamed. The oak desks, front bench, upright piano and crank telephone all glistened with a fresh coat of furniture polish and George Washington sat snug in a reglued frame. The globe lights were given new incandescent bulbs and the emergency lanterns filled with fresh kerosene. The windows were washed, the well pump primed, the cobwebs broomed out of the four-holers. A bag of lime was found in the woodshed, so the Broadwater brothers limed the BOYS and Danny Spencer, then Amanda limed the GIRLS and the Broadwater boys.

After everyone left, Abigail washed up at Evie's and sped off to the Turkey Ranch for supper. She was ravenous, having forgotten to eat lunch after her meeting with Mr. Bates and working hard all afternoon. She was also in a hurry to catch Mac and Tom at their evening meal before they returned to their landing to load another shipment of logs before nightfall.

She felt confident now. All the items on Hazel Brown's list were crossed off except the driveway and Evie said she'd take care of that. She hadn't figured out how to instruct six grades but Mrs. Brown had a system and had offered to share it with her replacement. She had two days to prepare before school registration on Thursday, so there was time to work out the loose ends. And she had friends, mothers to call for help.

The only mother she hadn't warmed up to was Delia Cole, and Abigail had been the cool one, not Delia. She was uncomfortable with Delia's involvement with Mac. Abigail regarded Delia as a rival. From her sorority experience in college Abigail had learned to distrust potential rivals.

Three scenes lingered in her mind, each occurring near the end of the day. One was funny, one was worrisome, and one was sad.

The funny incident happened when the kids were outside playing ball. There was a crash of breaking glass and a ball bounced off the piano and several desks before coming to a rest under the teacher's chair. Through the broken window the adults heard the kids' reactions to the misdirected play. Hank Broadwater's admonition was the clearest: "That's why I bat left, Amanda. So, when I tag it, the ball goes right over the shitter."

Ruby and Delia rolled their eyes. It was Carol Raker's turn to snicker.

The worrisome incident occurred while Delia was removing pieces of broken glass from the window frame. Mac and Tom had stopped at Evie's for a Coke. The Army six-by-six was loaded with logs and the kids raced across the road to gawk at the big truck. The popular brothers helped each kid into the cab to blow the air horn and pretend to steer.

Delia, watching the scene intently, sliced her hand on a shard of glass. Abigail saw it happen, saw her face as tears brimmed in her beautiful eyes, and she bit her lip in pain. But she did all that *before* she cut her hand on the glass.

The sad scene happened after everyone left the schoolhouse except Evie and Abigail. Evie pulled the ceiling trap open to the bell tower. She was going to ring any bats out of the bell, which she did. The lusty ringing bounced back and forth; off the ridges of Laurel, Blackwolf, Potash, and Bear, informing everyone therein the schoolhouse in Buttonwood was ready.

Just before she closed the trap, Evie smelled the rope.

Chapter 14 – That Vixen Julie

"Be still, Danny."

"Amanda's here, Mom!"

"When we're done you can go play."

"How long?"

"Not long. We're next in line."

Ruby Broadwater was standing in front of the teacher's desk, registering one of her brood. Julie and Danny and the mothers behind them and their restless children could hear every word. There wasn't much privacy in a one-room school.

"You remember Chucky, my next to the youngest? Keep an eye on him. He can be a little turd."

Delia Cole's face lit up with a wide smile. A ripple of giggles ran down the line. The former private secretary of Reuben Cole and current president of the PTA was sitting at a card table placed next to the teacher's desk confidently typing names onto file folders. The new teacher was at her desk interviewing the mothers and completing registration forms. Abigail's lips pressed tight as she tried to maintain her dignity, but she couldn't hold it and she smiled too.

"Well, he is," said the unruffled Ruby.

Danny squirmed under his mother's hands which were resting lightly on his shoulders.

"Can I have a hat like Chucky? For my birthday?"

"We'll see." But she really didn't think a coonskin cap would look right on her boy. It looked fine on Chucky.

Their turn came. The mothers in line stopped talking and shushed their kids. The three women involved with Jonathan MacEwen were together for the first time. Of the three, not one had anticipated this moment. Only their observers had thought ahead.

Abigail sat prim and proper in a belted dark skirt and light long-sleeve blouse. Delia was businesslike in a red and black two-piece suit. Julie was wearing a crisp white waitress dress, her order pad and pencil sticking out the right front pocket. Julie's outfit was the plainest but nothing about Julie was plain. This girl had it all, and didn't know it.

Abigail greeted Julie and Danny and was genuinely surprised.

"*You* are Danny's mother?"

"Yes."

"But I thought you were single."

"I am."

"Oh." Abigail paused to digest this information. Was Julie divorced, a widow, or what? Keep your mind on school, Abigail, she told herself. She concentrated on the registration form Delia had given her. "Danny's full name please," she said.

"Daniel Tyler Spencer."

"Date of birth."

"September twenty-fifth, nineteen forty-eight."

"So he's five now, almost six. That's young for first grade."

"I know. I think he can handle it."

"We will find that out shortly. Place of birth."

"Williamsport General."

"Family physician."

"Doctor Buckley."

"Has Danny had his shots?"

"Yes." Julie handed Delia the vaccination papers for Danny's file. Delia looked uncomfortable.

"Mother's name," said Abigail, reading down the form.

"Julie Spencer."

"Mother's maiden name."

Julie Spencer."

Another pause. "Father's name."

Julie felt her face drain of color, then flush. She heard some self-righteous whispers from the line.

"Father's name," repeated Abigail, ignoring a high sign from Delia.

Julie released Danny. "You can go with Amanda now," she said shakily.

Danny didn't go. "I want to know too, Mom," he said.

"Go, Danny."

Danny went.

Abigail waited, giving Julie a bewildered look that said the form required an answer. Delia's eyes blazed with anger. Julie's filled with tears.

"He has no father," she stammered.

Delia interrupted. "This is none of the school's business, Miss Whalen," she said pointedly.

This time Abigail flushed. Delia's rebuke stung. Why hadn't they told her in advance about Julie? She tried to salvage some of her dignity and looked to the form to bail herself out. "Let's leave that blank," she said. "For next of kin shall I use your mother?"

"Yes, Mary Spencer." This sharp response came from Delia.

The rest of their interview was a blur to Abigail and Julie.

———

Outside, Julie composed herself. Again Abigail had caught her off guard. Why had she been so insistent? Did she do it on purpose? Would Danny continue to ask about his father?

She found Danny being twisted in the rope swing by Chucky. Amanda was far away, petting one of Raker's heifers that had poked its head under the fence. Alarmed, Julie ran to the swing and pulled Danny from the seat a second before Chucky let it go.

The twisted ropes spun loose like an uncoiled spring, snapping the empty seat against the tree trunks with the jerky effectiveness of an executioner. Chucky was impressed.

"Come on, Danny. We're going."

"But Mom!"

"Come on, Danny!" She took him firmly by the hand and hurried to her car.

While Danny sulked in the front seat, sitting as far from his mother as possible, Julie remembered she had promised to let him stay and play with Amanda. Delia was to bring him home. But he didn't play with Amanda. Now he had to go home. She started the car.

It was the smug reaction of some of the mothers that got to her. "That vixen Julie" stuff again. A couple of them had gotten in trouble and had to get married but conveniently forgot about that. David Sheafer would have married her, too, if he hadn't been killed. He said he would after their one time. He promised her again in his last letter; as soon as he could arrange leave, he wrote. Then he fell off a truck servicing a plane and hit his head on the runway. Julie, just seventeen and three months along, grieved alone.

She had to quit school, of course. Posey gave her a job until she started to show, then took her back after Danny was born. She had worked at the Turkey Ranch ever since. She and her mother and sister raised Danny.

She never told anyone about Danny's father – not her mother, not Posey, not Missy, not Tom, not Fred or Aunt K. That way her shame was borne only by her and her family and the responsibility of raising Danny was her own.

She liked David's parents, especially Fred. He came in the Turkey Ranch regularly and always asked about Danny. Fred's interest was more than kindness, she knew.

She had bloomed after Danny was born. Strange, she never thought of herself as attractive. She had always been a freckle-faced girl, tall and skinny. Then she filled out and the freckles faded, except the few over the bridge of her nose, and Steam Valley tagged her as "that vixen Julie."

With her fresh beauty and down-to-earth personality she made good money. Customers tipped well at the Turkey Ranch. The Spencer's were no longer poor. And Posey paid her extra for keeping the books and doing the ordering. The truckstop owner was a great cook and promoter but a lax manager. Julie was an excellent manager. Posey said she could squeeze a dime into a quarter. They made a good team, she and Posey.

Julie knew the valley wives talked about her. Missy Morningstar kept her informed of the gossip. She was where men congregated, she was "experienced," and unmarried. It was bitter irony to Julie, "experienced" after one time.

Some of the wives had cause for concern. They couldn't trust their husbands. Julie was surprised at the number of offers...and refused them all. Another irony; the one they trusted least was the one they could trust the most.

She didn't want a man that would cheat. She wanted a man that wanted her like Jim wanted Missy. She hadn't had a man before David Sheafer and she hadn't had one since.

Then Mac came home from Korea. Betty Donachy had died and Julie had hired Tom and got to love him like a brother. But who couldn't love that rascal Tom? Someone had to keep him in line. Just the thought of Tom made her smile.

It was Tom that brought she and Mac together. She had known him before, of course. He was Major MacEwen, the war hero. She studied about him in school. He was the gifted local boy who went away and made good. Now he was back and she was all grown up and studying him as a man.

He was young, only ten years older, and he *was* interested. She would catch him looking at her with those captivating green eyes and *feel* his interest. Her mind couldn't grasp his thoughts but her body could. He wanted her and she wanted him, but two months had passed and he hadn't made a move.

Was she too busy? She was free on Friday's. Why didn't he ask her out on Friday? What was holding him back? Was it the gossip? Was it Danny? If it was, it wasn't fair. There was gossip about him too. The only difference between Delia and Mac and she and David was that Delia didn't get pregnant and Mac didn't get killed. She wouldn't have let Mac go like Delia did. Should she talk to him? The man was supposed to make the first move, right? If he doesn't, what do you do? Julie didn't know. She had spent her dating years working and raising Danny.

Abigail Whalen knew. Pretty, educated, aggressive Miss Whalen. Her son's teacher. Her mother's customer.

Her man's new interest. Her man? Get with it, Julie. Abigail had spent more time with Mac in the past week than Julie had all summer.

Maybe Mac had never been her man. Maybe she just imagined his interest because she wanted the relationship so bad. What she thought she had wasn't real.

But Abigail Whalen was real and she apparently wasn't used goods. She didn't have a son to raise anyway.

Julie felt a warm presence beside her. Danny was curled up, fast asleep, his blond head snug against her right thigh. She stroked his silken hair and soft face. He was an affectionate boy, Danny.

She guessed she'd better get her head straight about Jonathan MacEwen.

Chapter 15 – The First Day of School

It was Monday, the first day of school, and very gray, the morning sun hidden by a low-lying fog. Danny and Nan stood at the end of their drive waiting for the school bus. Danny clenched two of his aunt's fingers in a tight fist. All of a sudden going to school was a scary proposition. Aunt Nan was okay, more like a big sister than an aunt, but he really wished his mom was here.

He wiped his face across Nan's fingers. They had waited long enough that the fog moistened their skin. He could smell her Avon perfume. He knew it was called Avon because that was what the letters spelled on the saleslady's case. The lady seemed surprised he could read. Danny said he couldn't read, but his mom and Nan and grandma could, and they read to him all the time and taught him the alphabet. He just knew his letters real good.

Nan's perfume was nice, kind of rosy, but he liked Miss Whalen's better. Hers reminded him of violets he picked after a rain one time for his mother. His mom hadn't said, but he overheard his grandma tell Nan she was afraid Danny's teacher and Julie didn't like each other. That Miss Whalen wouldn't like him was a secret concern to Danny. But she had treated him just fine when they cleaned the school and when she brought her laundry.

The fog veiled their surroundings, making the larger objects ghostlike. He knew what they all were, old farm buildings and gnarly trees, but early mornings in Steam Valley were still scary. He could hear the occasional click, click of the windmill blades pushed by a fickle morning breeze. Soon the wind and sun would dry away the fog and he would be able to see the top of the windmill, and the blue sky, and the cotton clouds. He couldn't do that at school. It made you feel like staying home, the windmill.

From out in the fog came the vibrations of an approaching vehicle, a big one. Danny gripped Nan's fingers even tighter. He had never ridden a bus before. The headlights appeared first, just two misty yellow beams, then blinking red lights, then the vague outline of the bus growing more distinct as it drew closer and slowed to a stop.

The door folded open and Danny's wide eyes stared up the treaded metal steps to the jovial face of Sully Thompson. He knew him! Sully was the greeter at his church. He didn't know Sully was his bus driver!

"Good morning, Danny. Foggy, isn't it?" said Sully.

"Foggier than your head, Mr. Thompson," Danny replied, repeating a Tom Donachy-ism he had heard and never thought out.

Sully and Nan laughed. Sully knew where it came from. He had heard it earlier that morning at the counter of the Turkey Ranch. Posey was cooking breakfast and Tom was plaguing Posey.

Danny let go of Nan and climbed aboard, taking the front seat directly behind the driver. His feet didn't reach the floor so he supported himself by holding on to the pipe rail that separated he and Sully. He reminded Nan that they had promised to leave room for Amanda.

Sully drove north on 15, picking up the Broadwaters and the Ballards and a few other valley families. The noise level grew after each stop, excited kids banging their metal lunchboxes as they got on the bus, breaking in starched back-to-school outfits and creaky leather shoes.

At the turnoff to Williamson Road the bus turned west, rumbled across the covered bridge and labored up the incline to the Cole land at the top of the rise. Fog still hung over Blockhouse Creek, but higher, in the foothills, it had started to clear.

Up ahead, Danny could see Amanda and her mother waiting. Behind them stood their stately white house in the woods. In front of the garage Amanda's big collie strained against his chain. Danny knew Barney would go to school with Amanda if he could. He had before.

Sully stopped the bus and levered open the door. Amanda gave her mother a quick kiss good-bye. Behind them the collie reared against his chain, barking furiously. Amanda got on and took the middle space between Danny and Nan. "I don't know what's wrong with Barney," she said. "He's never acted that way before."

"I know," answered Danny. "He's barking at that man in the woods...right over there." He pointed to the trees beyond the garage.

The rest of them looked and couldn't see anyone, but the man *was* there. He blended in well, that man, but not well enough to escape the sharp eyes of first-grader Danny Spencer.

———

Ever since junior high Tom Donachy had carried a crush for prim and pretty Brenda Whitaker. She did not return his interest. Her dad was a bigwig at the tannery, she lived in a fancy Victorian in Fallbrook, and Tom lived in Tannery-town. That was a burden, Tom assured her one time, he didn't hold against her.

Each year he would ask for a date and each year get the same reaction: She would look at him in disbelief, tell him no or something worse, toss her yellow hair, and walk indignantly away. Tom called each fumbly attempt The Great Approach.

As they grew up it seemed she got prettier and he got homelier and perhaps that distinction was what affected the persistent Tom the most. She was unattainable. She wasn't always unfriendly; she was always...haughty. She represented a challenge that Tom could not resist.

They now sat in Senior English. Horseface, their teacher, droned on, lost in the nether world of the romantic poets. The old maid had forgotten her class. She was reading aloud John Keats' long poem *The Eve of Saint Agnes*. She had started reading to show the class *how* to read poetry, dove deep into it, and hadn't been up for air in five minutes.

You could tell she saw herself as the fair maiden Madeline, stolen away from a castle full of lusting, sleeping knights by the brave sneak-thief Porphyro. Tom hoped she would get her wish and go back in time and stay there; but what a dreadful surprise for poor Porphyro, to find Horseface under that veil!

It was the first day of school and already he was in trouble with the senior girls and their avowed protector, Miss Constance Abernathy, a.k.a Horseface. The girls had been acting coy all day, like they all had found boyfriends in Williamsport or Elmira or some other big city where the pickings were better. Then Miss Abernathy announced her annual futile quest to bring "culture" to Fallbrook High, especially to its Uncouth Boys.

To the Class of '55 culture meant poetry.

Her assignment had been for each of them to read aloud their favorite poem. She gave them a few minutes to make their selections, then started down Tom's row, which was at the far side of the classroom along the windows. Tom was fourth in line, behind three girls. In the rows directly across were Squeaky, Joe, Carol, and lastly, Brenda.

Tom liked poetry. He devoured westerns and mysteries but he also read poetry. His mother and Big Mike had raised him on nursery rhymes, fables, and poems, especially Scottish and Irish works. When it came to poetry, Tom Donachy knew his stuff.

The girls in front read their selections; all distressed damsel stuff, all picked to brownnose Miss Abernathy, and all delivered badly.

When Tom's turn came he was ready.

Summoning his best Gaelic brogue, Tom read Robert Burns' *To A Louse (On seeing one on a lady's bonnet in church)*, placing special emphasis on verses two and seven:

> Ye ugly, creepin', blasted wonner,
> Detested, shunn'd by saunt an' sinner!
> How dare ye set your feet upon her,
>   Sae fine a lady?
> Gae somewhere else and seek your dinner.
>   On some poor body.

O Jenny, dinna toss your head,
An' set your beauties a' abread!
Ye little ken what cursed speed.
    The blastie's makin'!
Thae winks and finger-ends, I dread,
    Are notice takin!

The guys broke up and so did some of the girls that could take a joke. A couple prisses, however, gave him looks that said they wished he was a board and they were sandpaper. Horseface was not pleased. Neither was Brenda. Tom could tell that by the way she tossed her hair. Some girls talk with their bodies, and Brenda was one.

Squeaky took the heat off when he flicked "something" from Monica Manikowski's shoulder and the fiery Monica turned around and cracked him over the head with her heavy Lit. book. The guys began leafing through their books for another poem like Tom's and the girls did the same to get even. Miss Abernathy restored order by announcing the class would read Keats and *she* would show them how. Then she became totally engrossed in the story of Madeline and Porhphyro.

When she got to the part in *Saint Agnes* where young virgins had "visions of delight", she slurred the words purposely. She didn't want those visions in *her* class. Heck, did she ever have them? Did she remember what they were?

By now most of the students had settled down to their math homework. Tom had some free time – he had done his math in POD. He glanced across the room at Brenda. She was following along with Miss Abernathy, also enamored with the handsome Porphyro.

Brenda was a responsible student, tied with Carol Raker for second in the senior class. Tom was first, as always an enigma. The academic side of his report card was all A's; the behavior side, however, was sprinkled with N's and U's, for Needs Improvement and Unsatisfactory. Carol and Brenda got a few B's mixed with the A's on one side and all Es and S's on the other, for Excellent and Satisfactory. Tom argued they didn't try hard enough. It took work to get the marks he did. All of them.

Carol was his best competition in Math and Science; Brenda almost his match in English and History. Brenda's yearbook biography was already written – she wanted to be a college English teacher. Tom hadn't gotten around to planning his future yet, survival came first, although Mac and Julie had started bugging him about it.

He thought Brenda's was a worthy goal, as long as she didn't end up a dried up old stick like Horseface. Romantic poetry, though, was juicy stuff and gave him an idea. If it worked for Byron, Keats and Shelley, why not him? T'was time for this year's Great Approach.

He checked on Horseface's whereabouts first. Porphyro had just sneaked into the castle and was headed upstairs, "brushing the cobwebs in the archway with his lofty plume." Now how can anyone sneak wearing a hat like that?

Tom borrowed a red pen from Squeaky and removed a five-dollar bill, the only bill, from his wallet. On the front side, near Lincoln's picture, was the word "tender." He circled it. On the lower right was the word "series," which he changed to "serious." On the reverse, in the clear space to the left of the Lincoln Memorial, he wrote a poetic message to Brenda.

He folded the bill so only the number five showed and whispered to Squeaky to send it over. The bill crossed the room, from aisle to aisle, just beyond the range of Horseface's finned bifocals, from Squeaky to Joe to Carol to Brenda. She was startled when she got it.

Back in the castle young Porphyro had been secreted to Madeline's chamber by a sympathetic old crone who hid him in a closet from which he could see his intended's bed. Tom noted strong resemblance between Horseface and the old crone, but she still saw herself as fair Madeline.

He checked on Brenda. She was writing something on his bill. Tom felt encouraged for the first time. At least she didn't rip it up like some others he had sent. That was five bucks!

Brenda finished her reply and the bill began its cautious trip home.

Meanwhile Madeline, unaware her beloved was peeping from the closet, began taking her clothes off. "She lowered her fragrant bodice, by degrees, her rich attire crept restlessly to her knees, like a mermaid in seaweed." Lucky Porphyro! Horseface sighed and drew a hand across her own rather droopy chest, subconsciously following Madeline's every move. If she didn't come to pretty soon her own blouse would be laying on the floor.

Squeaky handed Tom the note. By now the rest of the class had caught on to Tom and Brenda's involvement in another Great Approach. They put their math homework aside. In her chambers, Horseface, Madeline rather, "so pure a thing, so free from mortal taint," stretched out on her bed.

Brenda had refolded the bill so only the visage of honest Abe showed. The word TO was printed over his homely head, not a positive sign. Tom unfolded the bill and found Brenda's answer written on the right side of the Lincoln Memorial. He felt his ears grow hot. Her poetry was better, more pointed. She could be a minx, that Brenda Whitaker.

He was reading her reply a third time when the bill was rudely snatched from his hand. Tom looked up. Horseface hovered over him, a harpy from literary hell.

When did she get there? The last he knew Porphyro was creeping up to Madeline's bed. How could she ever pull herself away from a scene like that? No wonder she was an old maid.

For once Horseface had everyone's attention.

"Class, it seems Mr. Donachy and Miss Whitaker have been writing some romantic poetry of their own." She held up the bill. "Let me read it to you. I'll begin with Mr. Donachy's 'Ode to Brenda,' which was the earliest work":

O Brenda dear,
My heart aches for true.
If you go out with me,
I'll spend this on you.

98

The class howled, especially loyal buddies Squeaky and Joe.

Horseface continued: "My, but he's a generous suitor, isn't he? Imagine, offering five whole dollars! Let's see if Miss Whitaker is impressed. Her work is titled an 'Ode to Tom':"

> Thomas you're sweet,
> But you're not my honey,
> It's good looks I seek,
> So, here's back your money.

The class howled again. Somehow Brenda managed to flounce sitting down. When she tossed her hair at him Tom noticed her dainty ears were as red as his. He decided to steer clear of her for a while. In the meantime, Horseface had his five bucks.

The class bell rang and Brenda was the first out the door, followed by her teasing peers who wasted no time spreading the news. The Great Approach had failed...again.

Tom found himself alone with Miss Constance Abernathy.

"Did you learn anything today, Mr. Donachy?"

"Yes, Ma'am."

"What was that?"

"If I'd been Porphyro, I'd have gotten caught."

Horseface's tight lips turned up at the corner's a little. She returned his five dollars.

After school, Tom hurried off to help Mac at the log landing, but he needed gas. He filled up at Wally's Esson in town and, without thinking, paid with the five-dollar bill and left.

He should have charged it.

Wally's next customer was Sully Thompson. He paid with a twenty and got Tom's five back as part of his change. "Hey," he said, "the kids were talking about this on the bus." When he got home he gave the money to his wife.

For the next week the bill made its rounds. Mrs. Thompson bought groceries with it from Bob's Corner Market. Bob raided his cash register and paid a bet he lost to Harold Fabel, Sr. at the barbershop. Harold and Bob went to lunch at Woody's and Harold paid. Woody needed his restaurant trash taken to the dump so he offered Joe Ballard five bucks to load and haul it. Joe was behind two payments on Carol's engagement ring for Christmas so Bailey's Jewelers got the five. Thus it went, from merchant to merchant, finally ending up at Sawyer's Hardware as payment for a door handle.

Frank had been looking for the bill all week. He tacked it on the message board that hung on the wall across from his counter, directly above the loafer's bench and just below the set of trophy deer antlers everybody called Old Ebenezer. That was as public a place as any in Steam Valley.

Before the bill was retired it had been involved in several hundred dollars worth of transactions, proving conclusively the velocity theory of money, and finishing forever the one-sided romance of Brenda Whitaker and Tom Donachy.

Chapter 16 – The Dinner Pail

At 4:43 a.m. Luke Ballard reached from his bed and shut off the alarm clock, set for two minutes later. The alarm was a precaution left over from the tannery, where if he punched in five minutes late he was docked an hour. That alarm hadn't gone off once in seven years, since he left the tannery and started cutting timber on his own.

He felt Hattie's arm circle his waist, a waist that had thickened some when he passed forty. Her warm soft body nestled against his and a familiar wanting kindled. But she was just cuddling now, he knew. They never made love in the morning. That was reserved for night, an event antici-pated all day, after the kids were in bed, and after his back rub and shave and shower.

Hattie's hand left his waist and pressed on his shoulder for support as she sat up in bed. "Time to get going," she said, then threw back their covers. Luke felt the coolness of the room invade the small of his back and he sat up too. Hattie put on her housecoat, brushed back her dark brown hair, and went to the kitchen. She filled out a housecoat nicely, his Hattie.

Luke stood up and stretched; a brawny, hairy man in a cotton t-shirt and boxer shorts. A man with thick, well-developed legs. He went to the bathroom, washed up, then dressed in the clean work clothes Hattie set out for him the night before. In the fall he wore two pairs of socks, first cotton then light wool, a pressed flannel shirt, and denim coveralls. All his clothing was one size too large. Luke required freedom of movement to operate a forty-pound chain saw.

He went to the kitchen in his sock feet. Hattie's new ranch home was open to all, but if you had muddy boots, and loggers usually did, the boots stayed in the mudroom.

Luke passed through the kitchen on this way to the breezeway to check the weather. Hattie was bent over the refrigerator. He gave her backside a playful pat. "You stop that," she said, without meaning it. Two pots of coffee were perking on the counter.

At the breezeway Luke slipped on a pair of moccasins, turned on the porch light, and stepped outside. This was decision time. If it was wet, he stayed in his garage and sharpened saws. Dry, he went to the woods.

He first looked west, the direction the weather came from. The landforms were a wooly black, set against the lighter velvet of a clear night sky. A full butter-yellow moon hung over Bear Mountain, enhancing the peak's mystery. An old story had it the man who built the covered bridge had gone there and found enormous trees. He never made it back to cut them; he drowned at Jacob's Landing. Luke had never seen virgin timber. He wondered often about that story.

His attention shifted to movement on the moon. The irregular vee of a flock of geese, southbound, crossed the yellow surface. An outdoorsman, Luke never tired of nature's illusions. In the east a lavender crack appeared along the skyline, the break of a dry fall day. He would go to the woods.

For now moonlight prevailed, and would for another hour, reflecting off foothills and mountainsides chalked white with stiff frost. Frost covered everything. Even the spider web woven between two wrought-iron porch rails was coated. In the web, a frozen spider and a frozen fly. A good sign. Loggers celebrated the first killer frost. After that there were no more bugs, no more snakes, and no more leaves.

He looked low. Steam Valley was getting a double dose of refrigerant, frost and fog. He could hear the slow truck traffic on 15. He couldn't see it. Down there they were cursing the cold, the dark, and the mist. They didn't know it was a nice day.

From a quarter of a mile below him came the grinding of a starting car. Julie Spencer was on her way to work.

Simultaneously, a set of car lights blinked on across the valley in the foothills of Potash. The junkman's routine coincided with Julie's. Heck, he was probably up earlier.

Mort Fessler would finish his second cigar waiting for his morning coffee at the Turkey Ranch. Luke wondered if the affable miser ever slept. Probably not; too afraid of someone making off with his money.

Luke's feet got cold, reminding him of the task at hand. He reached inside the breezeway door for the workboots placed on the Rubbermaid mat the day before. He beat the soles of the leather hightops against the cement stoop, knocking the dried mud from the tread. He placed the boots back on the mat and swept the crumbling mudcakes into the yard with the porch broom. The fog crept uphill and Luke shivered. Back inside he was glad Hattie had insisted on the addition she called the mudroom, the place out of the wind to roll out filled pants cuffs and take off caked shoes.

In the kitchen, bacon was frying and a crock of oatmeal bubbled on the stove. Hattie added a cube of maple sugar to the oatmeal and cracked two eggs into the frypan alongside the bacon. Luke ladled a healthy portion of oatmeal into a bowl, added milk and another cube of maple sugar and sat down to the kitchen table to eat. Hattie poured his coffee and a water glass full of orange juice. Luke added milk and sugar to the steaming hot coffee, poured some of the mixture into his saucer to cool, then sipped his first coffee of the day from the saucer. The rest of the coffee he would drink from the cup. When the oatmeal was finished the bacon and eggs were ready. While he worked on that plate, Hattie packed his dinner pail.

In Steam Valley the morning meal was breakfast, the noon meal was dinner, and the evening meal was supper. Dinner was the day's eats packed in a box called the bucket or pail. Traditionally, the man's woman packed his pail.

Luke's dinner pail was made of aluminum, the metal dulled by scratches and dents and dings, two rectangular compartments hinged together at the back and accessible from the front by a makeshift hasp and cotter-pin assembly. It looked tired out but was still sturdy and suited Luke. A working man gets used to some things and sticks by them.

The pail's top compartment held a one-pint thermos and a thin weather almanac put out by the National Grange Insurance Company. The bottom part contained the fuel for Luke's day. Today was Friday which meant potato soup in the thermos, two ham and two roast beef sandwiches, a wedge of pumpkin pie, a green banana, a ripe Macintosh apple, and a Hershey bar. The full bucket was supplemented by a heavy-duty quart thermos with a handle. The second pot of coffee went in that.

Luke opened his pail four times a day: a ham sandwich and apple and coffee at nine; the other ham sandwich and one roast beef at noon, along with the soup and pie and coffee; the second roast beef, the banana and coffee at three. The Hershey bar was saved for the ride home at six, unless it was a hot day, in which case it traded places with the apple at nine. It required a lot of energy and organization to work in the woods.

Water was provided by Mac. Every morning he filled a new milk can with ice from the Turkey Ranch and spring water from the Tank. That was for the men. He filled two cans without ice for the draft horses and equipment.

Luke and Hattie's most personal conversations occurred while he ate his breakfast and she packed his pail. Today, Hattie started it.

"Joe sent his draft papers yesterday," she said.

Luke stirred his coffee. "He's eighteen. He's got it to do."

"Did you hear what Carol said? If they got married right away, he could get a farm deferment."

"Joe knows how I feel about that. They can wait. You and I had to." He glanced up at his handsome wife. Their eyes met and he grinned knowingly.

She smiled back. "I know. Abstinence makes the heart grow fonder. But it's not the same thing. We had two kids before you were sent overseas."

"He'll only be gone two years, he'll have leave, and there's no war. Why the big rush?"

"Girls don't think that way. If there's no war, why go at all?"

"Because he's got to, that's why. Just like me and Mac and Charley."

Hattie decided to drop the subject. Luke was adamant about duty and serving your country, but there was more. Luke wanted Joe to get away from the possessive Carol for a while, to see if the flame would burn steady without sexual fuel.

"Speaking of Mac," said Hattie, "is he taking Miss Whalen to the senior dance tonight? We're chaperones, remember."

"Mac will take his turn with the rest of us parents. I expect he's taking that Whalen girl."

"Missy Morningstar said she thought Mac and Julie had something going."

"I thought so too, but lately, Julie's gotten kind of distant."

"That Abigail Whalen sure hasn't. You know, she even calls him?"

Luke shook his head. "How do you find out all this stuff?"

Hattie demurred. "Trade secret. We keep tabs, just like you men do. That Abigail's a determined woman. Good teacher, too. But I think she's got bigger plans for herself and Mac than staying here. It will be tough on our girls if she leaves. They like her."

"Tom doesn't."

"That's what Joe said. That's odd. Tom gets along with everybody. Do you think it's because he's so close to Julie and Abigail's got Mac?"

"Probably. But I wouldn't count Julie out so soon."

"Why not?"

"Julie's got a secret weapon."

"Besides her looks, which are no secret, what would that be?"

Luke got up, gave his wife another playful pat, and said, "Julie packs his pail."

Leaving Hattie to mull that over, Luke went to his kids' rooms and bid each sleeper a silent good-bye. This was a poignant moment for Luke. Woods work was dangerous, and you never knew, you just never knew. He never left without saying good-bye.

In the breezeway he laced up his hightops, shrugged into a light duck jacket, and donned his brown felt fedora. It was an expensive hat, his only idiosyncrasy. The band was patterned with sweat stains and the fabric was beat like the dinner pail, but the hat fit perfect and still had lots of wear. It was the right hat for a gentleman of the woods.

Hattie handed him his dinner pail and big thermos. He leaned and lightly kissed her good-bye, not wanting his beard to scratch her face. "Just remember," he said, "Julie's the best thing he's seen all morning. He thinks of her every time he opens his pail. Thoughts like that grow on a man."

Hattie glowed. Luke wanted his friend to have what he had because what he had was so good. He was a loyal and caring man, her Luke. He was right, too, about Julie and the dinner pail. Abigail Whalen would never pack Mac's pail. But Julie Spencer would...and did.

Chapter 17 – The Cherry Tree

Luke broke a sweat with his first cut. The tree was a prime black cherry, two feet across and eighty feet high. Sunbeams piercing the tree's leafy canopy reflected off the shiny, oily sawbar, throwing a vibrant spectrum of color, a wood's crystal, then sprinkled and faded as the sawdust spewed out and the bar bit deeper into the wood. Within the spray was the rich smell of cherry syrup. The tree trunk seemed unaffected by that first cut, but the treetop quivered from the saw's vibrations and a family of doves, feeding in the upper branches, took their leave.

Unlike its maple, beech and oak neighbors, whose leaves had started their autumn turn, the cherry's leaves were still glossy green. The leaves remained to protect stems tipped with its tart purple fruit. The wild cherry was one of nature's delicacies. Unless a logger came along, though, only tree dwellers shared its bounty.

As he worked the tree, Luke noticed a whitetail doe and her two fawns browsing off a cherry top he had dropped the day before. The deer were within a treelength of him, unafraid when he ran the noisy saw. Animals got used to equipment quickly. But drop the saw and cruise timber quietly with your hands free, and the deer would scamper away. Danger was close when the woods were quiet.

It only took three precise cuts to fall the nice cherry. The first two cuts determined the direction of the tree's fall, the last toppled it.

The first cut was the undercut, a forearm-challenging horizontal slice at knee height through one-third of the diameter of the tree. The second was tricky but a bit easier, the angle or top cut, which began at thigh height and slanted down into the back of the undercut. Where the two cuts met a wedgelike slice of wood was loosened and knocked away, revealing a forty-five degree notch that opened in the general direction of the tree's fall. The third cut, the back cut, was the most precise because its effectiveness was measured not only by what it cut away but also what it left. The back cut began midway between thigh and knee height and sliced gradually down to one inch short of the point of the notch.

The cherry was now severed, except for a narrow diametrical strip between the back cut and the notch. This strip was the "hinge," which determined the specific direction of the tree's fall. Leaving the proper hinge was critical for the sawyer. If it was too thin, the tree could rock back and bind the saw; too thick, and it could split the tree.

He was cutting a level area, a wide middle bench on the east slope of Blackwolf, so Luke kept his hinge at an even one-inch thickness. On steep sides or with "leaners" Luke varied the thickness and angle of his hinge to help steer the tree. He never took chances. Luke followed a simple rule – choose the path of safety over convenience. It only took a few minutes to cut a tree out of the way, but it took forever to cut one off a man.

With the tree balanced precariously on its hinge, Luke quickly laid aside his saw and, taking a short-handled maul, drove a heavy steel wedge into the back cut until the hinge cracked and the cherry started to topple. Once the hinge broke and the severed trunk lifted slowly off the wedge, the science of treefelling was over. This was when the sawyer hurried out of the way and yelled TIMBER!

Regardless of all his skill and caution, Luke could never be absolutely sure where a tree would fall. Nature, by its nature, was fickle and unpredictable. A vagrant breeze could push a leafy top like a sail the wrong way; the heart of the tree near the hinge could be rotten and break early and the trunk would "jump the stump"; or a misdirected tree could bounce off another and the hapless logger would face the devastating rush of two "widow-makers" bearing down on him together.

The cherry proved cooperative, however, and crashed down between two maples, exactly where Luke pointed it. Amidst settling twigs and leaves Luke recovered his saw and prepared to limb the tree.

Before he started limbing, Luke completed one final felling operation that most sawyers didn't do but should –

cutting the hinge shards off the stump and butt end of the tree. Untrimmed hinges were ugly and dangerous. Early in his career, Luke found the body of a bear cub draped over a red oak stump. It had been playing in the woods and impaled itself on one of Luke's hinges. There it lay, food for the crows. Luke trimmed all his hinges after that.

Limbing was neatly shaving the branches off the trunk and topping the tree where the stem was too small to make a log. Luke revved the saw. The greenish-white chips started flying.

Unlike some owners who dragged their limbs and tops to a huge combustible pile and risked a forest fire, Mac let his lay. The downed branches provided browse and cover for wildlife and nurtured an entire generation of seedlings. A healthy forest required objects to hide under. It may not take a great picture, but it *grew*. No park-like European woods for Mac and Luke. To Luke, manicured woods were like a frigid woman; clean but cold, with no family.

Luke admired the way Mac harvested timber. The man loved the land. He refused to butcher it. Mac thinned a stand, taking half the cuttable trees. A tree had to be mature, at least sixteen inches in diameter to be cuttable. He never cut a den tree. He rarely took more than fifteen trees per acre, even though in these woods there were usually thirty harvestable and another seventy in various stages of growth. Actually, one of the reasons Blackwolf Mountain had such excellent hardwood timber was because it had been thinned out properly the first time, in 1851.

Mac was developing his land for the future. He built his log roads to last – narrow and canted to the inside for safety and good drainage. Wet spots were ditched and sluiced and corduroyed where necessary. A corduroy stretch prevented deep ruts and was made from poled cull trees laid side-by-side crossways in the road. Usually embedded in clay soil, it was amazing how much weight they took and how long they lasted; thirty years if built properly.

Mac harvested his timber to assure himself, his crew, and his land of a steady crop. With four thousand acres to cut, and four acres cut each day, it would take four years to complete the first stage. It would take another three years to swing back and harvest the remaining cuttable trees. By then another fifteen trees would have matured and the third stage would begin.

If that Abigail was counting on taking Mac to the city, she should first come up here and watch him run the bulldozer. He was as determined as she. If Mac was headed anywhere, it was two peaks west, not far as the crow flies, but far the gradual way they were taking, to Bear Mountain. Luke wanted to be with him when he got there.

After he severed the top, Luke was left with a tapered cherry pole fifty-four feet long. He oiled his chain. The saw revved to life again. His next task was to buck the tree.

Bucking was carving the pole into logs. It was here the skillful Luke made everyone money. Luke would not waste a tree. He was a master at getting the most value a tree had to offer. The crew was paid by production, by how much timber volume was delivered to the mill. Volume was determined by the number of board feet in a log. A board foot was a square of wood one foot to a side and one inch thick. The measurement was calibrated by a log rule, an ingenious yardstick invented in the early 1800's that told how many one-foot by one-inch squares of wood were in a tapered cylinder of log. Measuring a log with a log rule was called scaling.

The easiest way to buck the cherry was to cut it into three sixteen-foot lengths. The first log, the butt log, measured twenty inches at the small end and scaled 280 board feet. The second tapered to sixteen inches and scaled 159 feet. The third was twelve inches and 79 feet. Cut this way the cherry yielded forty-eight feet of log length, scaled a total of 518 board feet, and brought a price of 26 dollars. The remaining six-foot length, two foot short of being a log, was called a bolt and was left to rot in the woods.

But not when Luke Ballard bucked the tree. The veteran sawyer knew the Scribner Log Rule by heart and cut four logs; two sixteen-footers, one twelve, and one ten. He util-

110

ized the entire fifty-four foot length of tree, which yielded 574 board feet and brought 29 dollars. Having Luke on the job was the equivalent of a ten percent raise in pay for them all.

That difference added up. Mac was paid a contract price per thousand board feet. The price varied according to species; ash and cherry were the highest right now, oak and maple were in the middle, beech and other hardwoods and the softwoods, pine and hemlock, were low. Mac refused to skim the cream by taking only the valuable species. He took the timber as it came and was averaging fifty dollars a thousand, an excellent average due to the concentration and quality of the cherry. When they got up higher, where the oak and beech dominated, that average would go down. The crew's take would remain the same but Mac's profit margin would shrink substantially. And profit was what paid the bank and kept the equipment running. Luke hoped there was some nice ash up higher.

On a good day a normal crew would process and deliver forty trees, thirteen thousand board feet. Luke could run that total up to fifty and fifteen. Out of the fifty dollars per thousand Mac was currently getting, he paid his sawyer five. Charley Bower, his teamster, got three. Abraham Pierce, the hauler, was paid the same as Charley. Welcome Pierce, the loader, and a green hand, was paid two. Tom and Joe, who worked after school and on weekends, were paid the same as Welcome. Luke thought Tom was worth more but didn't interfere.

His son Joe worried him. He was just too damn careless. He hoped Joe's impetuous nature in the woods didn't carry over to Carol Raker, but he figured it did. It wouldn't surprise him one bit if those two made his deferment.

Abraham and Welcome Pierce were brothers from strict Presbyterian parents, sympathetically nicknamed Abe and Will in school. They looked alike but that was all. The older Abraham preferred Abraham. The younger Welcome preferred Will. They had six sisters, all born between Abe and Will. Abe was married and had a family. Will was single.

On a good day, cutting fifty trees into one-hundred-seventy logs scaling fifteen thousand board feet at the mill, Mac would gross $750. Luke got $75, Charley and Abraham $45 each, and Will $30. Luke made more in two days in the woods than he made in a week as maintenance foreman at the tannery. But then he didn't have rattlesnakes, copperheads, wasps, or nasty weather to contend with at the tannery.

The cherry was bucked – four beautiful black-barked logs gleaming emperor's red at the sawed ends. Now it was Mac's or Charley's job to drag the logs to a skidway or landing, an exercise called skidding.

On this job Mac acted as the floater, meaning he had several functions. The boss marked the trees, built the roads, serviced the equipment, skidded and filled in where he was needed. Mac was the best all-around logger Luke knew. Still a young man, Luke saw tremendous potential in Jonathan MacEwen.

Mac skidded with his diesel-burning Caterpillar bulldozer. Hitched to the drawbar was a heavy-duty chain, a chain with tentacles called grabs. Each grab could be hooked to one log. All four cherry logs could be skidded with one set of grabs.

Charley skidded with his oat-burning Belgians, Robert and Richard, Bob and Dick for short. Charley usually pulled with one horse, "trailing" two logs at a time, one chained behind the other. The teamster method was slower, but the horses were more maneuverable and damaged less young timber then the big dozer.

On a good day, like this day, it took both skidders to keep up with Luke.

The cherry logs were skidded down a trail to a skidway, a gradual earthen ramp mounded higher than the bed of the log truck. It was the loader's job to pile the logs on the skidway so they could be rolled off the ramp directly onto the truck bed. To accomplish this Will used pry tools called canthooks and pikes. It wasn't uncommon for scores of logs to be stacked high on a skidway, especially if the log truck broke down or had a long haul.

During the stacking, the cherry ceased to exist as a tree. Its parts were now piled with the sixteen-foot, twelve-foot, and ten-foot logs; four individual logs lost in the mass of a hundred other logs. Their last time together would be the same ride to the mill.

The loaded truck carried thirty to forty logs, scaled around three thousand board feet, and weighted about thirty thousand pounds. The six-by-six itself weighted another forty thousand pounds.

It took nerve to creep thirty-five tons of swaying wood and metal down a steep mountainside. The stoic Abraham Pierce seemed bred for the job. The stern church deacon rarely showed emotion; except when his black sheep brother acted up, then his reaction was rarely a smile, almost always a frown. Old-timer Charley Bower allowed that some sinner blood from way back must have infected Will, the poor sucker. Imagine, bein' happy all the while! A helluva burden for a boy so young. Just a burden, corrected Abe.

The load was contained by tall stakes made from tough white oak or ironwood saplings, which were driven into slots welded to the truck chassis. Cutting load stakes was a constant chore because one side of stakes had to be cut off each time the truck was unloaded to allow the stacked logs to roll off the truck bed. Abraham had to first make sure his load was chain-bound before he cut away a side of stakes. If he didn't, and the load sprung loose, fifteen tons would roll him out flatter than a wet shirt run through his wife's wringer washer.

Charley Bower regularly lectured Will and the boys to never trust a pile of logs. It didn't matter if that pile was stationary or being transported. It had a meanness of its own. It never moved until someone was in its way. Take those four cherry logs. They liked bein' a tree better. They're just waitin', conspirin' with the others. Lost a good big horse once to a log pile. Twenty hands high it was, the pile.

The wood uprights did not hold the logs, they just contained them. The load was secured by three huge steel chains wrapped around the ends and middle of the load and tightened underneath the chassis by chain binders. Crawling underneath the truck to bind those chains was a muddy task which the responsible Abraham did without complaint. A broke chain, a shifted load, a tumbling truck, and God forbid, Welcome was the head of the Pierce family.

Once the four cherry logs and their mixed brethren were secured, and Abraham had the truck in low-low headed toward Packhorse Run, the timbering process was complete. Out of his open side window the sweaty hauler could hear it begin again – Luke's saw biting deep, reverberating between Blackwolf and Potash, being felt as far west as the mysterious Bear.

Chapter 18 – Visitors

At noon the men gathered their buckets and thermoses and met at the skidway for dinner. Abe just returned from delivering the third load of the day to the mill. He handed Mac a brown envelope with Fred's letterhead on it. They all knew what it contained – the tally slip and check for that week's timber.

Mac, seeing Will fidget, took his time scanning the tally sheet. It had been a pretty good week.

Will couldn't wait. "Well, how'd we do?"

Mac pretended he didn't hear.

"Aw, come on, Mac."

Mac looked up and grinned. Will was as eager as a kid at Christmas. "Eighty-three-five," he said finally.

Will whooped. Eighty-three thousand five-hundred! His subconscious was already taking that footage total times two. A hundred and sixty-seven dollars, the biggest pay-check of his life! He whooped again. "How much did you get?" he asked, craning his skinny sunburnt neck to see the numbers typed on the check to J. MacEwen.

"Will! That's none of your business." Abe's rebuke was stern.

"Just askin'," replied the exuberant Will, not embarrassed at all by his forwardness.

Mac didn't tell him the figure, which was over four thousand dollars. It would be blabbed all over town if he did. Will was a likable fellow but too impressionable to be trusted. If Will was let in on a secret he couldn't wait to share it with someone. Abraham was entirely different that way.

Freshening his coffee from the thermos, Mac got his checkbook from the equipment truck, sat on the running board and wrote the paychecks.

"Put most of that by, Will," said Luke, folding his own check inside the almanac kept in his dinner bucket.

"Why?" said Will, whose mind already had him at the Ford dealership, showing off in front of Katrina Padleski.

To Will, money was like music, to be enjoyed right away. He felt the same way about Katrina.

"October starts day after tomorrow," reminded Luke.

"So?" Will couldn't see any cause for concern. It was a beautiful day. A Monarch butterfly bounced off the log pile, then rode a warm updraft into the trees and beyond, there displaying the primary colors of Indian Summer, orange and blue.

"Fall rains come in October," explained Abraham.

"And snow in November," added Charley. He continued: "Logs don't roll too well stuck in a foot of mud or two foot of snow. Do they Richard?"

With that he swiped Luke's apple from his bucket and gave it to the grateful Dick, who clopped nearby.

"Hey!" yelled Luke.

But Dick didn't understand hey, just gee and haw and a couple other choice teamster words. The apple was soon gone.

"I'll give you a chaw for it," offered Charley.

"You know I don't chew."

"I'll owe you then."

"You haven't paid for the last one you took."

"We'd be even if you chewed."

Luke grumbled and shut his bucket. He resolved to have Hattie pick up some horse laxatives at the feed store, if they had them. And a really big apple, a Cortland, from Bob's.

Mac shook his head at the friendly banter. Will may not be worried about the weather, but he was. He put his bucket in the truck, thought of Julie, and climbed on the dozer. Its roar to life was his signal that dinner was over.

———

At three o'clock break Tom showed up, hungry as usual. He cast a mournful look at Luke's open pail and Luke gave him his last sandwich, the ham. The sawyer munched on the Hershey bar.

"They let us seniors out early to decorate for the dance, so here I am, decoratin'!" Tom grinned.

"Why didn't Joe come?" asked Luke.

"He tried, but Carol caught us sneakin' through the guys locker room. Never thought she'd come in there."

"Led him right out by the ring in his nose, huh?" said Luke.

"Something like that," grunted Tom, his mouth half full of ham sandwich. Joe's mom made great sandwiches.

Luke mumbled something about his boy being hen-pecked and headed back to his chain saw.

Mac handed Tom his check. "Why didn't you stay and help?" he asked reprovingly.

"They didn't need me and I had helped already. I drew all the posters and put them out last week." Tom looked away. "I wasn't going to that dance anyway."

That meant he couldn't get a date, so Mac let the matter drop. His brother hadn't gotten friendly with Abigail so he was glad he wasn't going.

What had happened to everybody the past six weeks? Tom was cool, Julie was distant, and Abigail was pushy. Not like Carol Raker, certainly, but still pushy. He really didn't have time for relationships right now. He had to get this timber to market. Couldn't they see that?

He put Tom to work with Will piling logs and cutting load stakes, while he maneuvered the dozer toward a grove of cherry Luke was cutting. On the way he noticed the doe and two fawns working their way around him. The doe was agitated. Her long ears and white tail were up, she was stamping her front foot and sniffing. Luke's saw revved up and she loped off in his direction, the twins clinging close beside her. They were July fawns, small, and still had their spots. Like him, they had gotten a late start and may not survive a harsh winter.

Seeing no cause for alarm, Mac levered the dozer blade down and began clearing a skid trail to Luke. The doe was a sleek two year old, a first-time mother, and overprotective.

With luck they would make it. Mac told himself to start thinking more positive thoughts.

———

At the skidway, Tom and Will had a visitor. Spike Poorbaugh. The tall woodsman approached, a coiled leash chain and choke collar stuck in the belt that held the ever-present Bowie. Tom noticed he was letting his thick rust-gray hair and beard grow for the winter. Tom dropped the armload of stakes he was carrying, except one. He waited.

"Seen a dog lately?"

"What kind of dog?" Tom was wary. Will shrank back and let the two big men talk.

"Huntin' dog. Brown, like a cinnamon bear. Square head. Got some mastiff in him."

"We haven't seen him."

"He's around. If you run across him, leave him alone. He's touchy. Mighty touchy."

"How'd he get loose?"

The trapper didn't answer, but the cold look he gave Tom told him it was none of his damn business. "Just blow your horn if you see the dog. I'll come,"

Poorbaugh stalked away. He didn't get far.

From the cherry grove came a surprised yell from Luke for help. On the heels of that yell came the deep, heavy bark of an attack dog.

When they got to the grove Luke lay on his back in the tangle of a cherry treetop. The huge dog had Luke by the lower leg and was tugging at him, trying to pull him out of the protecting branches, so he could finish his kill. Luke struggled and kicked with his other foot, but couldn't knock the brute loose. The ripped bodies of the doe and fawns lay nearby.

Tom rushed forward, holding the ironwood stake like a ballbat to brain the big dog.

118

Poorbaugh caught him and angrily wrenched the stake out of his hands. "You don't club my dog," he said through clenched teeth.

Tom felt the steel-spring strength in the man, felt his own anger rise, and roughly shoved him out of his way. The trapper hadn't expected the boy's aggressive reaction, was thrown off balance, and fell backwards over an exposed root.

Tom picked up a rock the size of a baseball and heaved it at the dog. It bounced off the beast's flank without effect. Tom found a bigger rock...but couldn't complete the throw.

Mac had hold of the dog.

It was not the hold of a panicked or desperate friend. It was the hold of a trained killer.

Mac faced the dog. Each thumb was hooked in a corner of its mouth; the fingers of each hand gathered the skin behind the ears, purchasing a strong grip at the base of the dog's head. Straining, Mac slowly closed his grip, peeling the dogs lips from its jaw, skinning its face with his bare hands. The dog, trying to relieve the painful pressure, re-laxed its bite.

Luke pulled free. The instant the leg was removed Mac lifted the dog. One-hundred-fifty pounds gurgled and twisted and pawed, in excruciating pain as more skin was peeled as it was raised higher and higher.

The dog's bloody muzzle was even with Mac's chin before its back feet came off the ground. Mac could smell the musk of the deer and the leather of Luke's hightops on the brute's breath, he could see the uncompromising mean-ness in its eyes, he could feel his own adrenalin, his own fury, surging.

The dog relaxed a second to draw a breath, and when it did, Mac drew it in close, then viciously snapped it back. The head stopped but the body didn't and the dog's neck cracked, broken like a tree hinge.

A shudder ran the length of the dog, and Mac, his anger peaking, raised the dog's body high and smashed it down hard on the fresh-cut cherry stump. The dog had attacked before the hinge was trimmed. Blood and entrails spilled out

119

over the stump; the sharp splinter protruded from the splayed dog's back.

Hatred welled up in Spike Poorbaugh. Losing his meanest pack sire had not been in the plan. Automatically his hand grasped the walnut haft of his knife...but he was uncertain. He would have to stab MacEwen first, then the boy, then the others. If the strong logger timed his thrust, he could break his arm. He knew how. He would know more. He showed himself with the dog. Then it would be over. MacEwen would treat him, Samuel Poorbaugh, like the dog. Treat him like a dog!

Poorbaugh saw the green fury in MacEwen's eyes. His killer experience told him the younger man was taunting him, actually hoping he would try the knife. There wasn't one glint of fear or doubt in those green eyes. Only anticipation, hunger for another kill, for an excuse to split him like the dog and heave him out of the way. Well, he wouldn't give him the satisfaction, the son-of-a-bitch!

Still, he wanted to try it. He kept his grip on the knife, his gaze on MacEwen. Ever wary, his peripheral vision caught movement on his left side. The big kid, gettin' ready. He had killed five once, but he wore a helmet, had a rifle, a bayonet and a trench shovel then. All he had now was Jesse's knife. A knife wasn't enough to kill MacEwen and the big brother with the rock. Too risky.

He let loose of the knife. He shifted his gaze to the dog. It quivered on the stump. It had been a bad year for his dogs. But what galled him most was that the man was so sure. So damn sure! "You got a fancy way of killin', MacEwen," he said.

Alexander Alexander, better known as Posey for the lilies tattooed on his huge forearms, flipped the first fried egg of the day and broke the yolk with his spatula. It was no accident. The spreading yolk firmed on the hot grill and was formed into a square almost the size of a slice of bread. Mort Fessler was picky about his fried-egg sandwich. He objected when the egg stuck beyond the bread.

Leaving the egg, Posey turned Jim Morningstar's three slices of French toast and separated four thick strips of bacon from the various mounds of uncooked food warming on the "cool" part of the long grill. The four slices sizzled next to the French toast. They would be there awhile. Jim liked his breakfast very well done and covered with real maple syrup, which was stored in the kitchen cooler in a canning jar with a Pennsylvania Game Commission label around it. The label was marked: EVIDENCE. DO NOT TOUCH. THIS MEANS YOU, TOM DONACHY.

Posey returned to the fried egg, laid two partially toasted slices of buttered bread beside it, bladed the egg expertly onto one slice and topped it with the other. He put the sandwich on a seven-inch plate and slid the plate down the counter to Mort, who had a pepper shaker ready. The chewed end of his second cigar stuck over the edge of the counter ashtray. It was only there temporary.

Mort sat on stool number one next to the kitchen partition. Eleven other stools ran around the counter, four to a side, and when the regulars filled them first thing in the morning, Tom Donachy declared the Jury Was In. Posey presided as judge because he was the owner, Julie served as bailiff because she was the only one that could be trusted, and Tom was the foreman of the jury because...well, just because. The jury also convened on Friday and Saturday nights on the nail kegs at Sawyer's Hardware. Tom was foreman there too, but Frank served as judge.

It was obvious to the judges that the jury convened when its foreman convened it. Posey and Frank both agreed it was going to be godawful dull around Steam Valley after Tom left.

But that was the way it was in Steam Valley. The young men graduated, went away to the service or school or both, grew up somewhere else, sometimes came back, most times didn't. Where Tom was headed, he hadn't said. He probably hadn't decided yet. Tom lived for today. He didn't waste time bemoaning lost yesterdays or speculating about vague tomorrows. But Posey knew he would go. He had to. God, he would miss that boy.

Posey broke three fresh eggs on the grill and poured pancake batter from a two-quart pitcher kept on the lower shelf. He let the batter spread. Sully Thompson liked his one dinner-plate size buckwheat pancake topped with a large egg sunny side up and all coated with syrup, Jim's if he could steal it.

The other two eggs were for droop-eyed Ford Irish, who sat next to Mort complaining about Bud Cole, the tannery, his second job as township supervisor, his second wife, and life in general. He liked his eggs over easy, the same way he liked his workday. In this Ford was frustrated, rarely is anything ever over easy.

Ford had just worked the day shift, the evening shift, and half the graveyard keeping a recalcitrant boiler operating at the tannery. "When can a man sleep?" he said. "Now that damn Bud Cole wants me to meet some engineer at the steel bridge at nine. I wish to hell I never run for supervisor."

Mort, a thinking man, swiveled on his stool and blew a wavy ring of cigar smoke back toward the north dining room. He had only eaten a portion of his sandwich. Ford's whining was tiresome but informative. Why was Bud Cole playing politics with a Jackson Township bridge? One the tannery and milk plant didn't use?

Julie, pouring coffee refills around the counter, wondered the same.

The truckstop's doorbell jingled and the two tallest members of the jury walked in. Julie felt her heart quicken.

122

She went into the kitchen for more coffee. She didn't look at Mac. If she had she would have caught him looking at her.

Tom stuck his Yankees ballcap between the ears of the small three-point buck that Posey had shot and had mounted several years before. It was the only buck he had ever gotten and Posey was proud, giving the head a place of prominence high on the partition that separated the counter from the south dining room. Tom, when he came to work at the Turkey Ranch, had named the little buck Moose. The cap fit over the horns perfect. Poor Moose lost whatever dignity he had whenever Tom was around.

The brothers sat on the two stools to the left of Jim Morningstar. Julie returned with a fresh pot of coffee. There were still a couple of stools empty but that didn't matter, the foreman had arrived, the jury was in.

Tom started it. "Whew! Foggier than your head out there, Posey."

"Coffee's hot, smartass. Scald your tongue."

"That's a contradiction, Pose'. Smart is intelligent. Ass is stupid. I can't be both."

"For once you're right. Dumbass is better. Ain't it, boys?"

The jury laughed. Chalk one up for Posey. This verbal joust occurred every morning. Tom saw it as a challenge to razz the irascible former navy cook who had taken it from the best of them. Posey accepted the challenge, saying that as a pain in the ass Tom ranked high. They had a special friendship, Tom and Posey.

Posey set Jim Morningstar's plate and syrup jar before him. He bladed Sully's sunny side on the pancake and turned Ford's over-easy's, then broke four more eggs on the hottest part of the grill. Mac and Tom like their eggs firm. He dished Sully's and Ford's breakfasts, slid them down, and separated another dozen strips of bacon and a generous portion of sliced potatoes from their simmering mounds.

Mac tested the fresh coffee Julie had poured for him. Next she poured Tom's. It *was* hot. He set the cup down. The fragrance of her hair hung over the counter, and he breathed her in. He didn't look directly at her face. He started at the point of her chin, moved down her graceful neck to the full bosom that stretched the buttons of her blouse. It was there, just under the chin, he would begin. She was oh so close and oh so distant. Mac lifted his cup and drank in the sight of Julie as he drank his coffee. She was without doubt the most desirable woman he had ever known. She stirred him more than Delia, but Delia had *never* been distant. Here he was, dating one woman and desiring another. Abigail was attractive but she didn't affect him like Julie.

The doorbell announced another customer and Fred Sheafer came in. He took the corner stool next to Jim. Posey poured out a short stack of pancakes and threw on a slice of ham. Julie moved over to the corner and poured Fred's coffee. Mac's gaze followed her. Fred's greeting broke his concentration.

"How's Danny?"

Julie looked into familiar eyes of smoky blue. Must be Danny's eyes will darken as he ages, she thought. "He got his first report card," she said with a mother's pride. "All A's."

"Do you read to him a lot?"

"We all do."

"It helps."

Julie agreed and freshened Jim's coffee. Fred knew.

Hearing the talk of grades, Sully let his egg soak into the pancake and questioned Tom about his report card. Sully was one of those individuals who assumed you knew his business so he should know yours. "How'd you do this six weeks, Tom? Horseface mark you down for bad poetry?"

There were some snickers from the jury. Tom didn't take the bait. "Nope. Brenda and I both got A's. Her mom finagled a seat for her on the Library Board and I aced all her tests."

Sully was disappointed. He looked to Posey for help. Instead, Posey slid the brother's breakfasts down and Tom dug in. School conversation was something he and Posey wanted to avoid today.

Jim Morningstar had finished his breakfast. Opening the canvas duffle laying at his feet, he removed a wide spotted pelt and handed it to Mac. "Tell me what this is," he said.

Mac fingered the fur. As a boy he had spent a lot of time hunting and trapping with Charley Bower. This particular skin had been prepared by a professional, probably an Indian. Few white men could skin an animal without leaving any knife marks. "It's a wildcat of some kind, Jim, a bobcat or a lynx, but it's twice the size of any I've ever seen. From Canada probably. How'd you get it?"

"We raided a black market fur dealer in Lock Haven last night. He claims Spike Poorbaugh sold it to him, along with several bear cub pelts and two dozen paws. We found eight big ones and sixteen little ones."

"Two sows with two cubs each?" Tom's tone of voice indicated he regretted not smashing Spike's head with the rock.

"I think so," said Jim. "He tracks down the families, kills them, then sells their skins and paws and gall bladders."

Mac said, "I guess we know now why he's breeding those big hounds. Bear parts bring big money in the Far East. I saw black market traders in Korea."

"Where do you think he's getting the bears?"

"Behind Blackwolf. There's our land and Mort's and Great Marsh and the mountains further west. He's got fifty square miles all to himself. There are lots of bears in an area that large."

Jim said, "One day he'll slip up and I'll catch him."

"Don't ever go after him alone, Jim." Mac was dead serious.

Jim scoffed. "He's an old man. What could he do to me?" Jim was a fit young man, a former army M.P., and first in his warden's class. He had confidence in himself. Mac's warning offended him.

"He's not that old," answered Mac. "And he's not a poacher, he's a killer. Are a few pelts worth dying for?"

"You talk like you're scared of him."

"I am."

The sobering subject of Spike Poorbaugh quieted the jury, which deliberated over their breakfasts. Posey brought Fred his short stack and ham.

Mac finished his breakfast and got up to leave. Tom took his time nursing a second cup of coffee. It was too early to return home to shower and shave for school.

Julie came from the kitchen with Mac's filled thermos and dinner pail. This time their eyes met. Julie had overheard the conversation with Jim. Everyone knew Mac had killed Spike Poorbaugh's dog. Julie couldn't hide her concern. "You be careful," she said.

One by one the jury members went about their business until only Mort and Tom remained.

Posey's bulk filled the opening to the kitchen. Soon he returned through the batwings carrying a half-filled grocery bag which he handed to Tom.

Tom grinned and thanked him and told him he was alright, even if he did wear an apron. Posey told Tom to get outa here, and don't forget his hat.

"What was in the bag?" asked Julie, clearing the counter up to Mort. Posey was at the grill gathering food to take back to the cooler.

"Oh, just a lunch for a growing boy."

"But Tom gets his lunch at school."

"Not today."

Julie lectured her boss as he retreated to the kitchen. Tom had him wrapped around his little finger, she said, and Posey encouraged his shenanigans. Posey responded that they had made a business deal, don't get excited, to which Julie snorted and said, I'll bet.

Mort sat alone at the counter. He lit a third cigar. His fried-egg sandwich was only half eaten. He had remained quiet, contemplating Bud Cole and Mac, the steel bridge, and the junk business. Those two were proud young men with

126

conflicting objectives; they were bound to have at it. He was right in the middle... Sometimes ambition was bad for business.

He blew another smoke ring. This time he didn't swivel away. The smoke wafted over the customerless counter and rose toward Posey's little buck. Moose still wore Tom's hat.

Chapter 20 – The Cloak of Many Colors

Tom moved in a low crouch around the boulders strewn at the base of Caleb's Rock. It was a good place for a stalk. The red sediment that had shaved off the sandstone cliff's side was wet and crumbly. He could walk quiet.

He could hear rustling in the crisp leaves under the trees at Three Oaks Spring. He could see movement in the branches overhead but no clear silhouettes. The trees still carried most of their leaves, effectively concealing their occupants. He would have to sneak in close, and sit, and wait.

Charley Bower advocated stalking squirrels with a twenty-two as the best practice for deer season: "You practice for basketball season don't you? You have to be fit and sharp for deer, too. Besides, squirrels are a lot easier to find and carry and the weather's nicer. Gives you time to appreciate the Maker. He shows off on bright fall days you know."

Tom knew. He leaned against one tall boulder so his profile wouldn't show and scanned the timbered horizons. An immense sky of vivid blue bent over them. A bright patchwork of autumn foliage spread underneath. God *was* showing off today. Steam Valley lay under a coverlet, His cloak of many colors.

From his vantage point Tom the logger could cruise thousands of acres of timber. All he had to know was which colors the trees turned. The oranges were nut trees; oak, beech, butternut, and hickory. The reds were maples. The yellows were aspen, ash and basswood. The glossy greens were cherry. The dark greens were softwoods, pine and hemlock, which grew more somber as the days got shorter and the nights longer. The purple threads connecting this tapestry were wild grapevines, and the scarlets bordering it were shining sumac. There was a certain triumph in the mix of colors. Tom decided that on the morning of the seventh day, while He rested, God turned one final glorious stitch, and made Fall.

A nuthatch flew by, so close he could feel its wings flutter in his ear. It weaved and bobbed its way around the boulders to a dead tree. After landing, it swiveled and climbed down the trunk headfirst. The Lord sure put a different gyroscope in that little fella, thought Tom. Apparently the loose bark didn't house the proper insects because the nuthatch soon fluttered down to one of the giant white oaks and investigated the notches cut deep into its side. Its pert *ya ya* was answered by the chatter and bark of several indignant squirrels, who didn't take to intruders, even insect eaters.

If they keep that racket up they'll wake the Indian boy, thought Tom.

Three Oaks Spring was the sustainer of a grove of nut trees. The three white oaks guarded the spring, which gushed out from the cliff side, pooled, and overflowed into a small stream that wound its way down the foothill past the farmstead to Blockhouse Creek. The pool and first hundred yards of stream were ringed by nutbearers – white, red and scarlet oak's, shagbark and pignut hickory's, beech, butternut, and black walnut, and the stark skeletons of several great chestnuts that at the time of Caleb Skinner would have rivaled the three white oaks for dominance.

After the fall rains came and knocked the nuts to the ground, and the wildlife teemed in, the grove resembled a feedlot. That time was at hand. Today's tranquility would soon end. The smell of wet earth seasoned the persistent western breeze. Birds were lined up on the TV line. Too many squirrels foraged for food at midday. If he was going to fill a limit of squirrels for Missy Morningstar's game dinner, and cut a pickup load of wood for Evie, he'd better hurry.

The school's woodshed was crammed full, but Evie wanted to stockpile some extra. Signs were shaping up for a hard winter. The woolly worm's coats were thick this year.

The chuckling spring covered the sound of his approach. He settled down against one of the oaks, scraping his back against some of the notches in the process. The nuthatch flew back to the dead tree in the rocks.

Tom waited. He wanted a rest shot, a head shot at his last squirrel. The twenty-two lay in his lap, a scope-sighted Remington bolt action. The bolt was on the right side. Tom was left-handed but he shot right. He also batted right and strummed his guitar with his right hand. Sometimes he got his hands mixed up and looked awkward, like when he saluted the flag, or shook hands, or danced slow. He guessed God had given him a different gyroscope too. But he was adaptable. In a world made for right-handers, Tom Donachy made do.

It wasn't long before a fat gray came down from the upper branches and sat in the crook of a huge limb that extended over the spring. Tom was fifty feet away, on the opposite side of the pool. The squirrel's body was obscured by a cluster of shoots growing from the crook. Tom could make out the nervous bushy tail and the head, its cheeks bulging with two acorns.

Tom raised the rifle and sighted. Once he had the squirrel's head focused and divided into four parts he would shoot. The six-power magnification brought the rodent's dark brown eye very close. It blinked and turned its head, rubbing a cheek against one of the upright limbs to reposition an acorn. The limb was chalk white and was not wood. It was bone. The squirrel sat inside a rib cage.

Intrigued, Tom stood up and circled the pool to the big limb. The squirrel ran to a hole. A skeleton was wedged in the fork of the tree. Three other rib cages lay on the ground, moldy, and partially covered with this and last year's leaves. Tom dug in the leaves with his foot and uncovered a head. It had a long snout and large, sharp canine teeth.

Four dogs had died here, but how did one end up in a tree?

The cool shade told him. This particular oak grew directly under the ledge that stuck out like a splinter from Caleb's Rock. Tom looked up, peering through the branches of the oak. Five hundred feet above him hung the ledge. Those four got in one devil of a scrap up there and lost, he thought.

Tom's movements alerted the other squirrels. It became quiet as a graveyard at the spring, which in at least five respects it was. Only the uninterruptible constants, the flowing water and the west wind, made any sound. Eery. What had caused the Indian boy to fall? And the dogs? Or was this simply a dangerous place? Had they defiled the place by hunting here? Had he?

Tom decided to quit hunting today. He had gotten five squirrels. Added to what the others brought there would be plenty to thicken the stew for Missy's dinner.

Two quick shotgun reports went off below him. Squeaky and Joe were teamhunting the hemlock-lined fencerow next to Blackwolf Swamp. They probably flushed a grouse. Tom checked his watch. 11:30. They were to meet at noon at The Lady's. Tom followed the spring run down to the farmstead. Under one shagbark he picked a plastic bag full of hickory nuts for stuffing for the grouse. Missy was really good with grouse.

The Lady was Louisa Longsdorf. Evie told him her story many times...

———

When Louisa's grandfather Brenner came to Steam Valley, he found Caleb Skinner's bark shanty and hand-dug well. He replaced the shanty with a log cabin and walled up the well, which originated from the same artesian source as Three Oak's Spring. Along the spring run he built a grist mill, a granary, and a barn. With the mill, Brenner laid the foundations of the Longsdorf fortune. Later on he built a large frame Colonial farmhouse. Then Brenner died and his son took over.

Hermann expanded the mill and granary and fortune considerably, and displayed his prosperity by building a square Georgian mansion with pillars. After the pillars were installed the Mennonite Church excommunicated him and Brenner became a Lutheran. After his conversion he replaced the log cabin with a carriage house complete with a cupola and rooster weather vane. After Jacob Miller drowned Hermann hired Ike McFee to finish the timber job. He also retained Saul and Jesse Poorbaugh as bounty hunters. The next winter Hermann died and Louisa took over, making Ike foreman. The rugged Scot never drove timber again. The logs he had time to pull out were sawed locally. The Poorbaugh's retreated to a squatters' cabin deep in the mountains.

Ike McFee moved his family into the farmhouse. Louisa lived alone in the mansion. Ike rebuilt the well into a stone springhouse, added a dairy barn and a smithy. During the Civil War he and Louisa modernized the mill and expanded the smithy into a small foundry. After the war they dismantled and sold the foundry. Ike's first wife died, he remarried, and Evie was born in the farmhouse, attended to by The Lady. Evie's mother and Louisa then commissioned Ike to build the Buttonwood School. That was the last major project undertaken by Ike, who spent his remaining years managing the gristmill and dairy.

Louisa continued to beautify the Georgian, invested in railroads and factories, started the bank and hospital and library in Fallbrook. In time the locals dubbed her Lady Louisa. There was no formality to it. She earned it. She seemed it. A gracious, caring lady. Eventually her home, with its gleaming white pillars and reputation for hospitality, became associated completely with its owner. It too became The Lady.

————

At the springhouse Tom looked down the farm lane for Squeaky and Joe. On the left sat the carriage house, the tenant house and the mansion. On the right was the dairy barn, the hay barn, the mill and granary. Harry Raker's third cutting filled the mow of the dairy barn. Mac had extra equipment stored in the hay barn and granary. The rest of the buildings were empty. His buddies were standing on the wide stonerow where Mac had propped the iron gate. Joe carried a grouse.

Tom lifted the latch to the springhouse and went in. It was cool and moist inside and dimly lit by one bottleglass window. On its ledge sat Posey's sack lunch. Tom left the door open to let in more light. At the stone cistern he wound the rope that drew the bucket from the bottom of the well. The water was all of ten feet deep and clear and cold. Some said Steam Valley owed its splendor to its water. Each mountain seemed to contain a great underground reservoir of its own. They said it, the men who had been all over, nowhere in the world was there water like this.

The bucket appeared at the surface, filled with six cold bottles of Coke. Tom took the bag down from the window ledge. While he was transferring the Coke's from the bucket to the bag, a winged grasshopper flew through the open door and smacked against the opaque window glass. It fell in the water and struggled. It was a short-lived struggle.

The surface boiled and Tom was splashed as several trout darted at once for the big insect. The successful brown dove deep with its quarry. The disappointed ones flashed by the surface for a few seconds, then they too disappeared into the greenish-black depths of the cold spring.

The presence of the trout was a mystery to the brothers. Apparently they had been there for years. The water source came from deep underground. How the trout got there, no one knew.

Chapter 21 – As The World Turns

Storm clouds gathered over Steam Valley at noon while folks went about their business. The senior boys lounged on the porch of The Lady, the Buttonwood School kids swarmed out to recess, the Fallbrook Ladies' Garden Club convened at Delia's, and Spike Poorbaugh strung a seine line for turtles in the deep pool under the covered bridge. The wind blew out of the north in penetrating gusts, chilled feelers sent into the valley and side hollows to seek and destroy Indian Summer. The leaves still able turned up for the last time.

———

Squeaky was talking about life…as in what they planned to do the rest of theirs. Tom seemed content to delay that decision. They all had a future; it was out there somewhere, waiting. Why be early? A little uncertainty wasn't so bad. But Squeaky's life had to be in order. He had to *know*.

Squeaky sat with his back against the house wall. Tom and Joe sat against two pillars. They faced each other and passed around the grocery bag.

Squeaky spoke first. "My mom wants me to study for the ministry, but my dad says business school. What do you think, Tom?"

"I think if you keep skippin' school you won't be any good at either."

They laughed together but Squeaky persisted. "Give me a straight answer, Tom."

Tom scratched his long back against the pillar. "You're our point man, right?"

"Yeah. So?"

"So it's time you called some plays of your own. I'm not talking about basketball either."

"I'd like to be a minister, but I don't want to disappoint my dad."

"It's your call, Squeak. It's your life."

"I know. I've just avoided talking it out with dad. What about you, Joe?"

The sawyer's son had an announcement. "Live right here, I guess. If Mac and Harry can come to terms." He looked a little sheepish. "Me and Carol looked around some after stackin' hay one day."

Tom pretended to be surprised. Mac said to expect a lowball offer from Harry. Squeaky was surprised. He stared down the columns to the impressive portal of the house and whistled. "What are you and Carol going to do in a place like this?" he asked.

"The same thing they were doin' in the hay," interrupted Tom, grinning.

"Nah," said Squeaky, coming to his best friend's defense. The barber's son, short and compact with a face like a mouse, and inexperienced with girls, could be naïve sometimes. Tom, as inexperienced as Squeaky, was not naïve.

Joe tried hard not to smile. He didn't succeed but that was the extent of his giveaway. He never told tales about his times with Carol. "We plan to start out in the tenant house," he said.

"Start what?" replied Tom, smirking.

Joe threw the bottle opener at him.

Squeaky was satisfied. Joe was set. He would be once he had a heart-to-heart with his dad. He turned to Tom. "What about you, ugly?"

"I'm gonna strap on my guitar and hike down the road."

"Shi'it."

"You keep swearing like that you won't last long in seminary."

"The army will grab you, Tom," said Joe.

"That's not so bad."

"You got to have some goals," said Squeaky.

"I have goals."

"Oh, yeah? What are they?" Squeaky had to know now. Joe figured Tom would inform them when he was ready.

"Beat the town team, and get Ebenezer."

"I mean real goals, like becoming president or a great general or something."

"Something successful?"

"Yeah."

"Why?"

"Because that's what everybody expects."

"Everybody?"

"You know. Your family. Your friends. Society."

"So who decides? Me or society?"

"You do, I guess." Squeaky wasn't sure.

"What if I can't decide?"

"Then they decide for you."

"Hey Joe! Meet Squeaky Khrushchev."

"Darn it, Tom. You know this isn't Russia. We're free. We have choices."

"But I still have to choose. I'm not free. I'm just free to choose." Tom winked at Joe.

Squeaky was exasperated. Every time he got serious with the Class of 55's valedictorian Tom jerked his chain. "You know what I'm gonna do?" he said. "When we do the yearbook, I'm nominating you The Least Likely to Succeed."

"I'll second that motion," chimed in Joe.

"I'll third it," added Tom.

"You can't third a motion. It's not in the rules."

"The hell with the rules. That's what this discussion's all about, ain't it?"

Joe changed the subject. "Throw back that church key, Tom."

Tom tossed the bottle opener which Joe caught deftly. He pried the cap off his second Coke. "What did Posey charge for dinner?"

"Half a day each, butcherin' turkeys at the ranch. Thanksgiving's comin'."

"Oh God," groaned Squeaky. "I'd rather pay him triple than pluck turkeys."

"A deal's a deal," said Tom. He opened the lunch bag. "What kind of candy bar you want?"

136

"What are my choices?" asked Squeaky.

"A peppermint patty, a peppermint patty, and a peppermint patty."

"What'd you give me a choice for?"

"You wanted freedom of choice didn't you? If you don't choose, Joe and I'll split yours." Tom wore a broad smile.

"You can be a big turd sometimes, you know that?"

Tom tossed them their candy bars. "Joe," he said, "I'm really getting concerned about Harold's language."

"Me too," answered Joe, removing the foil wrapper. "Maybe you ought to go to business school, Squeak."

"You're both big turds," responded Squeaky.

The wind picked up, scattering the wax paper sandwich wrappers left on the porch. Tom held the grocery bag down with his foot. A noisy flock of birds swirled out of Blackwolf Swamp and joined with others perched on the TV line. The wire swayed with the wind and added weight. Several grew nervous and jumped to a dead elm whose brittle branches extended closer to the line. Beyond their black shooting-gallery profiles and miles to the north, lightning struck Bloss Mountain. The alarmed birds swirled out en masse into a black cloud, then dispersed and returned to their original places. Occasionally a flock became disoriented and chose the port most exposed to a storm. Better chase them back to the swamp, thought Tom.

He picked up the lunch bag. "Bring that Coke with you, Joe. That elm's Evie's firewood."

———

Abigail sat at her teacher's desk writing a letter. Hank Broadwater and Amanda Cole were taking their turns outside as recess monitors.

".....My research is going well, Mother. The preliminary results should interest you. These country kids can read! About half of the

137

third-graders and most of the fourth-graders read better than my fifth-grade class in Harrisburg. At first I thought the reason was the small classes. Five or six kids come up to a front bench at one time and there's a lot of individual instruction. (The little guys are especially cute. And I told Mr. Bates I didn't like primary!) I also thought it might be our practice of making older kids help the younger. The small classes and tutoring help, but they're not the answer.

"The answer is *how* they were taught to read in the first grade. Mrs. Brown used the old-fashioned alphabetic code. In Harrisburg I used look-and-say. The alphabetic code is simple. The alphabet letters are sounds; to read connect the sounds. The first rule these kids were taught was to sound the word out. When I started look-say with my first-graders you should have seen the stares. One first-grader named Danny came here able to read. He told *me* to sound the word out, it worked better!

"My training up to now has been all look-say. You know, word memorization and association, supposedly more exciting than the drudgery of teaching the alphabet. But this so-called drudgery is a fundamental. I realize now I have sounded the word subconsciously for years. It was a survival skill I learned on my own. But I was never taught this in school or college.

"I am meeting with Elwyn Bates to get permission to compare the academic development of the kids here in Buttonwood with the kids in Fallbrook who have learned under different generations of teachers, some still using the alphabetic code, others using look-say. I'm sure he'll give it even though my study will show he's skeptical of many modern methods and resists them. He stays with the basics. Maybe that's why his results are so good.

"This creates a quandary for me. The university establishment is tied to look-say and all that's modern and revolutionary. How will my thesis review committee react when I say their pet teaching-of-reading method is a crock? Can they refuse me my Master's?

"As to my personal life – yes, I know I talk too much school, Mother – I'm dating. His name is Jonathan MacEwen. He's 33. Just out of the service. A Colonel. An engineer. Holds a Master's from Penn State. Between jobs right now. I'm told practically every young woman in the valley has been in love with him. When you come up in four weeks you'll *see* why.

"Another man has asked me out, too. I haven't said yes to him yet. His name is Steve Heffner. Local bank manager. Late twenties. Good dresser. Cornell grad. Good family. Steadier than Mac.

"The gossip here is that Mac has been quite the ladies man, but he's always been a gentleman with me..."

...Darn it. Abigail leaned back in her chair to collect her thoughts. She checked the time. Recess was almost over. She would finish the letter after school.

Aunt K was right. When Mac was involved with a project he was a driven man. He rarely came out of the woods, and when he did he was more of an escort than a boyfriend. He was attentive, polite. He had never opened up about himself again. She did all the talking. His kisses were infrequent and restrained.

The man knew how to kiss. He could arouse her easily but he hadn't tried. What was holding him back? This relationship was not developing as planned. Maybe a date with Steve Heffner would move him off dead center.

The noise level on the playground increased dramatically, a sure sign of trouble. Abigail rushed outside. Amanda had Hank down and was pummeling him wildly. Hank didn't stand a chance. The sixth-graders were at the age where the girls were more mature than the boys. Amanda was a big girl, bigger than her teacher, and strong, and furious. It was all Abigail could do to pull her off.

"What happened here!" she demanded.

Neither Hank nor Amanda would answer. The kids gathered around. The sullen silence of not telling took hold. Hank had a bloody lip and a welt was raising on his forehead. Amanda's blouse had come undone and her bra was showing. She didn't care. She obviously wanted to finish the job. Her wrath was the righteous kind; Hank had somehow ignited it. None of the kids responded.

"Well?" Abigail waited. The wind raced over the fresh-cut stubble of Raker's cornfield. All of a sudden it was cold.

Finally, Rachel Ballard spoke up. "Hank told Danny to bring in some wood 'cause a storm was coming. Danny didn't hear him and kept playing. Then Hank got mad and called him a bad name." Abigail found Danny, who seemed confused by all the fuss. "Did he call you a bad name, Danny?"

The handsome boy looked up at her. "I don't know, Miss Whalen. What's a bastard?"

———

Delia opened the top drawer of her dining room credenza for more silver. The Fallbrook Ladies' Garden Club had their business meeting and lunch in the dining room, then adjourned to the living room for dessert and tea and their "story." Delia had come back to the dining room for extra utensils. In the living room the television was on, declaring the benefits of TIDE. The conversation centered on the next program.

Television was a new phenomenon to Steam Valley. Unlike most changes, TV was greeted warmly. The Cole's had a new Zenith console, got their reception off the line from Blackwolf Mountain, and improved that reception with their own signal booster installed on the southwest corner of the house. For most the TV picture was a crackly, snowy affair. You could actually see who was talking at Delia's.

For several weeks the ladies had been following the drama of Ellen Sloan, a pretty homemaker with short blond hair who was the principal character in a love triangle. Her husband Jim was a handsome army officer preoccupied with duty and his career. In the murky background was Roger, a successful businessman preoccupied with her. Jim was always in uniform. Roger always in a dark suit. Ellen never wore the same dress twice. On Monday her doctor con- gratulated her. She could expect her third child in April. Tuesday's program concluded with Ellen saying, "Jim, I have something to tell you." Today was Wednesday.

Maria Barbano, an expectant young homemaker herself, spoke in a soft voice. "I think she's going to tell him about Roger."

Bonnie Fabel disagreed. "I think she's just going to tell him she's pregnant."

Maria with the soft voice said, "Do you think it's Roger's baby?"

Freda Manikowski snorted, "Of course it is. Roger only comes around when Jim's gone. And he's gone too much."

Maria countered, "Yes, but she's married to Jim. They must be *doing something*."

Freda was certain of Ellen's infidelity. "She and Jim have twin beds."

"That's true," agreed Maria reluctantly. "But where would she and Roger…"

"I think it happened that time Jim was called to the Pentagon." This interruption was by Justina Whitaker, a bossy woman with a long memory. "Remember, in August, when she dropped the kids off at her sister's, and met Roger at that beach hotel for dinner? And had too much wine?"

Bonnie Fabel commented, "She sure acts guilty."

"She looks mixed up to me," proposed the sympathetic Maria. "I wonder which man she'll choose."

"She may not have a choice," snapped Freda, hoping the worst for Ellen as her punishment.

"Will Roger still want her if it's Jim's baby?" Maria was obviously hoping it was her husband's.

"I think he will," said Bonnie. "He really loves her."

Maria was solid for keeping the marriage together. "Jim loves her too. He just doesn't romance her enough."

"Well, somebody sure romanced her," declared Justina.

Giggles broke out from the semi-circle in front of the television set.

Delia wrapped the silver utensils in a linen napkin and moved to the doorway into the living room. Her guest's attention was riveted to the TV. All the seats were taken. She leaned against the doorframe and watched and remembered and held on to the silver. She didn't want to interrupt the audience. On her right the French doors to the garden shook as a gust of wind whipped against them.

The TIDE commercial ended, the story's musical prelude began, the TV picture showed the earth slowly turning in space, then switched to the Sloan household where Jim and Ellen faced each other.

Don't tell him about the other man, thought Delia. No matter how you feel, don't break up the family. She herself had chosen the amorous businessman over the distant serviceman. In her case there was no doubt who the father of her baby was. Mac had been gone too long.

She knew Reuben Cole and Jonas Pemberton suspected her of trapping the heir-apparent. Actually it was he who trapped her. Bud Cole wined and dined and romanced her aggressively after she went to work in the tannery front office. Giddy from the attention and money, and far from Mac, she succumbed. When she told Bud Cole of her pregnancy, he happily married her.

Soon after Amanda was born, however, her husband changed. Reuben Cole died and Bud became immersed in running the business. Before, she only had to share her husband with his sports. Now she had to take a back seat to business and sports. In his own way he loved his family, but he didn't put them first. Building an empire became a greater calling.

As the pressures on him increased, Bud Cole privately became distrustful and possessive. Delia's past relationship with his biggest rival began to gnaw at him. She had never been unfaithful, except in her mind. Maybe he sensed that.

Mac would never take her back, she knew. He was harder than Bud Cole that way. He gave his all and expected the same in return. You didn't get second chances with Jonathan MacEwen.

She ran into him last week at the train station. She watched him load some veneer logs onto a flatcar. She hadn't seen much of him the past thirteen years. He was bigger than she remembered, and more muscular. When he came to the station platform to sign the bill of lading, she was waiting. Maturity had made him even more striking. There were glints of silver in his black hair, his face was browned from outdoor living, and crow's feet were forming at the corners of his eyes, those emerald eyes.

She expected him to say why didn't you wait. She wanted to explain! But there was no anguish in his green eyes. He just said, Hello Delia, you're looking well. She fidgeted like a schoolgirl and said she was sorry about his mother. He nodded, a look of sadness drew over his face and she knew he was recalling their Irish families' closeness while they were growing up together in Tannerytown. She yearned to comfort him, to touch him, but held back. A sixth sense told her it was she who needed the reassurance, not him. Then the Edward T. Johnson roared to life, they couldn't hear each other, so they went on. Descending the platform, the realization hit her. His passion for her was gone. Mac was in love with someone else. Delia thought she knew who.

The TV wife was in her husband's arms, sobbing about the baby. He was smiling, which made Maria Barbano happy. When he was home they *had* acted as husband and wife. Delia also thought she was home free. Just keep your mouth shut about Roger, girlie, and buy a double bed. But Ellen Sloan was upset with at least a minute left to the program. "Jim, there's more..."

The Fallbrook Ladies' Garden Club sat on the edge of their seats. This was truly a pregnant pause. Before Ellen could continue, a strong gust of wind blew open the French doors, raised the curtains, scattered napkins and guests, and showered the room with pine needles and leaves. Delia rushed to the swinging doors and latched them shut. The TV picture turned to snow. The dialog disintegrated into electrical crackle.

"Oh, hell and damn!" swore Justina Whitaker. Then, realizing her place, she touched her fingertips to her lips. "Excuse my French," she said.

"Lightning must have struck the TV line," said Bonnie.

"Call Ruby Broadwater," suggested Freda. "She's on the Laurel Hill line. She watches this." Delia didn't move fast enough for Justina, who grabbed the phone and rang up the operator herself. Ruby was too coarse to be admitted to the garden club, but had a green thumb and was consulted in emergencies. This was an emergency.

———

But lightning did not strike the TV line. One wayward half of a split elm had fallen on top of it.

Tom Donachy pulled furiously on his stalled chainsaw. Squeaky and Joe supported themselves on the hood of his pickup, shaking with laughter. The paper bag that once held their lunch flew like a box-kite toward Blackwolf Swamp. Toward the birds.

Observed Joe wryly, "It'll be a while, Tom, before you can cut timber like my dad."

———

Bud Cole parked his Cadillac behind Spike Poorbaugh's battered Army-surplus jeep. Heavy raindrops splashed sporadically into Blockhouse creek, whose current was muddying already with runoff from the thunderstorm on Bloss Mountain. He strode into the covered bridge and leaned over the open crawlspace to the main deck beams. He used to snag suckers from there as a kid. "Poorbaugh!" he shouted. "I want a word with you."

Something thrashed in the deep water below him. A taut seine line seesawed in the current, first heading upstream, then down. The rain hit in bursts, machine-gunning the water on either side of the bridge. Whatever was hooked to the end of that line struggled to reach the rain. It was safe out in the rain.

A raspy voice called from under the bridge. "Come on down. We ain't goin' nowheres."

Bud Cole left the cover and minced down the slippery fisherman's path to the sand bar under the bridge. His brown herringbone suit got wet. Once under the bridge he wiped his broad face dry with a handkerchief.

Spike Poorbaugh stood in hipboots in the shallows, dragging in an old snapper. The feeding turtle had swallowed the stinkbait whole, the hidden trebles had hooked him deep. What the angry reptile was fighting for now wasn't life; it was for a few more hours of life.

Hand over hand the one predator drew the other closer, then lifted it up streaming water and blood and held it by the wire leader. The snapper's wrinkled neck stretched far beyond the protection of its knobby algae-coated shell, its razor-sharp beak clamped vainly on the wire, its clawed feet churned madly after its catcher, and its muscular ridged tail swept back and forth, seeking a target for one final defiant swat. It got it, striking the flat side of a bright steel blade being drawn from its sheath. The turtle wielded all his weapons at once without effect.

A practiced slash of the Bowie severed its head. Shell and squirming body tumbled to the creek bank, the clawed

145

feet dug into the sand. The head stayed hooked on the trebles. One beady black eye blinked.

"He don't know he's dead yet," said Poorbaugh, throwing the rebaited seine line upstream so it followed the current down to the muddy-green depths of a favorite summertime swimming hole.

The normally taciturn trapper then did a strange thing: He gave Bud Cole a biology lesson. "They eat their own kind, turtles. They eat most anything. They even eat some of the crap you been puttin' in this river. Someday, there won't be no turtles."

He grabbed the convulsing body by the tail, flipped it on its back on a flat rock, then split the underside of the shell with two knife chops. The turtle's body was removed, gutted, rinsed and carefully placed in a clean plastic bag, presumably ready to sell. Half of the entrails went in a smelly coffee can as bait. The other half went back into the bloody shell to be thrown in as chum for more turtles. He didn't waste natural resources, Spike Poorbaugh.

He stuffed the shell, uprighted it, and set it beside the bait can. "Lookit' there," he said.

Bud Cole edged closer and examined the shell, seeing nothing unusual at first. His expensive shoes sank in the sand. His feet grew cold, then wet, and he shivered. Then he saw the markings. What the hell?

The numbers 32 and 39 were carved on the shell.

Poorbaugh explained. "Caught him twice when he was a little fella. But he swallowed the hook today. If you get careless you don't get old."

The dates intrigued the factoryman. The turtle swam in that hole when he did. The number also indicated something else. He met the trapper's baleful gaze. "I heard you couldn't read or write."

"Jesse Poorbaugh taught me my figures so I'd never get cheated. Only dead men cheat Poorbaugh's."

He plunged the dripping knife into the sand bank to scour off the turtle slime, rinsed and resheathed it. The bone

146

handle was yellowed with age. "State your business, Cole," he said impatiently. "Turtles don't feed all day."

Bud Cole swallowed his irritation. This smelly no-account was busy! But he couldn't afford to alienate Poorbaugh. He needed him. For now. He stated his business. "Understand you had some trouble with MacEwen."

"He killed my dog."

"You going to do anything about it?"

"Someday...Someday somethin' will come to take him down."

"Are you that something?"

"Could be."

"Can you handle him?"

"It'd be close."

"Think I could take him?" Bud Cole's pride required that he get an expert's opinion.

The faint trace of a smile crossed the trapper's grizzled face. "If he ain't lookin', and you're lucky, you might. He's tough. He's been places and done things you got out of."

Poorbaugh's insinuation infuriated Cole. Still, he kept control. "He's coming your way," he said threateningly.

"I know."

"He plans to kick you out."

"He won't. He can't."

"Oh?" By his inflection Bud Cole let Poorbaugh know there was a chance MacEwen could.

"There's a paper," Poorbaugh replied firmly. "Signed by The Lady. Huntin' rights to us Poorbaugh's for cleanin' out the panthers and wolves. Saul took it to the courthouse."

"I've read it. Only binds Louisa and her heirs. The contract's over once the property is conveyed out of the family. MacEwen's not an heir so he's not obligated."

If this information bothered Poorbaugh he didn't show it. "You're not kin either," he observed.

"I'll deed the rights back if I get title. Better than before."

"Why don't I just ask MacEwen for 'em?"

147

"He'll never grant them to you again. You sicced your dog on him, remember?"

The trapper knelt down and felt the seine line for any bites that might be happening at the baited ends of the four leaders. In better times he'd hooked two turtles at once. It appeared his attention was fixed on the line. Watching it intently, Poorbaugh asked, "You want me to kill him?"

The casual tone of the question struck Bud Cole. Killing was inbred in this man. He was totally without pity or remorse or conscience when it came to destroying an enemy. Actually, he was kinder to the turtle, letting him go two other times.

Bud Cole answered vaguely. "I want you to stop him so I can get title. I don't care how."

"Alright."

"Good."

The trapper straightened up to his full height, half a foot taller than Bud Cole, a leathery throwback to Saul and Jesse, who also had shaggy rust-gray hair and amber eyes. Those eyes shifted to the bloody shell. "If you cheat me Bud Cole," his voice was as low and as clear as a hiss, "I'll split your head and carve on your face the date I done it."

Bud Cole shivered again, turned, and walked out in the rain. But some business was left undone. He meant to ask Spike Poorbaugh why he was staying low so late in the year.

Chapter 22 – Halloween

He came out at dusk when they did, the seven stars of the night hunter. Hot-blue and high in the east, they sparkled out of sequence over the Valley of Mist. On the Rock-From-Which-Blacksnake-Fell, the hunter stood watch.

Grandmother Songbird, a pure Seneca of the Bear Clan, said the stars were seven beautiful sisters chased by the evil spirit Tawiskaron, He-Who-Walks-On-Earth, in the form of a vast lusting bear. They were saved by good spirit Tarachiawagon, He-Who-Holds-Up-The-Sky, who lifted them to the heavens, far out of evil's reach. During the chase, the bear scratched the earth with his claws and made the mountains and valleys and hollows and caused the rivers and streams and swamps to spring forth. The longest scratch was the Valley of Mist, the deepest was Bear Hollow. Great Marsh was created when the bear made a high, snarling, futile leap skyward to snatch the maidens from Tarachiawagon's grasp and fell back heavily, denting the earth. Thus was made the hunting ground of the Bear clan.

Jesse Poorbaugh felt bad for the bear. That kind of longin' should not go unsatisfied, he said. Jesse himself had longed for his sisters-in-law and realized more satisfaction than the bear.

Songbird's Christian name was Sedalia, the name they gave her at the mission school at Kinzua. They taught her to read and write and gave her a Bible, but they couldn't turn her into a white Christian. Songbird became a red Christian, blending biblical and Seneca beliefs. She found the seven sisters in the Bible, where the tormented farmer Job was rebuked by the Good Spirit speaking out of Brother Whirlwind: "Can you bind the beautiful Pleiades? Can you loose the cords of Orion? Can you bring forth the morning star in its season and lead out the bear with its cubs?"

Jesse Poorbaugh scoffed at the Good Spirit. If he'd been Job, he'd a' asked the bear for a long rope, and snagged one of the pretty Pleiad sisters. They believed in different gods, the Poorbaugh's.

149

Songbird's great grandfather was Blue Jacket, chief of the Bear Clan, father of Blacksnake, his only son, the boy who fell from the cliff. Blacksnake's sister Lake Bird kept the family line alive.

But Blacksnake's spirit would not rest at Three Oaks Spring. It wandered on one of the four brother winds, screaming for revenge against what murdered it. Seneca belief required a relative exact revenge until the restless spirit was appeased.

There were cat tracks on the ledge, and a bare spot wiped clean by a long swishing tail. A heel print faced the clean spot. The boy had backed up until he plunged to the rocks by the spring. The four brother winds take turns carrying his scream.

For sixteen seasons Blue Jacket hunted his son's killer, then grew old and could come no more. Years later the Poorbaugh twins, whose adopted names were Pale Knife and Dark Knife, brought their Bear Clan wives to the Valley of Mist. Songbird, barely a woman, was the youngest of the wives. The men came for Jacob Miller's money. The women came for Blacksnake's revenge.

Saul and Jesse didn't get all the cats, so Blacksnake's spirit continued to wander. The hunting and trapping was better than at Kinzua so they stayed.

The twins had different lusts – Jesse's was for women, Saul's for killing. They changed places occasionally; Jesse had killed their oldest brother in a knife fight over the inheritance of a mule. But the twins got along. They shared their wives and daughters and chased off their older sons. Some of the daughters left when they could. Those that ran off went to Kinzua and other places.

The year the last wolf was killed Saul went off to fight for the Union. He limped back from Gettysburg carrying a minnie ball next to his backbone. The wound bothered and Saul grew crippled and died, but not before fathering Hannah by Songbird. When Saul could walk no more he begged his brother to put him out of his misery. There was some kindness in Jesse.

Jesse remained vigorous as he grew older and, when she was ready, took up with Hannah. The year neighbor Charley Bower went to Cuba, Hannah bore Samuel. That was Songbird's Christian name for him. His Indian name was Yellow Eyes, and the blood of both Saul and Jesse ran in his veins.

Songbird wrote everyone's name in her bible. Her line was Blue Jacket to Lake Bird to River Otter to Songbird to Hannah to Samuel. He had to memorize the names. Jesse frowned on his reading. He didn't want him leanin' Christian like Songbird. He didn't want him leanin' Seneca either. He wanted him leanin' Poorbaugh.

When he was twelve summers his father gave him Saul's bonehandled Bowie and taught him how to use it. Two summers later, he inherited the walnut-handled one. Jesse, who was slowing down, got trampled and slashed by a wild boar. Killed by one of their own damn loose pigs! His spirit rested after his son hunted and shot all the boars.

Songbird said Blacksnake's spirit had invaded the boar. It was angry with the Poorbaugh's for not killing all the big cats.

Saul and Jesse had learned a lesson after eradicating the wolves. There was no money for bounty hunters when the varmints were all gone. Blacksnake's plight wasn't so bad, argued Jesse. At least he wasn't boxed in a cold wet hole, or chained to a floor of fire.

Pigs were expendable so Samuel killed all the wild boars. Still, he wondered, who was right? Father Jesse? Or grandmother Songbird? Should a spirit rest or should it wander? Which was heaven, and which was hell? Who would avenge his spirit if he was murdered?

Songbird insisted...he must have a child.

He took up with his older sisters but no child came. Songbird urged him to go to Kinzua and bring back a young woman from another clan. Do not take one from the valley, she warned. The whites would not understand.

The year he reached his full height the whites came and sent him to war in France. He took Saul's Bowie because it held its edge longer. It was against regulations but Cap'n

Hayes let him use it. He earned the name Spike for his skill with the knife and bayonet. He was the best shot too. He took some women over there. There could be Poorbaugh's born after he left but he didn't know the mother's names. The best and worst of Saul and Jesse came out of him in France. After Armistice they sent him home.

The maple sap was running when he and Ernie Rollins and Cap'n Hayes got off the train in Fallbrook. The towns-people were waiting and honored Ernie and the Captain for being brave soldiers. But not him. Private Poorbaugh shouldered his pack and headed for the cabin on the backside of Potash.

No smoke rose from the chimney and no dogs announced his presence. The only greeting he got was Black-snake's howling spirit, which followed him up Potash then veered south to threaten the predators on Bear. The avenger had returned. Crystallized snow drifted over the front porch and piled against the front door. There were no tracks in the snow.

He felt true isolation after he opened the heavy plank door.

Hannah lay in her bed. Songbird sat in her rocker alongside the table. Mice had chewed their ears, but that was all. They had died during the bitter cold and hadn't thawed yet. Songbird's closed Bible lay on the table. A note stuck out the top.

The grippe. The grippe had killed his family. He saw some soldiers die from it aboard ship. The chaplain said some words and their canvassed bodies were thrown over the side. Spanish Influenza it was called. Killed ten times as many people as the war.

The Poorbaugh burial ground was froze over, so he wrapped Hannah's and Songbird's stiff bodies in burlap and stored them in the pelt shed. He burned the house and camped out in the shed. That was the coldest month he ever spent, the one in the shed. The livestock and dogs that couldn't get away had died from neglect. He burned them

too. He took Songbird's note to Cap'n Hayes, who read it to
him:

> "To Samuel if your stil alive. Rachel
> and Esther went to town for suplys. Came back
> with lung sickness very bad. Hannah burried all
> in the bog. Cannin's done. Traplines not set.
> To week to burry Hannah. Blacksnake wales."

When the frost went out he sank Hannah and Songbird in
the bog with Saul and Jesse and all the other dead Poor-
baughs. They had no markers. The only inscriptions marking their passage was imprinted in his mind and Songbird's
Bible.

He bought a team and some chickens and built a new
cabin, snugging this one closer to the steep south slope on
Potash.

He hunted the big cats and, for the most part, kept them
contained to the Big Woods. Their numbers were declining
but so was he. He was past his prime. He discovered that
when the Donachy kid upended him on Blackwolf. The boy
had the strength of an ironwood tree. There was fierceness in
him too. The kid was like he was when he was that age. If
he had a son he would be tall and strong like that kid. And
live long enough to carry out Songbird's mission.

He hoped for some of the Poorbaugh women to return
but none ever did. One summer, during the time the hoboes
walked the roads, he went to the Seneca nation at Kinzua.
They knew of him there and protected their women. In a
sour mood, he returned alone. Along the way he knifed three
tramps in the woods near the train station in Bradford. They
had boiled up a fine bluetick hound and offered him some.
They would not be the last men he killed over a dog!

Songbird was wrong. If he wanted a woman he would
have to take her from the valley. Bud Cole didn't know it,
but he had a robust woman there. He would take her and kill
that liar too. Deed him back the huntin' rights to his land!
There'd be nothin' to hunt. He'd been to Bloss Mountain.

He'd seen what a mess Cole made there. He couldn't let a miner or a logger get even close to the Big Woods.

Jesse warned of the day someone would come to take the land. Show them The Lady's paper first. If they came back be ready to fight.

He was ready. He had caches stashed in caves on Blackwolf and Potash and Bear and beyond. Charlie Bower was the only one that even knew there were caves.

An army couldn't find him back in there. He had spent enough time soldiering to learn that. He could go out at night and kill at will. It would be like the Argonne Forest all over again. For while the other doughboys were sleepin', he went huntin', and brought back Hun scalps and ears.

He leaned against the hollow chestnut that stood well back from the cliff edge. Long ago it had been a bee tree. Now it was like his ancestors in the bog, dead and rotting slowly. He resisted the urge to do what Blacksnake and the hounds did. The Rock possessed a magnetic force that compelled the watcher to brave the edge and look down.

This was the night when He-Who-Walks-On-Earth was strongest and the Seneca women stayed inside and Saul and Jesse would come to the rock to spite them and mock He-Who-Holds-Up-The-Sky. Songbird had begged Jesse to make Samuel stay home, but the old man just laughed and said maybe they'd meet up with the cat and settle this score once and for all.

His uncle's spirit wailed down low on Brother South-wind then rose up the black pit that began beyond the ledge. It carried glowing embers from below Three Oaks Spring. The embers rose high over the Valley of Mist and danced with the Seven Sisters, orange-jacketed soldiers at a ball with blue-gowned ladies.

Jesse would approve. His son stood guard at an officer's party in France one night and snagged one of the ladies.

The embers faded, turned into blackened wafers, and fell. But more came, and more, and more; until embers and sparks and finally smoke blotted out the Seven Sisters.

The Lady burned. Revenge against her for cheating the Poorbaugh's! Revenge against MacEwen for killing his dog, for taking his land! For the Poorbaughs, the best tasting revenge was the bitter, because it lasts.

The Lady and her fathers were dead and their spirits rested and maybe didn't care. But MacEwen was not dead...yet. He would care.

All The Lady built was burning except the springhouse. He let it alone. Behind a loose stone was a tiny survival cache wrapped in plastic – a Case pocket knife, a book of matches, a coil of clear fishline with a silver spinner. The Longstar spring never froze and his trout were always hungry.

Mac took the hat box from the top shelf of his closet and set it on his bed. He removed the cap and put it on. It felt tight, but not as tight as the first time he wore it after the shrapnel wound. He looked in the dresser mirror. He needed a haircut.

"So that's what a colonel looks like." Mac turned. Tom grinned at him from the open doorway. He was also dressed for the parade, wearing his denim FFA jacket over rumpled Sunday clothes. The practical Tom thought clothes should be clean but ironing wasn't necessary.

"You're supposed to salute a senior officer," replied Mac.

Tom snapped to attention, the top of his head barely missing the door lintel. "Aye, aye, sir!" he said...and saluted with his left hand.

Mac chuckled. "Someday a short bulldog of a Drill Instructor will have fun with you."

"Will big brother the Colonel help?"

"The D.I."

"Think I'll go to college and spoil your fun."

"We'll wait."

Tom stood beside Mac, looked in the mirror, and straightened his tie. He had never learned to tie one right. Try as he might the darn knot always pointed southwest.

He had seen his brother in full dress only one other time, when Mac was promoted to major and he and his mother rode a bus to Philadelphia for the ceremony. But things were missing today. Mac's uniform was decidedly spare. The adornments were the essentials – crossed rifles on his lapels, silver eagles on his epaulets, silver braid on the visor of his cap. That was all.

"No decorations?" asked Tom.

"None today."

Tom shrugged. "It's your parade."

"No," replied Mac. "It's your parade."

Tom had an errand, was running late, and only vaguely wondered what Mac meant. "I've got to pick up Danny and Nan."

"Why don't you ask Mary Spencer to press your shirt?"

Tom's chin touched his tie. "Why? I ironed the front. My jacket hides the rest."

Mac gave up. It was strange the traits men inherited from their fathers. Big Mike had been lackadaisical about clothes too. He switched to a more serious subject. "We're cutting on Longstar this afternoon," he said. "You coming?"

Tom winced. He had another obligation. He suspected his help was needed in the woods right now. Mac hadn't said, but evidence indicated money was tight. The spindle on their desk was thick with bills. Evie's slip for October's fuel was on the bottom. "We're butchering turkey's today," he said. "How are you getting away with Abigail's parents up?"

"I'm taking them out to supper this evening."

"At the Turkey Ranch?" Tom hoped not.

"No. The hotel."

———

Tom drove off in his pickup. Mac followed in his mother's sedan. At the traffic light Tom turned south toward Buttonwood. Mac crossed Fifteen to Main, on his way to the bank.

This week's check was light, barely enough to cover wages and November's loan payment, which was ten days late. The last three checks hadn't covered expenses as they slogged around in wet woods to haul what timber they could to the mill. Charley Bower suggested they quit and go duck hunting: least they'd have fun bein' wet and miserable, and wouldn't break any more equipment.

The fall rains and farm fire had really set him back. Ironically, the only good weather had been the day after the fire and today, both wasted production days. One he spent bulldozing smoldering buildings, the other would be spent marching in a parade.

Today was Veterans Day. Previous years saw November 11th celebrated as Armistice Day. This spring President Eisenhower and a vote-conscious congress changed it. It didn't matter to Mac what Ike called it. Ever soldier celebrated the end of war.

He was still kicking himself for not thinking to buy insurance on his equipment and the Longsdorf place. The insurance money would have covered his debt. As it was he didn't have the capital to replace the lost equipment or to build a shelter to maintain what he still had. Now he had to rent a place or hire the work done. Mort Fessler had let him use his garage nights but he couldn't impose on the junk man indefinitely. Mort didn't seem to mind, however. He was lonely and enjoyed the company.

Tom felt a closer kinship to the Longsdorf place than he did. Mac envied his brother's sensitivity that way, to quickly connect with a person or place. True, war had hardened him, but he had always been more detached than Tom. Again, brothers like their fathers. Terrance MacEwen had been cool and reserved. Big Mike Donachy was open and friendly.

Today's ceremony would show the impact of that friendliness. The man had been dead ten years and the town still remembered.

The fire had broken Evie's heart. The Lady was gutted. All that was left was the shell and columns, and the stone springhouse. Tom stopped him from dozing the house down. He and the FFA boys boarded up the openings with plywood. Evie paid for the plywood.

Mac felt the effort was a waste of time. Spike Poorbaugh would just come back some other night and torch the rest. They all knew Spike did it. They couldn't prove it. He would have to keep Tom away from Spike.

Mac knew what Spike had been – a scout sent to terrorize the enemy by killing and mutilating individual soldiers behind the safety of their own lines. Several of his kills were recorded. One example in a Ranger training manual described how a "breed" doughboy stalked and knifed a German sentry at night by trailing the smell of his cigarette smoke. Marine manuals also referred to the breed. Spike Poorbaugh had left a valuable, albeit bloody, legacy.

Spike's aggression was more than retaliation for the dog. He had met with Squire Hayes and learned the Longsdorf-Poorbaugh contract was void. The man thought in terms of clan justice, not normal right and wrong. It didn't matter to him that Louisa's journal revealed Saul and Jesse had frightened the document out of her. So she made a promise that bound her family but no one else. Family to family. Longsdorf to Poorbaugh. Sedalia probably didn't understand the document's limitations. Now that Spike did, he felt cheated.

Mac's soldier training wrestled with his conscience. His conscience was losing. The first chance he got he should kill Spike Poorbaugh. Kill him, bulldoze him in a hole, and never breathe a word to anybody.

———

The trim plain secretary filling in for an absent teller teased him: "I see you can still get in your uniform, Colonel."

Mac chided back: "And why aren't you dressed for the parade, Lieutenant?"

Helen Kuhl smiled, pleased that Mac remembered. She had been a WAC in WWII. Married to a former pilot, their military careers were cut short when he contracted polio. She pointed to her desk, piled high but neat with file folders. "Saturday's a busy day," she said. "Besides, some of the troops would object. It's a man's world you know."

"If I have to pull rank and make you, I'll do it."

"There was a time I outranked you, Soldier."

"If you had stayed in you still would. How about it? There's still time to change."

"Next year."

"OK. Next year."

Mac turned to leave but Helen stopped him. "My commanding officer wants to see you," she said seriously.

Steve Heffner stood by his window smoking an everpresent Lucky Strike. The curtain was drawn back and mid-morning sunlight streamed over his leather chair and cluttered desk and passed through his partially open office door. The banker watched the people gather for their little parade; little people with their little kids and little pleasures and dollar-a-week savings accounts.

He looked at the mess on his desk and wondered what the crisp army officer would think, what kind of impression he made on MacEwen, and realized that he was in control here and shouldn't care. But he did care. It made him feel a little better when he recalled that this officer was a warrior, not a manager.

The rectangle of sunlight in the hallway was blocked, MacEwen knocked on the door casing, and the banker told him to come in.

Steve Heffner felt it odd, the feeling he got when the ex-soldier opened the door wider and sunlight reflected off the braid on his hat. The banker had never worn a uniform. Too risky, that. But the uniform had its impact. Some men were born with all the luck.

It irritated him when MacEwen glanced at his desk and frowned. He smothered his cigarette in the ashtray and decided not to offer his customer a chair. "MacEwen," he said, "We've noticed you haven't made a payment this month."

"I just gave Helen the check."

"We notice your checking account is getting low, too." Whenever Heffner wanted to gang up on someone he used "we." The pretext of reinforcements, in this case just an illusion, made him feel stronger, and if there was a mistake he could blame "them."

MacEwen was matter-of-fact. "Production has been hurt by the weather and the fire. I drew my account down to replace lost equipment."

160

"I don't suppose there was any insurance?" Heffner, by implication, meant that any good businessman bought insurance.

"No, there wasn't."

The banker had expected MacEwen to be defensive, even belligerent. Other contractors he dealt with behaved that way. But not MacEwen. If anything he appeared embarrassed. "We want insurance on your equipment, MacEwen."

"I can't get it."

This was news. "Why not?"

"No company will take me after the fire. Said they wouldn't buy a claim."

Steve Heffner pondered that. Bud Cole had done his work well. Encouraged, the banker changed emphasis. He didn't need reinforcements. "I'm not loaning any more money," he said importantly.

MacEwen showed some consternation. "I'm not asking for any. What's the problem here? The trees are your security. I'll have that loan paid off by August."

You don't have that long, buddy.

The banker thought it. He didn't say it.

———

The veterans assembled at the tanyard. The sun broke through the factory haze, reflecting off the trappings of the Army, Navy, Air Force and Marines. From his second story office window Bud Cole peeked through the blinds and envied. Two particular reflections caught his eye – the silver flash off the braid of Army Colonel MacEwen's cap, and the white gleam off the handle of Marine Sergeant O'Conner's sword. He opened the window a crack to hear what was going on below.

He should fire that son-of-a-bitch O'Conner. The man recovered quickly from his beating and came right back to work. They figured he would linger on comp. He didn't. He worked harder than before. He had lost his arrogance and was slowly gaining the respect of the men. O'Conner was

161

getting even his way. He was surely a paid organizer. Pemberton checked his bank records. He made eighty bucks a week and deposited a hundred.

MacEwen didn't know it, but the noose was slowly being tightened around his neck. Steve Heffner's call just confirmed it. The trusting fool still thought he had ten months to pay off the note. The noose was tied to an invisible rope. Bud Cole yearned to yank it now and knock off his pretty hat.

Patience. Pemberton stressed patience. Mistakes happen when you get in a hurry. And secrecy. Absolute secrecy. A secret remains a secret only as long as no one else knows.

Bud Cole knew he had broken the gravest Pemberton rule. Someone else knew. But they were involved in parts of the plot, only he comprehended the whole. Steve Heffner was involved with the note and had probably guessed about the fire. Ford Irish knew Cole money was bribing the supervisors and the bridge engineer. Spike Poorbaugh knew he wanted MacEwen out of the way. It was all so neat. Heffner and Irish were too involved and too chickenshit to talk. No one would believe Poorbaugh if he did. Still Pemberton would disapprove, too many knew. Pemberton was old.

Most of the veterans were mixing freely in the yard – kidding, gossiping, reminiscing. Two stood below him, away from the others, along the shrubbery-lined side of the building. There was tension between these two. Bud Cole knelt closer to the open window. The venetian blinds made the perfect camouflage. One wore the armband of an army M. P. The other wore a combat knife that had killed its first soldier in the Civil War.

Jim Morningstar was heard first. "Last night a pack of dogs pulled down one of Sully Thompson's steers. Know anything about it?"

Spike Poorbaugh was deadly calm: "You askin' or accusin'?"

"I'm promising. When I catch that pack, I'm shooting every one."

The trapper put the image of that conflict into the warden's and Bud Cole's minds. "Be some good shootin'," he said. "Black o'night. Eight, ten hounds comin' at you. They eat rabbits for sport. What's to stop 'em from eatin' a rabbit cop?"

Jim Morningstar glared and walked stiffly away.

Sensing trouble, Squire Hayes had started over. Bud Cole kept at the window.

"What was that about?"

"Damn fool's gonna shoot my dogs!"

"What for?"

"Killin' one of Sully Thompson's beeves."

"Did they?"

"Nope. They was penned."

His listeners thought he was lying.

He wasn't.

———

Abigail and her parents stood in front of the bank waiting for the parade. Steve Heffner, who sat with her last week at a Lady Lutheran's ice cream social and started tongues wagging, came out and joined them. At first Abigail resented his intrusion, then decided it wouldn't hurt for Mac to know other men were interested in her too.

This was Abigail's first small town parade. She had told her parents it was no big deal but now the eagerness of the crowd affected them and each privately wished they could get closer.

They couldn't. The wide sidewalks of Main, from the Blockhouse Bridge west the three business blocks to the bank, swarmed with excited people. Even Steve Heffner's handsome but sallow face was beginning to show a little color.

The buffer between the business and residential sections of Main was the town square called The Green. Under trees stripped bare by the rainy weather were ordinary park fixtures; several wood benches, a gazebo, a fountain, a statue of

163

a WWI soldier, a flagpole. A temporary platform had been raised in front of the statue and rows of metal chairs fanned out from it. Here the parade would end and the formal ceremony marking Fallbrook's first Veterans day would be held.

Fallbrook had honored its veterans every Armistice Day since 1919. In that year two parades were held: The impromptu one in early March when the last three to return home got off the train, and the traditional one on November eleventh. Spike Poorbaugh hadn't been invited to the first one, most were disappointed he survived to be on the train. The Squire and Ernie Rollins corrected that slight and the trapper hadn't missed a parade in 35 years. With his vitality it was probable he would someday be the oldest living veteran.

A hush of anticipation quieted the crowd and Main Street grew still. A flock of pigeons rudely flopped their way from one building cornice to another. Then they too sat still. Traffic on 15 idled at the intersection with Main, halted there by two Pennsylvania State Troopers. The lined vehicles shut off their engines and 15 grew still. All looked east.

The vanguard of the parade stood silently at attention on the center rise of the Blockhouse Bridge.

The vanguard was the front unit of Fallbrook's high school band, whose uniforms were the school colors, blue and gold. Saluting at point stood sleek senior majorette Monica Manikowski, wearing a gold costume and holding a gold baton. Behind her was the color guard displaying the blue and gold school banner, and flanked on either side by flagmen unfurling the American and Pennsylvania flags. Behind the color guard, alone like Monica, stood the band director dressed all in blue, except for white gloves. Then in tight formation, brasses front, stood the mass that was the band.

The director raised his gloved hand. It grew quieter still.

Loud and clear he counted time...One! Two! Three!...and Monica split the blue sky with her gold baton.

It sailed high and silent, a gleaming arrow, and as it fell hundreds of people prayed she would catch it.

She did, and at that moment the band surged forward, full into John Phillip Sousa's "Stars and Stripes Forever."

Cheers swept in a wave down Main. Alarmed pigeons flew to a tannery stack that wasn't smoking. Excitement stirred the crowd. Kids were raised on father's shoulders. Older folks nudged their way to the curb. The parade was coming!

Behind the band came the color guards and post commanders of the American Legion and newly-formed VFW. The banner for the VFW was rolled up. It would be displayed after the post was dedicated.

Then came the veterans, marching in units according to the war they fought in.

The first was a single horseman riding a prancy chestnut gelding. He wore a sand-colored uniform and a wide-brimmed campaign hat. His mount carried the trappings of the First U.S. Volunteer Cavalry Regiment, 1898. Trooper Charley Bower waved to the crowd, at seventy-two one of the last Rough Riders.

Next came a contingent of WWI doughboys led by Captain Clarence Hayes and Lieutenant Fred Sheafer. All wore drab olive uniforms and steel helmets, except Fred, who wore a cavalry uniform like Charley Bower. Before the doughboys sailed east to fight the Germans, Fred went west to fight German-supported Mexican's under Pancho Villa. He ended up an officer under General Black Jack Pershing. But the most impressive veteran in this group was the tallest. His head and shoulders stuck above the rear line, thick graying hair covered his collar, and his sharp facial features were softened by a wavy graying beard. This private had stayed lean and savage for thirty-five years.

Martha Whalen asked her daughter who *he* was.

"You don't want to know him, Mother," replied Abigail sharply. There were times Abigail suspected her mother's female instincts were baser than her own.

The largest and most diverse group were the WWII vets. In this column were G.I.'s, sailors, air corps men, coast guardsmen, and marines. This group also had the most trouble fitting into their uniforms. Tailgunner Luke Ballard's flight jacket was open in front and his thick forearms stretched his leather sleeves. Sergeant Jacob O'Conner's marine dress blues were impressive, but the crimps in the belting indicated the wearer had once been a much thinner man.

Last marched a smaller squad of similar diversity except that three members in this group were in wheel chairs. Many of the Korean Conflict wounds were not yet healed. One of the taller veterans was a classically handsome officer wearing silver braid, one who could have marched as the highest ranking soldier in the previous group if he had wanted to. He drew stares, this man, especially female stares. Martha Whalen noticed this immediately. He passed within a few feet of the Whalen's. He smiled at Mrs. Whalen and winked at Abigail. Both were captivated by his intense green eyes.

"That's Jonathan MacEwen, Mother."

Martha Whalen didn't answer. She continued to watch Mac carefully. Abigail knew the look. Her mother saw a man in his prime, and was calculating already what her grandchildren would look like. The thought aroused Abigail, who turned to point Mac out to her father. He was deep in conversation with Steve Heffner.

The banker didn't stir her like the logger did. Heffner was safe. It bothered Abigail that one look from Mac would affect her mother so. And her, too.

After the veterans came an assortment of marchers and apparatus: The Steam Valley Hose Company, the Shriners, the Eastern star, the Rialto Theater popcorn truck, several ladies auxiliaries, two clowns on roller skates, Boy Scout Troup 50, the 4-H, and the Future Farmers of America.

Tom Donachy ambled along with the FFA. His big hands and wrists stuck out of the sleeves of a jacket he earned two years too soon. The popular youth mixed with the crowd, giving Tootsie Rolls to the kids and taking advice on love note etiquette, tree falling, pickup maintenance, deer hunting and basketball. Occasionally, he would look ahead, see the helmeted back of Spike Poorbaugh's head, and turn grim for a while. Seeing Abigail, he nodded but did not smile.

He tolerated her, she knew. He had penetrated deep into her personality and didn't like all he found. She bit her lip. Tom was a harsh judge and that hurt. Too harsh, she thought.

Just then she felt a small hand take her own. Danny had quietly approached through the crowd. His eyes were bright with excitement and his cheeks were rosy from the cool air. Abigail had purposely avoided making him a teacher's pet, but it was hard. If she ever had a boy she wanted him to be like Danny.

Abigail bent down. "Hello, Danny. Did your mother bring you?" She hoped not.

"No, she's working."

"She missed the parade? Too bad! Who did bring you?"

"Tom and Nan."

Abigail glanced up the street, saw Nan looking her way and waved. Tom was too close to Julie's family to suit Abigail.

"Know what, Miss Whalen?"

"What, Danny?"

"Mr. Bower is going to let me ride Duke. And Mac said I could wear his hat."

Abigail discouraged him.

"Oh, that's a special hat, Danny. You might drop it and scratch it." Abigail did not want her rival's son wearing Mac's hat in front of all these people.

Danny showed his disappointment with lowered eyes. "I'll be careful with it," he said stubbornly.

Abigail was just as stubborn. "I'll tell him you changed your mind," she said sweetly.

Danny's hand slipped out of Abigail's. His jaw was set. He hadn't changed his mind. He didn't have more to say to his teacher, either. Abigail waved at Nan again and pointed down at Danny. Nan got the message and came over.

"Where's Tom?" asked Abigail.

Nan nodded in the direction of the Green. "Mac wanted Tom to go with him," she said.

Damn, thought Abigail. She hadn't wanted Tom around today.

Nan took Danny and walked with the crowd toward the Green. Abigail and her parents and Steve Heffner followed.

Martha Whalen was curious. "Why can't the boy wear the hat?"

"Later, Mother."

———

The Veterans Day ceremony was military efficient and short. Squire Hayes presided. St. Bibliana's Father Rakoski, a WWII chaplain, gave the invocation. First Baptist's Reverend Klinger, a Korean War medic, was there for the benediction. The post commanders of the American Legion and VFW stood with them. The Legion commander held an American flag.

The Squire asked for Jonathan MacEwen and Thomas Donachy to come forward. Mac was grinning. Tom looked confused. The Legion commander presented Tom the flag and the VFW color guard unfurled their new banner. It read MICHAEL T. DONACHY Post #3780.

Tears streamed down Tom's rugged face and the crowd applauded warmly. The two commanders raised Tom's flag while the band played the National Anthem. The Legion Honor Guard shot off a twenty-one gun salute and the VFW bugler played "Taps."

Martha Whalen was impressed. She paid closest attention, though, to MacEwen, observing, "For a colonel, your Mac doesn't wear many decorations."

Ex-marine Jacob O'Conner, standing close by, explained: "Medal of Honor winners don't have to wear decorations, Ma'am."

"Oh," said Mrs. Whalen, giving her daughter a why-didn't-you-tell-us look.

Abigail was embarrassed. She hadn't known. She realized again she really didn't know Jonathan MacEwen. She had been talking and he had been listening. No one else had told her either. The people up here were open about some things and strangely private about others.

Abigail touched O'Conner's sleeve. "Where did he win it?"

"Korea. Heartbreak Ridge. It was big news. Made LIFE magazine. Where you been?"

In her own little world, thought her mother.

Mr. Whalen and Steve Heffner had overheard. Mr. Whalen was perplexed. He wasn't sure Abigail should get involved with an Army hero that was bankrupt.

On the platform, Reverend Klinger gave the benediction. Fallbrook's first Veterans Day ceremony was over.

Chapter 24 – Old Ebenezer

Ebenezer was a Michigan deer, the grandson of a sturdy northern whitetail brought in by the Game Commission in 1925 to improve the quality of the herd. The grandfather, who would have been exceptional in Michigan, lived ten years and was killed by one of the big cats in the mountains. Ebenezer's father lived nine years and was shot for trap bait by Spike Poorbaugh, who never told anybody. Ebenezer had lived twelve years, very old for a whitetail buck, and was in the last year of his prime.

Ebenezer had lived long enough to surpass his forebears in cunning, strength and size. He was a long, heavyset deer weighing just over 400 pounds. When he stood alert, his head held high, it was more than seven feet from the ground to the top of his magnificent rack of horns. His dark-stained antlers, the inheritance of his fathers, were thicker at the base than a large man's fist. The heavy main beams were almost three feet long and the same distance apart with six high tines to a side. When he was last seen, and sightings were rare, the witness, a trucker who caught the deer in his headlights crossing Rt. 15 near the Tank, described him as a monster buck carrying a rocking chair above his head.

Ebenezer got his name in 1933 when Spike Poorbaugh found a fresh set of shed antlers on the front side of Potash and carried them down to Mort Fessler's. Mort mounted the horns on an oak board and brought the massive set to Sawyer's store one Saturday night. Charley Bower helped him through the front door with the exclamation: "My, ain't he an old Ebenezer!" and the name stuck.

The rack was hung on the wall over the loafer's bench and ten penny nails and Ebenezer was hunted for the next twenty-one years.

Those horns had been shed by the grandfather. The current Ebenezer was the third Ebenezer, a fact known only to the mountains and Spike Poorbaugh, who wasn't talking and didn't care.

Most bucks were killed by their fifth year, so the mighty buck that was sighted occasionally over two decades was unique and took on legendary qualities. The experienced hunters argued sensibly that the buck that carried the rack on Sawyer's wall was long dead, that the current Ebenezer was a look-alike descendent, and would someday fall to a hunter's bullet. Tom Donachy belonged to this group and dreamed of being the hunter that took Ebenezer. Others, the less experienced or more romantic, argued there was a different quality to this deer, maybe he couldn't be taken. For most it was more fun to imagine Ebenezer as the Patriarch of the Mountains, a great graying beast, very very old, impossible to kill.

Ebenezer was a patriarch but he could be killed. Those special qualities that he had, qualities of extra perception and stealth and strength, were what ensured his longevity and survival. His natural enemies were disease, icy weather, a stronger buck, a pack of dogs, the big cats, and man.

So far he had avoided injury from disease, weather, and man. His left shoulder bore the faint scars of a youthful encounter with a cat. That attacker died of internal injuries after the whirling buck slammed the lighter cat into the trunk of a tree.

The jagged scar of his right flank was only a year old, left there by one of Spike Poorbaugh's dogs.

The pack, five young hounds led by their parents, a large male and a particularly vicious female, took Ebenezer's trail one bright fall night on Potash. The dogs were accustomed to exhausting their prey, catching it, and tearing it apart. The veteran buck, however, had a scheme of his own. He led them to Caleb's Rock, then doubled back. As the dogs were trying to sniff out his trail on the rock ledge, Ebenezer charged from out of the tall laurel, sweeping three off the cliff with his horns. Two of the younger hounds managed to scurry away.

The pair of adults, trapped between the angry buck and the cliff edge, attacked, the female leaping high for Ebenezer's throat, the male streaking low for the belly. Ebenezer speared the female, took the male's wicked slash across his flank, turned and kicked out with front hooves that had sledgehammer force, and sent the male spinning into the black void beyond the ledge. The impaled female hung over his head. It took until morning to scrape her off.

A mountain buck and a loner, Ebenezer preferred the wild, high backcountry and generally wandered at night. He ranged further than his more numerous counterparts in the lowlands who stayed in the thickets close to the farms.

Like all great patriarchs, Ebenezer sired sons and daughters. It was while engaging in that process he was in the greatest danger, for when the rut started, Ebenezer had to come down to find his does.

It was during that unheady season of passion and violence that Ebenezer was the most vulnerable. Then other bucks could challenge the patriarch for primacy. Few did. Usually Ebenezer drove off an aggressor buck. But if that rival chose to fight, Ebenezer would kill it. Over the years two of Ebenezer's own sons had fallen, victims of their fierce father. He had other growing sons and one would someday carry his mantle. For now Ebenezer reigned supreme.

Ebenezer was most vulnerable during the rut to man. When the fall weather stayed mild and the rut extended into December and deer season started, when he was caught low with his does; then he was in the greatest peril. With hunters in the woods, the seasoned buck's instinct for survival outweighed his instinct for procreation; then he hid in the densest cover in the valley. He hid in Blackwolf Swamp.

Chapter 25 – Blackwolf Swamp

The sun broke slow over Steam Mountain, its rays penetrating openings into the gloom of the evergreen swamp,
turning the rising mist to a yellow haze. At the lower end of
the swamp, a blue jay, the self-appointed herald of the
woods, announced the morning.

It had snowed steady during the night, a six-inch blanket
that hushed the woods. The jay was breaking that peace, his
harsh voice and brilliant plumage a sharp contrast to the calm
white of the snow and the deep green of the swamp.

Tom did not like blue jays. They reminded him of the
Miss Prisses in school, who, spying something or someone a
bit different, like Tom, felt compelled to alert the world to its
danger. *I'm gonna tell! I'm gonna tell!* they would shriek
happily. Tom hunkered closer against the uprooted hemlock
and hoped the jay would fly away.

It didn't. It flew closer, leaving its perch on a strand of
rusty barbed wire for a stunted beech sapling in front of Tom.
The tree's branches were covered with withered leaves, the
last to fall to winter, the rattling skeletons of soldiers that
refused to surrender. The jay had no respect, shaking the tree
and crumbling the brittle leaves with beak and claw in his
noisy pursuit for food.

That bird's going to find me out, thought Tom, and he
hunkered lower, trying to look like a bump on a log, exhaling
as he did so.

Bumps on logs don't breathe. Air does not spurt out of
them and condense into a finger pointing back to its source.
The jay spied this and flew off into the middle of the swamp
screaming an alarm. *Here! Here! Here!* – it seemed to say.

Disgusted with himself Tom considered changing stands,
thought better of it, and stayed put. On the first watch of
hunting season's first day he had broken Charley Bower's
first rule – don't let the chatterboxes of the woods know
you're there. The chatterboxes: the jay, the crow, the woodpecker, the red squirrel, are just like some people he would

say. They don't want you going anywhere or doing anything without them and their neighbor knowing about it.

It was Charley who suggested they hunt the swamp. He had found Ebenezer's track in the mud around some fresh cherry tops at their log landing near the Longstar Branch and in the orchard along the east border of Raker's Farm at the base of Laurel Mountain. Also, a trucker had sighted the buck at the Tank. And John Tate and Monica Manikowski had seen him in the white oaks beyond the overlook on Steam Mountain. These were late night sightings. What John and Monica were doing up there at that time they didn't say, and Charley, in return for the information, didn't ask.

The locations suggested a circular pattern of nighttime activity that ended near Blackwolf Swamp.

Charley, who taught the brothers to hunt, did not accompany them, saying his hip bothered him. It would be their first hunt together without Charley.

Knowing the brothers only had one deer rifle, Charley lent Tom his 30-40 Krag. Discontinued by the U.S. military after the Spanish-American War, the overproduced Krag was sold for a few dollars in the twenties and thirties. This carbine, though, had been Charley's meat gun since before the turn of the century.

"Don't forget, the front sight is mighty fine," he reminded Tom, as he removed the gun from its rack in the jeep. "If the front bead isn't snugged tight into the back vee, she'll shoot high. The bullet's heavy so aim for bone, the shoulder or backbone. Any time you hit bone your quarry goes down."

Charley would know. A commercial hunter in years past, he had also been a sharpshooter for Colonel Teddy Roosevelt.

———

Mac, stillhunting toward Tom, heard the jay coming and leaned against a hollow beech. The bird passed without taking notice of the swamp's other intruder. Mac could hear the nervous scratching of an animal denned up inside the old tree. Probably a porcupine or a raccoon, he mused.

He had been following the faint trail of a deer, a trail that came from Steam Mountain. The one detail that had not been erased was the unusual length of the stride. The snow-filled tracks themselves were indistinct, and getting harder to make out as the day brightened.

The beech stood at the edge of a tangled clearing created by a small twister. The clearing, about forty by forty, was walled in by a thick growth of stunted hemlocks, their branches weighted to the ground with snow.

Mac worked his way through the clearing, a snowy jungle of intertwined tree trunks, branches, blackberry briars and grape vines. His mind was on mud, money, timber, Abigail, Bud Cole, Julie and Tom; worry and responsibility dulling his hunting senses. He failed to notice that the faint tracks that entered the blowdown did not exit from it.

He groped into a cold, wet spray of snow and ground-cover as the huge deer exploded from its bed and crashed in the thick underbrush of the hemlock swamp, popping and snapping limbs and branches in its way. Mac, startled back into awareness, glimpsed a huge, thick-set buck, his neck arched back to allow the brush to slide off his antlers, weaving his way with surprising speed through the trees. Mac swung his rifle in front of the deer and fired, the kick of the 32 Special and the snow falling from the shot causing him to lose sight of his quarry.

Mac didn't feel good about the shot. He doubted the bullet got through. The continued snapping of branches told him the buck still labored in the dense thicket. It also told him Ebenezer was headed straight for Tom.

———

Tom jumped at the close shot. Immediately he could hear the sound of something approaching him, but was it a deer or bear? Never before had he heard an animal make so much noise. Whatever was coming was barreling out of there and since Mac had shot, it was probably Ebenezer. Tom's heart beat faster. He willed himself to keep his head.

He saw the flash of the antlers first, as the buck passed a sunlit opening. The treetops shook and snow fell marking the buck's passage, but it was too dense to make out his outline.

Tom raised the Krag and swung ahead of the moving sound, looking for an open spot. The only opening was at the old fence where the barbed wire passed through the trunk of a gnarled field cherry. It would be his only chance. Beyond the fence the ground sloped sharply away, down into the mouth of the Longstar Branch.

Ebenezer's emergence from the swamp surprised Tom. He thought he was ready but he wasn't. Tom had expected the buck to hesitate and duck under the fence but he didn't. For a prolonged period there were the sounds of Ebenezer's escape then, abruptly, silence.

It was Tom who hesitated, startled as the huge deer appeared in midair, clearing the remaining thicket and fence in one long, high bound, breaking the wire on his descent.

Tom aimed for the middle of the buck's back. The front bead was high in the vee. He fired. The solid thunk at the tree and flying bark signified a miss. The last Tom saw of Ebenezer was his bobbing rack as he struck the downslope and veered into the ravine.

A wave of conflicting emotions swept Tom, a mix of excitement, disappointment and wonder. Never had he felt anticipation as keen. Never had he seen an animal so majestic. Never had he wanted one more.

Mac walked out of the swamp, trailing Ebenezer. The brothers met at the fence.

"That was quite a jump," marveled Mac, noting the thirty-foot distance separating the tracks. "Did you hit him?"

"No, I shot high," grumbled Tom, pointing to the bullet hole in the tree. He didn't want to admit to his brother that he blew it. "How about you?"

"I don't think so," said Mac. "Let's see where he's headed."

They followed the tracks into the ravine and along the bank of the small creek until the tracks disappeared. The wily buck was wading the shallow watercourse, heading uphill.

But fate played a return trick on Ebenezer. Along the bank, by the last set of tracks, the hunters found blood on the snow.

Chapter 26 – The Bear Wallow

Ebenezer *was* hurt.   When he struck the barbed-wire fence, one barb had sliced open the inside of his upper left foreleg.   Strung between saplings in the 1880's to keep livestock out of the swamp, early barbed wire was a wicked tool.   A pointed triangular razor welded between two strands of steel and twisted into lengths called "ribbons", the barb cut deep into hide and muscle.

The wound bled freely, running down Ebenezer's leg and hoof. Bothersome, painful, certainly not fatal, the immediate problem for the buck was the telltale sign it left.   Blood on snow made the finding easier for the hunter and the hiding harder for the hunted.

Ignoring the pain, Ebenezer stayed in the shallow streambed, clambering over its small falls and slippery rocks. The cold water splashing up cooled and soothed the wound.

He came to a spot where a herd of deer had crossed earlier, heading south along one of the midway benches on Blackwolf.   He left the ravine there, mixing his tracks with the herd's, staying in their trail until it entered a thick stand of pines.   Here he found the herd, most of them bedded down on the soft dry mat of pine needles, the bulk of the night's snowfall piled on top of the natural roof of evergreen boughs overhead.

The herd was alert, having been driven out of the lower farm woods by hunters.   At sunrise they had numbered nineteen; seven does, eight fawns, and four bucks. Now there were sixteen, three of the bucks being killed during the flight out of the valley.   Had it been legal to shoot does, more would have died.

The remaining buck, a handsome eight-point half the weight of Ebenezer, let the solitary patriarch enter the pine grove unchallenged.   The leader of the herd, a large older doe more familiar with Ebenezer than the others, approached the huge buck and sniffed the bleeding wound.   The younger buck was their son.   Ebenezer rested with the herd a few minutes, then left them, walking on the pine carpet as far as it went, continuing his uphill course.

The pines thinned out on the crest of Blackwolf. Here, behind a web of grapevines slowly choking its spare hemlock host to death, Ebenezer looked back. Actually, he was smelling and listening back, depending on his more acute senses to tell him what was happening below.

The day was warming. The warm air was rising and carrying with it the information Ebenezer was waiting for. The man smell was in the rising current. It came from the crossing at the stream bed. In time the scent grew stronger, mixed with the scent of milling deer. The herd was moving out. The men had found his bloody track within the herd's and were approaching the pines.

The cut still bubbled blood. His leg was absorbed with it, leaving a red smear with each step in the snow. He needed a covert to hide and rest and heal.

He set a steady but careful pace across the timbered top of Blackwolf. Few men ever came this way, except the trapper. Ebenezer had lived long because he traveled as if the trapper was always around somewhere.

At the western crest of the mountain, where Blackwolf began its descent into the south fork of Longstar Hollow, Ebenezer paused again. This time the wind currents gave no news of his pursuers.

Leaving the timber, he followed a brushy corridor that meandered its way downhill to the glade and spring-fed pond at the head of the hollow. The brush grew right to the pond's edge, where it merged with a half-acre plot of tall dead cattails. Ebenezer kept to the corridor center, breaking a thin film of ice at the pond's edge when he plunged in.

The water was muddied immediately as the buck's hooves churned up the silted pond bottom. Again, cold water soothed the burning pain of the wound. He stayed within the cattails, pushing and breaking the brittle stalks, stirring the silt, as he waded through the chest-deep water.

When he emerged from the pond the lower third of his body was coated with black silt. He didn't shake himself off. He leaped quickly across the unfilled ruts of a long-abandoned log road and skirted the perimeter of the glade.

Here the hollow's opposite slope rose up suddenly before him. The bleeding had stopped, but the burning pain was still there, along with a gradual stiffening of muscle. Undaunted by the forbidding steepness of the slope before him, Ebenezer started up Bear Mountain.

———

While Ebenezer was climbing Bear, the hunters were about a mile back, crossing the top of Blackwolf. Mac was on the trail. Tom was flanking one-hundred yards to Mac's right. They both supposed Mac's shot had hit Ebenezer.

So far their teamwork had paid off. The canny buck had stumped Mac at the crossing and at the pines. Tom, swinging wide in a half-circle from the last sign, discovered the bloody track each time.

Deer were territorial, usually living within an area of less than four square miles. When chased, they would run and circle and hide, and when discovered, would run and circle and hide again. In this game of hide-and-seek the tracking snow gave the edge to the persistent seeker. Two good men could run down a normal buck in several hours, especially a wounded one. But this was Ebenezer.

Crossing Blackwolf, Mac admired his timber. The second growth, mostly hardwoods, had come in well on this mountain. Cherry and maple dominated the slopes. Oak dominated on the top where the soil was thinner. Beech, ash and basswood were mixed throughout. A few trees were almost three feet in diameter and ninety feet high. These had been the smaller trees left by Miller in 1850.

Mac did a quick mental tally. The marketable trees averaged twenty inches in diameter on the stump and their stems stretched sixty feet high. Looking one hundred feet to a side, Mac counted twenty-five cuttable trees in that acre. At four hundred board feet a tree, that made ten thousand board feet per acre, an outstanding tally considering he could make money at five thousand. At fifty dollars per thousand the timber up there would bring five-hundred dollars per acre. He had paid twelve dollars per acre for it! He could afford to select-cut this. But first he had to get it to the mill. If it stayed wet through spring he may have trouble paying that note off. He grimaced at the thought of losing all this because he hadn't negotiated for enough time.

There was something about this region that grew big trees. Miller, too, had noted that in his journal. Someday, Mac would return and find out why.

The evidence of Miller's effort was still here. Huge, rotting pine and hemlock stumps served as slow release fertilizer for the second growth. Cut with a two-man saw at waist height, and notched with a double-bladed axe, some of the stumps measured six feet across. Two of the trees of Miller's time contained more lumber than twenty-five today. They must have been something to see.

Mac willed himself to pay attention. The last time he digressed he lost Ebenezer's trail; before that, the buck surprised him in the swamp.

At the beginning of the downslope into Longstar's south fork, Mac stopped, intrigued by Ebenezer's practice of keeping to cover. Here the more rounded Blackwolf leaned against Bear, and was diminished by the higher, steeper mountain. That's where he's going, thought Mac, looking across the deep hollow and up the rugged slope.

Tom joined him. Mac knelt in the snow and studied the bloody track.

"He's not hit hard, Tom. He's able to go uphill. He keeps to cover and rough ground. He's not limping, and he hasn't laid down once. It bothers me that he's bleeding down the left leg. I shot from the right. I must have shot low and creased his bricket, making him bleed out the opposite side."

They followed the tracks, spreading out as before. Ebenezer's trail kept to the center of a patch of brush that switchbacked down the mountain. The patch was a jumble of thornapple and sumac laced with grapevines, obviously an old clearcut that had grown back in scrub.

There was a discernable swell in the middle of the patch. Mac dug with his boot heel and found it to be the black peat of rotting wood. Alongside the swell were scores of long snow-covered mounds scattered at random down the hill. These too were composed of peat.

"Logs," whispered Mac, talking to himself. "These were logs. Left to rot by McFee after 1851. And that center swell was a log slide."

Made of split logs fastened together to form a chute, log slides usually ended near the lumberjack's camp. He followed the swell just as Ebenezer did, wondering what was left of Miller's forgotten Bear Wallow camp.

Again the blood-smeared track led to water. The broken and bent cattails indicated Ebenezer's path. The cloudy water meant he hadn't been gone long. The buck's caution had allowed them to gain on him.

Tom, approaching the bank of the Bear Wallow, grinned, and motioned for the tracker to follow Ebenezer's path through the cattails.

Mac smiled and shook his head. He motioned for Tom to circle his side of the pond. Mac circled the other. They met where the tracks came out of the cattails.

The bloody track was replaced by a muddy one and after a few steps, the tracks were clear. Ebenezer's wound had stopped bleeding. Their admiration for the old buck grew.

Taking a break, the brothers explored the three-acre forest glade where Miller established his timber camp more than a century before.

They found a stone foundation with an unusual square pile in its center. Wiping the snow away revealed a rusty cast-iron cook stove setting upright on a well-fitted base of flagstone.

"One of those loggers was a pretty good stone mason," observed Mac. Then he remembered the "stone man" in Miller's journal who, along with four oxen, was killed by a huge mountain lion.

At the upper end of the camp Tom climbed a knoll some two-hundred feet long and twenty feet high. The two ends

182

were almost vertical while the long sides resembled a ramp. An odd assortment of plant life grew out of the knoll – a stand of white birch, some butternut, several apple trees with frozen fruit clinging to the branches, and lilac, forsythia and blueberry bushes bent over by snow. The knoll was criss-crossed with the tracks and diggings of foraging birds and animals.

Tom dug into the ramp to find a ground cover of winter-green, and a thick spongy moss feeding off a base of pure humus.

"Hey, Mac!" he shouted from the top of the knoll. "I'm standing on a log pile!"

Mac came over and walked around the knoll. It was a hillock made from hundreds of logs. At the far end, leaning against the steepest side, was the most unusual find of all – the wood-spoked wheel of a huge log cart, soft with rot, but still held together by its iron rim and bindings.

Tom climbed down beside Mac and gazed at the wheel. He stretched his long frame as far as he could and still couldn't reach the top. "It's almost as high as a basketball rim and that's ten feet," he remarked.

"Yeah, and sometimes one log was all it took," countered Mac.

He looked at the wheel, then back down the glade, at the log road that disappeared into the woods beyond the Bear Wallow. The deep ruts left by Miller's ox-carts were still there.

Tom saw the flicker of worry cross his brother's brow. Miller's problems were Mac's now. Mud was proving as intractable to bulldozers as it had to oxen. While he didn't have wild animals attacking his camp, he did have Bud Cole and Spike Poorbaugh to contend with, and they were worse. Was this a bad luck place? The evidence of Miller's century-old failure lingered; a year's work, a life's savings, decaying in the woods.

It was after noon and the brothers were hungry, so they ate their lunch; turkey sandwiches that Julie had packed for them, a Hershey bar and an apple. Mac rummaged through

183

the camp dump, found a flat bottle, rinsed it out in the flowing spring that fed the Bear Wallow, filled it, and shared the cold sweet drink with Tom. He kept the bottle, stuffing it in the side flap of his hunting coat.

Seeing the puzzled look on Tom's face, Mac explained: "It may come in handy later. We won't make it back tonight. Not if we want to find Old Ebenezer."

Chapter 27 – The Panther Patch

Bear Mountain loomed ominous before them; steep, rocky, and hairy with bare trees, its cliff rim peering over Blackwolf and Potash. Ebenezer's track headed straight up it, always seeking cover. There was no blood in the left track but the imprint of the right was deeper, indicated the right was taking the most weight. Ebenezer was limping. The hunters followed with renewed vigor.

It was to be a long, hard climb. Unlike the surrounding mountains that had six or seven benches at regular intervals up the slope, Bear only had three and the Bear Wallow was located on the first.

The second bench was a long, timbered slope littered with boulders that had fallen from the cliff above. Some years before an outcropping as large as a house had dislodged and cleared a swath almost to the Bear Wallow. It was up this splintered path that Ebenezer went.

The brothers followed, staying together now, negotiating the lower half of their climb without difficulty. They were both young men blessed with uncommon strength and ability. Still, Ebenezer and Bear Mountain tested them.

The final phase of their climb now confronted them, the near-vertical cliff face that circled and sheltered the top of Bear Mountain. Except for the waterfall on the western rim of the mountain, where Bear Run tumbled off the cliff edge into Great Marsh, there were no visible openings to the top. Slinging their guns on their shoulders, they started their climb, trusting Ebenezer to show them the way.

And show them he did. The cliff was pockmarked, its brittle sandstone and shale face scraped raw by the elements. There were gouges left from rocks fallen away and large cracks in overhangs that were about to. There were juts and rifts and cuts and, wherever soil had accumulated, a daring tree had taken root and projected itself outward, defying the cliff wall. Along these variations animals had made a path.

The day was clear and mild, which made the going worse. The midday sun was melting the snow, making the flat mossy rocks that lay underneath slippery and treacherous. Several times they lost their footing and slid backward. Once an ironwood sapling stopped Tom from sliding over a ledge with a ten-story drop.

"I'll never cut an ironwood again," vowed a shaken Tom, when he finally reached his equally shaken brother.

Mac had been in the lead and watched, helpless, Tom's scary slide toward the edge. He cursed himself for not recognizing the danger. He had scaled cliffs in Normandy on D-Day. A two hundred-foot fall smashed you just as dead here.

After Tom's scare they spliced their deer drag ropes together and tied the ends to their belts. They supported each other the rest of the climb.

Near the rim a huge outcropping nosed its way out over the cliff face. A widening crack ran vertically between the outcropping and the bedrock of the mountain. In a millennium or so the jut would find a new home near the bottom of Bear Mountain. For now a narrow path ran between the crack's deeply indented rock walls. Within these dents lay the dried refuse of the outcrop's inhabitants, deeper within lay the inhabitant's themselves. A seeking wind whistled through the crack, raising a dust devil of dried leaves and snakeskins.

Tom shivered. He wasn't cold. "I wouldn't want to come this way in July," he whispered, even though he knew the den's occupants wouldn't waken until spring.

Scrambling over the cliff rim, the panting climbers rested, ate some snow to quench their thirst, untied their ropes, and looked back the way they came. Below them a sparrow pestered a hawk, and further off, to the north, woodsmoke rose over Potash. Spike Poorbaugh was home, cooking lunch. "Good," said Mac. "We won't have to worry about him for awhile."

Ebenezer's track stayed west, passing through a stand of gnarled rock oaks, over a rise and into a high black wall. The rise was the highest point on Bear Mountain. Standing on the rise the brothers regarded the thickest expanse of laurel they had ever seen.

The laurel spread to the north and west as far as they could see. The patch's perimeter was so high and dense that from a distance it did look like a wall, a wall of evergreen.

Mac checked his compass. He would need it now. Once inside that maze there would be no landmarks to go by. Ebenezer had changed direction. He had entered the laurel and then slanted northwest. He turned to his brother. "Maybe he's starting his circle, Tom."

Then the prevailing wind blowing from the northwest hit Mac in the face and told him Ebenezer's purpose. Up on top the afternoon winds were more predictable. The buck was heading into the wind so he could smell what was ahead of him. He knew they were behind. He wanted to know what was ahead, too. But why was he so cautious up here?

The wind blew again and Mac sniffed the air. A good deer hunter can smell the musk of a buck if he's close. The breeze held no scent of deer, but he did detect the fragrance of pine. Somewhere beyond the laurel there were pines. He can hide his tracks there thought Mac, remembering their difficulty finding Ebenezer's trail in the pines on Blackwolf.

Again the wind blew and the men shivered. Up here it was ten degrees colder than the valley. The strenuous climb had caused them to sweat through their first layer of clothing. Now that layer was clammy and cold. They would have to move or find a place to camp and dry out.

Three hours of daylight remained. It was too early to make camp. The brothers followed Ebenezer, spreading apart as before. This time Tom took the trail.

Tom, wrestling his way through bushes taller than he, soon decided that God made laurel to give deer the edge. A cupful of snow plopped down his neck. A branch swished out of nowhere and stung his cheek. He tripped over a trailing branch and fell on his back. He never hit ground, the laurel absorbed his fall like a coiled spring. His wool hunting pants and coat were soaked. On a foggy wet day with no snow for a backtrail and no compass, he'd never find his way out.

Laurel, a camouflage maze of crooked brown branches and glossy green leaves, was a haven, a refuge. It was a barricade to man, a hiding place for animals. It was nature's version of a one-way window: what was inside could see out, what was outside could not see in.

But windows can be broken. In the thick laurel, movement is the window breaker.

Tom heard the brush pop to his left and raised the Krag, expecting Ebenezer. Instead, he saw two brown shapes bound ahead of him through the laurel.

Just a glimpse and they were gone. Two long, tan shapes. Two other deer hiding like Ebenezer. Tom kept on the buck's trail, not bothering to check further. Had he looked he would have discovered two more hunters after Ebenezer.

Ebenezer knew. He had caught their scent just before entering the laurel patch. Their paths had crossed before.

Normally they lived on the far west rim of Bear Mountain and hunted the Great Marsh and remote state-owned mountains to the west. The east side of Bear was too close to the trapper and his dogs. But the burgeoning deer population around the farmlands to the east promised easier winter prey and sometimes they ventured east.

Usually they gave Ebenezer a wide berth, but today he was hurt, giving the advantage to the predator. The climb had opened the wound and the wet laurel had washed away the caked mud. Ebenezer was bleeding again and its smell excited the hungry pair.

Four enemies were now converging on Ebenezer. One was on his backtrail, another to his right, and two more to his left. His intent had been to circle back to another covert on Potash, but that way was cut off for now. He stayed northwest, weaving his way through the laurel, heading for the misty evergreen hollow that hung on the dark side of Bear Mountain.

The brothers struggled through the wet laurel. When separated so they couldn't see each other, they signaled their location with the sharp find-me call of a young turkey.

Tom's three chirps were answered by Mac's two. They had spread too far apart, almost two hundred yards. Mac angled more toward Tom.

The brothers were good callers, so good in fact they attracted the other two hunters interest. Ahead of the brothers, they left Ebenezer's track and circled back, attracted to the easier prey. Despite their size, the largest weighing over two hundred pounds, they could move with ease and quickness through the thick growth.

Once they found the warm track of the humans, though, they paced back and forth in agitated confusion. Men were here, men without dogs, trailing the big deer. Curious, wary, hungry, intent; they kept their distance but stayed on the trail.

The brothers met at a small rock-strewn clearing in the patch.

Tom pointed out the jumble of tracks in the snow. "Ebenezer's joined up with some does again, Mac."

"How many?"

"I made out two shapes, no horns."

Mac knelt in the snow to sort out the mixed tracks. Ebenezer's were here and he was bleeding again. But something was wrong. The travel pattern of the others was not like that of deer. It was too wide, too nervous, for deer. One distinct print to the side told the story.

"That's a paw print, Tom!" Mac pointed to the round pug mark packed clearly in the soft snow. Incredulous, he added, "Panthers are still here."

Mac knew he was right. He had followed the tracks of several mountain lions when he worked for the Forest Service in Idaho, but he had never seen one. Even in the west, where the big cats were still viable, sighting were rare. In the west they were called cougars, in the east they were panthers. Whatever their name, mountain lions remained the most elusive big animals in North America.

In the northeast, lions had been considered extinct since the 1860's, exterminated by settlers and bounty hunters. Yet rumors of their presence persisted. In the 1870's a doctor making a night call on horseback disappeared near English Center. His horse showed up at its barn, claw marks down its backside, blood on the saddle. Mae Miller of Jew Hill, eighty years old and spry, told of one chasing her and her sisters along a stone fencerow while blackberrying near the Brick Church in 1880. And just last month, Major Bowes, in his Rovin' Rambler column for the Williamsport Sun Gazette, did an article on a nighttime sighting near Sully Thompson's place. No one paid the story much mind. The Major's source was a regular patron of The Pig's Ear in Trout Run and had seen the cat after the tavern had closed.

These places were no more than ten miles from Bear Mountain, only a day's hunt for the far-ranging cats. This was their home. Actually, in remote areas like Bear, areas ignored by man, there was no reason they should not have survived.

They followed the three sets of fresh tracks, staying closer together, noticing the cats were working Ebenezer's trail the same way as themselves. The smaller cat was staying on the buck's track while the larger was swinging wide to intercept him. Strange, thought Tom, predators, whether man or beast, hunt alike.

"They're probably a mated pair," guessed Mac. "I wonder how many still live here."

About one hundred yards farther the cats abruptly broke off their pursuit of Ebenezer and circled back toward them. The brothers exchanged knowing glances.

"They heard our turkey calls, didn't they?" whispered Tom.

"Probably," returned Mac. "But they thought we were turkeys, not men. When they get our scent, they'll back off."

Tom wasn't so sure and kept his rifle ready. "Who's hunting who?" he asked.

Mac just shrugged and kept going. He was thinking the same thing, but didn't say it.

They stayed on Ebenezer's track as it weaved through a section of taller laurel that marked the western perimeter of the patch. Here there was only one path. Here the plants were twice the height of men, and so tightly packed their canopies made an arch over the trail. They had to crouch down to get through it.

It was a dimly lit passage with a leaky roof, and a soft, quiet floor. A nice place for a cat to grab its prey, thought Tom, following Mac, peering around. It got darker and darker, an evergreen cave, and then the passageway made a turn. A moist breeze blew in their faces and, after the turn, a sky-gray opening appeared. The trail's surface was now a thick mat of extra-long pine needles. Pine needles?

Emerging from the passage, the brothers gazed in wonder at the forest before them. Ebenezer had led them to an older world.

Chapter 28 – Night In Bear Hollow

It was the forest primeval. Virgin timber. The Big Woods. Where the Indians hunted for hundreds of generations. What the European explorers described to their kings in the 1600's. What the King of England called "Sylvania", then deeded to William Penn. What the state later sold to the Scotch-Irish and Germans. Where Jacob Miller found his spar timbers in the 1850's. And what the timber barons destroyed by 1900.

Of the mystical forest land of Sylvania, this was the last of it.

It was an ancient evergreen forest and it was silent...formidable...and dark.

The day was waning, helped along by a metallic-gray cloud cover moving toward them from the northwest. The top branches of the towering trees blocked most of the remaining sunlight. The white snow became whiter as night bore down on the day. The tracks of Ebenezer and the cats disappeared among the tree trunks, a trail leading into a black hole. For the first time the brothers knew what the Black Forest truly looked like.

They yearned to explore the Big Woods, especially Mac, but the darkness prevented that. Tom had already followed panther tracks into one dark place, he wasn't too keen on following them into another. He didn't object when Mac suggested they find a place to camp.

They had emerged from the laurel at the head of a mountaintop basin that downsloped gradually toward the west. Between the laurel and the Big Woods was a transitional area that ran like a band around the basin. Here it was lighter, neither the thick laurel nor the tall trees dominated. The trees and plants were spread out and more diverse, somehow keeping the two squeezing forces on either side at bay.

They skirted the basin, looking for a place out of the wind to camp. A flock of grouse flew out of the laurel to their roost in a limby hemlock nearby.

Mac raised his rifle, took careful aim, and fired. The headless grouse fell noisily, bouncing off several branches, before piling in the snow. The other birds remained, nervous heads on plump bodies, peering down at their flopping companion. Obviously they had never been hunted by man.

Tom didn't shoot. He couldn't see the fine front sight at the end of the Krag's long barrel. He resolved to replace it with a shiny brass one like Mac's when they got home.

Mac levered another round and shot again. Another grouse flopped down. He picked their supper up by the legs and carried them along. "You can't say I don't provide for my little brother," he teased.

Tom gave it right back. "Grouse are out of season. Wait 'til I tell Jim Morningstar what you did."

"That "you" will change to "we" after you eat one of these grouse. Besides, he's after Spike Poorbaugh, not me."

"It would be safer for Jim to catch us than him."

Nothing more was said for a while. Both feared their friend's zeal for the letter of the law would get him in real danger with Spike Poorbaugh.

———

On the lee side of a rock ledge the size of a log truck they made camp. At the base, a lone lightning-scarred pine grew, its trunk and lower limbs passing within ten feet of the top of the ledge. It was snug and dry there, underneath the ledge and the pine.

Mac built a fire close to the ledge. The stone surface would hold and reflect some of the heat. Tom collected firewood and broke off fresh hemlock boughs for bedding. They would sleep against the tree, facing the fire and the ledge.

Mac let the fire burn down a little and helped Tom gather several large dead pine branches for the night's fuel. A fallen beech provided the hardwood for a longer-burning fire. Mac coated several yard-long pine sticks with the thick pitch that oozed down the damaged section of the stricken pine. "Torches," he explained. "If we have to leave in the dark we may want to see where we're going."

By now total darkness had set in. Mac lit two of the torches. One he stuck in a hole in the rock ledge to serve as a camp light. The other he took with him beyond the campsite where he foraged for wintergreen, a groundcover that grew abundantly in the high country. He soon found some and brought a pocketful to the fire, which had burned down to glowing coals and was ready for cooking.

He cleaned the grouse and put them on spits to roast. He packed the bottle he had salvaged from Miller's dump with snow and placed it near the fire. Using small round stones he ground the wintergreen pulp and poured the pulp into the bottle. Soon the tea water was boiling and the grouse were browning on the spits. The smell of the cook fire wafted skyward.

Tom made a high brush pile of firewood and lugged two large rocks for seats around the fire. He wiped their guns down with an oily cloth, checked the actions, reloaded them, and leaned the guns and several torches against the tree. Finally, he made their beds of hemlock boughs. He smiled at the thought of making his bed, a chore he overlooked at home.

Soon the grouse were done and the hungry men sat down to their supper, eating the roasted birds right off the spits. Mac split the extra apple Julie had packed him for lunch and handed half to Tom.

"Gourmet fare," he said with a grin, "fresh fruit, roast grouse, and herb tea." He took a sip from the bottle and passed it to Tom.

Tom allowed he never had a meal quite like this and they both laughed.

The warm food relaxed them and the fire's heat dried them out. A thoughtful mood prevailed as the night wind glanced off the top of the ledge and caused the drooping branches of the pine to sway. Twelve feet below, the fire flickered.

"Mac, do you love Abigail?"

A typical Tom Donachy abrupt approach.

Tom expected his brother to give him a none-of-your-business lecture but he didn't. Instead Mac poked a stick in the fire and said softly, "I don't think so."

Encouraged, Tom probed further. "What about Julie?"

Mac's frank reply had some anguish in it. "I can't get Julie out of my head. I've wanted her since I came home on leave two years ago. But she keeps me at arm's length and treats me like a brother. I don't want a sister for a wife."

Tom resolved to talk to Julie about that. Lately Mac had been too preoccupied to notice Julie's shy signals. Like the extra apple. But Tom sensed there was more. "What about Danny?" he asked.

"He's a nice boy."

"That's not what I meant."

"What did you mean?"

"I mean, does it bother you that someone else got her first?"

There was a pause. There it was, a big chunk of the problem anyway.

Mac poked another stick in the fire.

"Yes."

Knowing the stories about Mac and Delia, and loyal to Julie, Tom's next comment was caustic. "That's unfair. If Bud Cole can accept it, you can."

"I didn't say I couldn't accept it. I said it bothers me. It bothers Bud, too. It's why he hates me so much."

Mac stirred the glowing embers and sparks flew out into the night, tiny bits of short-lived brightness in a dark, starless sky. "You have to be careful what kind of fire you play with when you're young," he said.

Their conversation over, they banked the fire and settled down for a cold night's sleep.

———

They woke to a woman's scream.

At first Tom thought he was having a nightmare, but a second scream convinced him this nightmare was real.

Mac was already up, poking the glowing embers of the fire with one of the torches. The other hand held his rifle. Tom stood up, still a little groggy with sleep. The fire flared up as the torch was ignited. "Get your gun," Mac ordered. "They're here."

Tom grabbed the Krag as Mac held the torch aloft. Amber eyes gleamed down at them from the top of the ledge. Large amber eyes. Four amber eyes. Then two. A branch overhead snapped and creaked and snow fell in Tom's face. "One's in the tree," he whispered.

The panther on the ledge screamed again. It *was* like the haunting scream of a desperate woman. From the panther it was defiance, a warning. Tom fought off rising panic and raised the Krag. It was too dark to aim. It would be instinct shooting, just point and shoot.

"Wait," cautioned Mac. "Maybe they're just trying to scare us."

"They're doin' a good job."

"If they jump us, you take the one in the tree."

"Okay." Tom thought it might be easier said than done.

Stepping forward, Mac threw the blazing branch toward the cat on the ledge. For a brief moment both predators were outlined as the branch passed like a flare between them.

The cat on the ledge cringed and backed away. The cat in the tree leaped back to the ledge. With the quiet of the snow that sifted down through the pine, they were gone.

Mac built up the fire. Tom carried some wood closer. He carried the sticks cradled in one arm, the other stubbornly held his rifle. He was shaking. Mac appeared calm and brewed more tea.

Tom envied his brother's ability to react under pressure. Certainly his combat experience helped. There it had been lead, follow, or get out of the way, and Mac had led. Mac *moved* when danger threatened. He knew instinctively when to fight and when to run. When to *do* something. And his countenance never changed, except to grow more grim.

"Weren't you scared?" Tom asked.

"The scream startled me. But we had control. We had the fire and the guns."

"I almost shot."

"Probably no need. They scared us. They didn't hurt us. Kill only what tries to kill you."

"What about Ebenezer?"

"That's a different situation. We'll eat him. And mount the horns."

"If we get him, how are we going to get all that meat back home?"

"We can't shoot him up here. He's hurt and he can't hide. He will turn eventually. We just keep pushing him until he circles closer to home."

"What if he doesn't? He's different."

"Then he wins...but with this tracking snow, he can't win."

Mac was convinced the panthers wouldn't be back. Still, the brothers took turns keeping watch and tending the fire until daybreak.

When it was Tom's turn to take the last watch, Mac let him sleep. Mac was too excited to sleep anyway. In a few hours he would see Bear Hollow. See the Big Woods. Ebenezer had led him to it. He owed him something for that.

———

Ebenezer had heard the screams. He was in the Big Woods, bedded down within the bole of an uprooted pine, his back against the earthen wall, his rack a shield against a frontal attack. If they didn't kill something else, they would come.

They came in the inky blackness of predawn. When everything seems to slow down, even the turning world. The time the senses are dullest and demand rest.

They rushed him from the front because they had no choice. Two leaping cats, one ahead of the other. The first, the stocky male, went for the buck's neck. The second, the

197

tentative but compliant female, went for his back. She was a second or two late. Her lack of commitment saved Ebenezer.

Ebenezer stayed down and swung his rack in a powerful arc that caught the male in the face and sent him sprawling. The female landed on the buck's hindquarters, her extended claws dug in for a hold, her jaws opened wide to crush his spine.

Ebenezer raised up and rolled, kicking out furiously to protect his underside. He wanted to break his attacker's grip and crush it.

The hole that protected Ebenezer now protected the cat and she was able to scurry out from underneath him, but not unscathed. Pain coursed through her sensitive, partially crushed tail as she climbed the nearest tree to safety.

Her mate had regained his feet, but he was staggering. His body wasn't working right. The sharp ivory tip of an antler tine had pierced through an eye and into his skull. Half blind, half conscious, half dead, the predator became the prey.

Ebenezer was on his feet too, and he was raging. Ignoring the female, ignoring his wounds, Ebenezer attacked. He struck out with his flintlike hooves, slashing the cat's throat with one blow, crushing its skull with another. Ebenezer was a vengeful executioner. Even after the cat's convulsions stopped and its remaining eye glazed over in death, the maddened buck continued to pommel and toss the body.

Finally, his rage spent, the bleeding patriarch turned and walked stiffly away. He passed directly under the more fortunate female, who crouched in the tree and watched with feline indifference as Ebenezer finished off her mate.

After a while she slipped down, sniffed the body, ate some of him, and left.

Theirs had been a short courtship of five days. That was normal. Panthers preferred solitude, accepting companionship only to mate and raise young. The female was bred. The male would have left anyway. Other than procreation, there was no bond between them.

Even so, the female had screamed at her younger mate to avoid the humans and was uneasy about attacking the buck. Her fears were rooted in experiences of the past. She had lost a previous litter to a human, and a parent to Ebenezer.

Chapter 29 – Bear Hollow

Morning comes reluctantly to the Black Forest in winter. The woods give the impression they only tolerate the day. The early light contends with the mass of evergreen treetops, which finally relent and allow shafts of brightness to shine through. The woods floor is gradually illuminated as the inky blackness fades to shades of deep green and gray.

At first light Mac climbed the rock ledge for a view of the back side of Bear Mountain. The cloud cover persisted, layered sheets of slate, diffusing the sunrise at his back. It was going to be a cold gray day. There would be no glare, the dark shapes solid outlines against the backdrop of snow. A perfect day for cruising timber. And tracking Ebenezer.

Bear Hollow spread out before him, the mountaintop basin sagging toward the rim on the horizon to the west. Before the rim the hollow was hemmed in by higher ridges on three sides. The deep cut in the center marked the passage of Bear Run to its cascade over the rim and into the Great Marsh.

Within these confines lay a virgin forest. The trees formed a pattern according to the lay of the land. Pines dominated the ridges and higher slopes, hemlocks followed the watercourse, and hardwoods prevailed near the rim where the hollow leveled out. A few evergreens popped up over the hardwoods, and some hardwood branches could be seen among the hemlocks, but within the dense pines, nothing else grew.

Mac looked down the ledge to the base of the pine where Tom slept, sprawled out on his bed of hemlock boughs, his red wool stocking cap pulled down over his ears. He had conducted himself well last night. Mac wondered how he would have reacted at age eighteen.

Breaking camp consisted of waking Tom, throwing some snow on the remnant of the fire, checking their rifles, and walking away. They would stay together today.

They followed Ebenezer's trail into the pines, a trail the cats had followed, then left, and then rejoined.

"Looks like they decided to eat him instead of us," grumbled Tom, who yearned for a steaming hot cup of Turkey Ranch coffee.

"May take some doing," remarked Mac. "With all that screaming the one did, it might have pushed Ebenezer down out of here."

"Wonder where that is?"

"I've been wondering that myself."

The going was easier in the Big Woods. The snow was only half as deep and there was no underbrush. Only shade tolerant plants could grow under the immense pines but the pines weren't tolerant. It was a pure stand and it looked like the noble pines wanted it kept that way.

The nobility was plentiful on the high ridge. Forty trees to the acre grew there, ranging from two to eight feet across and two hundred feet high, twice the size of their second-growth counterparts on Blackwolf. The thick scaly bark was stained with streaks of pitch and had the rich purple hue that marked a prime, mature tree. Tall, straight, strong trees they were, growing along the shadowed north slope, the constant straining for sunlight making them taller, straighter and stronger.

On one they found a King's Arrow. Miller's timber brand was skillfully notched deep into the bark with an axe. Not the thickest or oldest tree. The straightest. The best. The one whose stem ran without limbs for 170 feet before a crown that ran a scant thirty. The one that was tucked in amongst less gifted brethren, like the palace guard protecting the heir-apparent.

Jacob Miller had found him, notched him, then failed to return and claim his prize, the main mast of a clipper ship that never made it to port.

"How would he ever get a timber that long out of here?" wondered Tom.

"There must be another way," replied Mac.

Near the stand's center, a freak of nature had occurred. Here three large branches, each as large as a single pine, grew out of a huge ancient stump. A fourth lay uprooted on the ground. Long ago one great tree had died and generated four.

"I could park my pickup on that stump," said the awed Tom, walking around it.

Mac noted that even in pure stands freaks were found.

It was Tom who discovered the dead cat. On the opposite side of the uprooted pine spread a killing field, its victim stretched out in the snow.

The kill was fresh and some of the corpse had been eaten. The dead panther resembled a magnified version of a tawny barn cat, except for the feet and legs which were overly thick and powerful. The prints of the cat that padded away were smaller.

"How could the smaller panther kill the larger?" Tom's question was based on his observation that the one had breakfasted on the other.

"She didn't," said Mac, assuming the survivor was the mate of the male. "Ebenezer did this. Looks like she ran off and came back after the fight was over."

"Fraidy cat, huh?" Tom's first smart-aleck remark of the day.

"Smart cat most likely," returned Mac with a smile.

The snow told the story like a book. Blood and gore sprayed out from the spot where Ebenezer had lain. The smaller cat had bloody paws and made it to a tree. The other cat's blood and hair was smeared against the trunks of several trees.

"He knows how to kill, that Old Ebenezer." Tom's comment held respect for the patriarch, some contempt for the unwise and very dead cat.

The smaller cat's tracks headed back toward the laurel. Ebenezer's went downhill. There was blood in the front and hind tracks now. Strength-ebbing blood. The buck's progress was steady, but all downhill. He chose the easiest route this time.

The brothers glanced at each other. Going downhill was the first sign of a badly wounded deer.

"Looks like we've had some help, Tom." Mac's tone was one of disappointment as they left the bloody battleground in the pines.

———

Below them the brothers could hear the constant rush of a turbulent stream, what the locals called a "roaring branch." Bear Run was a cold underground stream that poured out of a crack in the mountain and knifed its way through Bear Hollow to Great Marsh. Actually, this roaring branch was the creator and sustainer of both.

Hemlocks like water, and were especially at home along Bear Run, flanking the stream its entire course. The hemlock stand contained the same density as the pines but was more tolerant, permitting other species to mix with them. Hardwoods and pines were scattered throughout the rocky, uneven floor of the stand, their branches mingling with the thicker hemlock tops one-hundred fifty feet overhead.

Within these branches a wild chase was taking place. A gray squirrel was streaking for its life, pursued by a larger black predator with the same agility.

"Since when do mink climb trees?" questioned Tom.

"They don't. That's a pine marten. Old trappers used to call it a sable."

"They're a northwoods animal."

"It's still the northwoods up here."

"Then those black pelts Jim confiscated were sable."

"That's right."

"Spike Poorbaugh traps here!"

"All his life. And I'll bet those big spotted pelts he passed off as bobcat were panther cubs."

"The bastard." After last night Tom didn't care much for panthers, but he disliked the prospect of Spike raiding their dens worse.

"He lives by his own rules, and those aren't many," reminded Mac.

The chase ended. The squirrel had climbed to the end of a limber branch that hung high out over the stream. The marten joined him and the squirrel was trapped. But the end of the branch would not support the marten's greater weight. He couldn't quite reach the squirrel without falling off. There they hung, suspended, stalemated, facing each other, the squirrel chattering frantically, the marten just waiting, waiting, waiting.

Their observers moved on.

Tom felt welcome within the sturdy, long-lived hemlocks. Maybe it was the soothing sound of the rushing water. Maybe it was the misted shafts of light that penetrated the canopy like rays of grace. Like an open-air cathedral. Yet the hemlocks seemed more common than the majestic pines. They were the yeomen of the forest.

Then the brothers discovered the Boss.

Every woods has a Boss Tree. Virgin woods, second-growth woods, even city park woods, it makes no difference. Somewhere in those woods is a Boss Tree. One that's stood the test of time.

The Boss of Bear Hollow was a hemlock that encompassed a glacier-made hump set above the south bank of the stream. Several trees were a bit taller, which probably protected him from lightning. Others were straighter and prettier with no large limbs to make them look awkward. But none were sturdier. The Boss had limbs as big as the other trees and didn't seem to care how he looked. He had no honor guard, just lots of close friends, and two of these leaned on him for support. His trunk was rent and scarred with the marks of other falling trees; old friends that had leaned and died and rotted away while he had healed. The Boss remained; venerable, thick, and strong. The Boss had the widest shoulders in the forest.

Mac brushed the snow off one of the blocks of sandstone that peppered the hemlock floor and sat. Tom did the same. They weren't tired.

There was a reverent stillness around the huge tree. Finally, Mac broke it.

"He's watched the clouds go by for a thousand years."

"He's *that* old?"

"Maybe older. We studied one at Penn State that was 988. This guy's bigger." He continued. "You know, there's enough lumber in this one tree to build a barn."

Tom scoffed. "None of us know how to cut a tree this size down."

"I do."

Tom defended the Boss Tree. "Then you'd have the same problem as Ebenezer."

"What's that?"

"No way to get it out."

"With dynamite and bulldozers I can get it out."

"But would you?" Mac's answer was important to Tom.

"No. But Bud Cole would. He'd rip up these trees and leave them lay like his grandfather did. Then blow this mountain to rubble. Just to find some coal that may not be here in volume in the first place."

Tom's empty stomach churned bitter at the thought. "Can we stop him?" he asked directly.

"If I don't lose it, I can."

Tom noticed the shift from plural to singular and knew what it meant. His half-brother, who had deeded half of everything he owned to Tom, was taking all the blame for losing it. Like the Boss Tree, Mac was carrying the load, a burden weighing heaviest on his heart, that tender private place where all heavy burdens go.

Tom changed the subject. His brother had revealed more of himself the last two days than their entire previous time together. "It's been quite a hunt," he said.

"A good hunt," acknowledged Mac.

———

Ebenezer's trail paralleled the south bank of the stream. Wherever possible he angled into the wind. His injuries hadn't made him lose caution.

Tom deferred to the more experienced hunter. "Do you think he knows we're still following?"

"He knows. Our scent's behind him, but he can hear a twig snap a half mile away, and we've snapped our share. We don't want him to stop yet anyway."

Near the end of the hemlocks the stream's descent started to level off and grew wider and shallower. Here Ebenezer crossed to the other side.

"See what I see?" asked Mac.

"He waded across. He didn't jump back there at the narrows. Sign he's hurtin'."

The brothers crossed too, tying their hunting pants tightly over their insulated rubber boots to prevent wet feet. The current was deeper and swifter than it looked. The water was so clear it appeared shallow.

Ebenezer's trail left the stream bank and turned north. There was more light in the woods ahead. Soon they were in a stand of tremendous hardwoods, and the evergreen forest shut like a quiet door behind them.

The stand reminded Mac of the woods on top of Black-wolf. The same mix, the same density, but not the same size. Obviously, these were the parent trees one mountain removed. On Blackwolf the biggest trees approached three feet on the stump and eighty feet of height. The mature virgin hardwoods of Bear Hollow *started* there.

Oak, cherry, beech, ash and maple served a gray, leafless backdrop for an occasional pine or hemlock. Great trees, not as tall as the pointed evergreens, but straight and solid with canopies that spread a hundred feet. Prime hardwoods two to four centuries old. Five sixteen-foot veneer logs to a tree. More lumber volume than most current timber scale sticks could measure. Two thousand board foot per tree, twenty-five trees, fifty thousand board feet, twenty-five hundred dollars to the acre. Five times their best cut on Blackwolf! From trees like these luxury railroad cars, Victorian stair-cases, and Ragtime pianos were made. The Gilded Age died when the virgin timber died.

It was noisier in the big hardwoods. The midmorning breeze was more noticeable, bringing with it the creaking and groaning of brittle winter limbs. The snow was deeper. There were more animal trails.

The mast crop was good that year, acorns and beech nuts by the millions lay underneath blankets of snow and fallen leaves.

The animals had come to the harvest. Sections of the woods resembled a barnyard where squirrels, turkeys, deer, even a single small bear, had dug for food.

"Wonder if his mama knows he's not in bed where he's supposed to be," said Tom, pointing out the pudgy track.

Mac grimaced. "Might be the cub of the big sow that Poorbaugh killed and showed off last week."

"Who could shoot a sow with a cub?" Tom knew the answer before he asked the question.

"Bears were in season, Spike had a license, and she was worth money."

"He told Jim he was going to feed her meat to his dogs."

"All legal."

Ebenezer too had dug for food, pausing to nose out some white oak acorns. The scraped ground revealed that blood still seeped from his wounds.

"Good," said Mac, obviously relieved. "He's not hurt too bad to eat."

Tom began to wonder if *both* of them were hunting Ebenezer.

True to his furtive nature, Ebenezer sought the thickest cover, entering a grove of smaller trees and saplings that had sprung up from an ancient blowdown. The hunters, approaching quietly in the soft snow, surprised several squirrels intently working the grove. They scampered in different directions, abandoning their food.

Mac examined the spiney outer covering of a large nut that had ripened and split open that fall. The casing was empty, the hard shell and meaty nut inside buried somewhere by one of the squirrels. Mac knew what it was. Tom didn't.

"Chestnuts!" he exclaimed, kicking in the upturned leaves for more. "These nurse trees must have blown down before the blight. Then the seedlings grew after."

Tom knew of the beautiful chestnuts that were prized until exterminated in the 1920's by a killer fungus. A hard, rot-resistant wood, the dead trees still dotted the landscape, visible ghosts of a past grandeur. The Sentinel at the Tank was one.

Still, Tom found some irony in the situation. Here they were, in the midst of the most valuable timber imaginable, a logger's Utopia, and Mac gets excited about a half-acre grove of saplings.

Here also, was great temptation. Mac said he would save the pine and hemlock; could he afford to leave the hardwoods, too?

Tom bet he would. Mac wasn't greedy. He appreciated natural beauty. His immediate problem was to get the accessible timber to market before the note came due. That timber was the plentiful second-growth on Blackwolf. Mac had the timber resources. The resource he needed most was time.

Ebenezer and the chestnut thicket soon revealed another of Bear Hollow's secrets – the previous path of Bear Run.

The storm that toppled the great chestnuts had also changed the course of the roaring branch. The trees had fallen across the original channel, sending Bear Run in another direction. The path the stream now took to the falls was a relatively recent development of several decades. Mac realized then that Jacob Miller's journal never mentioned a falls.

The course that Miller followed was a gradual descent carved out by the stream over thousands of years and guarded by hemlocks to its mouth, where it emptied into the Great Marsh. As woods go, the ravine and its trees did not thrive after being abandoned by the stream that once fed it.

Ebenezer's trail led the brothers directly into the tree and brushlined gully. At one time it had been a series of short waterfalls, one after another. Now the former falls were like uncomfortably high steps, a two-thousand-foot staircase reaching from the top of Bear Mountain's west rim to its bottom.

Their descent wasn't nearly as treacherous as their ascent had been, but it had its discomforts. Near the base of the mountain the ravine was choked with underbrush, primarily blackberry bushes. From their tall, whiplike, thorny canes several nearby Briar Hills got their name.

Animals, mostly deer, had kept a low trail open through the canes. The brothers had to stoop down and stumble through, shielding their faces from the grasping briars. Before entering the canes they had donned their gloves, buttoned their coats, and raised their collars, anything to reduce the skin area exposed to the savage briars. Still, they received some painful facial scratches.

Several times they found tufts of gray deer hair sticking to a briar, tiny droplets of blood clinging to individual strands, telling who had passed through before them.

Mac examined the hairs closely. "He's been clawed high up. This is upper body stuff. I've never seen hair this stiff and gray. He's old. Old."

They hacked their way downhill through the canes, finally coming out where the former stream had emptied into the marsh. There was no visible evidence that a stream had ever been there. The marsh, a growing thing, had in fact raised its level and now covered the mouth of the old stream-bed. On the mountain, the heavy concentration of blackberry canes hid the ravine from view. Mac, conducting his perimeter survey last summer, had passed right by it.

It appeared the mountain and marsh had conspired, in the years after Jacob Miller, to keep Bear Hollow a secret.

Chapter 30 – Potash Mountain

Great Marsh spread out before them, soaking up the falls like an expanding sponge, its fifteen-thousand acre expanse broken by the raised mudstick hutches of muskrat and beaver, countless evergreen hummocks, and the bony frames of partially submerged trees. The mountains farther west were blurred, shrouded in the swirling whiteness of wind-driven snow. The mist from the falls moistened their faces, a cool balm for the cuts from the briars. Yet within that mist came stinging sleet. After that came a grainy snow. The northwest wind was bringing Mac an early Christmas present, an arctic storm to freeze-dry the mud.

With his way east blocked by his pursuers and south by the falls, Ebenezer was left two choices – west into the marsh, or north to Potash. The marsh held uncertain footing and more cats. Potash had solid ground and Spike Poorbaugh. Ebenezer chose Potash.

There was no hesitation on Ebenezer's part either. Once he left the gully, he immediately turned north along the firm, treelined bank that marked the present separation between mountain and marsh.

"He knows where he's going," declared Mac, reluctantly turning into the sleet. "If we can't gain on him, he's got us beat. This kind of snow covers tracks in a hurry."

Tom thought Mac seemed awful happy about *this* kind of snow. He wasn't so happy about it. Tom wanted Ebenezer. He admired the buck but he still *wanted* him. Within Tom was a strong competitive spirit that told him once he had his opponents cornered or weakened he put them away. In some ways Tom was like the youthful Ebenezer and Mac like the older one.

"Let's go then," countered Tom, taking the lead. He jogged along the buck's trail, unbuttoning his coat as he ran.

Mac followed. Ebenezer was taking a level course. Mac figured a stint uphill would tame Tom a bit. It would if the buck could still go uphill. If he couldn't and stayed low and followed the hollows, they were sure to run him down. Another Charley Bower axiom would be proved: "Keep him low in the snow and he's your own." Tom was counting on this. Somehow Mac knew Ebenezer would go high.

Ebenezer was hurt and tired, but he went high, bypassing the entrance of the North Fork and its easy gradual descent to Longstar, preferring instead the long, broad uphill slope to the ridge that circled Potash Mountain. Halfway up he hesitated, smelling danger in the northwest wind, and turned east along the ridge toward the high cliff where he had lured the hounds five seasons before.

The brothers halted their jog where Ebenezer turned uphill. Their wool clothing was crusted with icy particles of snow. Ebenezer's splayed hoofprints were filling steadily with fine grain, like sand in an hourglass. The timepiece favored Ebenezer.

Mac peered toward the ridgeline of Potash. It wasn't there. A thousand feet above them a real blizzard was blowing. "Run into *that* why don't you?" he teased.

"You don't want to get Ebenezer!" blurted Tom, frustrated at the prospect of their prize getting away, angry at Mac's casual acceptance of it.

Mac became serious. "Let's just say it's more important for me to get our timber than for you to get him."

"Let's do both," replied Tom stubbornly. He set a hurried, brooding pace up the lower reaches of Potash.

Tom felt a tinge of shame. "Their" timber versus "his" deer. He'd caught the meaning of Mac's rebuke. But this was a deer hunt, not a timber cruise! If Mac didn't want to kill Ebenezer why had he shot in the first place? Yes, the discovery of Bear Hollow had changed things, but they were so close...

His brooding was interrupted by a firm grip on his arm. Mac wasn't rough, just firm.

"Take it easy, Tom. We're in Spike Poorbaugh's territory now."

"Who cares?"

"He cares."

Mac took the lead.

———

The western slope of Potash was like Blackwolf's, related mountains actually, shaped by the same glacier. Their aspect was different because of their vegetation. Potash had been cut over and burned, hence the name "Potash", while Blackwolf hadn't. The timber on Potash was young and varied and close together. Bristly patches of blackberry, high-bush blueberry, and laurel grew within the trees, whose canopies weren't quite broad enough to block the sunlight and choke out the underbrush. Small game flourished on Potash as well as the furbearers that preyed on it. Ecologically linked with Great Marsh and Bear Mountain, it was a trapper's paradise. A paradise one trapper was unwilling to share.

At the midway point where Ebenezer had abruptly changed direction, they stopped. The climb had improved Tom's mood. The tracks were filling faster at the higher elevation, but the ninety-degree turn was still obvious.

"He starts north then turns east. Why?" Tom was genuinely puzzled. Ebenezer never went with the wind. "Is he getting sick?"

"No," said Mac. "A sick deer is aimless and falters. Ebenezer isn't wandering. He's got a place to hide during a storm. I think something spooked him. Whatever it is, he wants to be ahead of it. And us. The wind's at his back. He's more concerned now with what's behind than what's ahead."

Mac's analysis was interrupted by the distant baying of hounds. The insistent barking continued for several minutes then stopped.

Mac knew what it meant. "Spike Poorbaugh's dogs. This ridge runs above his place. The dogs are penned up. They just got a whiff of Ebenezer."

"Think Spike's home?"

"Probably. He knows nothing moves in a storm like this."

"Then he'll be waitin'."

"Keep an eye out."

Spike Poorbaugh wasn't home. He had known the storm was coming and had been out twelve hours, since three a.m., checking traplines that ran along the north bank of Great Marsh and the lower western slope of Potash. The fifty traps had yielded a mink, three muskrats, and three foxes; a gray and two red. The two red foxes were kept alive, roughly muzzled and bound by rawhide, their desperate faces staring over the front edge of the packbasket, their full tails bouncing out the back. If they survived, they would bring fifty dollars each from the Genesee Valley Fox Hunt Club. Dead, they would bring fourteen.

The trapper was on the return leg of the line when he heard his dogs. Where Ebenezer changed direction he discerned the cause of the dog's alarm. Alone and friendless, he studied the track and kept his own company.

"So, Spike, the old boy smelled you and went the other way. Hurt, too, favorin' his left side a little."

He crumpled a piece of packed snow absorbed with blood and smelled it. "Musky. Big guy's still in the rut. Flesh wound blood runnin' down his legs. Now let's see who the chasers be. Two men. Big feet. Long strides. One's tall, tall as me. The other's heavier..."

"MacEwen and his kid brother! Only one's it could be. Huntin' big game." He thought a moment. "Spike'll need a big gun to hunt big game."

Squaring the packbasket, he hastened downhill toward his cabin. On the line he traveled light, his only weapons being a .22 pistol, his walnut-handled Bowie, and a six-foot hickory staff. They were inadequate for what he had in mind.

The second baying of the hounds told him how far ahead the brothers were. There was still time if he could catch them on the ridge. The third baying of the hounds was his welcome home.

Entering the cabin he shucked the pack, kicked aside the struggling foxes that had spilled out of the basket, grabbed a scopesighted 30-06, some extra shells, and headed toward the ridge.

He wore the perfect camouflage for a winter stalk. His duck jacket and pants and buckskin gloves blended with the foliage; his stiff, shaggy, rust-gray hair and beard blended with the snow. His long, purposeful strides ate up distance with no seeming effort, the driving wind covered any sound of his approach. The only indication of his presence on the ridge was the musty smell of mink oil on his clothes and the fourth baying of the hounds when he left without feeding them supper. The wary buck caught them both, but for him the trapper no longer mattered.

Ebenezer crossed the open area on the ledge just when the full force of the storm hit the mountaintop. Some parts of the cliff were scoured clean by the wind, other parts were covered by snowdrifts two feet deep. By the time Ebenezer reached the windbreak in the sumacs all evidence of this trek across Potash was gone.

Ebenezer had won.

———

The brothers lost Ebenezer on Caleb's Rock. It was four o'clock, dusk a scant hour away. In Steam Valley incandescent lights glimmered through whirling clouds of snow, beacons set forth from the tame world to the wild one.

The stationary lights were houses. The moving lights were vehicles creeping in the snow. Directly below them a truck labored up the lane to Mort's.

The brothers leaned on opposite sides of a deep-rooted rock oak that grew close to the ledge. It was like the other trees up there – fighters past their prime, bent, rugged, not yet old. For a time the men were silent, contemplating the storm, where they were, where they had been. One had some growing up to do, the other had grown up too fast.

"Well, Tom, shall we go down and get Mort to buy us a cup of coffee?" Mac's question was really a decision. It mean the hunt for Old Ebenezer was over.

"You go. I'll stay here and watch for a while. There's shooting time left." Tom was still dreaming of that second rack on Sawyer's wall, his name in the record book.

"Give him up, Tom. He's won. If he showed up now it would be sheer chance. A lucky hunter should never get Ebenezer."

———

Spike Poorbaugh, hunting the biggest game, had the opportunity to score a double and lost it. He was crouched in the laurel, behind the bulk of a hollow tree, less than forty yards from the pair. Their backs were to him, silhouetted perfectly alongside the tree. It would be like picking tin cans off a post. MacEwen, the most dangerous, would go first, then Donachy.

He raised his rifle, looking for the center of MacEwen's woolrich in the crosshairs. He saw nothing. Lowering the gun he found that snow had filled the concave eyepiece of the scope. Swearing to himself, he blew the snow out and sighted again. Still nothing! His warm breath had filmed the lens. Quickly, he wiped the lens clear with a gloved forefinger and sighted again. The scope was clear. His first target was gone.

He swung to the left, scanning the area through the scope, and found MacEwen taking the downhill trail through the laurel. It would be an uncertain shot at an armed target moving sideways through the brush. His hatred urged him to risk it. His training held him back. Snipers didn't take shots like that.

Silently cursing Frank Sawyer and his Saturday night cronies to hell for talking him into a scope-sighted gun, the trapper waited. Soon the tall kid left.

The trapper let Tom get well into the woods before he ventured out on the ledge. Heights had a queer effect on him these days. He felt a tingling sensation in his loins whenever he peered over a cliff. It was a fatalistic attraction. Something he feared but couldn't resist.

He stepped cautiously out on the windswept shelf and peered down at Mort's. The headlights of a truck blinked out in front of the house. Probably old Bower, there to pick up the loggers. He looked past the house at the rows of snow-

215

covered junk cars and recalled the rumors about Mort Fessler's money. This winter he would find out where Mort hid his money.

Feeling braver, he stepped forward and looked straight down. Five hundred feet below him swayed the bare branches of the three oaks. Underneath those branches was Blacksnake's grave. Within those branches he had found the bodies of his lost hounds.

A sharp snap in the laurel thicket startled him into the realization that right now he was as vulnerable as they. Would that mean old buck do the same thing to a man? To him?

He knew the answer and turned swiftly, expecting a charging Ebenezer. The buck wasn't there, but the sudden turn loosened a large flat rock underfoot and he felt himself being carried toward the edge. He lunged toward the oak, grabbing hold of an exposed root with his free hand. The flat, sedimentary rock slid over the edge and fell intact until it struck the corner of a lower ledge, where it broke into smaller pieces which rattled the rest of the way down the uneven face of the cliff.

His adrenalin surging, Spike Poorbaugh scrambled off the ledge and into the laurel where he sat against the hollow tree. He didn't make many mistakes in the woods, but in the past hour he had made three. Maybe he was getting old.

Recovering shortly, he regarded the hollow tree and probed inside. A bee tree. In the summer its upper length supported several colonies of bees. The lower level remained snug and dry.

Heading home from Caleb's Rock an idea began to form in Spike Poorbaugh's twisted mind.

Chapter 31 – Fessler's Junkyard

Mac was almost to the house when Tom took the logging trail that switchbacked behind Caleb's Rock down the mountain to the converted pasture where Mort lined his junk cars. Disappointed, tired, hungry, and suddenly anxious for company and that hot cup of coffee, Tom took a shortcut through the sumac grove that grew between the timberline and the lowest leg of the trail.

Within the sumacs Mort had placed his largest wrecks. The trucks and tractors were arranged in order of their demise with the older units located in the upper end of the yard. He kept a good distance between them to accommodate future wrecks of similar vintage. Mort Fessler was a well-organized man.

Tom entered the upper section of the sumacs. He immediately tripped over the buried tongue of a bent hay wagon with saplings growing through its rotten wooden bed. The foot-deep snow muffled the sound of his stumble and he regained his balance without falling, stepping more carefully now.

In front of him loomed the burnt hulk of a well-drilling rig that hit gas one day instead of water, and beyond that the high mass of an antique iron-wheeled tractor. They were covered with a thick blanket of snow. The smaller, dark, blocky object positioned between them was not. A shower of stones rattled down the cliffside and the object moved.

Ebenezer raised up and turned his head toward the rattling sound, then stood still as a magnificent statue until the rockslide stopped. Tom had blundered into his hiding place. Mac had passed right by him.

It made sense really. The sumac's were a snug, secure covert. The hard winds bounced from peak to peak and didn't intrude into Mort's comfortable vale. And no one, absolutely no one, visited a junkyard in the winter. The junkyard, set between two high mountains and above a river, was the most ideal place for a home in Steam Valley.

217

Ebenezer was facing away from Tom, the buck's attention riveted to the threat from the ledge. His heart pounding, afraid he would shake too much if he shot offhand, Tom took a rest across the fender of the burnt truck. The end of the long barrel steadied, the entire front sight was buried in the darkness of Ebenezer's front shoulder. He didn't need the fine bead. At fifty feet it was a sure kill.

A luck hunter should never get Ebenezer.

Once again Tom was flooded with conflicting emotions. There was glory and recognition for the hunter that took Ebenezer. What was there for the hunter that let him go?

There was always Ebenezer.

Tom let the Krag rest on the fender and drank in the sight of the majestic deer, etching that image forever in his mind. Ebenezer was part of Bear Hollow. Tom Donachy could not cut him down.

A vagrant breeze stole up the valley, carrying the smell of woodsmoke and the sound of approaching voices. Ebenezer lowered his head, sneaked along the bed of a Ford stake body, melted into a thicker stand of sumac, and disappeared.

Tom left the sumacs and met Mort and Charley coming up the field road.

"Was he in there?" asked Mort.

"Yeah," answered Tom, surprised. "How'd you know?"

"He's come with every storm for the past five years. I told Charley when you didn't come back last night. We figured if you didn't get him he'd lead you back here."

"How bad's he hurt?" asked Charley.

"Clawed up some. He's going good though. Mac creased his leg."

Charley snorted. "Mac didn't do that. I tracked you in the swamp. Ebenezer cut himself when he jumped onto that wire. There was deer hair all over it."

Tom smiled at the irony of that.

Charley had another question. "He take you up to Bear Hollow?"

Tom didn't answer. He just nodded. He could see the gleam of a shared secret in Charley's blue eyes.

"His granddaddy led me on a merry chase too. I lost him in the Marsh."

"Why didn't you shoot?" Mort's tone indicated he was glad Tom didn't.

Tom took his time answering. "He's so grand. Let's just say...I got buck fever." Tom winced at this lie. He was still getting razzed about his wreck and the poem to Brenda. Now a buck fever story. Ebenezer would give him recognition all right. A buck fever story was like Posey's pancake yeast. It never died.

Charley let him off the hook. "I got a better idea," he said. "Let's just say...nothin'."

Mort readily agreed. He had rued the day he brought that rack to Sawyer's store. There's substance to this boy, he thought.

"Let's get back to the house," suggested Charley. "Hopefully the fireworks will be over by the time we get there." The grin on his face meant he really hoped different.

"Fireworks?" Tom was puzzled.

"Julie's there. Come up with me. She's fretted all night and all day about you two bein' gone. Even sent Jim Morningstar out lookin'."

Mort chimed in, not above enjoying the younger men's current domestic trouble. "We can't figure who she's maddest at. Mac for keeping you out, or you for keeping Mac out. Expect we'll find out directly."

Tom groaned.

The warmth of the woodstove hit Tom full in the face when he opened the front door. Julie's hair gleamed gold as she stood in front of the light in the kitchen. Mac sat at the table, ignoring the full mug of coffee he was fingering absentmindedly with both hands. He sat looking intently at Julie, his face black with a three-day growth of beard and controlled anger.

Julie was just finishing her lecture when Tom ambled reluctantly into the kitchen. He could tell by the muscle

219

movement of Mac's jaw that he wasn't taking this well. Tom heard the word "irresponsible," followed by a wrap-up question.

"Do you hear me, Jonathan MacEwen?"

"I hear you, Sis," was the restrained reply.

Chapter 32 – The Baying of the Hounds

Something was awful wrong. Something hot had entered his throat, leaving a bitter aftertaste of metal and blood. He choked. He felt for his neck and discovered the slit in his parka. His gloved hand was immediately soaked by an open faucet of warm blood.

His blood.

He couldn't see very well. The dismal darkness of winter dusk and the swirling wind-driven crystals of snow spared him one last image of horror. He choked again, this time vomiting a river of blood.

His blood.

The hounds that had announced his presence bayed loud their frustration. They wanted out. They wanted him.

They smelled his blood.

The blurred outline of a tall figure waited between him and the pen. Just...waited. He hadn't seen him before. He should reach for his gun, he knew. He should put up a fight, but shock and enveloping weakness prevented that. Besides, the fight was over.

He wanted to breathe but couldn't breathe. He wanted to scream but couldn't scream. He wanted to stand but couldn't stand. Most of all, he wanted to turn back time and not come up here. Oh God!

Missy!

His last earthly sensation was the clamorous baying of Spike Poorbaugh's hounds.

———

The trapper let the body bleed out. Less load to carry that way. The dogs were in a frenzy, the ambush occurring right by their pen. They were already hungry. He would have to feed them when he got done.

He entered his cabin, lit a kerosene lantern, stuffed the two captured foxes back into his pack basket, and carried the lantern and full basket to the pelt shed. In the shed he dumped the day's catch in a corner and reloaded the basket with four heavy steel traps – two bear and two beaver. He shouldered the basket and grabbed a coiled 16 ½ foot length of chain, which was part of the booty Saul and Jesse had recovered from a survey party they killed one time on Potash.

Carrying the lantern and heavy load he broke a path through the deepening snow to the quicksand bog. He deposited everything and returned toward the buildings, tramping an easier path, veering off toward the dogpen and warden's body. The lantern gave off an eerie amber glow back at the bog.

He picked up Jim Morningstar and carried him the two hundred yards to the bog. He laid him down gently, only because he didn't want to kick up snow and snuff out his light.

He went through the warden's pockets and wallet and took his cash – eight dollars. He didn't take the holstered pistol; it was weight. He needed weight. He wound the body with the survey chain and clamped a bear trap over each foot and a beaver trap over each wrist. The trap chains were hooked to the survey chain. It would be months, even years, before the sprung trap jaws would grind through the bone. Properly weighted, no body had ever risen from the bottom of the bog.

Traps and chain were expensive but he had the warden's cash and the two foxes to offset that loss.

The body secured, he heaved the warden into the bog. The quicksand, crusted with snow and thickening from the cold, parted in two wet-cement like waves, then gathered and sucked the intruder in.

Taking the long chestnut pole that was always propped against the hemlock at the head of bog, the trapper probed until he felt the body and pushed it down hard, sinking it faster into the unknown depths whose bottom only the dead had ever found.

Grandmother Songbird would object to the body of an enemy defiling their burial ground. Saul and Jesse wouldn't

222

care.   Songbird hadn't known it but the surveyors were buried there too. Tonight they were getting their chain back.

Brother Westwind roared and swung low and mean down the north fork of Longstar, bringing new snow and churning up what had already fallen in front of it. By midnight all evidence of Jim Morningstar's visit would be erased.

The trapper picked up the lantern and pack basket and walked toward his cabin. Sensing his return the hounds bayed once more. Reminded of their hunger he stopped at the smokehouse and, with Saul's bloody Bowie, stripped off pieces of meat from the fat sow bear he shot the week before.

Chapter 33 – Christmas in Steam Valley

"Mom! There are twenty-three cheerios in my bowl."

"If you eat four how many are left?"

Without hesitating Danny answered, "nineteen."

His mother, washing breakfast dishes, was pleased. Nan was drying. Standing next to her sister she realized Nan had grown as tall as she. Danny had been too excited earlier to eat. Now he sat on his knees on his chair at the kitchen table, still in his pj's, divebombing his bowl of cereal with a spoon, having fun and making a mess. Julie decided to overlook the mess.

"Thanks for getting us the television, Sis." Nan whispered this, not wanting to shatter a little boy's illusions about Santa Claus.

"Don't forget, Luke and Joe are coming at three to hook us up to the TV line. It's wintry out so have some pie and coffee ready."

"Yes, boss."

Julie got the hint. She didn't have to order Nan around like some of the waitresses at work. Nan was dependable, steady. Getting prettier too. It was hard being fifteen years old and taller than most boys your age. "Who was on the phone? I heard it ring twice."

"Sally, then Tom. Monica got her ring last night. Carol did too."

Julie looked at her hand in the dishwater. She wore no rings. Marriageable girls kept track of such things at Christmas. Not long ago she too had hoped for a ring at Christmas.

"Got five that time, Mom!"

"How many are left now?"

Danny cheated and looked in the bowl. "Fourteen. They're the lucky ones, so far."

"Well, get them all in the next few passes and finish your milk. I want to wash that bowl."

"Okay."

Under the table Nan's calico cat licked spilt milk from the linoleum floor, then crouched patiently for more splashes from the air and sea battle raging overhead.

"Is Tom coming over?" whispered Julie. "Danny's missed him."

"After dark. He called from Evie's. Getting gas in the log truck. Then back to the woods. You know, that was a pretty song he sang last night."

"He has a voice, that Tom."

Julie could sing too and at one time took lessons from Aunt K. There she was noticed by Airman David Sheafer, home on leave.

Tom had sung the Negro spiritual "Sweet Little Jesus Boy." A simple song to sing, really. Tom was a gentle baritone and when he sat down there wasn't a dry eye in the Brick Church. Julie sneaked a glance at Mac, who rarely showed emotion. His eyes were brimming too.

Mac was leaner. Maybe she hadn't noticed it before, when he came in every day. He had spent the first week of December bulldozing trails for the search parties looking for Jim Morningstar. The next two weeks had been spent in a frenzied effort getting timber to the mill. The ground was firm. Snow was a lot easier to work in than mud.

They had concentrated the search on Blackwolf and Potash, Jim's snow-covered four-wheel-drive being found at Mac's log landing on lower Longstar. The most accessible path was the wagon road up to the Poorbaugh homestead. But why didn't he drive up there? He either thought he would get stuck in the deepening snow or he wanted to sneak in under the cover of the storm. He could have gone anywhere but he probably went there.

Julie had overhead his last words to Missy. He called her from the counter phone: "Hi! Remember me? The guy you married a while back?...Yeah, it's snowy. Really comin' down. Don't wait up. I'll be late. Kiss the girls for me."

Today a donation jar set on the counter for the education of the Morningstar children, for the twins and the one on
the way.

It took Mac two days to open the trail to the Poorbaugh place. Spike said he hadn't seen the warden and
wouldn't help look. As cold and blowy as it had been, he
said, Morningstar was probably under a hemlock windfall,
stiff as a board. Only a damn fool would have gone out the
second night of buck season.

Mac warned him to stay off his land and Mort's too.
Spike knew he was being baited and shrank back, obviously
not wanting a confrontation there. He said nothing more,
except that Mort should do his own warning. The searchers
standing around said the dogs made an awful racket. They
wished the dogs could tell what they knew.

After a cold hopeless week Jim's dad asked the Game
Commission to call off the search. Squire Hayes started
action to have him declared legally dead and Missy moved in
with her parents. They had a funeral and a headstone was
placed on the family plot at the Brick Church. Jim's name
was on it and so was Missy's; her signal that she would lie
with no other man. It didn't seem final to Julie. Jim's was
the only recent grave there that wasn't mounded up.

Missy didn't blame Julie for Jim's disappearance,
which somewhat relieved Julie, who was blaming herself.
But she had asked Jim to look for Mac and Tom, not spy on
Spike Poorbaugh. Jim had been looking for a reason to raid
the trapper's home but she never thought he would go there
alone. She distinctly heard Mac tell him never to go after
Poorbaugh alone.

Now Mac was goading the trapper. Oh, Mac!

Danny finished his cheerios, climbed down off the
chair, and handed his empty bowl and sticky spoon to his
mother. He hugged her leg, then Nan's leg, sticky hands and
all, then ran to the living room to play with his new toys and
probably wake his napping grandmother.

Julie wiped the table and chair with the dishcloth,
washed and rinsed Danny's bowl and spoon and handed them

to Nan. She checked the kitchen clock above the refrigerator. Time to get ready. She took the evening shift this day because it was the busiest.

Mac and Tom weren't the only ones working on Christmas.

———

If you didn't have anybody you came to the Turkey Ranch for your Christmas dinner. That's the way it seemed to Julie anyway.

Two long-haul truckers shared space at the counter with two bachelor farmers. They were talking freight rates and futures prices and the truckers were having a good year. The two farmers weren't. They were notorious poormouths, those two, and too stingy to ever get married. The truckers seemed unattached but you never could tell about those guys.

Four gussied-up widows were smoking and gossiping happily at table four. They had added one to their number since summer. Gerald Leidy, a dignified widower and semi-retired car dealer from Fallbrook, sat alone at table five. Julie had sat him there on purpose. Mr. Leidy usually ate in town at the diner but Woody was closed today. The widows were not displeased and he didn't seem bothered by the hens bustling near him. Who knew? One of the widows might gain an escort and Gerald might sell a car. Maybe four cars.

The round table by the stone fireplace had again been reserved by Fred Sheafer. He and Aunt K had reserved that table every Christmas since David died. By rights she should have them at her home so they could share in Danny's Christmas. One of the toys under their tree came from Fred – a jet fighter. Fred knew, and if he knew, Aunt K did too. There was no denying Danny's growing resemblance to his father.

Joining Fred and Aunt K would be Evie Todd, Mort Fessler, Charley Bower, and Mac and Tom. All were strays. Evie, Mac and Tom were recent strays. Mort and Charley had lived alone a long time. Charley's wife and daughter had

227

died in the flu epidemic of 1919. Mort's wife had run off with a shoe salesman during the Depression. A rumor persisted that Mort had a son somewhere. The junkman never said. Mort was closemouthed about his personal business.

She hadn't seen much of Mac. Lately he got his breakfast at the diner and packed his own lunch. Evenings he worked and ate at Mort's garage, with Mort coming down for take-outs and Mort paying for it. Mac was obviously overextended and working frantically to keep caught up. He still owed Evie for October's fuel and Posey for November's meals. Privately his friends were starting to express their worry; for *him*, not the debts.

She told herself he was just making every awake hour count, that days were short this time of year, but deep down she knew he was avoiding her. Her stinging rebuke at Mort's had not set well with him and taught her something – Mac was very sensitive to criticism. And he could hide his feelings as well as she. Shouldn't they talk this out? Did it matter now? She had lost him to Abigail. It shouldn't matter, but it did.

Abigail hadn't seen him either. They had supper together at the hotel the night before Abigail left to spend the holiday with her parents. Abigail had caused a local stir when she went to the Cole Christmas party with Steve Heffner. Evie said the person that hadn't seemed stirred was Mac, which was interesting. Abigail's intent was otherwise and it backfired. Julie couldn't help feeling pleased by that, but she wasn't exactly being encouraged by Mac either.

Nor had Tom been around. The judge and jury had not convened since Jim died. Between school and basketball games and daylight to dusk in the woods on weekends, Tom hadn't time for socializing. Julie had seen him at Jim's memorial service and heard him sing last night and had taken Nan to a home game, but there was no opportunity for conversation. She worried that Tom was upset with her too. Sure, she had gotten scared and chewed them out and maybe went too far. But she loved them and her reaction was natural. Couldn't they see that?

228

The doorbell jingled and Julie looked that way. A tall figure stood in the dark, tentative about entering. Tom, she thought, you know better. You're letting the cold air in! She didn't speak out and admonish him like she normally would have done. He was here, he was early, she would take a break and they could talk. She started forward to greet him.

Spike Poorbaugh closed the door.

Shocked, she somehow maintained her composure. "There's room at the counter," she said.

Poorbaugh nodded and walked slowly to the corner stool usually occupied by Mort Fessler and sat.

Posey was working the counter. The trapper ordered a steak, explaining he didn't get much beef meat where he lived. He wore clean corduroys and a red and black checkered wool shirt. His thick long hair was neatly brushed and hung to his shoulders. His powerful, knobby hands rested on the counter.

Posey said he hadn't ever seen him come in in the winter.

Spike said he'd never been plowed out before.

One of the truckers asked him his business.

Furs, he said.

Was he having a good year?

No. Prices were down.

Spike noticed the glass jar almost filled with cash and change and asked what it was for.

The sign says Morningstar Children Fund replied the trucker, but he didn't know the story. Did he know about it?

Spike said a little, and reached into his shirt pocket and brought out some bills, a five and three ones. The five went back into his pocket.

He put the three ones in the jar.

The trucker allowed that was pretty generous, furs being low and all.

Trouble came in the form of a warm south wind which, like an unwelcome visitor, stayed too long. The thaw officially began when a drop of water fell from a clump of snow packed in the crown of the tallest pine on the highest ridge on the northern-most slope of Bear Hollow. That drop was normally created in mid-March; this year it formed and fell two months early.

The drop wandered downslope a night and a day until it slid off a mossy rock into Bear Run, joining trillions of others whose journey hadn't been quite as long. Once in the roaring branch it covered distance rapidly, gaining speed as it traveled the length of Bear Hollow, finally spewing out as spray over the falls and settling into the widening pool that was eating away at the winter ice covering Great Marsh.

The marsh ice blackened and rotted and crumbled away and the mudstick hutches shrank lower as the water level grew. It would be months before air could return and dry out the hutches' central cavern and their inhabitants, and the trapper began to worry about next year's cash crop.

The seasons skipped January and February but the human calendar stayed in effect and the humans got behind. They couldn't believe they were having spring when they should be having winter. The wild animals adapted better. The trapper's fears were unfounded. They somehow knew that spring, which usually lasted three months, would this year be extended to five, and reacted accordingly.

In Steam Valley, the ice went out of Blockhouse January 10th; the frost began leaving the day after the final snowmelt on the 15th. Blockhouse ran high but stayed within its banks, its muddy rapids lapping a few feet below the flood stage marks painted on the abutments of the township bridges.

The thaw affected people differently; some gained, some lost.

Bud Cole gained. Late one night he got rid of several thousand gallons of nasty effluent Pemberton had budgeted as a trucking expense that the high water took for free. Frank

230

Sawyer gained. He ran a special on overstocked zipper artics and knee-high boots and sold every pair. Harry Raker lost. He tried to prepare his Buttonwood cornfields early and destroyed a new set of plows. Fred Sheafer lost. He was forced to buy logs at higher prices from other mills because his loggers couldn't get timber to him. In fact, all of his loggers shut down except one, Jonathan MacEwen.

Mac was losing. He'd barely covered his interest payments for November and December, January looked worse, and the loan balance, almost $40,000, was due February 16th. A muddy hour didn't pass without reminding him what a fool he'd been to figure he could pay $8,000 a month *plus interest* on that loan. He'd have to extend that note another six months and pray to God to drain the woods before that time was up. He'd never get another extension. Bud Cole would see to that, he and his patsy banker.

They told Mort and Luke what they found in Bear Hollow. Charley already knew. They all agreed to keep the timber resources up there a secret. Mort vowed he'd never let them lose it. Mac figured he could borrow a few payments from Mort if he had to, but he hated asking.

Today was Friday, payday, but there wasn't much pay. Luke was down to cutting and bucking twenty trees a day. That was low for Luke but the rest of the crew couldn't even keep up with that. The dozer was almost always chained to the log truck, which floundered constantly in the deep soupy ruts. Twice the truck had tipped over when a section of road suddenly gave way. Luckily no one was hurt and there was only sheet metal damage – the one advantage of working on soft ground. Most of the skidding was being accomplished by the horses. They were managing to drag 4000 feet a day to the skidway. And Abe was somehow managing to deliver the two light loads they created to the mill.

He couldn't make it on 4000 feet a day. He owed Evie and Frank and Posey and Mort and the bank. He hadn't paid Tom or their home utility bills. So far the only ones to dun him were the utility companies and the bank. He kept current with this crew.

He hadn't seen Abigail or Julie. Abigail complained about being stuck in her apartment and started seeing Steve Heffner. Julie kept her distance and he kept his. He didn't have time for a woman anyway. He worked dawn to dusk in the woods and dusk to midnight in the garage. But he missed seeing Julie. And missed her packing his pail. He didn't miss Abigail.

Something broke every day. Today it was the winch cable to the dozer. Yesterday it was a punctured gas tank on the log truck. He prayed the horses didn't get hurt or sick. He remembered then that he owed Charley for their feed. Charley hadn't said a word about the money.

Tonight would be his first evening off since Christmas. He had to quit early and pick Tom up at the Turkey Ranch, which was the stopping place for the team bus after away games. Good. He'd take time to talk to Posey about what he owed him. He wouldn't see Julie, though. She didn't work on Fridays.

The first financial victim of the thaw was Will Pierce. He hadn't put any by, got behind on his pickup payments, and lost the truck and Katrina Padleski the same day. Charley Bower was philosophical: Will'd get over it. Sad thing though, losin' a nice pickup thataway.

At dusk they met at Mort's, where Mac wrote their checks for the week's work. He gave Abe's check to Will. Abe had left earlier to deliver a load of logs and Mac included that volume in everyone's pay. Other contractors would confirm that volume with the millowner before paying off on it, but Mac and Fred never disagreed on scale.

The men were standing in the yard, talking and warming their hands over a tar barrel fire, when Abe unexpectedly returned. He hadn't had time to unload.

The firelight showed the anger and concern on Abe's normally taciturn face. "Ford Irish wouldn't let me cross, Mac. They've posted the bridge."

———

232

Ford Irish was in the middle of supper when Mac knocked on his door. He invited Mac to his office, which consisted of two filing cabinets and a metal desk in a corner of his enclosed front porch. He had been expecting Mac's visit and had the engineer's report handy.

Mac scanned the paper quickly. "This is nonsense, Ford. A ten-ton limit? That bridge will support forty-five easy."

"Not now it won't."

"How long you keeping it posted?"

"The report says 'til high water is over."

"That's months from now. May."

"I know."

"Those abutments will withstand five times the volume going through now."

"Not according to our engineer."

"Let me see the drawings. I'll calculate the stresses myself."

"Won't do you any good, Mac. We've decided." The supervisor was a heavy-jowled man. The set look on his face told Mac the bridge posting had more to do with politics than physics.

"I see," said Mac.

They were interrupted by a call from the kitchen: "Ford, you said you'd be at the milk plant by seven."

Ford took the report back and set it on his desk. "I have to go, Mac. Got some fixin' to do for Bud Cole."

"Looks like you got some done already," observed Mac, and he left.

The supervisor returned to the kitchen and his cold supper. Lately he and his wife had not been getting along. She was a prickly woman, his Etta.

"You just lost a friend," she said.

"Just doin' my job!" he protested. "I can't let him break down the bridge."

"Bull," she said.

At the Turkey Ranch, Julie had returned to table six.

"Where's Erma?"

"Home. She called in sick today."

"You done same time as Erma, Blondie?"

Julie ignored the burly driller's question. She leaned over and poured second cups of coffee for the other two at the table. As she reached the big man held his empty cup up and brushed by the front of her blouse. He pressed in with the back of his hand. Julie backed away and filled his cup. He watched her. She watched his cup.

"When you're done, just drive on down to cabin 7, Blondie."

"Sorry."

"Well, maybe it ain't on your way, like it was for Erma."

So *that's* why Erma called in sick, she thought. Julie returned to the kitchen for their orders. Those three had been working on Erma all week and the big one must have gotten to her. Paul probably figured it out. They had three kids, she and Paul!

She brought out a tray loaded with the three orders, set it on an adjacent empty table, and started to serve their dinners. The smell of stale beer and cigarettes and peanuts and crude oil emanated from the three. They hadn't bothered to clean up after work. They cashed their paychecks at the nearest bar and stayed there for hours, until it was time to get a late supper and proposition Erma.

As she served the first dinner to the burly man the headlights of a high vehicle canvassed the south dining room. Must be the team bus, she thought. Hope Tom helps me serve that bunch. She started to serve the second dinner to the medium-built driller. She was laying the plate down when the third driller, the tall skinny one, ran his hand up the back of her skirt and squeezed.

Julie smashed him in the face with his buddy's dinner. Her momentum pushed him back, the wooded chair legs broke, and he went down. The other two jumped up. The skinny one stayed on the floor. He wrenched the table cloth

234

off, scattering dishes and drinks, and wiped his face. "Bitch," he said and started to rise, glaring at her.

A strong hand grabbed her arm and pulled her away from the table. The newcomer stepped between her and the drillers.

"Now that you've had your supper, I suggest you leave," he said.

Mac! When did he come in? She saw Posey rush from the kitchen with a butcher steel. He knew how to use that steel. "I've had it with you three!" he said. "Get out." He pointed to the door with the steel.

Julie wasn't sure what convinced them to leave. They were rough men, accustomed to trouble. Maybe it was Posey's steel. Maybe it was a thread of remorse. She doubted that. She noticed they paid most attention to the stranger, the tall, fresh-shaved man with the steady voice and hot green eyes.

The big one, the leader, left first. "See *you* later, cowboy," he said.

They stalked out. The drilling rig started up, backed onto Fifteen, and headed south toward Trout Run and the Pig's Ear.

Julie, shaken but under control, knelt down on the floor and started picking up dishes. She had to find something to do. Posey helped her. She felt Mac's gentle touch on her shoulder. She liked it better than his firm grip before but that had been welcome too.

"You okay?"

Her eyes brimmed and she nodded yes.

Mac straightened up. "I'll be back," he said. "I left my lights on."

A moment later Julie stood up. The one-ton's light's still illuminated the south dining room. She looked out the window. Three black shapes bobbed and weaved alongside Mac's truck.

"Oh God!" she cried, and ran to the door. Posey grabbed his steel and followed.

The team bus pulled into the parking lot just as Julie and Posey got outside. There was lots of light and plenty of witnesses to the brutal action occurring by Mac's truck.

Sully Thompson stopped the bus. Tom had already levered open the door and jumped out, Joe Ballard right behind him. Coach Anderson was third because he thought to grab the first aid kit.

None of them got there in time to stop the fight and the injuries required treatment beyond Coach Anderson's abilities.

The skinny driller lay sprawled on his back, eyelids fluttering, blood trickling from his nose and ears. The big driller lay curled up on his left side, sick, and holding himself between his legs. Mac's last blow was an expert kick to the downed man's bent right knee. His intent had been to rupture two places, crotch and knee, and he succeeded. The big driller screamed and fainted.

Then Mac reached inside his truck cab and shut off his lights.

Shortly, the third driller returned to find their ruse had not worked out as planned. "I'm calling the cops!" he said.

"Better call an ambulance first, you fool," replied Sully Thompson.

The ambulance and police came. There were no arrests. The troopers were regular patrons of the Turkey Ranch and knew Mac and Julie. The fight was a clear case of assault and self-defense, they said. The third driller didn't think it was so clear. The black-haired guy didn't have a mark on him! Then the police reminded him that Julie could file charges against the skinny one, if he lived. She could probably file charges against you and the big guy as well. All the charges may not stick, but some would; it could be a while before you got back to West Virginia. The driller got the message and shut up.

The skinny one would live but that was about all, for pieces of the bridge of his nose and splintered off into his brain. The big one's knee was shattered and he would never father children. The ambulance sped north with two cripples. Neither would be able to molest a woman again.

———

Spike Poorbaugh, prowling the foothills of Potash, saw the red lights and wondered if he had been spotted. When they raced through Buttonwood and disappeared around Big Curve, he was relieved – there must have been a bad accident on Fifteen.

If he got caught he would say he was pulling muskrat and beaver sets but the water was too high. Damn, he hated to lose good traps. This, of course, was a lie. He had retrieved his traps two weeks ago.

He had just come from scouting Cole's, now he was watching Mort's. He'd resumed his visits since the snow left. Tracks in soft ground were hardly noticeable. By now he knew that Bud and Delia went out every Friday and their housekeeper stayed with Amanda. The collie dog stayed inside. They fed that dog too much but he was alert. He'd sensed the trapper's presence every time. Someday he would have to deal with that dog.

He knew Mort's habits too. The junkman worked in his office late and got up early. Until now, Mort had treated him fairly. During the second war he earned extra cash loading and unloading black market tires for Mort. Now he didn't want him on his land. He hadn't said it direct but MacEwen did, so it must be true. The Squire said the Poorbaugh's had squatter's rights to the cabin and surrounding land but they couldn't claim the whole mountain.

What good was the cabin without all the land? He had seen what happened to The Lady's land after she died. Nothing. All his for more'n twenty years. Mort didn't have anybody. Probably the same thing would happen if he died.

Brother Southwind blew balmy up Steam Valley, stirring a fishworm smell of wet spring earth. Riding high on that breeze was a staccato of bird calls.

237

Honkers. Mort heard them too and stepped outside. There was no way he could see them or him, it was too cloudy and dark. Still, the trapper crouched behind a junk car. The flock was coming north then veered west over Bear Mountain to the open water at Great Marsh. They had been there before.

He had never seen geese return this early. Jesse saw it once, the year he and Saul came down from Kinzua. That had been a muddy trip. Said they had a helluva time gettin' crost the cricks and rivers.

Chapter 35 – The Drive

The drive began with a bet, a log, and a jug of hard cider...

Every fall Mort and Charley made a barrel of apple cider. They claimed their own blend, "pasture squeezin's" Charley called it, derived from a wagon load of drops picked from the untended orchard next to Harry Raker's heifer barn. The keg was tapped and cradled on its side in Mort's root cellar, which stayed at a constant 55 degrees. When required, the contents were drawn off into a one gallon stoneware jug and stopped by a cork that had floated a year in the previous mixture. Cider's bouquet, said Charley, had to be just right, and began with the cork. The brew's "kick" was determined by taste and time ranging from "sweet" when the leaves turned to "mild" in deer season to "fine" by the first of the year.

By the third Friday in January, the day the supervisors posted the bridge, the cider was "mighty fine."

Mort and Charley had met on Friday's before supper ever since the new managers of the Hotel Fallbrook advertised an end-of-the week cocktail hour for their "sophisticated" customers. Mort owned stock in the hotel, received as payment for capital and inventory provided during the dark days of Prohibition. Before the change in management it was called the Fallbrook Hotel, locally shortened to the Hotel. Mort became concerned about his investment and wanted to see what this cocktail hour was all about. He took Charley with him. Charley told the story best:

"Me and Mort sat at the bar and next to me was this bald skinny fella and next to him was this pretty girl who snorted when she laughed. I told Mort to put out his cigar this was a fancy place, and I winked at the girl even though I was probably older than her grandpa. The skinny fella was awful proud about how good he'd turned out, tellin' the girl he was a reporter for the newspaper and radio station. His shoes

239

were real shiny and his tie was hangin' loose around his neck like he'd worked hard all day.

"That tie, it had one of them picture-book scenes, you know, the kind that tell a story? It had a black velvet background and a silver moon and a waterfall and a shimmerin' pool. I was fascinated with that tie. Finally the fella turns to me and asks what I was lookin' at. I said I was waitin' for the mermaid to pop her head and breasts out of that pool, where was she? The girl snorted and he got mad and remarked that maybe me and Mort didn't belong in a place like this. I said if you're gonna wear a tie you ought to wear it right, so I tightened it up real good for him and we left.

"On the way home we figured that cocktail hour was really a couple of high-priced drinks after work. We could relax cheaper in Mort's kitchen. But Mort decided to keep his stock because at those prices the Hotel Fallbrook should start showin' a profit, and by darn he was right. Been gettin' a dividend every quarter, ain't you Mort?"

This particular Friday Mac had just rushed off to confront Ford Irish, which the two older men rightly considered a waste of time. Best to sit back, have a glass of cider, and think. The Pierce brothers, upset because the bridge posting meant no income until dry weather, were invited to join them.

Abe wasn't sure but Will reminded him they were done early and had time for a visit before Rebekah served supper. They sat at Mort's kitchen table, next to the iron cookstove. It was lulling warm, the first real warmth of the day for the loggers.

Charley poured four water glasses full of cider, which was cool and a little cloudy. Its taste was tart and musty with a trace of dusty keg and cobwebby cellar. Charley declared it had a good bite and Mort agreed. Will and Abe thought so too, without really knowing what bite was. Soon Charley suggested a second round, Mort said okay, and Will didn't mind if he did either. Abe thought they ought to head home but Will observed they would still be early and Rebekah would fret about the bridge. Charley emptied the jug in Abe's glass and went to the root cellar for more cider.

They were on the second round of the second jug, reminiscing about old times, when Charley recalled that when he was Will's age driving logs meant going down the river not the road. Why the drive would start at Jacob's Landing at sunup and make camp at English Center at sundown. Took fifty men. Average a mile an hour they did.

"Naw," said Will, who always doubted Charley's stories.

"Two bucks says I'm right," said Charley.

"Gamblin's sinful, Will," cautioned Abe.

"I ain't goin' to hell over two dollars. What's the bet?"

"The creek runs next to the road at Flooks Run. From the steel bridge it's a little more'n a mile. We throw a log over the bridge. If it shows up at Flook's Run in an hour, I win."

"You're on."

"We'll need your spotlight, Mort."

"What we gonna do for an hour?" asked Mort.

"I'll fill the jug," said Charley.

At 6:33 p.m. the log was dropped into Blockhouse. At 7:26 it showed up at Flook's Run.

At 8:00 p.m. Mort and Charley took the Pierce brothers home. Charley asked Rebekah Pierce to remind Will, when he woke up, that he still owed him two dollars.

———

The spectators at the bridge watched the last log slide with an icy splash into swollen Blockhouse Creek. It bobbed in the swift current, its brand, a King's Arrow, showing clear against the mudcaked ends of the log. Soon the mud dissolved and the brand blended into the butter-yellow surface of the sawed end. The log twisted toward the rapids, making a valiant attempt to catch up with the thousand other logs that had gone before it.

The log had been delayed. Before its departure Squire Hayes had shown up and handed an antique stamp and hammer to Jonathan MacEwen. They shook hands and Mac branded the log. Pushing hard with his canthook Mac sent it on a fast roll down the streambank to the water.

The log slowed in the riffles of the widened area known as Jacob's Landing, got a directional push from an FFA volunteer with a pry pole, then dipped and disappeared into the boiling rapids at the narrow southern end of the landing where Blackwolf and Steam Mountains pinched together.

It was a small white pine log, only eight feet long and one foot in diameter. At nightfall, when it reached Sheafer's Mill seven creek miles away, it would receive special treatment. Fred would saw it into sections and stamp each with a King's Arrow and the year. All involved in the log drive of 1955 would receive a section. The two end sections, the ones that made the trip, were reserved for Charley Bower and Mort Fessler.

Tom had planned to paint a cider jug on Mort and Charley's sections but Aunt K found out and overruled that idea.

———

Mac and the crew hadn't wasted a minute in the week since Charley suggested they float the logs to market. They set to work getting the downed timber out of the woods to the creek bank. Luke quit cutting and worked with Charley and the team skidding logs to the main landing on lower Blackwolf. Will and Abe cleared brush along the creek bank from the steel bridge to the southern end of Jacob's Landing. Mac and Tom and Joe Ballard built a road joining the two landings, Mac operating the dozer and the boys laying corduroy spans over the soft spots.

By Monday morning Abe and Will were trucking logs from Longstar to Blockhouse, a short haul of one mile, dumping the logs and arranging them lengthwise along the creek bank in close piles the oldtimers watching from the bridge called a "rollaway." Mort helped out at the rollaway. He was shut down until the weight restrictions were lifted from the bridge.

On Tuesday Mac got a break. The weather turned cold, not quite freezing, and the ground firmed up. The mountains continued to pump water into Blockhouse but the rate abated.

Perfect, said Charley. Logs float better when the water's level. When she floods and swells up in the middle and grows a fin, she scatters and beaches the logs. Stay out of the way when that happens.

With his crew busy feeding logs to the rollaway, Mac went to the mill and borrowed Fred's dozer. At the gravel bar below the mill, on the mill side of Blockhouse, he gouged out a shallow one-acre pond. With help from the mill crew he built a floating log boom across Blockhouse. Simply constructed of long oak logs lashed lengthwise together and anchored to posts set on both banks of the creek, the boom would divert the downfloating logs into the mill pond. Grabs attached to the dozer's winch and cable would snake the logs from the water. Mac then cleared the gravel bar of brush and flood trash to make room for a temporary log landing, and built a skidway ramped high enough to accommodate Fred's biggest log truck. That truck could carry extra large loads. Finally, he opened a wide access lane from the gravel bar to the main road for the short three-quarter mile haul from the gravel bar to the mill.

By Thursday the sending and receiving areas were ready. The shorter hauls and firmer ground eased the burden on equipment and men. That evening Mac found he didn't have any bookwork or equipment to repair, so he had a quick supper at the Turkey Ranch and went to basketball practice with Tom. Julie and Posey figured it was his first recreational break since buck season.

By Friday the rollaway was piled ten feet high and extended two hundred yards below the steel bridge. The unique effort attracted attention and the word got out that Mac was "driving timber" on Saturday, folks could see it all from the bridge.

Public sentiment went strongly against the supervisors for posting the bridge. Many privately suspected the involvement of Bud Cole, and the three elected officials were bluntly told this would be their last term. The posting explained some of Mac's brutal anger at the driller. But he should be careful defending Julie Spencer. After all, hadn't someone seen her leaving Cabin 7? Granted, it was late at night and foggy, but who else could it be?

Also on Friday Mort Fessler ambled unannounced into Steve Heffner's office and guaranteed Mac's loan. The banker made sure no one else heard Mort's comments and assured him he would take it to the Board at their February meeting. Mort left satisfied and Heffner called Bud Cole. Angry, and bitterly disappointed, the tanner ordered him to leave that item off the agenda. They both knew however, with the junkman behind him, Mac couldn't be stopped.

When the last log dipped from view the crowd dispersed. The weekend drives would continue until the runoff receded. For now the action shifted to the millpond, where it was rumored Mort and Charley had set up a log roll between Will Pierce and Bravo Burton. The two old schemers had bet Bravo ten bucks and a jug of cider that Will would roll him into the drink. Bravo worked nights in the tanyard, which is where the bet was made. Katrina Padleski was his new heartthrob. Bodythrob reportedly remarked Will, whose comment became the basis for the contest. The tanyard men who saw Mort nudge Charley figured Bravo was going to get wet.

Two women remained on the bridge. They were bundled up against the cold and were talking and watching a towhead boy running along the creekbank toward Mac and the Squire. The boy was delivering something. Overtly the parent and the teacher were discussing the child; yes he was doing well in school. Covertly each was uncomfortable with this meeting.

The boy reached Mac and handed him his dinner pail. How domestic, thought the teacher. The boy pointed back to the bridge. Mac looked at the women on the walkway and waved and smiled. Both women were glad to see the smile. Mac was obviously pleased with the success of the drive. He was an incredibly attractive man, especially when he smiled. Each then wondered who he was acknowledging with that wave and smile.

Chapter 36 – The War of Words

It all started in late January when the Town Team issued its annual challenge to the Varsity for a game. The challenge came, as it had in years past, with an article in the Fallbrook Agitator describing the Varsity's record that basketball season and comparing it to the Town Team of that year. All the bigger towns within thirty miles had high school teams, and "town" teams comprised of older ball players, mostly former high school players. Competition between towns was strong. In Fallbrook tradition dictated that competition between the Varsity and the Town Team be strong as well.

The Varsity had never beaten the Town Team. Historically the game had been a rout, with the stronger and more experienced Town Team running up the score mercilessly against the high school boys. Last year's Varsity had came the closest, losing by 10 points, but with strong showings from juniors Bobby Richards, Tom Donachy and Squeaky Fabel. This year the three boys were back as seniors, had good support from the other team members, and had won their league and district and regional playoffs, losing a heart-breaker by two points at states to a much bigger school from Scranton. Squeaky had gotten sick and missed that game. Their record was 23 –1.

The Town Team had dominated the Bi-State (NY & Penn) League, defeating teams from Elmira and Williamsport mainly on the strength of a couple of prudent imports by player-coach Bud Cole, who took his basketball seriously. The Town Team was 18-0.

Their mainstays were: burly Bud Cole, who doubled as coach and power forward; hulking 6-5 center Big Jake Callahan, who worked as the new pasteurizer operator at the milk plant; flashy and quick-tempered guard John Tate, just out of the service, who was a foreman at the Tannery; steady wingman Wilson Klinger, a Baptist minister with six kids and known by all as The Preacher; and the other wingman, herky-jerky Jeff Wheeler, the morning disc-jockey at the WBEN radio station and contributing sports editor for the Agitator. He signed on and off as DJ.

DJ threw down the gauntlet when he predicted in his Sunday article that the game would be another rout, men against boys, a case of giants wading through the muck and mire of a high school game, squashing tadpoles.

The Varsity countered in The Beacon, the school newspaper. Tom D. was the sports editor. He knew DJ to be a vain, opinionated fellow whose mother, whom he lived with, called him "Jeffrey." He wore the latest in mens fashion bought on credit at Straus' in Williamsport and was balding prematurely.

The Beacon responded that tadpoles were slippery and hard to catch, especially by those with soft feet and bald heads.

Tom had struck a nerve. He got the predictable response. The Agitator editor, feeling insulted, demanded a retraction and an apology.

The Beacon responded with a correction and the apology. There had been a typing error, Tom explained. They really meant bad feet and soft heads. Sorry.

The Agitator editor, agitated now, hit back at school loyalty, noting the cheerleaders had boyfriends and brothers on the more mature squad and would probably cheer for the Town Team.

The Beacon responded that while the cheerleaders did indeed love their older brothers and boyfriends, a poll had been taken and girls had voted to support the team with the most hair. Until they graduated they wouldn't cheer for anyone whose hair part began just over the right ear.

Both papers were read by the locals who enjoyed the banter but also knew there were deeper rivalries beneath it.

Bobby Richards had broken John Tate's scoring record that stood for six years, MacEwen and Bud Cole having it before them. Bobby had also dumped John's youngest sister Sally, or she had dumped him, their stories differed, the kids had suddenly quit talking, but there was bad blood between families.

Moreover, the Varsity was in Mac's camp. Until he got busy on Blackwolf Mountain, Mac had helped coach them. Most of the Town Team were Bud Cole men. The town itself felt, even relished, the tension between Mac and Bud Cole. At one time they wanted the same woman and the same land, maybe they still did, conflicts creating excitement, speculation and rumor.

The cheerleaders *were* split. Their advisor was a secretary to Bud Cole. Senior Monica Manikowski was engaged to John Tate. Moreover, she had dated Bobby Richards for a while and made the mistake of telling her fiancé about it. Sophomore Sally Tate admired Tom Donachy, had a growing affection for Squeaky Fabel, and wanted to be free of her overprotective brother. Senior Sharon Sullivan was going steady with Varsity wing Jim Levandowski, but was having a secret fling with a married Town Team man. During the regular season there were no split loyalties. For this contest, there were.

Chapter 37 – The Locker Room

Friday night was slow downtown. There was lots of traffic, all streaming uphill to the school gym. The steady, pouring rain had slacked temporarily to intermittent sprinkles, the drizzle and rising mist diffusing the blue-white glow from the top of the hill where the gym lights mixed with the headlights of scores of cars.

Frank, knowing there would be no more business that evening, decided to close early and go to the game. Mort, having no interest in sports, no one else to talk to, and half asleep from sitting too close to the overwarm coal stove, stood up to go home. Stretching, he saw Tom's five-dollar bill tacked to the message board and decided to take it down. He inserted it in the large roll of cash in his pants pocket, handed Frank another five, and left.

Frank watched him shuffle off and shook his head. Mort was one of the gifted few who had the knack for making money. Besides the junkyard, Mort did a nice business making small loans, collecting the bulk of his weekly payments Friday and Saturday nights at the store. He just sat there on a nail keg and pocketed the cash. Some nights he brought in more than the store.

————

In the locker room the Varsity was subdued, except one. Bobby Richards, in uniform already, admired himself in the mirror and combed his wavy blonde pompadour. Cocky, over-confident, self-centered, he didn't feel the tension the same as the other players. "When you were a baby you were adorable, in grade school you were cute, as a young stud you're adorable again. Know what that means?" he asked no one in particular.

"Yeah," interrupted Tom. "It means you're back to being a baby."

Everyone laughed, except Bobby.

It raised his hackles, but Bobby let it pass. He knew better than to challenge the big, powerful Tom. He'd tried it once. The quickness and brutality of that thrashing was etched deep in his memory. Bobby saw a fight as a fair thing, like a basketball game where you play rough but by the rules. Tom saw a fight as a fight, there were no rules.

Bobby knew Tom just tolerated him. A selfish grand-stander, Bobby's objective had been to win the league scoring title, which he did handily, breaking the school record in the process. It brought him the recognition he craved. Normally lazy, on the court he was an aggressive and effective ballplayer. He had a great shot, played hard defensively and wasn't afraid to mix it up inside. His weakness was passing; he didn't do it enough to get good at it. Tom knew when Bobby got the ball to head for the basket and the rebound if he missed. The system worked well; Bobby got the spotlight but Squeaky was the playmaker and Tom the court general. By the time the opposition figured out there was more depth to the team than a one-man scoring machine it was usually too late.

Bobby was husky and handsome with bright blue eyes and a devil-may-care attitude. He liked the girls and they liked him...for a while. He liked to score with them too, then brag about his conquests at school.

The bragging ended earlier that season after he told tales about a tryst with Sally Tate, a perky, impressionable, first year cheerleader liked by everybody, especially Squeaky. The girl was crushed. That private confrontation in the locker room also rankled Bobby.

Tom: "We hear you went all the way with Sally."

Bobby: "So? What's it to you?"

Squeaky: "You told everybody."

Bobby: "Not everybody...Some."

Tom: "You've got to make it right."

Bobby: "Make what right?"

Tom: "Stop the gossip about you and Sally."

Bobby: "How?"

Tom: "You gotta lie."

Bobby: "What?"

Tom: "You gotta lie. Say you didn't do it with Sally. Say you made it all up…and apologize."

Bobby: "Who cares?"

Tom: "We care."

Bobby: "What if I don't?"

Squeaky: "You'll never get the ball."

Bobby lied.

Chapter 38 – The Roll of Drums

Coach Anderson swore to himself. He hated this game. Time-honored tradition demanded he play it. The game was almost like a rite of passage. The stronger Town Team gives his boys a public beating, the boys take it goodnaturedly, "like men," then join the Town Team after graduation and repeat the process to the next group of boys down the line. It reminded him of the distinction between plebes and upper-classmen when he was a cadet at West Point.

Coach swept his hand through his thick iron-gray hair, parted at the middle. He looked like a school principal, which he was. His earlier military background had made him used to delegating authority and he had delegated a lot to Tom Donachy. He had never seen a player that competed with the force of Tom. Mac came the closest. He wondered what the half-brothers shared that made them that way. Whatever it was, his coach's instincts told him this rite of passage could prove difficult.

The Varsity came out nervous and tense, their lackluster warmup drill consisting only of a meager display of layups and jump shots.

The Town Team came out with a fast-paced drill they had worked on all week, and another surprise, new uniforms. These were of the latest tighter-fitting style, a white back-ground with red trim, Cole Enterprises in prominent lettering above the number on the back of each jersey. In contrast, the Varsity wore uniforms left over from the forties, loose fitting jerseys and baggy shorts in faded blue and frayed gold. If plumage counted for anything in this game the Varsity had already lost.

Bud Cole, whose number was his age, 35, turned on the charm. He sought familiar faces in the gathering crowd and waved and pointed and turned thumbs down at the Varsity; just kidding, he laughed. His winning smile was infectious, convincing most that Fallbrook was fortunate indeed to have such a generous and successful citizen. What would they do without the Tannery and Bud Cole?

The new gym was filling fast, the combined din of bouncing balls, cheering cheerleaders, slamming bleachers, and milling people echoed off the bar joists and blasted through the gym doors and into the lobby. It was an exciting greeting.

Mac came in with Abigail and sat directly behind the Varsity bench. Coach Anderson, drawing on Mac's experience as a university player at Penn State, had asked him to assist.

Abigail, who had called Mac at the last minute after declining an earlier offer from Steve Heffner, wished for a less conspicuous spot. She decided to make the best of the situation; beggars can't be choosers. She couldn't help but note the contrast between the new high school facilities and her one-room elementary down the road. She smiled at the thought of her girls asking to go to the "ladies room."

Delia Cole came in dressed like the regal society queen, Amanda in tow. Amanda, with her outgoing and mischievous personality, received the most attention. Abigail noticed that Delia was patient and obviously proud of her tomboy daughter. They sat on the Town Team side.

Julie Spencer came in with her stringbean sister and walked to the Varsity side. Mac, forgetting Abigail, watched her intently. She was wearing a beige sweater and dark slacks, her tawny hair hanging almost to her waist. Male and female heads turned. The cheerleaders paid special attention to Julie. She didn't seem aware of any of it.

It was then Abigail realized that the standard of beauty for the valley was not set by the classic cameo elegance of Delia, or by the crisp modern attractiveness of the new elementary teacher, but by the earthy, natural loveliness of the ponytailed waitress at the Turkey Ranch.

Abigail edged closer to Mac, who by this time was more involved with Coach Anderson than with her.

People were still streaming in from the lobby. There the fund-raisers were taking place, the practical reason for the Varsity-Town Team game. The Varsity Club boys, athletes of sports other than basketball, were selling admission tickets for fifty cents. The Junior High Cheerleaders were selling popcorn, the smell of their concession permeating the lobby. The VFW, Steam Mountain Rod and Gun Club, and the Fallbrook Hose Co. Ladies Auxiliary were all selling raffle tickets for their worthy causes.

The women of the Polish and Irish Catholic churches were selling sausage and canned goods, bingo being cancelled for that night. And the Protestant Ministerium was taking donations toward their summer tent crusade. Their booth wasn't doing so well. Then someone told Revered Klinger, who left his warm-ups, came out into the lobby, and stirred things up, convincing the Catholics to donate a portion of their stock so the Protestants would have something to sell. The gregarious and sometimes irreverent Preacher was popular; he mixed it up in his community just like he mixed it up on the basketball court.

The lobby emptied and the crowd finally filled both sides of the bleachers. At the opposite end from the lobby was the stage, occupied by the band and cheerleaders.

The band members, in their uniforms of blue and gold, were warming up too, creating a disjointed symphony that made their parents uneasy and squirm in their seats. Tom, shooting a foul shot on the stage end, observed the similarity between the Varsity and the band. They both seemed ragged right now. Fallbrook High really had a good band, and a good varsity. But when the drummer rolled his drums, he wondered who it was for.

On the ledge of the stage in front of the band bounced the symbols of school spirit and sexuality. Hair done, makeup right, voices clear, dressed in soft white sweaters, short blue skirts, and saddle shoes dyed to match, the cheerleaders did their pom pom and gymnastic routine. Monica's graceful cartwheel and Sally's high backward flip reminded Tom they were really athletes on a par with the boys, but they definitely weren't boys.

Her part of the routine done, Sharon Sullivan, a pert blonde cutie with red lipstick and a falsie-filled sweater, left the stage. She walked sprightly along the sideline toward the lobby, the scent of her perfume lingering in the air. As she passed the Town Team bench, she gave her married lover a provocative extra wiggle. Like a yearling doe leaving her sign, thought Tom.

Sharon's high-school steady, Jim Levandowski, whom everyone called the Polack, saw it. So did the wife's best friend. The wife, home with two small children, would hear about it tomorrow. Everyone knew, but Sharon and her lover, like all deceivers, thought no one knew.

Tom shot with indifference, studying instead the down-court Town Team, noting their weaknesses. Big Jake couldn't shoot outside. The Preacher was nearsighted and his glasses kept sliding down his nose. John Tate lacked confidence going to his left. DJ dribbled too high. Bud Cole couldn't jump worth beans.

Tom received a ball from Squeaky, drove to his deep corner, and shot the long practice jumper. The ball rolled cleanly off the fingertips of his left hand, flew with good arc and, swish. Tom was on. He noticed however that Bobby was off. He hadn't hit a single outside shot during warm-ups, and the Polack's normally accurate two-handed set shot was flat.

The play buzzer sounded calling both teams to their benches. Everyone stood as the band played the National Anthem, the cheerleaders led the Alma Mater, and The Preacher intoned a blessing for safety during the game. The crowd settled expectantly back into their seats and the refe-ree's shrill whistle called the ten starters to center court.

The game was on.

The matchup at center court *did* look like men against boys, the exception being the heavily bearded Tom who hadn't shaved in two days. Still, hound-jowled Big Jake at 6'5 and 260 weighed forty pounds more than Tom. Squeaky, at point guard, looked timid against the determined John Tate. Bobby, the shooting guard, would have his hands full defending the savvy Preacher. The Polack's mind was on Sharon's suggestive sashay around Earl Steinbacker and not on the sneaky DJ. And Joe was taken in by the friendly handshake of solid Bud Cole. "Let's have a good game," he said smiling, and slapped Joe loud on the back.

The tone of the first quarter was set right there. The Town Team was ready but Tom, checking to see if his men were in position, was not. The rightside referee tossed the jump ball high at the backslap, Big Jake went up with the ball as DJ and Bud Cole hustled downcourt, the ball was tipped hard to DJ, who scooped it up and made the easy layup.

The surprised Varsity hadn't moved. DJ, Bud Cole, Big Jake and the rightside ref, a manufacturer's rep who called on Cole Enterprises, exchanged obvious knowing glances. The crowd loved it.

The Varsity took the ball out. The Town Team was on them immediately with a fullcourt press. Squeaky, rattled at the unexpected defense, made a bad pass which was intercepted by the Preacher who relayed it to John Tate for another score.

The Varsity took the ball out again, determined this time to break the press. Tom went to center court to take the high hard pass he knew was coming, pivoted and passed to Bobby at the wing, then broke for his foul line, expecting a return pass or to screen for Bobby there.

Bobby didn't make it. John Tate and DJ had converged on him for a two-man trap. Bobby was caught upright and couldn't pivot out. John Tate grabbed his arm and knocked the ball loose, which was picked up by DJ who passed to the

Preacher at their foul line. Canned for another two, the Town Team led 6-0.

Bobby cried foul. So did Coach Anderson and Mac. The rightside ref said he didn't see it and Bobby got mad. Coach called for a time-out.

"Get your heads into this game and play ball!" he exclaimed, slapping his clipboard for emphasis. "Don't force it. Hit Tom in the center. If they're doubleteaming Bob that leaves the other wing open."

But the ball handlers didn't hit Tom or the other wing. The Town Team's aggressive pressure defense continued, neither team settling into a normal offensive pattern. It became clear the Town Team's defense was their offense. They meant to capitalize on the turnovers made by the frustrated Varsity players. And capitalize they did, scoring eleven more times before the Varsity scored once.

The harried Varsity finally broke the press near the end of the eight-minute first quarter. Tom drove around a panting Big Jake for one score and screened for Squeaky for another. He noticed Squeaky was regaining his composure and the Polack and Joe Ballard were getting into the game. Bobby Richards, however, doubleteamed and fouled continuously by DJ and John Tate, had lost his cool and was out of it. The quarter ended with a charging foul called on Bobby for trying to break out of one of their traps. The score at the buzzer was Town Team 22, Varsity 4.

―――

At the quarter break Coach Anderson encouraged his boys. "Look, there's a lot of time left in this game. They're not in shape to stay with the press another quarter. They'll go to a zone, probably a 2-1-2. We'll do the same."

He instructed each player: "Tom, work on that big center, he's lagging. Bobby, you stay out front with Squeaky on defense, watch the fouls, head downcourt for the fast break. Jim, (Coach just couldn't call him Polack), I need some outside shooting from you. Make sure your rebounders are in position. And Joe, box out Bud Cole. Let's give these showboats a game."

Tom outjumped Big Jake easily, tipping the ball to Squeaky who passed long to Bobby at the Town Team three-quarter line. Bobby took the ball in, thought he heard footsteps, hesitated, and missed the easy peeper. The Polack, hustling downcourt, put the ball back up for the score. They were his footsteps that Bobby heard.

Tom knew Coach had given Bobby the fast break assignment to give him some layups and restore his confidence. Bobby had responded by missing the first easy opportunity offered. DJ and John Tate, sensing weakness, continued to dog him hard, John Tate running alongside him yelling trip! trip! trip! every time Bobby got the ball. Bobby was rattled. The biggest contribution he could make until he settled down was as a decoy.

The Town Team, true to Coach's prediction, abandoned the press and set up a tight zone, posting Big Jake in the middle to plug the lane. Comfortable with a 16-point lead, the Town Team decided to play the crowd instead of the game.

First, DJ tried a fancy behind-the-back pass that was intercepted by the Polack, who passed downcourt to Squeaky for a short jumper and score. Next, Bud Cole tried an "alley-oop" to Big Jake; a high pass to the basket rim, the receiver catching the ball and ramming it in. A real crowd pleaser.

The pass was good. Jake had good position and momentum but Tom was there too, and Tom was a leaper. He jumped, his hand extending above the rim higher than Jake's, and like stealing fruit, plucked the ball from Jake's outstretched hands. A strong baseball pass followed to Bobby, who made his first score.

Big Jake, his pride hurt, cried foul. Bud Cole yelled goaltending. The rightside ref, confused, said, "Well, which is it?" causing a ripple of disapproval from the Varsity fans. The leftside ref, whose call it was, said nothing. He had decided to even things up a bit.

The Town Team guards brought the ball upcourt. The score was 22-10. The ball went to Bud Cole in his deep corner, who faked a jump shot and baselined Joe, driving neatly around him toward the basket. Here he was met by the craggy figure of Tom, who had position and wasn't going to give it up. Bud Cole decided to shoulder him out of the way, driving his 240 pounds into the boy. The young oak bent but he didn't budge and the leftside ref blew a charging foul against Bud Cole.

Inwardly seething at the rejection, outwardly smiling and shrugging "oh, well," Bud Cole decided to get even by humiliating the boy and pulled down Tom's shorts. He had gotten away with circus tricks like that before. About half the crowd laughed at the sight of the rangy, hairy boy standing there awkwardly in his underwear. The other half plainly thought it was a cheap trick. They all looked for the reaction from Tom.

Tom pulled up his shorts, jogged downcourt to his foul line, and made the free throw.

Bud Cole paid in that exchange. Some crowd support had shifted from his team to the Varsity, and his face hurt from the beard burn he got when he collided with Tom. That angered him more because he knew Tom would have gotten that tip from Mac.

The Varsity began cutting the Town Team lead. Squeaky hit Bobby with two good passes for outside jumpers and Bobby made them both. He's getting his composure back, thought Tom. DJ and John Tate, who had been singly screened off Bobby by Joe, went back to doubleteaming him. This freed the Polack on the wing and his long two-handed set shot went in for another two. The Town Team lead was down to five, 22 to 17.

The Town Team called time out. The Varsity had hit them with eleven unanswered points. Their comfortable lead had disappeared. The Town Team bench stirred with disaffection; if the Varsity kept this close, Bud Cole wouldn't let them play. Bud Cole, ignoring his bench, conferred with his starters, especially his guards. After receiving instructions from their coach, DJ and John Tate had their own personal conference.

When the Town Team came back they found the Preacher open along Joe's side for two. It became obvious that they would emphasize Joe Ballard's side and keep away from Tom. Big Jake, blocking with his heavy body and arms, was trying to keep Tom behind him, enabling the Preacher and Bud Cole to stack on Joe's side. But Joe, fooled by Bud Cole twice, was not about to let them down his lane. He conceded an occasional outside shot to the Preacher but stuck to his assignment – boxing out Bud Cole. DJ and John Tate stayed out front.

The Preacher hit two more jumpers and the Varsity countered with two, the Polack netting another set shot and Tom driving by Big Jake for a score.

Then it happened. The Preacher missed a long jumper, pushing it left. The ball sprung high off the rim and the Polack grabbed it at the foul line. He threw it hard down-court toward their basket, expecting Bobby to be there for the fast break.

He was. And in good position too, just ahead of his two defenders, DJ to his left and John Tate directly behind. All were running at full speed. The ball bounced once ahead of Bobby who took it in stride, ignored his defender's footsteps, and leaped high for the backboard, his body extended in perfect layup form.

He was hit immediately, DJ crashing into him high and John Tate undercutting him low. Bobby crumpled in midair, like a gamebird shot in flight, his feet sailing higher than his head. He landed hard on his shoulders and skidded headfirst into the cement wall at the base of the stage. His knee drew up, then straightened, and he lay still. The anxious gasp of the crowd and leftside ref's whistle calling the foul signaled the end of play.

Bobby's team members crowded around him. Coach Anderson and Mac rushed over. His parents came down from the stands. Irascible Doc Buckley shouldered his way in and checked the boy's eyes. "He's unconscious," he said, "probably has a concussion." Then, to reassure his anxious mother he added, "He'll be all right, but he's done with basketball for a while."

As two men carried Bobby to the nurse's office a murmur of resentment swept through the crowd.

Ted Jones came in for Bobby. Ted was the youngest of the Varsity players, a sophomore, a boy of medium height and slightly built. But he played so much backyard basketball that he had developed into one of the best shooters on the team. He was a mild-mannered boy and popular. His dad owned the five and dime in town. His granddad was the Squire.

DJ and John Tate smirked at the foul line as the nervous kid missed both of Bobby's free throws. Their maneuver had paid off.

The Preacher didn't approve and had said so at the timeout. Bud Cole, unaccustomed to criticism, threatened to bench him. The Preacher, the team's most reliable scorer, responded with scorn. "You do that and you'll lose," he retorted. Bud Cole couldn't stand losing at anything so the defiant Preacher stayed in. He thought the Preacher was making a big deal out of nothing. Who cared about one cocky kid anyway?

But the Varsity did care. Bobby, with all his faults, was still one of their own. He had been savagely taken out and anger was setting in.

Two minutes later it happened again.

The Town Team had the ball and a bigger lead, having gotten two scores from John Tate, who was no longer preoccupied with Bobby Richards. DJ got caught napping at the wing and found himself covered in a two-man trap by Squeaky and Ted. He couldn't get out so he got them. Taller than both boys, he first knocked Squeaky back with a left elbow to the breastbone, then swung his right elbow high at Ted. It caught the fair-haired boy over the right eye and opened an ugly gash the length of the eyebrow. DJ's malicious reaction was a flagrant double foul, ignored by the rightside ref, but not by the crowd. The leftside ref called a timeout as Ted staggered toward the Varsity bench, the majority of the crowd roaring its disapproval.

Doc Buckley was rousing Bobby when his parents and Mac brought Ted in. Pete Jones was furious. On the way out he told Bud Cole that Main Street would never support the Town Team again. Bud Cole just laughed.

Harry Krotzer came in for Ted. A short, stocky senior with deceptive speed and all-day endurance, Harry could handle the ball but couldn't shoot. He was captain of the soccer team and had a mean streak in him. Coach used him when he wanted to dog somebody. His assignment was to dog DJ. But the Preacher suggested that DJ sit out, Bud Cole agreed, and Earl Steinbacker came in. Harry and the Polack switched places.

With less than twenty seconds left on the clock the Varsity worked a screen play for the last shot of the quarter. Squeaky hurried his outside shot and it caromed wide off the rim toward the stage. Tom had rebounding position and went toward the out-of-bounds line for the ball, intending to pass to Joe who was standing open underneath the basket. The Preacher was yelling "Watch low! Watch low!" meaning for Big Jake to cover Joe. Big Jake and John Tate, however, followed Tom, intending to shove him out of bounds. Tom knew why they were there. He leaped toward the stage, grabbed the ball, twisted, looked, and threw a high hard pass that struck John Tate square in the face, flattening his once-noble aquiline nose.

John Tate, who in that last instant had seen the fury in Tom's eyes and realized his intent, reeled back, dizzy with pain, his thick blood spattering the white sweaters of the cheerleaders sitting along the stage ledge. It was running in alarming amounts down his throat, choking him as he tried repeatedly to tell the leftside ref "He did that on purp..., he did that..., he did..." But the words just wouldn't come and the quarter buzzer announced the end of the first half.

The scoreboard read Town Team 32, Varsity 21.

———

The cheerleaders led an enthusiastic greeting when the Varsity returned from halftime break. The girls' loyalties were no longer split. Monica and Sally, making sure that John Tate suffered nothing worse than a broken nose, rallied the girls, including Sharon Sullivan who decided too late that Jim Levandowski had more appeal than Earl Steinbacker.

Of the Town Team, whose return greeting was polite applause, only the Preacher saw special significance in Sally Tate's emphatic cheer just before the game buzzer sounded: "Tom Donachy he's our man! If he can't do it..." here she paused and looked directly at Tom... "no one can."

At center court matchup the Town Team met a grim and well-conditioned squad of suddenly older boys. Harry Krotzer set the tone when he patted the bald spot on the top of DJ's head. "I'm gonna kick your ass," he whispered to the surprised DJ.

All eyes were on the leftside ref when he tossed the ball high at center jump. Tom jumped off Big Jake's foot, clucking him hard under the chin with his elbow as he went up. He reached the ball at its apex, sending it long downcourt to the Polack who easily beat his defender for the score. Big Jake, his tongue cut, slobbered like an offended St. Bernard.

The Town Team took the ball out and immediately ran into an intense man-to-man press. This defense required a lot of stamina. The Varsity's obvious game plan was to take it to the older, flabbier squad.

With their playmaker John Tate out of action, the Town Team relied on DJ and Earl Steinbacker to move the ball out front, working it to Big Jake in the middle and the Preacher and Bud Cole at the wings. The offensive plan made sense but didn't work.

DJ, without John Tate to back him up, was intimidated by the stocky soccer captain whom he knew by reputation and recent example to be real nasty. Earl was uneasy being guarded by his stronger rival, the Polack. Big Jake, with a swelling tongue and bone-bruised foot, was worrying about

263

making it to work tomorrow. This left the Preacher and Bud Cole to carry the load.

They couldn't do it by themselves as the Varsity pressed the Town Team relentlessly, scoring five times off DJ's and Earl's turnovers. Bud Cole sulked and, like a snake striking itself, stubbornly refused to let fresh men play. In less than six minutes they lost their big lead, the Varsity gaining the advantage 33 to 32.

Then, on a signal from court-general Tom, the Varsity backed off the press, allowing the Town Team to work their first offensive play.

The ball went to the Preacher, who was being guarded by Squeaky. Bud Cole set a pick on Squeaky, allowing the Preacher to drive toward the basket. The lumbering Big Jake missed clearing the lane and Tom loomed before the driving wingman, his right hand high. The Preacher decided to take his layup to the opposite side, using the rim as an obstacle to Tom's certain block attempt and draw a foul. The ruse worked, the Preacher looked good as he jumped and made the tricky shot that regained the lead and drew the foul, but he learned soon afterward *who really* planned that play.

Tom's right was hindered by the rim but his left wasn't and as they descended together his left hand deftly plucked the glasses from the Preacher's face and dropped them to the floor. The Preacher stepped on his own glasses when he landed.

"Dang it, Tom," he said. "Now I can't see."

Tom's answer was a portent of things to come. "Goin' easy on you, Preacher," he said.

The Preacher missed his foul shot badly and took himself out of the game. This was an instance, he decided, that nearsightedness probably was the Lord's blessing.

Bud Cole called for a time out. He had two men to replace as the suffering Big Jake sat down and like a spent horse refused to get back up. Bud Cole was getting tired too, but his competitive nature wouldn't let him quit. He replaced Jake with tall big-eared dairy farmer Bill Short and the

Preacher with Barry Johnson, the truck vendor for Windy View Egg Farm.

The subs were good players and fresh, but no match for Tom and Squeaky who still weren't breathing hard. Bud Cole decided to try a different tactic. He motioned for the rightside ref.

Play resumed with neither team scoring until the last ten seconds of the quarter. On the run, Tom intercepted a DJ pass at the top of the key and, finding himself all alone and ahead of any defender, dribbled the length of the court. The crowd noticed, many for the first time, that there was no awkwardness in the way he ran and handled the ball, nor in the way he leaped, holding the ball high in his big left hand, his forearm and elbow clearing the rim and jamming the ball home. The crowd roared its approval.

The effort signaled the Varsity had a lot of energy left with a whole quarter to go. At the buzzer the Varsity had the lead 35-34.

———

At center jump it was Bud Cole against Tom Donachy. They shook hands late, Bud Cole intending to hold on to Tom's hand, jerking him off balance as the ref threw up the ball. But the youth's big, work-hardened hand encased the man's in a grip of anger and iron, and squeezed so hard the pain forced Bud Cole to let go.

Tom got the jump, tipping it to the Polack who hit Squeaky downcourt for the score.

Bud Cole reproved his guards, "Can't you stop those guys?" he shouted.

DJ and Earl, knowing the Varsity had scored seven times in the third quarter to their one, weren't sure. The quicker team was capitalizing on their weaknesses bringing the ball down; Squeaky or Harry stealing the ball when DJ dribbled too high and Polack picking off Earl's telegraphed passes.

It was more of the same as the Varsity guards converted two more Town Team miscues into scores. Then, inexplicably, with a seven point lead, Tom called off his dogs.

The Varsity went to their zone defense, Tom staying higher in the post then before. They used the same formation on offense. In each case Tom stayed high and worked DJ's side.

Bud Cole, seeing the corners open, switched with Bill Short and soon after hit a long jumper for two. He kept complaining to the rightside ref about the roughness of the game and that ref obliged by calling two cheap fouls on Tom. The crowd showed its disgust by booing the ref.

After the third bad call on Tom, the scorekeeper buzzed an angry summons to the rightside ref. The scorekeeper was Mr. Bates, a pugnacious little man, a sports nut, a nut in general, but as Superintendent of Schools, a powerful nut. Knowing the salty nature of Mr. Bates, every spectator present yearned to hear that conversation.

"Brewster, if you keep that crap up you'll never referee in this county again."

"What crap?" responded Brewster, trying to look innocent.

"You know what I mean," snapped Mr. Bates. "You and Cole are as obvious as rat turds on the kitchen floor. Understand this. No one fouls out. I repeat, no one fouls out. Let 'em play their game. Got it?"

The rightside ref got it.

Play resumed. Mr. Bates' interruption enabled Bud Cole to gain a second wind, drawing on a reserve of strength, willing himself to ignore his bruised hand, beardburned face and blistered feet. He remembered Tom's wry crack about soft feet and bald heads and unconsciously felt his own receding hair line. In contrast MacEwen could go all day and had thick hair. The truth of Tom's prediction made him angrier.

He felt better after DJ hit him with a pass for another successful corner shot. That score and the one foul shot that was converted earlier brought them within two points of the Varsity. They could still win this game.

Tom promptly answered Cole's score with one of his own, a long clean jumper from the top of the key. Bud Cole gritted under his breath: "I didn't know he could shoot from outside!"

DJ brought the ball upcourt. He dribbled high toward Tom's side of the key, looking for Bud Cole or the egg man to get open underneath. Reacting swiftly, Harry and Squeaky pounced on him, catching him in a two-man trap, and knocked the ball loose. DJ, characteristically, shoved Squeaky out of his way and dove for the ball, his right hand reaching out to bring it in. Things were a jumble for DJ after that.

First there was the flash of a black sneaker, leaving behind the stale smell of canvas and rubber, then a stab of pain as Tom's other big foot descended upon DJ's wrist and ground it with a sharp crack into the hardwood floor. DJ rolled and looked at his right hand, which hung at an awkward angle, and yelled out in fear and pain: "Time-out! Time-out!" Then he yelled out again as he automatically tried to make the sign of the T with his hands.

The rightside ref blew the time out.

The crouching and moaning DJ was taken to the nurse's office, which by now was beginning to look like the emergency room at the hospital. Doc Buckley, who had just stuck a second ice cube on Big Jake's swollen tongue, asked what the score was and groused about missing a great game.

Bud Cole protested to the rightside ref, who told him to take his complaint to the scorekeeper.

"Did you see that!" shouted an indignant Bud Cole as he approached Mr. Bates.

"I saw that loudmouthed DJ stick his hand where it wasn't prudent," was the reply.

Bud Cole swore at Mr. Bates and stomped back to the bench.

Mr. Bates, who allowed no disrespect, buzzed him back. "Bud Cole," he said, his blue eyes blazing under bushy gray brows, "you asked for this game. Now play it." He paused for effect then added, "By the way, this is your last timeout."

In the stands directly behind Mac and Abigail were two college scouts sent there to recruit Bobby Richards. Seeing Bobby shut down in the first quarter they had decided to leave at halftime, but the exciting comeback engineered by Tom changed their minds. They were now scouting Tom. Abigail overheard their conversation.

"How does it stand now?" Said the one who had just returned from a quick trip to the men's room.

"Still four to two in favor of the big kid," responded the other.

"There's only one starter left for the Town Team," observed the first. "That fathead forward that thinks he's a coach."

"I know. I'll bet the big kid goes low the rest of the game," predicted the other.

"I'd bet on that too," said the first.

Abigail, no student of the game, and who had laughed when Bud Cole pulled down Tom's shorts, asked Mac what "going low" meant.

Mac had heard the scouts too. Coaches themselves, they had first noticed when Coach Anderson had given Tom his head. The Preacher had caught on next. Bud Cole hadn't figured it out yet.

"Going low means he's going to play closer to the basket," explained Mac, adding, "Against Bud Cole."

"This isn't a game, this is a fight!" retorted Abigail angrily.

"Which they started," countered Mac, finishing Abigail's sentence to make his point. He wondered if Abigail knew whose side she was on.

When play resumed, the rightside ref giving possession of the ball to the Town Team, Tom was low, standing next to Bud Cole.

Chuck Wetmore, a mechanic at Forbes Chevrolet, replaced DJ at guard and promptly threw the ball away, his wide eyes telling the Varsity he would rather be working under the hood of a car than playing in this game. Bud Cole saw it too and gave Tom a hard shove, a mindless act of exasperation. The crowd's roar of disapproval drowned out the leftside ref's whistle calling the foul.

It was at the foul line, while Tom calmly shot his two free throws, that the truth dawned on Bud Cole. Looking around, he realized he had lost his team, lost the crowd, lost the town, and as the second foul shot dropped cleanly through the cords for a six-point lead, lost the game. He lost his temper, too.

The score was Varsity 45, Town Team 39. Less than four minutes remained in the game.

In that time Bud Cole did what he could to get Tom Donachy. Jumping up behind Tom for a rebound, he came down on Tom's back, his weight knocking the youth to the floor. On another rebound play he clawed Tom's neck, leaving four ugly parallel welts that glistened with sweat and blood. In both instances Tom managed to score, increasing the lead and Bud Cole's frustration. It was leg to leg, hip to hip, elbow to elbow, shoulder to shoulder; Bud Cole struggling like an older lion to retain dominion, but the younger lion prevailed, the crowd watching their conflict more than the game.

Meanwhile the Varsity started running up the score, which they did by running. They ran constantly, their fast unrelenting style of play allowing the floundered Town Team no time to recover. They scored on fast breaks brought on by steals. They scored from retrieving their own rebounds. They scored from a complicated three-man weave play at the foul line that confused the Town Team defense and made them look foolish. They scored and scored. With less than a minute remaining, the Varsity led 59 to 39.

Worse than losing was losing bad. Losing by more than twenty was losing bad. The Varsity poured it on, telling the Town Team they were going to lose bad. The Town Team responded with renewed vigor, doing their best to prevent that kind of a rout. Bud Cole particularly couldn't accept a rout.

The game got out of control. The Preacher yelled at Bud Cole to take himself out. "For God's sakes man! Stop this nonsense before someone else gets hurt!"

Bud Cole stayed in, hoping for a chance, any chance, to hurt Tom Donachy, to get him out of the game, to prevent losing bad.

With twenty seconds left the Town Team secured possession of the ball. Chuck Wetmore finally hit Bud Cole with a pass in the deep corner, the corner by the stage. Bud Cole took the shot, but a tall figure leaped in front of him and caught the ball after it left his shooting hand. Bud Cole was livid, no one had ever rejected him so easily.

Tom came down in front of Bud Cole, holding the ball with both hands at chest height. Tom looked downcourt and exposed the ball, allowing it a little too far forward, and glanced back at Bud Cole. At that instant Bud Cole lunged for the ball, knowing the trick, knowing it was a maneuver taught the youth by Mac. He just couldn't resist one more chance at the boy and the ball.

Tom turned to the left as if to avoid the steal attempt, hesitated, then swung his shoulders swiftly and powerfully back, carrying a vicious high right elbow that caught the oncoming Bud Cole square in the mouth.

The hushed crowd heard the impact, a squishy smack of hard on soft tissue, like meat being tenderized by a cleaver. The blow knocked Bud Cole off his feet and he sat bloodied and dazed on the floor, his winning smile gone forever.

Tom threw a long baseball pass to Squeaky who made the layup for the final score. The buzzer sounded the end of the game, Varsity 61, Town Team 39. Bud Cole's front teeth crunched under Tom's right foot as he walked off the gym floor.

Chapter 40 – The Robbing of Mort Fessler

Jesse Poorbaugh admired the rattlesnake. Nothin' kills better with so little risk to itself, he declared. The snake plans his ambush then attacks. He coils up where he can't be seen, lashes out, then coils up again. Hunts best at night, when his eyes widen into catlike ovals. And he stays quiet when he kills. His rattlin's a warnin'. Just like a man. If he's talkin', he ain't killin'. He's threatenin'. Quiet ain't peace, it's danger.

So Samuel, when you're huntin' and waitin', think of yourself as a rattler. Time and comfort mean nothin' to a snake.

———

Behind Mort Fessler's cellar door he coiled and waited. Light from the hallway streamed through the cracks around the door. His own catlike eyes had grown used to the dark, now he had to get them adjusted to the light. He peered through the crack. His prey wandered between the kitchen and office, passing within inches of taut-muscled and patient danger. Within inches of one cold-blooded oval eye getting used to the light.

At present he was relying most on sound and smell. In the kitchen to his right was activity. The hinges of the woodbox creaked as the cover was lifted and stove wood removed. Later the stove's cast door was opened and some wet wood placed on sputtering coals. Then tap water gushed into a kettle.

All this took time, but time meant nothing to a rattler.

Actually, it hadn't been a long wait. Mort had returned from town early, deviating some from his pattern. Still, he was ready.

He moved his head a bit and peered through with the other eye. He was waiting for sounds to his left, one in particular. He had been in the cellar before. Mort would take his tea into the office, light a cigar, and open the safe.

271

When the floorboards groaned over the cinderblock posts supporting the safe, the rattler would strike.

He closed his eyes. Mort passed by the door to the office. The cup and saucer clinked together on his desk. A match was scratched and the acrid scent of sulfur came through the crack in the door. Soon after came drifts of cigar smoke. Then the tongue-and-groove creaked by the safe.

The rattler uncoiled, began his stalk.

————

Mort was pleased. Considering the circumstances; the game, and the Tannery down to four days, the night's take had been pretty good. He knelt down and turned the safe dial. Right three times, left twice, right once, then left to open. He could feel the tension when he found the correct numbers, a spring load within the door. If he missed a number the tension released and he had to start over. Not so tonight as the heavy door clicked open to reveal an inside steel door painted with fancy scrollwork that said the safe was patented in 1887, in December.

He swung that door open to reveal wrapped stacks of cash filling compartments according to denomination – hundreds, fifties, twenties, with one compartment for unassorted small stuff. There was also some gas ration stamps left over from World War Two. The lowest compartment held account books and a couple folded canvas bank bags. He reached for the loan book. A draft stirred the loose papers in the safe, bringing with it the pungent odor of the cellar. Charley must not have latched the door. He'd see to it directly. That draft was cold.

Yes, it had been a good night. Bravo Burton had finally paid his bet and insisted on a rematch. He'd gotten Tom's five and would give that to him tomorrow. He wished he'd had a boy like Tom. He wasn't sure where his own son was.

Yes, it had been a good week. The crew had a goodly pile of timber ready for tomorrow's drive. Mac would best that cocksure Bud Cole. Shut them down would he?

Yes, it had been a good...life.

———

Saul Poorbaugh's Bowie quivered with the body. Spike left it there, stuck at the base of Mort's skull. If he pulled it out the wound might bleed.

He went through Mort's pockets, removing his car keys and cash. He stuffed all the wrapped cash from the safe into one of the canvas bags. He left the small stuff and didn't bother with the other items. He couldn't read what they were anyway.

He left the house and put the money bag in the front seat of Mort's Chrysler and opened the trunk. He put Mort's coat on him, carried him to the car, and carefully laid him in. He didn't want any blood in there either.

He returned to the house and closed the safe. He wore tight leather gloves. He knew about fingerprints. He emptied Mort's cup and placed it back with the saucer. He let the teakettle whistle on the stove. He let Mort's cigar burn down in the ashtray. The house would look as if Mort planned to return soon and didn't.

He closed the cellar and front doors, left the lights on, and drove off in Mort's car. Years ago Mort had taught him to drive and later picked up his jeep for him at auction. His name was in Mort's book, too, but that loan was almost paid off. Mort never had to dun him for money! He always paid on time.

He felt no remorse. Rattlers didn't have any. Mort was going to kick him off the land and give it to MacEwen. Now the land was like The Lady's, no one's but his for twenty more years. He still had a score to settle with MacEwen. He wondered if he still owed for the loan.

He stopped the car in the parking area before the steel bridge. It was dark at Evie's store. Few lights were on in Buttonwood or in the foothills. Most folks were at the doin's in town. There were few vehicles on 15 and none on Williamson Trail. Lightning flashed to the north from a thunder-

273

storm on Bloss Mountain. That storm would be here soon. Time to move.

He pulled Mort out of the trunk and closed the lid quietly. He removed the knife, wiped it on his trousers, and sheathed it. He shouldered the body, carried it along the walkway to the center of the stream, and dropped it over the railing. Blockhouse was swelling already from the storm up north, running swift and black and oily. Ford Irish had probably opened the milk plant's sewer valves again.

He went back to the car, transferred the keys from the trunk to the ignition, grabbed the moneybag, and walked away. Only then did he remove his gloves.

The setup looked good. Poor Mort: came down to check on the rollaway and high water and fell in. Pointed limb rammed into his head.

He walked along the creek bank to the rollaway, then took the log road up to the lower landing on Blackwolf, crossed the foothill to the junkyard and climbed the switchback to Caleb's Rock. The steep side by Three Oaks was much more direct and quicker but dangerous at night. He didn't want to plummet into Blacksnake's grave or end up a skeleton in a tree with his dogs.

———

He did not venture far out on Caleb's Rock. That red shale was slippery near the edge. Cars were streaming down 15. Must be the doin's at the school were over.

He found the hollow chestnut and stuffed the moneybag high up inside. He kept Mort's roll in his pocket. Must be three hundred in there. That would stand him a good while.

The storm hit him hard as he crossed Potash. The cold driving rain plastered his hair to his face and neck and soaked him to the skin. He didn't shiver. Rattlers never showed discomfort. Blacksnake rode point on Brother Westwind, roaring like a locomotive pulling a cargo of rain. Rain that would wash away his tracks and the few drops of Mort's blood. Songbird would say it couldn't wash away his sin. Jesse would say how many rattlers give a damn about sin?

He felt an irresistible urge to laugh out loud, and he did. In that laugh was more mania than humor. It was threatening, like the snake's rattle. Madness, creeping madness, was funny.

Chapter 41 – The Flood

Storm clouds whirled above Steam Valley at night while folks went about their business. Squeaky, Tom and Joe were headed for a victory celebration at the Turkey Ranch. Mac and Abigail were off to her apartment. Bud and Delia Cole had scheduled an emergency appointment with their dentist. Julie and Nan were taking Amanda to spend the night with them. Spike Poorbaugh wandered in the rain on Potash. And Mort Fessler floated in the rain down Blockhouse. The creek, the clouds, and the people were uneasy.

———

The boys were bunched together in Tom's pickup, near the end of a slow-moving line of traffic southbound on 15. Squeaky spoke first: "Bet you don't ever play for the Town Team, Tom."

"Probably not," agreed Tom.

"Bud Cole's gonna think of you every time he puts his teeth in a jar," said Joe.

They laughed.

"Wonder what he'll do?" remarked Squeaky.

"Something," said Joe. "You can count on that."

Squeaky, sitting in the middle, felt Tom tense up. He changed the subject. "What did those scouts say, Tom?"

"Offered a scholarship. College deferment. Job. The works."

"A free ride?"

"Yep. A free ride."

"What did you say?" asked Joe.

"I'd think about it."

"What did Mac say?" asked Squeaky, exasperated at his friend's indecision, hoping the older brother would put some sense in Tom.

"He said it was my decision."

"Jeez. A free ride," repeated Squeaky. "You'd better take it, Tom."

"We'll see."

They were quiet for a while, each occupied with his own thoughts. Rain pelted the pickup. The windshield wipers beat steady against the rain. The surface water from the road sprayed the floorboards of the truck. Finally, Joe said it: "You know, this was our last game."

"That's sad," said Squeaky.

"That is sad," said Tom.

———

Several cars back, Julie was sorting some things out in her own mind. Delia had found her after the game and asked her to take Amanda for the night. While talking they noticed Mac escorting Abigail from the gym. Julie had seen them when she came in and had a whole game to steel her emotions. Julie Spencer was expert at controlling her emotions.

"It appears that Mac has made up his mind," observed Delia.

Julie took a breath. "Looks that way."

"Talk to him, Julie. She's pushy. You're not."

"That's hard."

"Not as hard as losing him. Mac does not express his feelings. I know. I pursued Mac. Bud pursued me. I knew Bud loved me. I never knew with Mac. I still don't. A woman's got to know."

Delia's beautiful dark eyes glistened. She bit her lower lip and looked away. The evening's conflicts were telling on her too.

"How is Bud?" asked Julie.

"Raving."

"I'm sorry."

"I'm not. Bud's had it coming. He's had it coming a long time."

Driving home Julie analyzed what Delia said. She said Bud loved her. She didn't say she loved him. Delia was still in love with Mac.

Julie tried to examine the situation practically, unemotionally. The solution made her want to cry, which she couldn't do with Nan and Amanda in the car. Three women loved Jonathan MacEwen. Two had had babies by other men. One was as fresh as a spring daisy. And she was aggressive. She had the edge.

Delia was wrong. It wouldn't do any good to talk with Jonathan MacEwen.

———

Protected by the wide front porch, Mac and Abigail said goodnight. The rain poured heavy around them. Mac returned her umbrella. Abigail was reluctant to end their evening so early. She didn't care what Aunt K or the neighbors would think. "Want to come up?" she said brightly. "I'll put on a pot of coffee."

"I'd better not. I should be with Tom and the team."

...But not there with me, she thought.

She knew she blew it at the game. She never quite understood the rivalry between the brothers MacEwen and Donachy and Bud Cole. Her disapproval showed.

She stood on her tiptoes and kissed Mac goodnight. The dim porch light hid her hurt feelings. She heard him slosh out in the rain, open his car door, start up and drive off.

Her head told her what her heart was increasingly reluctant to admit. She was losing Jonathan MacEwen. She went upstairs and went to bed. Had Mac responded as planned she would not have slept alone.

———

Mac did not go directly to the Turkey Ranch. Before leaving town he went home and made a phone call.

A tired voice answered: "Hello?"

"Mrs. Spencer? This is Mac. Is Julie home yet?"

"No."

"Tell her, if she wants to, I'll come by and take her to the game party."

There was a pause, and a disappointed sigh. "She won't be able to, Mac."

"Oh?"

"Danny's sick...just a stomach bug. But he needs his mother right now."

"Will you tell her I called?"

"Sure."

"Thanks. Goodnight."

"Goodnight."

Julie arrived a half hour after Mac's call, right when Danny became violently sick in the bathroom.

Distracted, Mary Spencer forgot to tell her daughter Mac had called.

———

The clouds continued their whirling and folks went home and slept. By midnight most lights were out in Steam Valley.

Meanwhile the rain poured down and Blockhouse started to swell. Mort Fessler was carried to the log boom and dutifully diverted to the millpond, which was beginning to lose its placid nature. Mort slept an eternal sleep.

High up on Potash, Spike Poorbaugh rested in a cave. He did not sleep.

He sat on a flat rock, wrapped in a wool army blanket taken from the cache in the cave, and stared out at the slanting rain. The light of one candle flickered from its niche along the cave wall. He had not built a fire. There was no place for the smoke to go. Blacksnake no longer wailed. Even he had taken cover from the rain. The night belonged to the clouds and the rain.

Grandmother Songbird said demon spirits were afraid of rain, that the Good Spirit had used water to flush evil from the earth one time. Jesse allowed He done a bad job of flushin', 'cause badness sure as hell was still here. He-Who-Walks-On-Earth must 'a found a high dry place and sealed

279

himself in for forty nights and days. Then came out and started raising hell again. How else could badness be explained?

Songbird didn't argue.

The trapper figured the storm would let up by dawn. But this was an unusual hard rain. It should be snow. He thought it was still February. Blockhouse would be on a tear come mornin'.

They may never find Mort Fessler.

———

The flood of '55 started from a cloudburst that lingered over Bloss Mountain. The ground had already absorbed all the water it could and rejected the rest. The rejected rainfall ran halfway down the mountain and ponded in Cole Enterprise's deepest strip mine. Bud Cole had laid the dragline crew off because of the wet weather. His order caught them by surprise and they left without cutting any drains.

The long trench filled with restless water, becoming a restless mountain lake one thousand feet above the head of Steam Valley; a lake contained by a breastwork of loose mine tailings and uncompacted fill.

Water from a cloudburst has an urgent purpose about it. It cannot be contained. It has a goal, a destination. This particular group of clouds wanted to regroup in the Chesapeake Bay and got lucky. They had unleashed on the south side of the mountain. If the rain had let go on the north it would have been a much longer trip.

The persistent water permeated the base of the breastwork, softening the soil under a large boulder on the outside surface of the trench. The boulder loosened, tipped, and started rolling down the steep slope. It started fast, like it wanted to be the first to get out of there.

It was, but just barely.

A geyser of mud and black sludge blew out of the hole left by the boulder and spewed further as the hole grew bigger. Other geysers followed, exploding in sequence like planted charges of dynamite. The water sliced through the bottom of the breastwork and one-half of the strip mine, one-eighth of the side of a mountain, slid in pursuit of the boulder.

Blockhouse Creek began as a roaring branch on the south slope of Bloss Mountain. A powerful stream, it had carved out a deep gully down the mountain and foothills and high side banks through the valley. Fallbrook, after a half-century of bad experiences with the unpredictable creek, had protected itself in the thirties with a stone-walled levee. The dike could withstand a flash flood carrying a twelve-foot wave.

The slide caught up to the boulder just before it bounced into the gully. The slide spilled into the ravine, filled it, and jetted downstream, a thick, churning, ten-foot high mixture of earth and water, but mostly water. The boulder became a miniscule part of the mixture.

A flood is measured in terms of human suffering. If a whole lot of people aren't cruelly affected the event is more a disturbance than a disaster. Such was the case with the flood of '55. Three feet higher, though, and the governor would have called out the National Guard.

The only folks adversely affected were Bud Cole, Harry Raker, Jonathan MacEwen and Mort Fessler. Bud Cole inevitably benefited from the flood. Harry and Mac were hurt by it, Mac particularly, and Mort Fessler required a closed casket at his funeral.

The flood surged through Fallbrook before sunrise, just as the rain let up. Constricted by the high levee walls, the flow swelled in the middle to a sharklike fin that sliced and smashed whatever it was able. It rammed the boom from the dragline into the bottom of the main street bridge, and blew muck and flood trash back through Cole Enterprise's sewer drains into the milk plant. Ford Irish had fallen asleep on the job and failed to close the plant's gate valves.

Although the entire main level of the plant had to be cleaned with disinfectant and repainted, Bud Cole still gained. The dragline was insured and the slide exposed a new vein of coal that justified Bud Cole's investment and made borrowing for operations and expansion easy. It also heightened the tycoon's desire for more coal-bearing mountains.

Downstream, a huge rock split the channel just north of the covered bridge and saved the bridge from the finlike wave. Normally the rock was a small island. The stream split, rolled along either side and rejoined behind it. This time the fin hit the rock at an angle, deflected into the east bank and around the bridge, and scoured a six-foot deep trench through the road and a thousand yards of Harry Raker's best bottomland. It then joined the main channel north of the steel bridge in Buttonwood. It would take Harry and Carol and her husband ten years to reclaim that land. Like Bud Cole, the Raker's had the resources to withstand their loss.

Jonathan MacEwen and Tom Donachy did not.

Mac had been right about the steel bridge. It was built strong. The main current ran against the east abutment, then swung along the west bank of the creek the entire length of Jacob's Landing, before being forced to the center by the narrow notch between the bases of Laurel and Blackwolf mountains. The current and high banks made the west side the perfect spot for the rollaway.

The fin took the same route and the grinding collision of the swift abrasive water against the stationary concrete abutment awoke Evie Todd. The bridge scraped and creaked and groaned and held firm, and the fin, containing untold tons of weight and pressure, veered off and raced away.

For a few seconds Evie was glad. The next sounds, though, made her sick at heart for Mac and Tom.

The fin ran hard against the west bank and undercut the rollaway. The sickening sound Evie heard was the din of a thousand rolling logs tumbling into the frenzied water.

The fin had lost some height coursing through the valley but entered the notch carrying new weight and power – a thousand battering rams. The constriction through the notch raised it higher, and the added volume from Packhorse Run joining from the east ran it faster. It was ten feet high again and gaining when it reached Sheafer's mill and the wider, flatter expanses of Little Pine River.

The fin snapped the log boom like a matchstick, converted the millpond into a whirlpool, and swept all the logs stacked and unscaled at the mill landing downriver. Mac's logs would end up beached and irretrievable, many floating as far as the Susquehanna River. A few became driftwood in the Chesapeake Bay.

A misty daylight prevailed. People drove by the stream, curious to see the damage done. Several carloads of gawkers stopped and watched the battered body circle around and around and around the whirlpool. Finally Luke Ballard hooked it with a set of timber grabs attached to a long rope. God, he prayed it wasn't Mort. But who else could it be? His car was parked at the bridge and he wasn't home.

It has stopped raining. Overhead the sun was trying to break through the clouds. Menacing clouds they were, lean and gray, like rats, on their way back to the Chesapeake.

Chapter 42 – The Brick Church

Mort Fessler was buried at the Brick Church. Squire Hayes, his executor, made the arrangements. Durwood Klinger conducted the service. Aunt K played the organ. Tom struggled through another farewell song. Mac and the timber crew acted as pallbearers. The church was packed. The affable junkman, who dealt squarely with the rich and the poor, the honest and the not-so-honest, the believer and the heathen, had a big funeral.

At the gravesite the Preacher committed Mort's soul to heaven and his body to earth. No next-of-kin made it to the funeral. Grimfaced Charley Bower threw in the first handful of dirt, Julie Spencer the second, Posey Alexander the third, the crowd followed suit and somberly left.

The Squire stayed by the grave and threw in the last handful of dirt. For the first time he noticed the day. The sun hung low in the south, diffused by a frosty winter haze. There was a stiff breeze, the temperature was just above freezing, a warm day for February. That was good. Squire never heard anyone say they wanted to be buried on a cold day.

The Brick Church sat on a high meadow, had a tall white steeple and could be seen for miles around, a beacon for the living and the dead. The gravestones were arranged in neat rows, almost surrounding the 125-year-old church. Their non-conformity added to the beauty and mystery of the place. Little Joyce Bower, who died in 1919, had a stone that was scarcely a one-foot cube. Zebulon Cole, who died the same year, had a monument that was also a cube. His was a concrete mausoleum ten foot high and wide and frescoed with angels blowing horns. The display had a purpose. Zebulon needed to impress the angels. Little Joyce did not.

The headstone of Jim Morningstar was next to Mort's. The Squire had settled Jim's estate as well. His grave looked like it had been there for years, yet Jim had been gone less than three months. The ground should be disturbed like Mort's. Of course the stone was only symbolic; Jim did not lay there. His son, James, Jr., was born Sunday. Missy had delivered early.

Damn you, Samuel.

Charley Bower was convinced Jim and Mort were murdered and Spike Poorbaugh was their killer. But Jim was only presumed dead and Mort's death was ruled accidental.

Bull, scoffed Charley. Mort's hat still hung on its hook and the safe only contained 352 dollars. Mort was bald and didn't like the cold. He never ventured out without his hat. And he always kept at least ten thousand in that safe.

The state police said that wasn't enough to convict a man of murder.

The attorney caught the subtlety in the police response. They said convict, not suspect.

The Squire suspected him too. He feared for his friends in Steam valley. He feared for anyone coming in contact with the trapper. He feared also for his friend, the trapper.

Samuel was his friend. He owed his life to Samuel. He was Samuel's only friend. His loyalty to his captain was what kept him restrained all these years. Apparently those restraints had worn thin over time and recent circumstances.

Samuel Poorbaugh was an accomplished killer. He came from a line of killers. Saul and Jesse killed out of hate and lust and greed. They were always fighting someone and always had women and money. Folks often wondered where the money came from. The bounty hunter's money was more booty than bounty, but they had never been tried for a robbery or killing. The Squire doubted their progeny would either.

He recalled an incident they covered up in France.

The girl had been the belle of the ball and sneaked off into the woods behind the chalet with her officer escort. She returned hysterical and alone, her blue gown torn and soiled. Her lover lay gutted under some trees, his orange tunic and wide leather belt slit cleanly through. The killer had "taken" her she said. He was very tall and very strong. That was all she could say. Tall and strong. Tall and strong.

They moved out the next day. The officer had been a political appointee, not a real soldier, and was married. The girl was a local coquette and only sixteen. The French high command was embarrassed. The guard on duty was the Rainbow Division's tallest, strongest, and most ruthless scout. He was needed on the line. His captain never assigned him to duty near civilians again.

The lawyer shivered but not from the cold. Samuel Poorbaugh was around civilians again and was not heeding his captain.

The wind picked up. The Squire moved over to the Cole monument and leaned against it, out of the stiffer breeze. The excavation contractor had installed the cover over Mort's vault. He turned his backhoe, and with the shovel end started backfilling the grave. Soon they could all go home.

Two tombstones side by side. Samuel's work. He had controlled his urges for almost forty years. Now he was reverting back to a composite of Saul and Jesse. He had killed Jim out of hate and Mort out of greed. Who would he kill out of lust? Did that passion still rage within him? It had for Jesse, who remained robust and only died after a feral boar slashed a leg artery when he was a very old man. Compared with his father Samuel had at least three decades of vigor left. He may even be tougher. He had Indian blood and had managed to survive four decades in the mountains alone. Who could stop a man like him?

The only one capable was Mac. Charley Bower might have, in his younger days. Although an adept woodsman and former soldier, Charley was not a trained killer like Samuel or Mac. Charley did have the older man's good sense to know that Poorbuagh should be ambushed and let lay. The trapper had turned into a predator, a mankiller that had to be eliminated. Mac was too highminded to take the law in his own hands. He would react if attacked. Samuel was too deadly to be given that advantage.

The law! Sometimes it didn't work. Mac was civilized. Poorbaugh was not. In this case the law inhibited justice.

Mac was the root of the problem. His return unsettled the lives of Samuel Poorbaugh and Bud Cole. In each case Mac's threat was more imagined than real. Unprovoked, Mac would not have taken away Samuel's hunting and trapping privileges. The area was too vast and rugged to control anyway. And he was not after Bud Cole's wife. He just wanted to be left alone, get to know his brother, and develop his land. Neither Poorbaugh nor Cole would accept intrusion into what each perceived as his domain, with the result that their holds on their respective domains were weakening.

Tom Donachy's elbow broke more than Bud Cole's front teeth – it broke the factoryman's chokehold on the town as well. Tom put on a show the town would never forget. Bud Cole was powerful, but no longer unchallenged. There were other factories, other jobs. Cars were available and affordable now, the men could drive to their jobs. The first-shift men, led by O'Conner, were openly talking union. The second and third shifts weren't as militant. Eventually they would come around. Tannerytown would soon be demanding more from the tannery, not vice versa.

When Bud Cole's team was defeated it signified he was vulnerable. If the upstart Varsity could win, the upstart union could too.

The factoryman continued to scheme. He didn't give up easy, Bud Cole. Mort hadn't been dead a day before Jonas Pemberton called about buying Mort's land on Potash. The state police commander, a crony of Cole's, had seen the will. Jonas said the Cole's never did like the junkyard near their estate. While that was probably true, they never tried to buy it from Mort either.

That reason was a smokescreen. Potash Mountain offered an easier access to Bear Mountain and its coal. With the flood taking Mac's timber they probably thought Mac would give up and they could buy him out. But Mac was connected with the land now. He'd never sell. It bothered Squire that Cole Enterprises was willing to spend a lot of effort and money just to get close to Bear Mountain.

Cole and Pemberton were overlooking the greatest risk – Samuel. He might tolerate logging because he feared Mac-Ewen and knew Mac's methods wouldn't hurt the hunting and trapping. But he wouldn't fear Bud Cole. And he would never tolerate strip mining. Never. Bud and Jonas were risking a lot more than Cole Enterprises money. An *awful* lot more.

They were scheming at the bank too. Steve Heffner had been sly and evasive. Rom Barbano had not been his usual hearty self. Something was on his mind. The shoemaker was the swing vote on the five-member bank board. Bud and Jonas had been courting him since August, since the Squire assumed ownership of the Longsdorf bank shares.

The bank's annual Reorganization Meeting was a month away. Bud Cole wanted to retain his chairmanship even though tradition awarded that position to the largest share-holder. Tradition, not charter. The directors could choose someone else but had to gain the support of a majority of the shareholders. Even if Rom voted with Jonas and Bud, Squire felt he would carry the majority of shareholders.

Squire wanted the chairmanship mainly because he didn't want Bud Cole to have it. The bank president reported to the chairman, which gave the factoryman access and influence the other directors did not have. The president and chairman ran the bank until they were held in check by enough dissenting directors or shareholders. That occasion had not arisen. Yet. Squire still touched base with Helen Kuhl every day.

Rom owned enough stock to be sought-after, but not enough to be threatening to Bud Cole. He could be made into a pawn. He was never dependent on the tannery, but now his son worked there. The Sunday paper featured Lundy and Maria and their new baby boy while announcing Lundy's promotion to purchasing agent. Lundy was rising fast. Two more-experienced executives had been passed over and the office wives were buzzing. Lundy and Maria would have to move from the bungalow they shared with Rom in Tannerytown to a house in Fallbrook proper. They didn't have any money. Rom would have to buy it for them.

Squire shut down Mort's junk business and started compiling his assets. He hit three quarters of a million before adding the junkyard and two thousand acres on Potash. He had to find out what a junkyard was worth. Did it increase or decrease the value of the land? Besides the rows of junked vehicles the yard contained a good house, a large barn, and a new repair garage. He let Mac continue to use the garage. In return Mac agreed to maintain the place.

He had to admit the complex was the perfect location for the headquarters of a strip mine. But why buy the headquarters before buying the mine?

He hired a detective agency to find Mort's heirs – the wife who deserted him and the son she took with her. She was much younger than Mort so she was probably still alive. They had never divorced. The son would be a young man now.

Wife and son split everything. The will was in the safe, unchanged since the Squire wrote it for him in the early thirties. He waited twenty years for her to come back. She didn't and there was no contact from the son either. Maybe she had turned the son against his father.

There were indications Mort was changing his mind about his estate. On the back of the envelope containing the will were penciled notations giving $25,000 each to Charley Bower, Julie Spencer, and Missy Morningstar. To Jonathan MacEwen and Tom Donachy went the junkyard and Potash Mountain. The commander hadn't seen the envelope.

The notes weren't signed or witnessed. Mort hadn't lived to formalize the changes. Squire wished he could declare the notes valid changes, but knew he couldn't risk it. Mort's footloose wife could successfully challenge him in court.

That was the trouble with handling estates. The ones whose companionship and business you enjoyed were dead. The ones you preferred not to associate with weren't.

The grave was filled in. The backhoe operator changed from the shovel seat to the tractor seat, lowered the wide front-end bucket and backbladed the grave until it was level. Then he raised the bucket and backed carefully down the path between the rows of gravestones. Squire tipped his hat to Mort's marker and followed.

G. Morton Fessler, March 18, 1885 – February 10, 1955, was buried.

Chapter 43 – The Note

Bud Cole brooded at his corner table in the Hotel Fall-brook. The banker, typically, was late. He ordered his lunch and his second double scotch. He wasn't much of a drinker, a few beers sometimes with the boys after a game or a match, but lately he had developed a fondness for the smoky taste of scotch. The strong whisky took some of the edge off. Helped him think.

Every morning the factoryman took stock, examined how he stood, and prioritized his day. Mort Fessler's funeral interrupted his routine. With Heffner being late he had time to think.

Where did he stand? What were the pros and cons? Usually, for him, the pros outweighed the cons. The scales tipped in his favor. They always had.

There were those the business gods favored and those they didn't. One could fall in a pile of goose shit and find a golden egg. Another could fall in a nest of golden eggs, break them all, and emerge only hanging on to a turd.

The hostess brought his drink, smiled the suggestive smile of an opportunist who knew a good tipper and was willing to offer more for the money, then swung back to the bar. She was in her twenties, and shapely. Her backside swayed provocatively and he felt a twinge of desire. And caution. She was a homewrecker, that one.

He always transferred that desire to Delia and was rarely disappointed. He sometimes felt her appetite that way was stronger than his own. He recalled Pemberton's advice to his father and grandfather regarding getting caught in infidelity: "Deny, deny, deny; they *want* to believe you!"

So far he hadn't needed Pemberton's advice on that subject.

He stirred the ice in the scotch then took a sip. The drink was good; iced charcoal that started out cold then ignited on the way down. He put the woman out of his mind and got back to business, back to the pros and cons.

He ran down the pros first. The coal vein the slide exposed on Bloss Mountain; the credit line approval from Dauphin Deposit; Mort Fessler's death; the new order from Hanover Shoes.

The credit line and Hanover order they'd worked hard to get. Now he had some working capital; he could put the men back on six days. He could buy whatever he wanted. The coal vein and Mort's death were gifts from the gods. His feelings were mixed about the junkman. Mort had treated him kindly when he was a boy and he'd always liked him... until he got friendly with local hero MacEwen.

He took another sip and ran down the cons. The rail line, the milk plant, the union, Bear Mountain...McEwen.

The Fall Book Line had suffered major flood damage. If he didn't buy it New York Central would shut it down. Pemberton advised buying the line and repairing the tracks. But trucks were the coming thing. Railroads were on their way out. Sometimes Pemberton couldn't let go of the past. Bud Cole wanted a fleet of trucks. The Edward T. Johnson, stranded in the tanyard, would leave by truck.

The milk plant was now losing money and also needed extensive repairs. He refused to give up on the plant. He rarely gave up on anything. Maybe they should switch from powdered milk to cheese. The garlic and spaghetti eaters in Tannerytown would like that.

The union. O'Conner was raising the rabble again. The trouble was concentrated on first shift. The Company was quietly training an extra beam house man on third right now. When that man was trained he got the third shift job, the regular man on third went to second, and second went to first. O'Conner went out the door, heaved out by his boss. With O'Conner went the union.

The union advocates got busy after the Donachy kid decked him. They figured he'd crawl off into a hole for a few days. He hadn't. He got temporary caps on his front teeth that night and went to work Saturday morning, supervising flood repairs. Jake Callahan and John Tate couldn't get out of bed. The pansies!

He took a big sip and sloshed some of the ice around the inside of his sore mouth. It felt good. Cool then warm. He was still tender from that elbow. He'd gotten knocked on his ass by an eighteen-year-old boy. In front of the whole town no less! Publicly he would have to shrug and smile his new smile and admit he was getting too old for that stuff and say oh what the hell, it was only a game. Privately he had plans for that boy. He would pay.

Bear Mountain. Careful plans were being made to gain control of that land. MacEwen and Poorbaugh would have to be evicted. He had MacEwen in the bag. Poorbaugh stumped him.

The easiest access to Bear was the trail by the Poorbaugh cabin. Originally he had intended on wrangling a right-of-way from Mort. Now he could buy everything cheap and get rid of that unsightly junkyard. Now he had the money to buy it.

If Poorbaugh killed Mort, he did it to tie up the land. That made the trapper a serious problem. He had shrewdly bought time and control without paying one dime for it. That made Poorbaugh a very smart, very bad man.

He doubted the trapper did it. He wasn't that shrewd. He was simply an illiterate hermit with a bad reputation, one he inherited from his outlaw ancestors. People just heeded the Squire's advice and let him alone. Mort wasn't murdered. He just drank too much cider, went to look at the high water, and fell in.

He dismissed Poorbaugh as a significant con. He'd bulldoze the smelly bastard out of the way when the time came. Hell, the man had to be in his late fifties. Maybe he'd die up there and solve a problem for him like Mort had done. Become another blessing from the business gods.

He took another sip. The whisky was tasting better, was warming him and numbing the pain in his mouth. It was helping him think.

MacEwen was the most immediate threat. All the other cons could wait. Mac had to be dealt with first. Mac was proud and honorable. If it looked like he stiffed the bank for a lot of money his pride would be shattered. He'd leave. His kid brother would leave. Maybe Amanda's teacher would leave too. Heffner sure hadn't made any headway there. She showed up at the game with MacEwen.

Mac could have her. She was too skinny for him. He preferred the busty calendar girl types that adorned the walls in Rom's shoe repair shop. Women with bodies like that hostess or Delia or Julie Spencer. If he lost Delia, he'd pursue Julie Spencer. Why wasn't Mac bedding Julie Spencer?

Was it Delia? Did they have a thing going? She had gotten friskier since Mac came back. He'd heard of that. The ardor of the female increases when there's competition. Was she accommodating two men? Or was it coincidental? At the beach house they had discussed having another child. More than discussed, actually. They, he, wanted a boy. She was probably trying to give him his son. But did she still love Mac? When they made love was she pretending to be with him? He'd always wondered that.

He didn't want to lose his wife. He loved Delia. And Amanda. He may not say it or show it but he loved them. If she did go, he'd take her back. He wouldn't wait in vain for twenty years either. He'd find her and go get her.

Pemberton advised forgiving once. They're always loyal once they've been forgiven. Pemberton had some experience here. He'd outlived three wives.

Yes, he'd take her back. He'd forgive her. But he would never forgive the man that took her! He'd kill that man, and have the right to do it.

Could he kill MacEwen? He had never killed. What was it Poorbaugh said under the bridge? "If you're lucky, and he ain't lookin', you might do it." The insolent son-of-a-bitch! What the hell did he know?

Mac had been merciless with those drillers. Maimed them on purpose. He knew how; he was a commando for chrissakes!

Bud Cole set down his near-empty glass and examined his thick forearms and hands. The fighting they were trained for was brawling. He'd just lost a brawl to Tom Donachy. The older brother was heavier and stronger and had killed in the army. That's what all his medals were for – killing.

If MacEwen didn't leave, maybe he'd have another talk with Poorbaugh. Challenge the leathery bastard. See if he was as mean as they said. Give him another chance.

Poorbaugh had not kept their bargain. MacEwen was still in business. The trapper hadn't stopped him as agreed. Different methods were required to stop MacEwen.

His subconscious ramblings were interrupted by Steve Heffner pulling out a chair. Dammit! He wasn't done yet!

"Mourning the death of our biggest depositor, Bud?"

Bud Cole composed himself and looked up. "I liked Mort," he said, thinking back. "But I'm not sad he's dead."

The banker smelled whisky breath and realized his boss was mildly in his cups. He sat down and lit a Lucky. "Hard to believe, a junkman leaving a hundred grand in cash."

The remark offended Bud Cole. Bankers should have money. Junkmen shouldn't. The snooty ass! Bud Cole dug him a little. "That's just in our bank. Some of the locals spread their money. Jonas said Fessler had accounts in every bank in two counties."

"How'd he get it?"

"Made it and saved it." Bud Cole himself had trouble with the latter. The banker did too.

"How much?"

"Half a million, at least."

"Who gets it?"

"Wife and son and government."

"I didn't know he was married."

"Few did. Wife ran off with a sharpie when I was a kid. Mort kept his mouth shut and folks forgot."

The hostess brought the factoryman's lunch and a martini for Steve Heffner. The banker was a more regular customer and single, yet she rubbed against Bud Cole like a purring cat. The extra attention the shapely golddigger paid the married man irritated the banker. She was after big money, not his.

Little did she know! Mort Fessler kept more on deposit than Bud Cole. Heffner ordered quick. He didn't want her and her distractions hanging around. After she left he leaned closer to Bud Cole: "Jonas mention anything from the Squire about Fessler guaranteeing the note?"

"No. I never told Jonas either."

"Good. Fessler obviously didn't leave any record, so we're the only ones that know."

"Friday's the due date, right?"

"Right."

"And that extension is destroyed, right? We can't have our boy proving he has six more months."

Heffner nodded his assent and sipped his drink to cover his lie. He did not have a poker face and knew it. He wished martinis came in thick tumblers like Bud Cole's scotch. You could see right through a thin martini glass. He'd searched for that paperwork since August and hadn't found it. Hopefully it was buried as deep as Mort Fessler.

"So when does the hammer fall?" asked Bud Cole, tipping this glass and chewing the ice.

"Next Saturday. I typed and processed the demand myself. Cover letter even gives him an extra week to come up with the principal."

"All of which he'll never receive."

Heffner grinned maliciously. "Things have been known to get lost in the mail."

The hostess brought the banker's lunch. She noticed Mr. Cole had barely touched his. She was about to offer him something else when his appetite suddenly returned. While eating Bud Cole ordered another round...to celebrate.

Chapter 44 – The Sheriff

The doorbell rang and Tom answered. The county sheriff stood on their porch with Steve Heffner. Behind them were the two deputies he had trouble with after his mom passed away. Tom felt a nervous pang shoot through his stomach.

The sheriff was polite, even deferential. "Is Colonel MacEwen at home?"

"Yeah."

"We need to see him."

Tom opened the door wider and the four filed into the living room. Tom was in his sock feet. He'd just gotten home from work, had just removed his boots and winter coveralls. He'd trucked logs with Abe Pierce all day. The supervisors had lifted the weight restrictions on the steel bridge so they could cross their own heavy loads to repair flood damage upstream. Tom was cold and tired and looked forward to an hour in the recliner with a soft blanket, a mug of hot chocolate, and a Luke Short western.

The blanket and novel lay on the recliner. Half of the hot chocolate lay in his stomach, churning and curdling. Every time they overcame one trouble another reared its ugly head. Standing in his mother's living room was a four-headed hydra of trouble. "Mac's upstairs," he said. "I'll get him."

Tom got Mac and followed him downstairs.

Mac was puzzled. "What's going on?" he asked.

The sheriff handed him a sheaf of legal papers. "You've defaulted on your note, Colonel. The bank's taking possession. You have one hour to pack your personal belongings and get out."

Tom towered over the sheriff. "I'm not going anywhere," he said.

———

Roby Tucker was a likeable man. He was also a Democrat and a Catholic, both outnumbered five to one in rural Tioga County. The sheriff didn't say he was a Democrat; he said he was a New Dealer. FDR and the WPA gave him work during the Depression and, by God, he was staying loyal.

He didn't say he was a Catholic either; he said he was a Freethinker, attributing this ideology to another popular dead president, Abe Lincoln. His wife was a Catholic so he followed her to St. Andrews. Went to church every Sunday by God, because he was loyal. Drew the line at confessing though. Confession had no political benefit. He could only keep the priest's vote by lyin'. But then the majority Protestants would lose hope of him ever converting to their side and they wouldn't vote for him, and he'd lose his job and die of a broken heart and God would send him to hell for lyin'. Whoever said confession was good for the soul was not a politician.

This would bring waggled forefingers from the female faithful; a stout Polish babushka, maybe, or a spare Puritan from the WCTU. Shame on you, Roby Tucker! Then the sheriff, a short round man with merry blue eyes, would wink and smile, peck the offended on the cheek, and whisper the best part of politics was kissing the mothers and hugging their babies. He'd get a gasp, a giggle, and a vote.

The county sheriff didn't set the tax rates and didn't make policy so it was safe to vote a Democrat into that office. All the sheriff did was serve the court's papers and the county prisoners their meals, and Roby Tucker let them think that way. He was the highest vote-getter and fundraiser and he did quietly make policy. He had the mandate and the money and the job because he kept in tune with the voter.

There *was* peril in this seizure but it wasn't from the big stubborn kid standing over him right now. It was the public's perception of what he was doing. He preferred that contentious parties talk and settle, but the bank president didn't want to talk and had insisted on surprise. To his chagrin the

298

court went along. Bud Cole called the county clerk and the clerk called the judge. Three debts would be paid off with this deal – one business and two political.

Merchants and Farmers obviously didn't want to settle; they wanted to *take*. They wanted this to hurt, which didn't make sense to Roby Tucker. Sheriffing the sons of Mike and Betty Donachy would linger long in the memories of Tannerytown...

He knew these brothers. In 1944 his oldest son had written from England telling of the transfer of another Tiogan to the 2nd Ranger Battalion. That was just before D-Day and Jeff's last letter home. Lieutenant MacEwen's subsequent letter said their son fought bravely and well.

Mrs. Tucker will not be pleased.

Tom Donachy was more popular than himself locally and a rascal to boot. The sheriff felt a kinship with the boy. They shared an attitude about life. He was defiant now, a head taller than the tallest of them, and young and desperate and strong as a bear.

His deputies edged forward. They had jailed Tom once before and were eager to repay him for the thumping they got while bringing him in. They weren't bad men, those two, just full of themselves. They worked cheap, which left more for him and the missus. Give some men a badge and a belt-loop of keys and they were content. But not smart. They were about to see history repeat itself and embarrass him again. The sheriff waved them back: "You two hold still," he said sternly.

He spoke gently to Tom. "That's a court order, son. I have to enforce it. You have to obey it. We can't do anything different. I'm here to take possession and inventory. that's all. I'm not here to get hurt or hurt you."

Mac had been scanning the papers. The cover paper read Action in Ejectment. Tom had discerned their meaning without reading them. Hearing the word "hurt" broke Mac's concentration. "Back off, Tom," he said.

"Mac! They're taking our house!"

Mac corrected him. "They're taking everything, Tom. House, equipment, land...everything."

"Why? What've we done to deserve this?"

Steve Heffner interrupted: "You haven't paid."

"We've paid twelve thousand plus interest," replied Mac. "This is wrong, Heffner. We agreed to a six-month extension on that note."

"Produce it then," said Heffner smugly.

"I took your word. You said you'd change the note. Why didn't you?"

The banker ignored the question. "Enforce the order, sheriff."

Roby Tucker felt helpless even though he was the authority here. "I'm sorry, Colonel."

Mac turned aside for a few seconds, struggling for control. He was angry, scared, embarrassed, and confused, but none of this was the sheriff's fault. It was his. He wanted to fight but this wasn't his kind of battle. He needed help. He took a deep breath, exhaled slowly, regained control, and faced the sheriff. "We have an hour?"

The sheriff nodded.

Mac went to the phone and called the Squire. This was one of the few times in his life when he really didn't know what to do. He silently prayed for the Squire to be home.

———

When Squire Hayes arrived his fierce hawk eyes fixed on the banker. He wanted to speak with him in private, right now!

They went into the kitchen. The Squire closed the door.

"Foreclosure is a board matter, Mr. Heffner."

The banker tried to meet the direct gaze, to stand his ground. "I have a majority."

"Bud, Jonas, and Rom?"

"Yes."

"Why didn't you contact Fred and me?"

Heffner looked away. "I only needed three."

300

"You mean you only wanted your majority to know. You avoided us deliberately."

"The policy book says I need a board majority to foreclose. I got a majority and I foreclosed."

"Policy also directs legal action to be done through the solicitor."

"The majority can overrule the solicitor, Squire. We thought it was a waste of time going through that process."

Squire's heavy eyebrows raised. "We? Whose interest are *we* protecting? The bank's or Bud Cole's?"

The banker got testy. "MacEwen's in default, Squire. He's done here."

"We'll see...We'll see who's done here."

———

The Squire dismissed the banker and asked for Mac and Tom and the sheriff to come in. Mac was to bring the served papers with him.

In the living room Steve Heffner lit a Lucky. His hands were trembling. He paced the perimeter and dropped his cigarette. He ground it out on the worn carpet and lit another.

Who the hell was he, ordering him out that way? He wanted to barge back in there and tell the lawyer off. But he wasn't good at bluff and bluster. He would have to face that penetrating gaze. Squire's eyes cut too deep for Steve Heffner.

———

The mood in the kitchen was sober. Squire Hayes took time to review the documents. Finally the sheriff pulled out his pocket watch. "Time's running short, Squire."

"Listen for a few minutes, will you Roby?"

The sheriff closed the cover and slipped the watch back in his vest pocket. "I'm listening."

301

The Squire told of Bud Cole's losing bid, of the coal on Bear Mountain, of the uninsured loss to the farm buildings, and of Pemberton's offer to buy Mort Fessler's property. Like everyone else, the sheriff knew of the bid and farm arson. The coal discovery and the proximity of the Fessler land thickened the soup. Squire ended by pointing out the carbon copy of the demand which was part of the foreclosure papers. "Where is the original of this?" he asked. "The cover letter gives you a week to come up with the money."

"I never got it," replied Mac. "I would have gone to another bank if I had known, and had a week."

"And gotten the money, and out from under Heffner and Cole," added the Squire. "They didn't want that."

"So they didn't really send the demand." This was Roby Tucker, finishing the story.

"Exactly," said the Squire.

"If you can prove it, this is an illegal seizure."

"It's all conjecture right now, Roby."

"Then I'll have to execute that order, Squire."

"Can you give us more time?"

The sheriff checked his watch again. It was six-fifteen. They'd already been there an hour. "You know, I could use a cup of coffee. I'll take Heffner with me but I won't enjoy the company."

"Thanks, Roby."

The sheriff started for the door. He had to pass by Tom who had listened to everything and hadn't said a word. Roby Tucker was sympathetic: "Bad business, isn't it, son?"

"What else do you call sending the law to steal?"

Tom's contempt set the sheriff back. He'd expected some understanding from the boy and hadn't gotten it. It made him angry. Then he realized his barb was the harsh truth. Cole and Heffner *were* using him to steal. He hadn't seen that until now.

———

The banker pitched a fit about the sheriff's casual abandonment of seized property. He went along when reminded he would be left alone in the living room with Tom Donachy.

The hour-long conversation at Woody's was uncomfortable for Steve Heffner. The sheriff appeared his normal genial self, gladhanding the other customers, asking about their families and jobs, and vague about the nature of his business. In between interruptions he asked several disturbing questions. He was probing. The acid in Heffner's stomach responded bitterly to each probe. Heffner left the diner with the queasy feeling that the Squire had gotten to Roby Tucker.

They returned to Tannery Hill at dusk. The streetlights blinked on and spread and by the time they turned on Highland Avenue the town boundaries were outlined. The banker and two deputies didn't notice any patterns, but the sheriff did.

Fallbrook proper was a lit gridwork of squares and rectangles. It lay low and flat and organized and sedate. Tannerytown however was a lit cone, a series of concentric half-circles that shortened nearer the hilltop. It lay on a slant, was cramped and haphazard and restless. Tannerytown reminded Roby Tucker of a beehive.

Invading the Donachy home this way would start the hive buzzing.

They arrived as the brothers were leaving in the red pickup. Tom was driving. The back was loaded and covered with a canvas tarp.

This was not Steve Heffner's picture of them going. He had imagined them walking to the bus stop, droop-shouldered, with a suitcase in each hand. This was too dignified. "Stop them, Sheriff! That vehicle is bank property!"

The sheriff pulled them over under a streetlight. They got out and approached the pickup. Tom rolled his window down.

"You can't take this truck, son. It's the bank's now."

Tom opened the glove compartment, withdrew a dusty envelope and handed it over. "The title, sheriff. It's free and clear. That bank jerk forgot to ask for it, and I never offered it, or any of *my* stuff, so what's mine is mine."

The sheriff unfolded the title, saw it wasn't encumbered, and returned it to Tom. He grinned. "Sorry, son. We were misinformed."

Steve Heffner persisted. "Look under the tarp, sheriff. See what else they've stolen."

"They haven't stolen anything, Heffner. You don't have this truck secured."

"You can't be sure until you look."

Sighing, the sheriff motioned for his deputies to remove the covering.

The tarp was held down by two long wooden containers filled with frozen dirt. They were heavy. It took two grunting deputies to lift one. Mac and Tom got out and rolled back the tarp.

There, under the streetlight, the deputies searched Tom's pickup. Blinds and curtains parted in the surrounding houses and Steve Heffner felt a smug satisfaction. The sheriff was disgusted. He knew they wouldn't find any bank property and they didn't. All they found was luggage and sports equipment and tools and boxes of family and business records.

The brothers calmly recovered their load and replaced the heavy weights; Mac lifting in one, Tom the other. The deputies shook their heads. They got back in the pickup and Tom started it. The sheriff leaned down and spoke quietly so Heffner wouldn't hear: "Where you going?"

"Mort Fessler's," said Mac. "The Squire's waiting at the house. He has the keys."

The sheriff noticed tears welling up in Tom's eyes. He had just kicked this boy and Colonel MacEwen out of their home. His own eyes misted and he squeezed Tom's shoulder and turned and walked toward the patrol car. Would Jeff understand and forgive him? Would the missus? It was Saturday. He'd drop these three off and visit Father Duncan after confession.

Heffner and the deputies followed. "What were those weights?" said one. "They were heavy as lead."

"Flowerboxes," answered the sheriff. "Everybody grows flowers up here."

Chapter 45 – The Ad

At the traffic light Tom turned south on 15. He'd take the long way to Mort's. He'd be damned if he'd take the shortcut by Bud Cole's. If he did he might pay the man a visit. Break a few more teeth. He wished Roby Tucker had left that fishface banker at the house. He'd still be smelling the hole he burnt in his mom's carpet. He wiped his eyes on his coat sleeve.

Mac took the blame. "I'm sorry, Tom."

"They can do that? Just barge in and throw us out? Take everything?"

"If we don't pay on time they can. I swear to God we agreed to six more months on that note."

"I think Cole and Heffner wanted our land and found a way to take it."

"That's about it."

"So what do we do now?"

"Something we've never done before."

"What's that?"

"Depend on someone else."

"The Squire?"

Mac nodded. "The Squire. Let's unload and get a quick bite to eat. The Squire wants to see us at 9:30."

———

Squire Hayes' conference room smelled of bookbinding and furniture polish. The four walls were covered with dark oak shelves crammed with books; law books and classics. The Squire was a reader. In the room's center sat an oak library table with six sturdy oak chairs. Four of those chairs were occupied; the Squire at the head, Mac and Tom, and across from them, Helen Kuhl.

Helen spoke first. "I typed that extension, Squire. I'm sure Steve okayed it."

"Can you prove it?"

She hesitated, thinking back. "No."

"Then it's your word against his. He has documentation. You have recollection. He'll say you're disaffected because you were passed over for the job he got."

"And fire me."

"He might try. I doubt Jonas would support that." He rubbed his chin thoughtfully. "I wonder what Heffner did with that extension."

"I hadn't attached it to the note yet. He signed it, I witnessed his signature, he took it, and I haven't seen it since."

"Looks like he destroyed it."

"He probably did, but..." She paused.

"But what?"

"He's so disorganized. You've seen his desk. He could have lost it, Squire."

"Small chance of that."

"I'm not so sure."

"Why?"

"Well, he's been reviewing files for weeks. Says he wants to familiarize himself with our customers, which he should have done earlier. He could be looking for something he misfiled."

The attorney pointed an emphatic finger. "You start looking on Monday."

Helen nodded, and he turned to the brothers. "I bought us some time, but you two are going to suffer."

"How so?" asked Mac.

"Cole and Pemberton were prepared to pay your note off tonight. In return for your assets, of course. I stopped them. Claimed collusion between the board and the bank and threatened a suit. The sheriff backed me. Said he didn't like the looks of the deal and neither would the judge. Cole didn't want to but Pemberton made him withdraw the offer. Now what you pledged will be auctioned. Public sale."

"The whole town will know!" exclaimed Tom.

"That's what I'm counting on," replied the Squire.

"When?" asked Mac.

"Next Saturday. They're not wasting any time."

"What do we do?"

"Cooperate with Roby. Bring your equipment in..."

Tom interrupted. "Why should we help them?"

"Lessens the chance of damage, Tom. If you get it back it won't be broke."

"We'll do it," said Mac. "Then what?"

"Get other work. And pray that Helen finds that extension or I can prove the seizure was illegal."

"If you can't?"

"Then you start over. That's the worst. You can start over now or wait a week. There's still a chance if you wait."

"We'll wait," said Mac.

———

The Squire hadn't been gone two minutes before Steve Heffner approached her desk. "Business as usual, Helen?" he asked, with more than his normal dose of sarcasm.

"You know better, Steve."

He picked through her stack of work, expecting to find MacEwen's file there. It wasn't. Monday morning's Agitator was, though, the classified section folded open to his full-page Foreclosure Sale ad. It was running all week, in all the area papers. Beside the paper was the preliminary agenda for March's Annual Stockholder's Meeting.

Helen rolled her office chair back, folded her arms and let him look, let him be Boss, let him bait her.

"Awful quiet around here this morning," he said curiously. He began leafing through the agenda.

"None of us like what you're doing to Mac and Tom. The bank hasn't sheriffed anyone in years."

"The bank has to protect its interest, Helen. MacEwen had too much against him."

"Just you and Bud Cole."

Her directness surprised and piqued him. "My, aren't we being insubordinate today? Ever considered looking for a new job?"

"No. But you should."

"Oh? Tell me, how does the secretary fire her boss?"

Her frankness took the bite out of his sarcasm. She wasn't intimidated. Not one bit. "By changing your bosses, Steve. You've divided the bank into two camps – Bud Cole's and the Squire's. The board reorganizes in three weeks." She pointed to the agenda. "You're holding the stockholders list. Add up the shares."

He went back to his office and closed the door. The door glass rattled within its frame. He still hadn't gotten around to having it fixed. In fact he'd forgotten about it. It had become another everyday sound in the busy bank, blending in with dings of typewriters, the ringing of phones, the opening and closing of cash drawers, the flushings of the commode. He'd ceased to hear it. The rattle belonged.

He sat at his desk and read the list. Merchant's and Farmer's only had fourteen shareholders, had only ever issued 10,000 shares. Each share represented a vote at a stockholders meeting. The charter required an annual meeting in March and authorized special meetings called by the board for emergencies. Only one special meeting had been called in the twentieth century – when FDR declared a "bank holiday" and closed all banks for almost a month in 1933. Merchant's and Farmer's was solvent, thanks to the conservatism of Clarence Hayes and Jonas Pemberton, and reopened as a member of the FDIC.

When he was hired in June Bud Cole assured him the annual meeting was a mere legal formality, more like a party than a business meeting. The director whose term was up that year was reelected unless he had died or became senile, a dividend was declared if the bank had made money, and management was slapped on the back and given the mandate to go out and make more. If there was any left after capital was boosted and dividends paid, management got a bonus. His predecessor had bonused every year since 1946. Bud Cole assured him it was a good job. And a good bonus.

On an accounting sheet he listed the stockholders names and their shares. At the top of two other columns he printed HAYES and COLE. The Squire's 3,300 shares went in his column, as did Fred Sheafer's 1,000. Bud Cole's 2,500 went in his column, as well as Jonas Pemberton's 1,700 and Rom Barbano's 500. So far so good. But when he finished allocating the remaining shares his hands were trembling too much to light a calming cigarette.

On the present board Cole outnumbered Hayes three directors to two and 4800 shares to 4300. Romolo's support was pivotal. But at the annual meeting where the shareholders elected a new director and the new board elected a new chairman, Hayes' supporters outnumbered Cole's 5100 to 4900. Worse luck, this year Cole's mainstay came up for reelection – Jonas Pemberton.

The five directors were elected for staggered terms of five years. One director came up for election each year. The Squire had the votes to remove Jonas Pemberton as director and Bud Cole as chairman. In three weeks Clarence Hayes would assume control of the bank!

Helen Kuhl had already divulged the plans for the bank president.

Why tell him now? Simple. They wanted to rattle him and they had. Make him sweat for three long weeks.

What could he do? He searched the list for a math error. None. He liked being the president of a bank. He could issue more stock and possibly change the balance but that required time and director approval. He checked his calendar. He only had eighteen days and the Squire could block him by accusing him of insider trading or watering the stock.

He scanned the list again. He could buy a big block from someone on the Squire's side. He'd have to pay a high price but that was better than not having a job. Besides, it was a good investment. He couldn't lose money. He wished now he'd insisted on some stock as part of his employment package. The list disappointed him. There wasn't one person even remotely disloyal to the Squire. Not one would sell.

But Mort Fessler was dead. Squire undoubtedly had control of those 200 shares. If he didn't, that made a tie, which meant compromises. They might have to keep him. Those heirs may sell. But where were they? The Squire hadn't found them yet…or hadn't said if he did. He wouldn't until after the stockholder's meeting.

The Squire had the inside track. He was being boxed just like he boxed MacEwen. The only difference was, he was being told ahead of time.

Proxy statements had been mailed in January with Jonas recommended for another term. Helen's notations indicated none of the proxies had come in. And they wouldn't. These rubes brought their proxies with them! Like Bud Cole said, the meeting was a big party. With this MacEwen foreclosure everyone would be there. Squire's majority would have his head. Screw them! Screw Bud Cole!

Mister Big would have to make sure a couple of Hayes supporters didn't make it to the meeting. That was the only way.

He finally got his cigarette lit and took a deep drag, surprised at the way his mind was working these days.

———

Julie was finishing her books when Erma brought her a cup of coffee and the evening paper. Their friendship had been strained since the incident with the drillers. Gossips still speculated about who frequented Cabin 7. Julie kept her peace and so did Erma. She and Paul were working through it, for the kids. Erma was an impulsive woman with an earthy, sensual manner about her. She sat in the chair across from Julie's desk. "Haven't seen much of Mac lately, have you?"

"I saw him at Mort's funeral. I've been busy helping Missy."

"Yeah. And changing schedules so you're not here when he's here."

"There's been a lot of sorrow lately, Erma."

"I know. I've had my share. I've brought some on you and I'm sorry. But you're making some for yourself. I'm not smart like you, but I'm here to tell you something and I want you to hear me out."

Julie closed her ledger. "I'm listening."

"Well, you've been giving Mac the cold shoulder when you should be showing it to him."

"Erma!"

"I know. I shouldn't talk. But I've been thinking about something."

"Which is what?" asked Julie curiously. Erma had a tendency to act and then think. This was a welcome change.

"I waited on Tom's table the night the Varsity beat the Town Team. Tom told Joe that Miss Whalen called as they were leaving for the game and asked Mac to pick her up."

"So?" said Julie, trying to sound disinterested. But this *was* interesting.

"So then Mac came alone to the game party. He didn't bring her. I heard him tell Tom you couldn't come 'cause Danny was sick."

"Danny was sick."

"How did Mac know that?"

"I don't know."

"I know." She rested her elbows on the desk and looked at Julie intently. "He called for you. He was asking you out. Why are you giving him the cold shoulder if he called?"

"He didn't call me, Erma."

"He had to. There's no other way he could have known about Danny." She stood and peered out the office window to the kitchen. Posey was motioning for her. He had an order ready. "I've got to get back. Before you leave you might want to check our ads for tomorrow."

"Thanks."

At the doorway, Erma paused. "You're too proud. Pride chills a bed, Julie."

After Erma left, Julie phoned her mother. Why, yes, Mac did call the night Danny got sick. She was preoccupied with him and forgot to mention it. Sorry, dear. Was something wrong?

Julie sighed and said she'd be home in half an hour.

She wanted to go home now but first she had to check those ads for Tuesday's specials. Page one of the classified gave her a start. The whole page glared out the Foreclosure Sale of the assets of Jonathan MacEwen and Thomas Donachy.

She hadn't heard. She *had* been busy with Missy. She had been avoiding Mac and Tom. She had given Mac the cold shoulder. She thought he'd chosen Abigail.

But Mac had called. He had asked for *her*. He had wanted her with him at the game party. He didn't want Abigail. He wanted her.

She didn't know! And she made herself unavailable.

She thought of Erma's comments. She wasn't experienced like Erma. Erma's experience told her to throw away her stubborn pride. Consequently, she still shared a bed with her husband. Julie slept with her pride in a double bed. One side was always empty and cold.

Julie re-read the ad and picked up the phone. This time she called Posey's banker in Williamsport.

———

Abigail corrected papers at her desk in her apartment. She gave lots of homework so she had lots of homework too. She had purchased two file cabinets to separate her school assignments and thesis research. Daily she committed an hour or two to her research and the four file drawers had filled rapidly. Teaching in a one-room school was a great education for Abigail.

Lately, though, she wished she didn't have so much time to spend on schoolwork and research.

Her expanding subject matter came from teaching six grades. The "thesis" cabinet was filled with file folders; files marked Discipline, Homework, Chores, PTA, Phonics, Tutoring. The fattest file, files actually, their subject taking up a whole drawer, was Phonics.

Phonics, teaching reading by emphasizing the alphabetic code, was the focus of her thesis. Simple, basic, and effective, still favored by Europeans and gray-headed American teachers, the phonetic method had been abandoned as old-

313

fashioned by education experts in the thirties. They wanted revolution and they got it – a generation that couldn't read.

Remediation and literacy programs were springing up nationwide and the revolutionaries were now wondering what this generation was coming to. Why so many slow kids? Was it genetic? Abigail Whalen, twenty-five and a country school teacher, said no. It was simply the wrong direction the "slow" students had been pointed when they entered first grade.

The one crammed file drawer was documentation proving the discarded phonetic method was more effective than the modern sight-say technique. Abigail's thesis would urge return to phonics.

Buttonwood School kids taught by Hazel Brown went to seventh grade in Fallbrook and none ever required remedial reading classes. Kids taught sight-say in Fallbrook Elementary did, unless they learned on their own to break a word into pieces as a survival skill. This was true of senior Brenda Whitaker, who was going to college to be an English teacher.

Abigail had tracked other students as well. Mr. Bates and Constance Abernathy had been very helpful. Last week she compared the first year records of Tom Donachy and Danny Spencer, the top senior and top first-grader in Fallbrook School District.

Tom had attended Fallbrook Elementary, but his mother was a Steam Valley girl taught by Hazel Brown. Tom had come to first grade fluent in his ABC's, already able to figure out words by sounding out their letters...just like Danny Spencer, whose mother was also taught at the Buttonwood School. Julie, until she quit school in her junior year, was also the top student in her class.

Abigail had learned to accept the truth in her research, even when it revealed information she preferred not to believe. Danny's success indicated his mother spent a lot more time with him than with dates arranged at the Turkey Ranch. In truth, there were no dates. Research, and female intuition, also told Abigail Danny's mother had set her cap for one man, and only one man. She was not aggressive, and kept her feelings a secret. Yet many knew. Julie Spencer was truly beautiful, and it wasn't all physical. Abigail feared Julie Spencer.

Finishing her schoolwork, she set it aside and cleared space for her research. In doing so she had to move the ribboned stack of forty valentines she got two weeks before; thirty-six standards from her kids, nice ones with notes from her parents and Aunt K, a naughty one from Ruby Broadwater, and an expensive one from Steve Heffner.

Steve was persistent. Steady and successful and persistent. Her father liked him. But he was not exciting. Not like Mac. Her mother liked Mac. Mac excited a woman, women actually, even older women like her mother. And loyalty? Mac engendered loyalty. From women and men. It was a quality he had.

A valentine remembrance from Mac would have been nice. She wondered like a jealous schoolgirl if Julie Spencer had gotten one.

She had to agree with her father that Steve offered more security. Certainly Mac's prospects weren't the brightest right now. She had seen the ad in the paper and made a beeline for Aunt K. Actually she heard Mac's name mentioned through the open floor register, knelt down and eavesdropped, then found the ad and went to Aunt K.

She had an inkling that Mac's routine was different earlier today. For two weeks she had heard the loaded log truck make its labored turns south on 15 and, two hours later, return. Today it turned north. She looked out and saw it carried the dozer. She thought he was hauling it somewhere to get repaired. The truck didn't return.

A bitter Aunt K explained what happened. Mac and Tom had been sheriffed by the bank, shut down, and put out of their home. The justification for the foreclosure was questionable but legal. They were staying at Mort Fessler's. On Saturday they were to be sold out. Fred and Squire Hayes were backing them, but it didn't look good. Tom was taking it hard. Mac was under control; God help Cole and Heffner if he lost it, and God help her for wishing he would. Mac

315

was starting tomorrow as woods boss for Fred. The job paid good money and Fred needed him bad. The mill had just won a big state contract on Oregon Mountain. It involved some travel. He'd be leaving early and returning late. Fred was getting too old to ramrod that kind of job. Mac's whole crew was going with him. Be patient, dear.

Back upstairs, Abigail realized she had never sensed the seriousness of the conflict between Mac and Steve Heffner and Bud Cole. Mac's adversaries played for keeps and what they were keeping was Mac's. There was no question jealousy was involved. Like it or not Mac set a standard few men could reach. He gave Cole and Heffer a chance to knock him down and they did, taking his home and business and dignity with them. It appeared to Abigail that Mac had been rather gullible and trusting in his dealings, especially with Steven Heffner.

Then again, so had she.

She removed Heffner's card from the stack and threw it in the trash. She wished she'd never encouraged Steve because it drove a wedge between herself and Mac. And she sensed with some desperation that gap was widening. She had created an opening for another woman's affections.

But maybe Mac's downfall was a hidden blessing. Maybe he was just working for wages until Tom graduated and went on his own. Then Mac would leave. Her research would be done by then and her teaching contract completed. She'd leave with him. She'd have her man and her career and her home in the suburbs.

It was a happy thought.

———

Luke Ballard's chainsaw roared to life and the thousand crows enjoying the cloudless vista atop remote Oregon Mountain flew up. The evicted crows and the working saw made a raucous music. The crows lyric could be heard above the saw. The man's could not. Mac knew it was there just the same; he had seen Luke mouth the words many

316

times...*undercut-topcut-backcut-down!*   *Undercut-topcut-backcut-down!* Luke's cadence changed with the terrain and size of the tree.

The saw droned loudly on, the crows circled and cawed their objections, a tree crashed to the ground, and the echoes of a clearcut for a fire tower bounced from Oregon north to Potash, south to Sugar, and east across Great Marsh to Bear.

The flock gathered and flew east toward another high roost on the backside of Bear Mountain, five miles away. As the crow flies, five miles. For a walker, meandering the uncertain footing of Great Marsh, at least ten, possibly twenty, miles.

Halfway across, the flock dropped down to investigate a long evergreen-clad island that rose from the Marsh. What a murky five-hundred acre den that looked to be! A place at once swamp-ugly, swamp-dangerous, and swamp-beautiful. It was truly the final sanctuary. The final refuge for the cats and bears and great bucks like Ebenezer. And renegades like Spike Poorbaugh. There, someday, the refugees would contend against the island and each other and the winner would be the last to die. To the professional soldier the island was like a medieval hill-fort, surrounded by a huge booby-trapped moat.

Beyond the island rose the misty western rampart of Bear Mountain; the black notch in the skyline the high opening to Bear Hollow, where the roaring branch spilled over the cliffside. There also was the next-to-last refuge for the cats and bears and Ebenezer's and Poorbaugh's. And the last refuge for the great trees like Jacob Miller's arrowed pine and the aged Boss of Bear Hollow.

Until Saturday he had controlled that mountain, had decided to keep it a refuge. He had come to see himself as the protector of Bear Hollow and would somehow preserve all that was ancient and wild and forgotten about it. He would preserve it by keeping it forgotten.

But he had failed. Someday Bud Cole would come with dynamite and dozers and draglines. He would blow the top off the mountain and bury Bear Hollow. The miners would find soft coal and iron oxide and underground springs, and the roaring branch would run rust red.

The refugees would retreat to the island. Great Marsh would suck up the polluted water; then it would rust and weaken, brittle and die.

Finally, the surviving refugee, whoever or whatever it was, would die.

Mac felt sick. Sick at heart and soul, sick in mind. He had thought, when he returned home, that he was finally out of danger. Instead, he let his guard down, trusted too much, and was taken in by enemies at home. What a fool.

Bear Hollow would now have to rely on its previous protector. There was no question he would kill to preserve it. He already had. Bud Cole probably didn't have any idea what he was buying into. Inevitably though, Cole, or someone like him, would win.

Bear Hollow would last as long as the trapper lasted. He would be forced out of his cabin. He would become a guerilla fighter and kill and run and survive in the woods. That would take its toll, even on a man as hardy as he. Time and exposure wore out every man, even the seemingly ageless Spike Poorbaugh.

The flock rose up from the island and headed toward Bear, reducing from a black cloud to a black speck in an amazingly short time. Mac turned his attention to clearing the rim of Oregon Mountain.

He was familiar with cliffs. A twenty-story height on Oregon felt like the sandstone ones off Caleb's Rock or Bear Mountain, or the seaside chalk cliffs above the Isle of Wight, or the gravel ones towering over the beaches of Normandy.

His Ranger instructor on the Isle had a saying: "When hanging by a thread, pretend it's a rope." He was climbing a cliff much like this at H-hour, D-Day. Jeff Tucker was beside him. The Germans rolled grenades over the side and one exploded above them. His line was frayed. Jeff Tucker's broke. He was one of 87 that made the fighting on top. Jeff was one of 148 that didn't.

His line had held, until Saturday, when it broke.

The Fallbrook Ladies' Garden Club held their Wednesday meeting at Delia's. The business part was brief, the only
item being the purchase of bulbs from Hansel's Nursery for
the club's spring-time flower planting on the Green. They
took their dessert and tea to the living room but no one turned
on the TV. Real-life drama was more riveting.

Freda Manikowski announced it was a travesty for the
bank to sell out MacEwen, him being a war hero and all.
And Monica came home worried about Tom. Losing everything like that was too big a burden for an eighteen-year-old.
Her husband Stan was a day-shift foreman at the Tannery.
The men, especially the veterans, were wondering why
Mac's note wasn't renewed. The word on Main Street was
he had made all his interest payments and paid a good part on
principal. Why, Bud Cole and Jonas Pemberton had arranged
new terms for plant workers lots of times. Why not the same
for Mac and Tom? Was Bud Cole getting revenge for losing
the game? Or was it that new bank president who's sweet on
Abigail Whalen, who obviously sweet on MacEwen?

Justine Whitaker was unsympathetic. MacEwen made a
bad business deal and lost, taking that rough-as-a-cob
younger brother down with him. Her husband Henry was
senior accountant at the Tannery and reported to Mr. Pemberton. Jonas told Henry they tried to arrange a quiet private
sale but Squire Hayes blocked it. The brothers brought this
all on themselves. Anyway, it was better for everyone if
Cole Enterprises got it. Cole had the resources to develop it.
Word from the front office had it there was coal on Bear
Mountain. Even so, the bank wasn't sure how much equity
they were getting – after all, a lot of timber was cut and the
Longsdorf Farm burned – so they took the Donachy house
and contents too. They had the right. As for her, she
wouldn't miss the sale. She had always coveted that maple
teacart of Betty Donachy's. It was one of the items listed in
the ad. Justine was sure they had all seen it. Freda said she

wouldn't miss it either. Probably all of them would go. She may be a dumb Pole but she knew better than to bid on anything at that sale.

Justine sniffed and sipped her tea. There was a strained silence as the rest took cover behind their teacups too.

Outside, Barney began barking furiously. Delia had him on his chain because he was overly friendly and rambunctious with visitors. But this barking was not friendly. He was growling and angry. Delia rose to see what he was up to. She could use the break from the tension.

Freda and Justine were opinionated matrons whose personalities and backgrounds clashed. They also had pretty, senior-class daughters who clashed.

Justine was Fallbrook prim and proper, Eastern-Star and DAR, who had an ancestor on the Mayflower, she thought.

Freda was like herself, a second generation transplant from Tannerytown who married someone important at the factory. The club flourished after Delia was admitted and she sponsored other ladies from the Hill. The bluebloods were afraid to challenge the wife of a Cole. Delia and the other hilltoppers smoothed their feathers by sharing family secrets for growing flowers. After all, it was a garden club.

The majority of club members sided with Freda. In fact, Justine's only ally might be mousey Maria Barbano, whose husband also reported to Jonas Pemberton, and whose father-in-law Romolo sat on the bank board. The Barbano's were Old Country Italians. Maria knew better than to defy Papa. Or speak up at all.

Delia sighed. She *had* defied the head of her household, and it created the worst row of their marriage. Bud had stomped out and had stayed at the tannery's guest house in Fallbrook since Monday night.

He had been drinking and all but accused her of infidelity. She protested vehemently but failed to convince him. She wasn't guilty. She didn't say she could have been if Mac had encouraged her. She said enough. With Bud gone these past two nights, though, she discovered she missed her husband. She did not enjoy sleeping alone.

320

She parted the sheers in front of the French windows. Barney barked and strained on his chain. She looked in the direction he was pulling and saw movement in the trees. Just a flicker, nothing more.

She didn't like it when she and Amanda were here by themselves. After the meeting she would call Bud and entice him home.

———

The intercom broke into Constance Abernathy's senior English class: "Mr. Donachy, please come to the office."

This frequent announcement usually brought suppressed smiles and usually Joe Ballard and Squeaky Fabel were invited along. Usually they knew why. Today there were no smiles, Tom went alone, and he didn't know why.

Once Tom was well down the hall the class gathered around Monica Manikowski and Carol Raker. Monica was class vice-president, Carol class treasurer. Monica presided when Tom wasn't available. Today they made sure he wasn't.

Miss Abernathy, senior class advisor, and co-sponsor to their plans, checked creative writing assignments and the hall for Tom. Mostly, she checked for Tom.

At the office Tom was directed to the section occupied by Mr. Bates, who was waiting for him.

The superintendent hadn't seen much of Tom since the game. Tom's elbow was one of the meanest, slickest strokes he had seen in sports and he had cheered lustily when Squeaky Fabel had taken Tom's pass and scored at the buzzer. But Mr. Bates was cheering more for the blow than the score.

He hoped Bud Cole's sneakthief revenge hadn't taken the spunk out of the boy. Some feared it had.

Tom filled the chair in front of him, respectful, attentive, but the glint of pixie was gone from his eyes. Instead Mr. Bates saw hardness and anger. Right now he shared Tom's hatred for Bud Cole.

He began by explaining the reason for the summons. "Tom, I'm writing an article for the paper about our graduating seniors. You're valedictorian. What are your plans?"

Tom shrugged.

"I've written college recommendations for Harold and Brenda and several others. But none for you. Why is that?"

Tom shrugged again. "No money."

"Malarkey. There are scholarships. You can work. Mac'll help. Every week we get inquiries about you. You haven't even applied to a school."

Tom opened up. "Mr. Bates, I'm not sure I want to go on to school. I really haven't had time to figure out what I want. All we do is work and sleep." He bit his lip. "From the results it looks like we slept too much."

"Even the strongest have to rest sometime, Tom."

"We're being wiped out and we can't even fight back!"

Mr. Bates got them back on track, feeling deeply Tom's frustration. "You let Clarence Hayes fight this one. You and Mac sit down and make plans for your future."

"Mac's got enough on his mind without worrying about me."

"And you will add to his burden if you don't involve him in your plans."

Tom was adamant. "I can make my own. I did before Mac came back from the service. I buried my mom without him."

"Mac was in a field hospital when that happened, wasn't he?"

"Yes."

"Being a little hard on him aren't you?"

"I guess."

"Do you blame him for what happened with the bank?"

Tom fidgeted. "Some."

"What would you have done different? What could he have done different?"

Tom thought for half a minute. "Back out. Not try at all, I guess."

"Since when did a MacEwen or a Donachy quit trying?"

Tom's tight lips relaxed. "I get your point, Mr. Bates."

The superintendent changed the subject. He'd gained a little. "You running track?" he asked. Tom was their miler.

"I'll be around."

"Then what?"

"Graduate. Hit the road."

"Which road?"

"We'll talk it over and let you know, Mr. Bates."

Bud Cole looked out his office window toward the depot. The Central had agreed to rent the facility to the tannery until he made his mind up about buying it. He'd buy it someday, at his price. Who else could buy it? But the train would never run again. He just wanted the trackage that ran alongside him and the in-town right-of-way. The 49½ foot wide strip that began north of town and ran to Blossburg could grow up in weeds for all he cared.

Roby Tucker stood on the depot platform, clipboard in hand, presumably checking off the items seized for tomorrow's sale. MacEwen's log truck, dozer, one-ton pickup, Big Mike's wrecker (stored in his garage since 1943), and Betty Donachy's Plymouth sedan were lined up behind the depot. The logging gear, garage tools, and household furniture were displayed inside. The auctioneer had expressed some worry; there had been few pre-sale lookers. He'd agreed to cut his commission to 5% because of the real estate value but demand for the other stuff looked low.

Bud Cole assured him it would all be sold.

The Squire's campaign was having its effect. Helen Kuhl's avowal that Mac had a six-month extension carried weight, more than he and Heffner had expected. She had no proof so the board majority backed Heffner. But Rom and Jonas refused to fire her. They had trusted her with their money too long. They explained away her stand as misguided loyalty to her old army friend. Mac had the damnedest knack for getting people on his side, especially women.

His bank president was the weak link in the scheme. Squire's promise to unseat Jonas unsettled him. It unsettled them all because it appeared he had the votes to do it. Jonas would not serve a twelfth term as director. Tannery attorneys were checking now to see if they could block the Squire from voting the Fessler shares. They also were searching for Mort's heirs, but the Squire controlled the timetable of the probate process. By doing nothing he had control. And they couldn't issue more shares; there wasn't enough time and they couldn't control who'd buy them.

He'd buy them! He'd outbid everybody. They had three weeks! Damn lawyers never operated on schedule. If he ran his business the way they did his hides would rot before they were tanned.

The stockholders meeting was now two Friday's away and the Squire had them. Had him, and Jonas, and Heffner, by the short hairs. He'd be out as chairman; Jonas, a friend of the Squire's, would be out as director; and Heffner would be out of a job. He'd have to create a position for Heffner.

Strange, Pemberton wasn't mad at the Squire. Business sometimes worked that way, he'd said. But he *was mad* at him. If you had listened in the first place none of this would have happened. You're losing control, Benjamin.

The four o'clock whistle blew. The shifts changed and the men mingled in the tanyard, then half went to work and half went home. In the middle of the mix was that sonofabitch O'Conner, talking union. For sixteen seconds a day, eight at seven and eight at four, that whistle trumpeted Cole control over Fallbrook and Tannerytown and Steam Valley. The first-shift wives fixed supper, the second-shift wives made their beds. Used to be the men hurried to work or hurried home. There were no agitators. Lately, they lagged.

He had lost his hold over them, but did it matter? Tomorrow he'd be rid of Mac and have Bear Mountain. He could buy back the town's esteem, regain control, in time. His grandfather Zeb had fallen from grace and used money to regain stature. Fallbrook hated him when he brought in the ethnics and built Tannerytown. But that hate subsided with

324

time and prosperity: "Build them a library or a hospital or a public toilet, Benjamin, and they'll praise God for sending you."

He'd regain control of the bank, too. The other directors were over sixty. Someday, after the right ones died, he'd give the boot to Helen Kuhl.

The sheriff left the platform, got in his car and drove up Tannery Hill, presumably to see if the Donachy house was empty. Roby Tucker was going through the motions. He was not an ally. He'd bucked him too. Someday, he'd get a Republican elected sheriff.

It pained him to look at the depot. It had since October 10th when he saw Mac and Delia standing there together. She waited on the platform, watching him load logs onto a flatcar. She waited a long time. Then Mac came to the platform and they talked.

He'd reminded her of that meeting last night. She had called on Wednesday and begged him to come home. He made her wait a day. When he arrived Amanda got to him first and rebuked him for hurting Mac and Tom. He told her she was too young to understand, she sassed him, he backhanded her across the mouth, and she ran off with Barney. The big collie would have bitten him if she hadn't intervened.

Delia said he was overreacting and they got into it again. He was drinking too much. His judgment was impaired by booze and greed and jealousy. Let what was in the past stay in the past.

He accused her of meeting Mac on the sly and she denied it. What about that time at the depot? That was a coincidence, she said. They just bumped into each other. She told him she was sorry about his mom. Like hell, he said. Then he accused her of trapping him with Amanda and she slapped his face.

He went out on the patio to cool off. Where the flagstone ended he found a boot track in the soft earth. For his bulk he had relatively small feet. Size 10. His shoe easily fit inside that track. He followed the imprints to the edge of the woods. MacEwen was a tall big-boned man. He'd been

325

coming over here from Fessler's, the nights he was gone. And she told him she was lonely!

He went back inside and slapped his wife's face. He didn't say anything about the track. He didn't call her a tramp and liar. He didn't say a thing.

He left in his Cadillac and drove to the Hotel. Ordered scotch and a steak and propositioned the hostess. She followed him to the guest house at eight and didn't leave until nine...the next morning.

That was earlier today. The first time he'd been late to work in years. They had another date tonight.

He'd gotten even with Delia. Tomorrow was MacEwen's turn.

Chapter 46 – The Sale

Bud Cole came to the sale armed with a hangover, checkbook and million-dollar credit line. He set the tone with the first item on the block – Mike Donachy's old wrecker. Big Mike had built the rig himself from a 1937 Ford truck chassis. Those that researched its value knew it had a low of $950 and a high of $1,200. The locals knew it was worth the high because Big Mike had owned it.

Colonel Newby Guy, Esquire, the white-hatted auctioneer brought in from Lancaster County, started the bidding at a thousand even. Edward's Brothers from Bloss bid ten-fifty, Wally's Esson in town bid eleven-fifty to keep the Sinclair dealer honest, the dealer countered at twelve-fifty, Wally bumped him to thirteen, and Bud Cole took it for fourteen hundred.

A murmer ran through the large crowd, which filled the depot lot and spilled over to the tanyard. Now what did Bud Cole want a wrecker for? They'd heard he was going in the trucking business. Everybody's gonna have to buy a car now. Won't be no railroad.

Cole's overbid was the astute auctioneer's signal that this could be a profitable sale. For him. Business had been terrible since the wet weather began in January. He ostensibly agreed to cut his commission to five percent because of the real estate value, but he actually cut it because he needed the work and had a hefty income tax bill due in April. His business card advertised no minimum fee. He worked on pure percentage. Five percent was low but five percent of big numbers could add up to a good day's pay. Better, maybe, than expected.

Newby Guy was quick with numbers and would keep track of his progress in his head. That wrecker brought $1,400. His commission was five percent. For fives, figure ten percent and halve it. For ten drop the last aught – 140. Halve that – 70. Seventy bucks from that wrecker was his. Another way was to drop all aughts and multiply the remaining figure by the commission. That was 14 times 5.

Five 4s were twenty. Drop the aught down and carry the two. Five 1s were five, add the 2 makes 7. Drop the 7 down back of the 0. 70 bucks. Ok system for sixes, sevens, eights or nines. But for fives, and he never went less than five, halving was quicker. The auctioneer had a good eye for figures, mathematical and otherwise.

Colonel Newby Guy, Esquire wasn't a military officer like MacEwen, or an attorney like Squire Hayes. The colonel title was honorary, a perk of his profession, stemming from post-Civil War days when Union military colonels were assigned to auction spoils of war. The Esquire designation was pure promotion, intended to make him look like a country gentleman, which he did. A tall portly man in his late fifties, on sale day he wore a gray wool suit, white shirt, string tie, horseman's boots and a white Stetson. He commanded attention with a broad wave of his white hat or a sharp rap of his gavel, which was more like a hammer than a gavel.

Betty Donachy's '50 Plymouth four-door was next. It booked for eight-fifty. Carol Raker bid eight-fifty, Bud Cole ran her to ten-fifty and out of money, and took the car for eleven hundred. Carol was so mad she cried. Joe, and several class members standing near, consoled her and urged her to try for some of the furniture later. The ten-fifty was their senior trip money. Justine Whitaker fumed and demanded her family's contribution back, until Brenda intervened and told her she had voted with the majority. "And Mother," she added, "don't you dare bid on that teacart!"

Tom thought Carol wanted the car for herself and Joe and protested when he found out. Monica told him it was their money, the vote was unanimous except for him, so shut up. Tom was moved and covered his emotion by grousing he'd owe each classmate a trip to Washington D.C. Hotel rooms would probably cost a hundred bucks a night by the time he got the last one paid off. Folks laughed at that.

The logging equipment came next. Fred Sheafer and two Potter County mill owners bid against Bud Cole. Fred's objective was similar to the senior's and his success the same. With each item the factory man bid way over market and won.

Bud Cole was sending a message: Money couldn't buy everything, but it could buy out MacEwen.

The high prices made two participants discretely happy – the auctioneer and the banker.

Colonel Guy smelled the fire company's chicken barbecue and money. People attended auctions to socialize and find bargains, or vice versa, he never was sure which came first. Stuff was expected to sell low, way below market. Foreclosures especially were distress sales. The presence of the sheriff at an auction always depressed prices. But this stuff was going high, twice what low would be, meaning his five percent would yield the same return as what he normally expected from a ten percent contract. He wondered if the trend would hold through the real estate offering, where the real money was. Probably. This wasn't a foreclosure sale. This was a grudge sale. That rich factory owner was nursing a grudge against the whole town. When folks get emotional with their money they spend it. Might as well get my share. Nurse your grudge with money, Mr. Cole. Line my pockets.

Steve Heffner felt a smug satisfaction. Retaining the high-powered Newby Guy had been a smart move. Bud Cole had tried to steal everything earlier by paying off the $38,000 remaining on the note. The bank would have had its principal back, plus interest, which showed the bank a small profit. But not the profit Bud Cole and Newby Guy were creating. If he ever got another shot at a bank presidency he could point to Merchant's and Farmers first quarter in 1955 – the best in bank history. His forced resignation was political. He was the casualty of feuding directors. His termination had nothing to do with competence. Look at the money he made!

———

Mac and his crew, taking their first Saturday off in months, stood silent as Bud Cole bought a logging business for fifteen thousand dollars. With them stood Fred Sheafer and Squire Hayes. Both felt as mentors who had failed a friend. The *last* thing Mac deserved was this humiliation.

Now all Bud Cole needed was some timber to cut. That was seventh on the handbill, after the property on Highland Avenue.

Mac seemed cool and impassive, standing there, "taking his medicine." But Tom knew better. Mac's jaw muscles were working. That meant anger, controlled anger. Someday Cole and Heffner would regret this affair.

They'd talked things out last night. Made some plans. Resolved to start over. Both had expected to leave Highland Avenue someday and build a country home of their own. Mac borrowed money from Fred to buy back the family heirlooms. From the way Bud Cole was bidding they hadn't borrowed enough. But they already had their family records and scrapbooks and memories and each other. They had things to take with them that could not be destroyed.

But they could save nothing of Bear Hollow. It pained them to lose it, especially Mac. Tom had fallen asleep late in the night, wishing he was a rich man so he could buy Bear Hollow back for his brother.

The auctioneer announced the Highland Avenue house and repair garage were being sold as one unit. Was he bid seven thousand?

Bud Cole said "Here." He was sitting on the top step to the platform and looked bored.

"I have seven thousand. Am I bid seventy-five hundred?"

A hand raised from the center of the crowd.

"I see that hand. I'm bid seventy-five. Do I hear eight thousand?"

Bud Cole was looking to see who bid against him but the hand had gone down. Damn! "Eight thousand."

Good, thought the Colonel, I get five bucks a hundred. That's a hundred bucks a minute if I keep 'em bumping on five hundreds. "Eighty-five. Do I have eighty-five?"

The hand raised again.

"Thank you. Eighty-five hundred from the lady in the brown scarf." The hand went down. "Do I hear nine, nine?"

Bud Cole was trying to locate his competition. He looked over the crowd. There were lots of women and lots of scarves. It was a clear, brisk day. Across the road several kids were trying to raise a kite in the parking lot of the milk plant. That was dangerous with those wires overhead. Some people don't watch their kids. He wouldn't let Amanda do that.

"Eighty-five hundred once, eighty-five hundred twice..." Newby Guy mouthed the words carefully giving Bud Cole time to regain his attention. Those kids were costing him money.

The factoryman came around. "Ninety-five!" he shouted.

Several in the crowd laughed. The auctioneer had asked for nine. A mental lapse at an auction can be costly.

Bud Cole pointed toward the milk plant. "Someone pull that kite down before your kid gets fried!" Under his breath he added, "And I have to buy a new transformer."

The crowd turned to look and Herm Broadwater raced across the road, shouting at his boys. The kite came down.

"I have ninety-five, ninety-five. Who'll give me ten, who'll give me ten?" intoned the auctioneer. The crowd turned back around.

The same hand rose from the center.

"That's a thousand more than its worth," growled Bud Cole, trying to intimidate her. Homemakers were more easily intimidated than businessmen.

"Ten thousand," affirmed the lady in the scarf, loud and clear.

"Ten-five," countered the factoryman. Who was that girl? He squinted for a better look. The midmorning sun was bright. No!

By now Fred Sheafer had elbowed his way to the center. "How much you got, Julie?"

Her voice broke. She was determined, but nervous. "Eleven thousand. That was all I could raise."

"Posey in on this?"

"I didn't ask him. You know Posey. He'd throw in his retirement money if I let him."

Fred was impressed. Most of the people here couldn't raise that much on their own. But Julie the waitress could.

"I have ten-five. Do I hear eleven?"

Julie spoke up. "Eleven thousand!"

Bud Cole held up the handbill. He spoke over the crowd. "Says right here, cash or good check, young lady."

Becky Raker was standing close by. "Her money's as good as yours, Bud Cole! If she says she's got it, she's got it."

"Eleven-five then," said Bud Cole.

"Take him to fifteen," whispered Fred. "That's twice what it's worth. Kate and I'll back you."

"Twelve thousand!" shouted Julie.

Colonel Guy knew when to keep his mouth shut. He just shifted his attention from one bidder to the other. Two tall men, one was very tall, were working toward the center of the crowd. The going was hard. The smaller older man had had a lot less trouble.

"Twelve-five," bid Bud Cole, getting angry.

"Thirteen," answered Julie.

"Fourteen," growled the factoryman. "Those truckers must tip pretty good at the Turkey Ranch is all I can say."

Julie colored and bent her head. The crowd gasped at the insult.

"That was uncalled for Bud Cole!" This came from fiery Monica Manikowski whose fiancé was a foreman at the tannery. So was her father. The boss decided to have a talk with those two.

Jonas Pemberton reflected that times were changing at the tannery.

"Keep bidding," whispered Fred to Julie. "Make him pay."

She raised her head. Her eyes glistened. "Fifteen thousand!" she called.

The crowd cheered.

332

"Sixteen," countered Bud Cole.

There was no response from Julie, Mac and Tom were still trying to get to her. They heard sixteen once, sixteen twice, and their home was sold for sixteen thousand dollars.

Julie felt hot and embarrassed and turned to leave. Fred grabbed her arm. "Wait it out," he said.

She untied her scarf and shook her hair. The blonde tresses tumbled over her shoulders and she drew stares. But Julie always drew stares. These, however, were admiring stares. From men and women.

That vixen Julie had made quite a stand.

———

Up front Bud Cole was getting a stern lecture from his mentor. "You're wasting money, Bud! You don't need any of these assets!"

"Relax, Jonas. I've only spent thirty thousand or so. Besides, I'm enjoying myself."

Colonel Guy, sipping coffee a few feet away, overheard and ran his own confidential tally. You've spent thirty-three-five, Mr. Bigshot. Drop the last aught leaves $3,350. Half of 50 is 25. Half of 33 is $16.50. That's in hundreds. $1650. Add the 25 - $1675. Not bad for the sticks. And the big one's next.

The scent of done chicken wafted over from the lunch tent. His stomach responded. He hadn't eaten in five hours. He'd sell that acreage then take a break. That woman who lost the house was a real looker. He'd inquire about her at the tent.

Two raps with the gavel grabbed everyone's attention. The elderly gent in the baggy black suit climbed carefully down the steps. On the way he grumbled, "If we had offered seventy-five thousand for that land in the first place we could have avoided this nonsense."

Seventy-five thousand. For land? The auctioneer had his cue. Ten percent was seventy-five hundred. Half of that, thirty-seven fifty.   Add the sixteen seventy-five; fifty-four twenty-five.   Enough to pay the taxman and a good down on the beachfront bungalow in Saint Petersburg.   Oh, those warm Gulf breezes during the winter at Saint Pete! Wouldn't that blonde look great down there?

"I have four thousand acres, plus or minus," he declared. Best to start them at sixty percent of his goal. He did some quick mental math. "How about ten dollars an acre? Is ten dollars good up here? Am I bid forty thousand dollars?"

Bud Cole raised his hand.

"Forty-five!" responded a male voice in the crowd.   The bidder waved and the auctioneer recognized Harry Raker. The last time he'd seen Harry was at the Bloomsburg Fair. Sharp buyer.   Got skinned by a carney kid at a sideshow though.

"Fifty," countered Cole.

"Fifty-five," returned Harry.

Newby Guy kept quiet. Save his voice for later.

"Sixty."

"Sixty-five."

"Seventy."

"Seventy-five."

Gotcha!

"Eighty," said Bud Cole firmly, resolving to go by tens if Harry kept this shit up.

Harry faltered.   Fred Sheafer edged up beside him and Becky. "How high you going?"

Becky answered. "Seventy-five was it."

"I'll give you fifty for the timber."

"Eighty thousand once, eighty thousand twice…"

"Ninety thousand!" shouted Becky.

What the hell? thought Bud Cole. The Raker's had only bid forty at the estate sale. Now he's bid double that and she's bumped him by ten. They've found out about the coal! Jonas thought Hank Whitaker had blabbed about the coal. He would have a nice "chat" with Whitaker too, on Monday.

"…Ninety thousand twice…"

"One hundred grand!" shouted Bud Cole.

The crowd tensed up. Newby Guy took his time; allowed the bidders time. This was big money.

"One-ten," countered Becky.

"Take it easy, woman," whispered Harry. "Go fives."

"One-twenty," offered the factoryman. "You make the pants and she wears 'em, right Harry?"

"One-thirty-five!" shouted Harry.

Becky whispered, "We're ten over, dear."

"One-fifty!" boomed Bud Cole. "There, damn you."

Again Harry faltered. He'd have to mortgage his farm if he went higher.

Fred Sheafer whispered again: "I'll split with you. Take him to two hundred."

"One-hundred-fifty once..."

"One-seventy-five!" shouted Harry.

"Two-hundred!" responded Bud Cole. "Go to hell, Harry. And find another plant to buy your milk."

Harry came prepared for that. "Sunnydale's pickin' us up tomorrow, Bud. Listen folks! Sunnydale Dairy is payin' fifty cents more a hundred than Cole here. If us farmers set up a co-op we can get seventy-five cents more."

"Count me in," said one farmer in the crowd.

"Me too," said another.

"And me," said a third.

Harry noted who his supporters were. All substantial producers. Others would follow. He shouted toward the platform: "You've been a public fool, Bud!"

Bud Cole ignored Harry's comment. Pemberton didn't. If enough farmers followed Harry, Cole Enterprises was out of the milk business. Milk was not highly profitable but it was good cash flow. Bud had just alienated his source of supply. Coal veins ran out but cows gave milk every day. They had mortgaged the milk plant and tannery to get the credit line. The profits from Bloss Mountain were six months away. The profits from Bear Mountain, if any, were years away. They were paying ten times for Bear what they paid for Bloss. All borrowed money. All based on one scared geologist's knapsack of samples. He poked his protégé's leg with his cane. "Fred Sheafer just ran you up a hundred thousand. I hope that coal's there, Benjamin."

"It is," he growled.

The crowd got antsy. Colonel Guy took control. The last bid was two hundred thousand. Five percent was ten thousand dollars!..."I have a bid for two hundred. Do I hear two twenty-five? Two twenty-five?"

During the Cole-Raker exchange a car ran the red light at Main and Fifteen, raced across the bridge and stopped at the entrance to the milk plant. A woman jumped out, left the door hanging open, and hurried around the crowd. The auctioneer was irritated; she'd partially blocked the entrance to the parking lot. But the bidding was too hot to worry about her right now. She probably thought she was missing the household auction.

Steve Heffner saw her too. Watched her skirt the crowd, locate a sheriff's deputy and show him a paper. Together they rushed toward the platform, toward the sheriff.

The banker opened the door to the depot warehouse, ran to its back door and exited it. Telling himself not to panic, he skirted the side of the crowd opposite the sheriff. He walked fast. He told the deputy watching that side he needed something from the bank, which was true. His car was parked just inside the entrance to the milk plant. Thank God Helen hadn't blocked it entirely.

Outwardly, Colonel Newby Guy, Esquire was at two-hundred thousand. Inwardly he'd hit eleven thousand six seventy-five. His greatest payday ever. Two hundred went once, twice, he raised his gavel, and...the sheriff stepped in front of him.

"Stop this! Stop this sale!"

Chapter 47 – The Bank Board

The crowd stood stunned. Then came a few peripheral stirrings. At the barbecue pit four firemen turned a basket of chicken on the count of three. In the crowd Ruby Broadwater's youngest was ready to go home. Across the road a car door slammed shut. Everyone else waited on Roby Tucker.

He explained: "Colonel MacEwen's assets were illegally seized. Any property sold must be returned. This sale is over! Folks, let's have some chicken and go home."

Most of the crowd cheered. The few out-of-towner's wondered who was running this show, the sheriff or the auctioneer. From the stricken look on Newby Guy's face they soon decided the sheriff.

Friends of Mac and Tom shook hands and patted them on the back enthusiastically. Others near Harry and Becky and Fred congratulated them. Julie Spencer found herself surrounded by well-wishers and embarrassed by comments such as Hattie Ballard's "It's about time, Julie!" Over the din the sheriff and the auctioneer could be heard calling for Steve Heffner. Had anyone seen Steve Heffner?

After a while the crowd settled down and broke up. Most were attracted to the lunch tent. A few returned to their cars. Jonas Pemberton climbed the platform to confer with Helen Kuhl and Squire Hayes. He stepped by his protégé, who remained sitting on the top step, publicly pretending it was easy-come easy-go, privately sick with hangover and dread and vowing to kill that incompetent pansy-ass banker. Bud Cole was one of two who saw his car cross the Blockhouse Bridge.

The brothers finally reached Fred and Julie. The men grinned broadly and shook hands. Julie was shy and subdued and embarrassed and beautiful. The weight of defeat had been lifted off the shoulders of the brothers MacEwen and Donachy. The glint of pixie had returned to Tom's eyes. A glint of hunger gleamed in Mac's.

He reached toward her and gently stroked her flushed cheek. Julie turned and pressed her face against his light touch. Their eyes met. The waiting was over. She was his. He was hers. Mac offered her his arm and nodded toward the lunch tent. "Would you join me for dinner, Miss Spencer?"

Tom interrupted. "Mac! What about our stuff?"

His brother never took his eyes off Julie. "It can wait."

———

Two other attractive women mingled with the group returning to their cars. Both wore scarves. The taller somewhat older woman wore sunglasses.

They met at the gate where two milk plant workers were pushing Helen Kuhl's car out of the way. In her rush Helen had taken her keys.

Delia spoke first. "I would say Mac is a very fortunate man. Wouldn't you agree, Miss Whalen?"

Abigail bit her lower lip, nodded a reluctant yes, and kept walking.

Delia paused at the gate and looked back. On the platform the sheriff had his finger under Bud's nose and Bud was paying attention. Then the auctioneer butted in and Bud backhanded him so hard he fell and his white hat went sailing. The blow was a typical reaction for Bud, which might have been tolerated a week ago. Not now. The sheriff called for his deputies who escorted Bud into the Depot office, Pemberton in tow. The sheriff helped the auctioneer to his feet and one of the Broadwater boys retrieved his hat. Funny, she hadn't pictured him a bald man.

Bud had some answering to do today. And not just to the law and the bank. To her. She had stopped at the guest house earlier. She wanted to talk this problem out and put her family back together.

Bud had gone already said the sleepy, busty young woman who answered the door.

———

What he needed at the bank was cash. There were two essentials right now – cash and gas. He'd have the cash in a couple of minutes. He looked at his fuel gauge. Half a tank. Enough to get him into New York State.

338

He wasn't leaving much behind; some furniture and clothes and golf clubs and Abigail. He had never really possessed Abigail, just wished it so. Still it hurt to know she didn't want him. They had seen each other as he was leaving. She was standing at the crowd's edge, on the raised railroad bed, to get a better view. She didn't speak but her message was clear. You're a disappointment, Steve Heffner.

She had her flaws too! Like encouraging him to make MacEwen jealous, which backfired. He pounded the steering wheel and ordered himself to pay attention, to stay in the present. He didn't have time for recriminations. He had to get away from here.

Going up Main he remembered putting his golf bag in his trunk a week ago. His shoes were there too. That made him feel a little better.

He parked behind the bank, for the last time in the space marked "President," and unlocked the back door. The two tellers on duty weren't busy. Most of the bank's customers were at the sale. He told them he was in a hurry, the auctioneer needed cash to make change, and opened the vault. As he went inside one of the tellers asked if he'd seen Helen.

They knew.

He answered no and stifled the rising panic that they might shut him in. No, they wouldn't do that. They thought he was going back to the auction and Helen and Squire Hayes and the sheriff. They'd let them do the dirty work. The hell with them.

He had $475.85 in his checking and $1734.48 in his savings, amounts he verified daily. He grabbed two packs of hundreds, four single fifties and one ten, leaving the odd packs in plain sight for the teller. He brushed by her and told her to write down $2,210 and close the vault. As he rushed down the hall he heard her tell the other that wasn't a lot of change for an auction.

He entered his office and wrote a receipt for the money. He was no thief! The bank could keep the change. At the bottom of the receipt he wrote "I resign," signed it, and placed it on top of the mess on his desk.

339

He stuffed the cash in his jacket pockets, grabbed the carton of Luckies from his desk drawer, and left.

He sped up side streets on the north side of town, entering 15 at the borough line. He would travel north into New York, then northwest. At Buffalo he'd cross over to Ontario, then head northwest again to Alberta. An oilfield was being developed in the Athabascan Valley. His college roommate was wildcatting with his father there. He had written they were doing some tomcatting too, did he want to join the fun? Fort McMurray was a boom town. They needed an accountant he said. They were too busy making money to take time to count it.

They had no hard evidence of a conspiracy. The extension agreement was all. He could stay and say he forgot signing it and lost it and might even pass a lie detector test because the statement was half true. Cole certainly was behind the Longsdorf arson, but he didn't know how. Rumor-mongers claimed Poorbaugh did it, but the big trapper was blamed for every unsolved crime in the valley, even murder. They had nothing substantial. All he and Cole had to do was keep their mouths shut.

Cole could do that. But he could never withstand the scrutiny of the Squire. He'd spill his guts and end up in jail. The Squire was going to fire him after the annual meeting anyway. Best to get away. It galled him though. Cole and MacEwen would still have their property and women and stature, while he had shit. Well, Cole wouldn't have much stature after this. Not after the Squire got through with him, he bet.

————

The Bank Board met at two and had two invited guests – Helen Kuhl and Roby Tucker. The MacEwen file lay on the table in front of Helen. Clipped neatly on top was the extension agreement with Steve Heffner's signature on it. The bank president's chair, by tradition to the right of the chairman's at the head of the table, was empty. Steven Heffner's file laid in front and clipped on top of that was his hasty resignation and receipt for funds taken.

The sheriff had compared the signatures and they matched.

The chairman and secretary-treasurer's chairs were also empty. Jonas had called saying they would be a few minutes late. The two had been sequestered in the tannery offices since noon, presumably conferring by phone with Cole's Harrisburg attorney. Squire Hayes and Roby Tucker had given them a lot to confer about.

On the wall behind the head chair hung the somber portraits of all the board chairmen. Except for haircuts and suit styles the men looked alike, and they should, for three generations of Cole's were displayed there. In each generation it was obviously forbidden for business scions to smile. Brass nameplates told their bank history.

Zebulon Cole had served from 1888 to 1938; Reuben Cole from 1938 to 1943. They died in office. Benjamin Cole had been a very young man when his tenure began in 1943. He would not die in office.

The next chairman resolved to have all the portraits taken down. He had gotten along with the hard-driving Cole's but had grown tired of them and their monuments to themselves. The ones who really belonged up there were Louisa Longsdorf and Jonas Pemberton. Too bad Jonas was tainted by this mess.

The Squire was seated at the opposite end of the long table, where the solicitor always sat, traditionally and symbolically as far away from management as possible. That disdain for the law had finally bitten the Cole's, for whom principle was subordinate to profit as long as you didn't get caught.

Helen Kuhl sat patiently to his right, and next to her, even-tempered Fred Sheafer. The sheriff sat impatiently to his left and next to him, the impatient and apologetic Romolo Barbano. The left side of the table wanted blood.

The Squire pointed to the extension: "Where'd you find it?" he asked Helen.

"Ernie Rollins' file," she said. "After he died I started a new one for his widow and daughter. Both files were on my desk along with Mac's the day we closed the Longsdorf deal. Steve signed the agreement and somehow stuck it in Ernie's file instead of Mac's. I stored Ernie's file with our inactive accounts in the basement. Steve never thought to look there. I didn't until this morning, when Mrs. Rollins came in to deposit a pension check."

Ernest Rollins. Squire's thoughts turned to his WWI trenchmate whose life was once saved by Samuel Poorbaugh. Samuel wouldn't appreciate Ernie saving MacEwen even though Mac was far better for Bear Mountain than Bud Cole. That understanding required rational thinking. He feared Samuel was beyond that.

The trapper hadn't been seen since Christmas but that didn't mean he wasn't around. Mort Fessler's death was indication of that. Samuel would be down soon. He'd need supplies.

He doubted Samuel was sane. But was he *ever* sane? When did the insanity occur? During a childhood spent with Jesse Poorbaugh? During combat in France? During one of almost forty winters spent alone in the mountains? Was it gradual or sudden? He recalled the Melville classic *Billy Budd*, where the transition from sanity to insanity was likened to the passage between colors of the rainbow. Just when did one color become another? Or was Samuel simply, coldly, brutally sane, a savage guided by a different set of rules?

Just then Bud Cole and Jonas Pemberton came in and took their respective places. Squire's attention turned to them. No pleasantries were exchanged. Each person at the table felt their own form of discomfort. By pre-arrangement Fred Sheafer, the vice-chairman, called the meeting to order.

The first item of business was the acceptance of Steve Heffner's resignation. All voted in favor, without regrets, including Bud Cole who wanted him as far away as possible.

The second item of business was the promotion of Helen Kuhl to bank president. All voted in favor except Bud Cole.

Helen then moved to the president's chair next to the chairman's. Her first official act was to hand him a typewritten document that required his signature.

Bud Cole read it, scowled, and scribbled his signature. Zebulon and Reuben looked over his shoulder as he signed.

The third item of business was the acceptance of Benjamin Cole's resignation as a director of Merchant's and Farmer's Bank. Bud Cole abstained from voting. All voted in favor, including Pemberton, who seemed to stoop lower today. The Squire had expected more emotion from Bud Cole.

The offended Romolo supplied the emotion. When his turn came Romolo voted "Yes, gladly," adding, "My boy, he won't be to work on Monday, Mr. Cole. I told him to go to the foundry in Bloss, even if he has to start by wheeling sand. I'm not voting for you at the annual meeting either, Mr. Pemberton, and I'm telling all my customers they need a union."

Pemberton shook his bald and wrinkled head. All the workers frequented Rom's shop. He was a true With-Out-Papers rags-to-riches success story. The swarthy wop shoemaker was the voice of close-knit Tannerytown. Until today he had sided with management. Now Bud Cole had been caught cheating a pair of Irish boys. Protestants true, but still Irish, and still Tannerytown. O'Conner's union was in.

And when Pemberton learned what else the Squire had in mind, he realized he himself had no hope of gaining a twelfth term as director of Merchant's and Farmer's. Such was the business life. He was past ninety and getting wobbly. It was time to retire. He would withdraw his name rather than suffer the indignity of being booted out like Benjamin. He glanced up at Zebulon and Reuben. Take a good look at your third generation, gentlemen. I told you.

Bud Cole rose to leave.

"We're not done yet, Bud," said the Squire.

"You got all you wanted, damnit!"

"Not all."

"What now?"

"You are to sell your stock to the bank on Monday."

"Like hell."

"If you don't we'll bring Heffner back and file charges." The Squire's hawk eyes were fierce and determined.

Bud Cole jeered at him. "Heffner's gone. Without him you don't have a case." He thus made it clear he *had* been in contact with his attorney.

The Squire turned to his left. "Sheriff?"

"Mr. Heffner was seen buying gas in Painted Post an hour ago. He's now headed toward Buffalo, then probably Canada. I found a letter on his desk from a friend in Alberta. The Mounties have agreed to tail him after he crosses the border."

"What's the selling price?" asked Jonas.

"Par."

"Par!" scoffed Bud Cole. "They're worth four times that! You're stealing my property."

"No, Bud," replied the Squire. "We're paying a legal price that you will agree to. Just like you and Jonas trying to obtain the Longsdorf property by paying off MacEwen's note."

"What are your plans for the shares?" asked Pemberton, smelling a good retirement investment.

"Sell them. Use the proceeds to rebuild the Longsdorf place." Having anticipated Pemberton's interest he added, "Sorry Jonas, directors, past or present, can't buy."

"You can go to hell," said Bud Cole vehemently. "My money's not helping MacEwen."

Immediately the sheriff rose from his chair. "That does it! I'm having Heffner picked up at the border."

Pemberton sighed wearily. "It's sell or face a trial, Benjamin. You can't win this."

The sheriff pointed his pudgy finger at the factoryman for the second time that day. "Understand this, Bud Cole. You've caused me a lot of trouble lately. I *want* to bring Heffner back here. I *want* you to suffer the consequences."

Bud Cole's countenance remained stubborn and defiant, but he backed down. "Jonas will deliver the certificates

Monday morning," he said. He couldn't resist one final parting shot before walking out: "But I'm pulling my money out the same day."

Helen Kuhl shot right back. "We'll survive."

Squire Hayes excused himself for a few minutes and followed the former chairman down the hall. "Bud!" he called. "I need a private word with you."

The tense and burly man stopped. The two tellers craned their necks toward them. Mr. Cole looked like he wanted to hit the Squire.

The lawyer was not intimidated and motioned toward Steve Heffner's former office. The two went inside. The Squire closed the door and the glass rattled. He resolved to remove that window today. He would remove that irritating rattle and name at the same time.

The office was a disorganized mess, which was not caused when the sheriff conducted his search. "He was something of a pig, wasn't he?" observed the Squire.

"What do you want now Squire?"

"Delia called me earlier. Asked me to represent her. Seems she found a young woman at your guest house this morning."

For the first time desperation crossed Bud Cole's stolid face. "She talking divorce?"

"I can get her half of everything, Bud. Maybe more."

The Squire's prediction was a test that the younger man passed. The figure didn't seem to matter much right then.

"I only did it to get even. She's been with MacEwen."

"I don't believe that."

"Damn it, Squire, I found his tracks! He's been at my house, I tell you."

The lawyer was incredulous. "You found tracks? You'd wreck your marriage because of tracks? Whose tracks? Delia *saw* that girl, Bud. Have you seen Mac at your house?"

Bud Cole bowed his head. "No."

"Then I suggest you reconcile with your wife before you lose her."

"When she loves another man she's already lost, Squire."

The Squire was both gentle and firm. He did not like Bud Cole but he did like his wife and daughter. "Talk to Delia, Bud. I don't believe she really wants a divorce."

The big man's countenance changed from one of desperation to hope. Faint hope, with some jealousy and anger and stubbornness mixed in. "I'll talk to her," he said. "But you tell Mac to say away. None of this would have happened if Mac had stayed away."

Bud Cole stalked out of the office and out of the bank. It was three o'clock. One of the tellers locked the vault. The other pulled the shades halfway and hung the closed sign on the heavy front door.

Squire Hayes remained by the president's desk. Bud Cole's jealousy of Mac had completely warped his judgment. Delia said he hit her; now he knew why. He found the other man's tracks!

Bud Cole did his own yard work, was good at it, enjoyed it actually. But when he got busy at the plant he would send a workman to the mansion to catch up the landscaping. Usually it was Ford Irish who came. Ford was a big man. Tracks! The jealous fool hit his wife because of a big man's tracks.

The Squire found the desk phone and called his son-in-law. Pete Jones was the stockholder favored by the board to replace Bud Cole. Pete was Main Street. Pete was solid. They needed to seat the new director before seating the new chairman.

Pete answered the phone. He'd been expecting the call. The Squire asked him to come over right away. He'd watch and unlock the back door for him. And bring a screwdriver. They needed to remove a doorglass after the board meeting was over.

"Goin' to the prom, ugly?"

"Yep."

Squeaky's eyebrows raised. Tom had never been on a date, let alone THE PROM. "You are? Who with?"

"None of your beeswax."

"Joe, who's he takin'?"

Unlike Squeaky, Joe could mind his own business. "I don't know. I feel sorry for the girl, though." He handed his empty plate to the camp cook. "Slide that last trout on there, would you, Tom?"

With a spatula borrowed from Posey, Tom loosened the fat, crisp brookie and gave it to Joe. He then set the sizzling fry pan aside and put the teakettle on. He'd borrowed that from Evie. Their whole picnic, except the main course, came from items scrounged from Evie and Posey. He returned to his seat on the porch and waited for the water to boil. Tom had developed a fondness for tea after a meal, had since that night spent in Bear Hollow.

The school cafeteria served fish on Friday but it was bland fare. When he suggested they observe the tradition somewhere else his two buddies eagerly agreed. So here they were, on the front porch of The Lady, devouring a mess of fresh trout caught from the springhouse pool.

The dwelling and springhouse were all that remained of the farmstead. Gutted and stained by the fire but structurally sound, the house stood vacant, boarded and secured from the weather. The bank had gotten a price to rebuild the property but Mac and he decided to use the money to reduce their loan. Evie was disappointed but it took the pressure off Mac. Reconstruction of The Lady would have to wait until the Day of No Debt, whenever that was. He knew it would someday be his task to restore it. He promised Evie. Mac didn't have the affection for old homes that he did. Old trees, yes. Old homes, no.

Full and warm and content, Tom sat against a pillar and closed his eyes. "I wonder how the poor folks are doin'," he said with a satisfied sigh.

Joe smirked.

Squeaky wasn't fooled. "You're always doin' that," he said. "You piss me off."

"Doin' what?" returned Tom, feigning innocence.

"Changin' the subject."

"Do I do that, Joe?"

"Do what?" replied Joe, wolfing down the last of his trout.

"Change the subject."

Joe thought a moment. "What was the subject?" He, too, was a master at exasperating Squeaky. They'd been doing it for six years, ever since junior high.

"You do it too, Joe. You both piss me off."

"What? What do I do?" This time it was Joe feigning innocence.

"You go along with him. Haven't you noticed he never tells us anything? We talk but he doesn't. The important stuff he keeps to himself."

"Finish your fish, Squeak," interrupted Tom. "It's good brain food."

Joe laughed. But he *had* noticed.

Squeaky finished his lunch but he did not give up. He ran down the list of desirable girls. "Let's see. Joe has Carol, I've got Sally (Squeak was awful proud of having Sally), Monica's engaged. Who's left?" Mentally, he reviewed the list again. "Brenda! She doesn't have a date. You didn't ask Brenda?"

"I told you, Squeak. It's none of your business."

"The prom is everybody's business. Always has been."

Joe glanced over at Tom. "You know, he's got something there."

Just then a car pulled into the farm lane and stopped by the fencerow. Julie got out and spotted them. After shaking her finger at the hooky-players she walked underneath the tall bushes that lined the fence and started clipping branches.

348

"What's she up to?" asked Joe.

"Aunt K likes pussy willows," answered Tom. "Today's Julie's day off. She's gathering some for her." Tom knew Julie planned a visit with Aunt K. It was he who recalled her fondness for that particular spring flower.

Squeaky butted in. "There you two go again. Changin' the subject!"

Tom relented. "You mean about who I'm taking to the prom?"

"Yeah."

"Nan. I'm taking Nan."

———

It was pleasant there, in the shade of the pussy willows. An aimless breeze wandered out of Longstar, drawing with it a sweet blend of Steam Valley smells. They were also secure smells; fresh-cut wood from the timber landing, blooming lilacs from the springhouse, wisps of smoke from the cookfire. She had Mac's dinner pail in her car and fifteen minutes to spare before they were to meet for lunch at the landing. Just enough time to savor the day and pick a spray of wildflowers.

The breeze pushed down the limber branches, enveloping her in the softness of a thousand tiny pillows. Aunt K's favorite spring flower was really a bud, a furry white bud that felt good. The delicate kitten-toes caressed her neck and face and reminded her of Mac's gentle touch. That such a physical man could be so gentle had surprised her. And stirred her. Excited her almost to the point of losing control. Almost. In June, after Tom graduated and moved on and they were married, there would be no restraints.

———

After school Abigail and Julie met unexpectedly at Aunt K's. They hadn't talked since that cold winter morning when they watched the log drive from the steel bridge. Abigail was

349

crumpled and dusty from a rowdy spring day at school. Julie was crisp and flushed and lovely, reminding the envious Abigail of a model in a fashion catalog.

Abigail carried an armload of books and files, homework for the weekend. Julie carried a wide spray of pussy willows. Julie had the lightest load so she opened the first-floor door. When she did, Abigail saw the unmistakable flash of a diamond. It was a small flash from a small diamond but still a diamond, the same one Abigail herself had desperately yearned for.

Danny had said he was moving after school was out. Now she knew where. Abigail kept her composure, thanked Julie, and started upstairs. Her heavy load seemed to grow heavier. Julie knocked on the Sheafer's door. Aunt K answered and made a fuss over the pussy willows. She did not notice Abigail resting two-thirds of the way up the stairs; resting, and listening. Julie said, "Aunt K, we have to talk," and the door closed behind them.

Entering her apartment Abigail dumped her schoolwork on the couch and knelt quietly over the floor register. It was open. The two women were directly below her, at the kitchen table. Aunt K served lemonade and they began talking.

At one point Aunt K left the kitchen for the dining room. When she returned Julie said, "I don't recall this picture of Danny."

"This isn't Danny. This is David."

Neither spoke. Both were obviously drawn to that compelling photo of David Sheafer as a child. Julie reacted first.

"You've known. I thought maybe you did."

"We've suspected it for a long time, dear. Have you told Mac?"

"Yes."

Thus Abigail was the first outside the family to learn the answer to the oft-asked questions regarding Danny Spencer, namely who his real father was and who his step-father would be. The knowledge did little to console the young teacher.

Chapter 49 – The Taking of Amanda Cole

Usually he could kid a customer who'd eaten raw leaks and whose breath smelled like sour milk. But Frank Sawyer did not kid this customer. Kidding was foreign to this customer.

Spike Poorbaugh swiveled the metal display rack roughly, picking his garden seed by the pictures on the envelopes. He talked to himself. He rambled. "Cucumbers, I need cucumbers. And beans. I need beans. Too late for peas, too late. They don't keep anyway. Where's the sweet corn? Damnit, where's the corn?"

Frank had heard him ramble before but he was never this agitated. Never this loud.

The loafer's bench was full and uncustomarily quiet, its occupants ill at ease. Frank wondered if the trapper knew he was a regular subject of their discussions. The conversation, muted now, would be lively after he left.

Friday lingered muggy and buggy and hot, drifting in the calm between afternoon and evening. He'd almost sold out of fans and had sold out of flypaper. The fans he had left were all running, which kept the air moving and their price tags fluttering. He and the bench hoped he'd sold the last one, hoped he'd priced them too high.

Over the drone of the fans they could hear Spike Poorbaugh's harsh voice. He wanted to get his seed planted before the rain.

The trapper was dressed for the weather, wearing moccasins, stained jeans, and an unlaced buckskin vest. No shirt, just the vest. Frank didn't know a half-breed could have so much hair.

Spike Poorbaugh hadn't yet trimmed his winter's growth. His thick locks hung loose and to his shoulders. His beard was heavy and wavy. His torso, front and back, was matted with coarse hair, bronzed skin showing underneath. The color was wolfish, dark gray, highlighted with patches and streaks of rust.

The everpresent bowie, in its beaded sheath, was strapped behind his back. Over the years Frank had distinguished two knives, one with a wood handle, the other of bone. The Squire said his favorite was the bone, the one he took with him to France. He carried the bone-handled bowie today. Spike Poorbaugh aged like that ivory. His eyes, his teeth, his long nails, all yellowed and hardened menacingly over the years.

He was sweating and the thick wild onion smell seeped from his pores and clung to his body. He wasn't unhealthy, far from it in the physical sense. He was simply different, a throwback to another time and place. Jackson Township's history credited Jesse Poorbaugh for killing the last wolf. Frank maintained he'd actually sired the last one.

Normally the trapper's spring order was worth the odor. On his rare trips to town he stocked up: traps, ammunition, tools, and garden seed from him; flour, salt, and sugar in bulk from Bob's; a haircut and shave from Harold; a visit with the Squire.

But not today. Just garden seed today. Few provisions and much talk. He didn't seem lonely. Seemed content keeping his own company. Odd.

His selections made, the trapper placed the envelopes on the counter. Frank rung him up. "That will be three seventy-nine, Spike."

Spike handed him a five.

Frank laid the bill across the open drawer and started counting the change. His eyes wandered across the bill and his heart jumped. There was writing on that bill! Tom's note to Brenda! He'd given it to Mort the night he died. Now Spike was giving it back.

Spike, who had seemed distracted earlier, was now focused on him. Money grabbed his attention, always had. "Somethin' wrong?" he asked, aware of the delay.

Frank tried not to stammer. "No. Just miscounted your change. A dollar twenty-one, right?"

The trapper's coarse gray eyebrows grew together in a frown. The cold yellow eyes slitted suspiciously. He counted his change.

Frank slammed the cash drawer shut and put the seed envelopes in a paper bag. "Looks like a nice evening coming on," he said, wincing immediately because it wasn't.

Spike took the bag and disagreed about the evening. "Can't you smell it? It's fixin' to rain. I got to get this seed in before the rain." He turned and walked out.

Frank breathed a sigh of relief. He then hurried to the sidewalk to see what direction the trapper had gone. Charley Bower was right – Spike Poorbaugh had killed Mort and taken his money. There could be no other explanation. And Mort had been a friend! What a crazy cold-hearted son of a bitch!

The jeep traveled east on Main then turned south on 15. That too was strange. Why take the busy highway? Williamson Trail was closer and less traveled, more to the shy man's liking. Stranger still, Squire Hayes was walking down the sidewalk with that day's mail and Spike drove right by him without any acknowledgement. He always stopped for Squire Hayes. Frank could see the Squire was puzzled as well.

When the lawyer reached the store Frank pulled him inside and showed him the bill. He told him of his ramblings. The Squire went directly to the phone and called Roby Tucker. It was one of the times the lawyer regretted the county seat being an hour away.

———

The jeep lurched and backfired through each gear. It needed a tune-up, something Mort used to do for him free in the past. Now he'd have to hire it done. Well, he had Mort's money, which made up for not havin' Mort.

Grandmother Songbird said every man should leave a son. It was in The Book. *Like arrows in the hands of a warrior are sons born in one's youth. Happy is the man*

354

whose quiver is full of them. It sounded different in the
Bible she had. She had to translate it for him.

Jesse said it was fun, fillin' that quiver. But when his
boys growed they turned testy, mighty testy. Got themselves
killed, they did. Killed each other, mostly. All 'cept you,
Samuel. Don't you turn testy.

Songbird said Jesse would have killed those men that
came and took their surviving son to war. But Jesse'd been
dead some seven years and his son wanted to see some places
other than these mountains. He did.

He'd fought and sowed some wild oats. Squire got him
out of a scrape or two. Could be he left a Poorbaugh over
there. He didn't know for sure. He'd heard the French girls
had a way of killin' their babies before they were born. He'd
resolved to ask Songbird what The Book said about that kind
of killin', but she was dead when he got home. He had to be
sure. He was the last of the Bear Clan. He was the last
Poorbaugh. He should leave a son.

He took the turnoff connecting 15 and Williamson Trail
and parked inside the covered bridge. From there he could
watch the Cole place and not be seen. And still have the
jeep. If someone came along he'd just get out of their way.
He was watchin' for turtles, a rain was comin', and turtles
came out when it rained.

When he drove by earlier the girl was mowin' the lawn.
Had shorts on. Then she was close to the house. Now she
was down by the road. She'd had to tie her dog. He wanted
to play and she had to work. It was good he was tied. He
was too fat, that dog.

———

Bud Cole worked out back, picking up pine cones that
had blown in the yard. He had taken the Squire's advice and
reconciled with Delia. He'd dumped the hostess, cut back on
the booze, and came home. So far he slept in the guest room.
He wasn't getting in their bedroom without an invitation.

But he'd caught some signals recently that it wouldn't be too long.

He heard the mower down by the road. Delia worried Amanda might get hurt by the mower but she was a big girl and strong. Thirteen now and as tall as her mother. Sure, they could afford a groundskeeper but the girl needed to learn how to work. What better place than the yard? Barney was tied to his chain from the garage. He was too much of a pest when she mowed. He pranced and barked every time she passed by the front of the house. This time, though, he bristled and growled and reared crazily, and Amanda was way down by the road. Curious, Bud Cole turned the corner.

Spike Poorbaugh stalked his daughter.

Amanda, intent on keeping the rows straight, the mower revved on high, was oblivious to her danger.

The trapper strode up from behind, clenched a fist, and hit the back of her head. She folded and slumped down. He picked her up and carried her toward his jeep. The mower drowned other sounds.

With a bellow Bud Cole ran toward them. Barney, jumping and straining violently, pulled the chain fastener out of the wall and tore through the yard. His chain burned Bud Cole's ankle as he raced by him.

Poorbaugh, his back to the yard, was almost to his jeep when the furious dog jumped him. The speed and weight of the heavy dog sent all three sprawling. Recovering quickly, Poorbaugh drew his knife. The dog and the trapper whirled and fought. Amanda lay still.

Spike Poorbaugh was familiar with attacking dogs. The bowie flashed as Barney growled and jumped and clawed and bit savagely, then let out a shrill yelp. Then another. The trapper disabled him first with a thrust that broke a hip, then ripped him open underneath, belly to breastbone. Barney's hind feet became entangled in entrails and chain and he whimpered and flopped toward the still form of Amanda.

Poorbaugh rose up in time to see Bud Cole rushing him, head down, like a raging bull. He thought the father to be a damn fool: he had no weapon, just his rage and youth and weight and beefy hands. The older man was half a foot taller, though lean, was big-boned and actually weighed more than Bud Cole. He too was maddened, first by lust and next by pain. The fat dog had split his right ear with a fang slash and had clawed him deep along his side. His ear bled and his ribflesh burned. Poorbaugh crouched and snarled and his yellow eyes ignited and he resolved he wasn't going to give any ground or woman to Bud Cole.

He set himself for the rush, crouched lower, and when they crashed together, straightened the charging man up. He jerked the bowie flat and hard between the third and fourth ribs and when the hilt struck flesh, he twisted. A rib cracked and he withdrew.

Bud Cole got his hands around Spike Poorbaugh's throat. His thumbs sought the Adam's apple but the trapper lowered his head and butted him in the nose. Cole's nasal passages filled with brine and blood and pain. He was aware of another sharp pain in his chest. He kept his grip but he held more neck than throat. The bowie slashed in front of him and lanced his forearm open elbow to wrist. He lost his hold and was shoved back. Another deep thrust ripped across his groin and Cole stumbled to the ground. The fresh-mowed grass was wet with blood and getting wetter. He screamed and pushed himself toward Amanda, to shield her, but the going was hard, and futile. His one good leg kept slipping over the wet grass.

The fight was over but the trapper kept low, fearful of being shot from the house by the mother. Maybe she couldn't shoot. She may not have seen. She couldn't have heard. The mower drowned out the howls and yells. He hadn't expected that damn dog to get loose. Or Bud Cole to get there so soon. Damn dog. Slowed him up. Now they were dead or soon to be. All he wanted to do was breed the girl. They could have had her back. Damn dog.

He approached the limp form of Amanda. Had he cold-cocked her too hard? He'd been taught that by Jesse. You could breed them out cold but it wasn't as much fun, he said.

He wiped the knife blade across the heaving coat of the dog, sheathed it, and lifted the girl. He carried her to the jeep and dropped her in the back seat. Her bare legs excited him. The females he'd known all wore skirts or dresses. Never showed much leg. She was solid, too, and shaping up to be a wholesome woman.

He jumped into the front seat and drove off. His long hair was spongy with blood from his split ear. He'd have to stitch that together later, after. He didn't look back. The jeep backfired when he hit second and third.

He didn't see Delia rush from the house. She'd gone to the basement for some canned goods for supper. When she returned to the kitchen she looked out the window to check on Amanda...and witnessed the last few seconds of Poorbaugh's ravaging of her family.

When she got to Bud he was curled up on his left side. She turned him over and gasped. He lay in a black puddle of blood. He was conscious. He knew she was there. He mouthed words she couldn't hear because of the mower. She ran to it and shut it off. The resulting quiet permitted other, more distant sounds; a chain saw buzzing on Blackwolf, a vehicle backfiring on Williamson Trial. She held her husband close so she could hear. Cole spoke in a hoarse whisper. "He took Amanda," he said. "Get Mac." Then he faded out.

Frantic, crying, overwhelmed with disbelief, Delia did as she was told. She jumped in the Cadillac and raced to the timber landing praying aloud to God to help Amanda, praying for Bud's life, and praying for Mac to be there.

Behind her, Bud Cole lay very still, and Barney kicked his last.

Chapter 50 – The Battle of Potash Mountain

Delia arrived as the crew was loading up to go home. She stumbled out of her car screaming for help. Her blouse and slacks were smeared with blood. Mac got to her first.

"Oh Mac! Spike Poorbaugh took Amanda. And Bud's hurt real bad."

Mac held Delia by the shoulders. Her knees were rubbery. "Did he hurt Amanda?"

"I think so. He carried her to his jeep. She wasn't moving."

Charley spoke up. "Poorbaugh drove by a few minutes ago. I heard that jeep backfire. He's headed to his cabin for sure."

Mac felt Delia's weight increase. She was near collapse, on the verge of hysteria. He pulled her closer, made direct eye contact with her. "Does he know you saw him?"

"I don't think so."

Mac drew her closer, held her a few seconds, thought the situation through. The trapper had gone over the edge. He had to be dealt with, now. Amanda, Delia, and Bud needed help, now.

The shocked crew waited expectantly. The order would come soon. There would be no discussion.

"Abe, take Delia home and get help for Bud. Tell the police to bring dogs and not to bunch up in one vehicle. The rest of us are going for Amanda."

Abe hurried Delia to the car and sped off. Mac continued: "We'll take two vehicles. Keep fifty yards apart in case he finds out we're following and ambushes us. Will and Charley ride with me. Tom, you ride with Luke. Get the guns. Make sure they're loaded."

Since the incident with the bear dog they had carried weapons in their trucks. Mac kept his .32 Special in the one-ton and his Army .45 in the log truck. Luke kept a scope-sighted .270, Abe a 30-30 Winchester, and Charley, the 30-40 Krag. Will grabbed the 30-30, Tom the .45.

Charley returned, belting on the Krag's scabbarded bayonet. This usually hung from the gun rack and came in handy as a can opener and pry tool. It was added protection today. "A man like Poorbaugh," he explained, "can get close, mighty close."

Will was following along but his wide eyes showed fear and bewilderment. Will had never experienced true meanness. "What'd he take Amanda for? Ransom?"

Charley snorted. "He didn't take that girl for no ransom."

Guns checked and loaded, they got in their trucks. Mac led off in the one-ton. Luke followed. He pointed to the .45 automatic. "Can you shoot that thing, Tom?"

"I can shoot it. I can't hit anything with it, though."

"I carried one in the war. I couldn't hit anything with mine either."

"This has all happened kind of fast. What are we going to do when we get there?"

"Mac's working that out right now."

"He split us up on purpose. The brother's aren't together."

"I noticed that."

"Spike used that big knife on Bud, didn't he?"

"Bud Cole's probably dead by now, Tom."

"You scared?"

"Yep."

"Think Mac's scared?"

"Sure. But he's mad too. And Mac will keep his head. Poorbaugh's accustomed to folks being scared of him and losing their head. That won't happen this time."

———

He parked the jeep beside the cabin, a double-planked one-story with a slant roof, an open porch running the width of the front, and an enclosed woodshed attached to the rear. He'd rebuilt the cabin after the first war, after the flu killed

360

his family. He'd returned a fair rough carpenter, one of several skills he'd honed in the army.

The front and back doors were also made of plank boards, hinged to open in and bracketed for oak bars for additional security. Sash windows salvaged from an abandoned farmhouse allowed light and air from all sides except the back. Each window was hinged for inside plank shutters, which could also be barred if necessary. The windows were open and unshuttered today, with adjustable store-bought screens filling the openings.

The cabin faced south and gained heat in the summer. On hot nights he took his bed to the porch and chained a dog near to protect him from prowling snakes. Jesse admired the rattler, but he wouldn't tolerate one around his house. Nothin's more lowdown, quick, or quiet, Samuel. But he's lowdown first.

The only opening out back was the door. He'd snugged the north side of the cabin closer to the steep slope of Potash and allowed the laurel to grow high and dense against it. He kept a low path cut through that tangle all the way to the ridge. Every snake had an extra hole and that was his.

East of the cabin, also snugged against the slope, set the pelt shed and dog run. A low path ran to them, too. It worked good the time he stalked Jim Morningstar.

In the clearing in front, facing south and warmth, was his garden, all spaded and raked, with the rows hoed for planting. Next to the garden stood the smokehouse. To the west, at the edge of the hemlock grove that semicircled the clearing, was the privy. Deeper within the hemlocks, banked by tall ferns, was the bog, the Poorbaugh burial ground.

The girl moaned in the back seat and the dogs clamored. They heard a stranger. They smelled a female. They did not approve of her. He reached down and ran his hand through her thick auburn hair. He found the big lump on the back of her head and felt of it. Her skull wasn't cracked. She was just knocked out. She hadn't seen her dad or dog get it, hadn't seen anything, which was good. He didn't have a whole lot of time. If she came to early she might be coop-erative. He doubted it, though.

He leaned over, wrapped one long arm underneath her chest, lifted her out, and dragged her inside. She was ches-tin' up real good, better'n his sisters. The dogs pitched and clawed against the wire sides of the run. They sure wanted to smell of the girl.

The law'd be comin' soon. They'd lay the knifin' of Bud Cole to him. He should breed her, lock her in the pelt shed, release his dogs to kill their dogs, and be on his way.

Kind of quick, what he'd done. He'd only planned on watchin' her from the bridge. He'd watched her lots of times. He'd really only planned on gettin' his garden in.

She reminded him of that girl in France. That Frog officer raised her dress, he saw her bare legs, and he stepped from the bushes and took her. Happened all the time in the woods. A female frisks around a courtin' male, then a stronger, no-nonsense male shows up and breeds her. The Frenchie didn't even try to fight, ran off with a slit belly.

It wasn't quite the same today. This girl wasn't friskin' and her dad wasn't courtin'. In the army he'd found most folks weren't urged that way. Just Poorbaugh's. He'd really only planned on gettin' his garden in. But those bare legs urged him.

This was a good place but he'd have to leave. He'd hole up by day and travel at night. Go back to Kinzua. There was lots of godforsaken land up there. Maybe get a Seneca woman with child. Make double sure there were Poor-baughs. He'd have money this time. Cash money. Mort's money. The tribe always needed money. He didn't have cash money the last time, when hoboes walked the roads, and the tribe sent him away. He'd sneak back to the Cole place in a year or so and see if this taking took. See if he had a son. He didn't care back in France. He was young then. He thought there was time. There was, but it went.

He laid the girl on her back on the steel-framed bed. He unsnapped her shorts and the dogs clamored again. Some-thing rasped against their wire and they went crazy. Had that male Airedale bit his way through? If so, he'll be tearin' through that open door. He straightened up, headed for the porch and a club…and saw movement beyond his jeep. A man ran through his garden! He'd just gotten that ready!

He closed the door, barred it, went for his guns.

———

He grabbed a 10-gauge shotgun and a handful of shells. Double aughts. Heavy buckshot that ripped a hole to and through his target. A true poacher's gun, used when his hounds treed big game at night. He'd blown cats and bears clean out of the tops of pines in Bear Hollow, long distance shootin' for a shotgun. Some of those trees were sixty yards high. That man behind his smokehouse was less than thirty.

If he peeked around the corner he'd get a face full of buckshot. Hell, he wouldn't have a face. If he ran for the privy he'd hold his fire. Wait 'til he hid behind that narrow building and thought he was safe. Then send two belt-high rounds right through it. He'd only single-planked that privy. It would keel right over and so would the man.

There had to be two men. One at the dogpen, the other at the smokehouse. Who were they? How'd they get here so fast? There hadn't been enough time! Damn!

He'd drop the one at the smokehouse then circle out back. Stalk the dogpen from the laurel, the same way he stalked the warden. The dogs wouldn't yammer any different than now. Catch him in a crossfire, would they?

He crept to the porch window, the one with the best view of the smokehouse. The man behind it did not look his way, did not know he was the target. With his knife blade he slowly raised the window off the screen, making a slot to poke the side-by-side through when it was time. Sons of bitches. Take his woman, would they? He sheathed the knife, shouldered the gun, and watched the smokehouse.

It was old glass. Stuff Mort had given him from a house he tore down one time. Had bubbles in it. Distorted your view. Made a difference with a rifle but not a shotgun.

363

The cage rattled again. That wire was taut. Sounded like a blade against a sharpenin' steel. The pack barked and growled furiously.

A diversion. He wasn't fooled! The man behind the smokehouse would move now, and he did, sprinting for the privy.

Donachy! With a handgun! So the loggers worked late, did they? Saw him go by. No matter. When he reached the privy he'd blow it and him in two. Then go out back for the brother. Would have to be a lot more careful with the brother.

He slid the double barrel out of the window. Aimed for the left half of the privy door. The big kid would grab the rear corner post to stop his run and when he did he'd flatten against the planking and end up with a door latch in his belly. Almost there...

Something darkened the window like a part-drawn curtain. He looked up. No! The window pane smashed and he was clubbed hard on the left shoulder. Sash and bone crunched in the same instant. The shotgun went off as he was knocked away from the window. He fell backwards still holding the shotgun. Glass and framing rained in on him. He scrambled to get up as MacEwen stepped through the window. He had a round left if he could get the gun up in time. He was still off balance when the gun was booted out of his hands. MacEwen wouldn't shoot in here. Wouldn't until he knew where the girl was. He got up finally but was butt-stroked and knocked backward again, seeing flashing blue streaks as he tumbled over the stove. The pipe let loose. Black soot billowed up like smoke and filled that section of the cabin. He landed hard behind the iron stove and lay dazed and still. The soot swept over him and he stifled a cough.

————

All Mac could see were Poorbaugh's bent legs. He decided to shoot both knees, to prevent him from going

364

anywhere, but his rifle wouldn't fire. He'd broken it, jammed the action during the clubbing. The trapper was down, probably out, certainly not dead. Mac wanted him dead but his first duty was to Amanda. He had to get her out of there.

He tossed his rifle out the window and stepped to the bed. Amanda was unconscious. He threw her over his left shoulder and tramped through the broken glass toward the front door and spreading cloud of dust. He yelled he was coming out. The black grime stung his eyes and someone coughed, he thought Amanda. He felt for the bar, lifted it, found the latch and pulled the door open. The light and incoming air turned the black to gray. He stumbled crossing the threshold and felt the unmistakable bite of sharp steel. He grunted and flinched and heard Poorbaugh swear. He drove himself forward, ran off the blade. He clambered down the porch, fell behind the jeep, and covered Amanda. Gunfire erupted around him.

———

Poorbaugh retreated behind the door as bullets splintered and holed the planking and crisscrossed in search of him. MacEwen's whole crew was out there! He dropped to his stomach, ignored the pain from his broken collarbone, and wormed along the floor through the grime and glass to the woodshed. He stretched between two stacks of firewood and was thankful for the short winter. Bullets from three sides penetrated the main part of the house. A few strayed to the woodshed and made several unsplit two-footers jump. None entered from the rear, from the ridge. He cracked the back door open slowly and just wide enough for him to crawl out. The laurel looked impenetrable. He moved a thick branch, revealing a low tunnel underneath the leafy canopy. He crawled in it.

They continued to shoot into the house so they didn't know he was gone. His escape was marked by vibrating limbs and leaves and grunts of effort and pain. Halfway up he felt confident he was safe and started talking to himself again.

The path opened at the spine of the ridge beside a truck-sized boulder. He stood against it to get his breath and looked back for a view. The laurel was high but scattered, the cover not so good. He reeled sideways as sandstone exploded by his face and embedded in his cheekbone. The sound of the shot followed him over the ridge. They'd got the girl, the bastards, and almost got him. Someday, he'd get them.

———

With Poorbaugh routed the crew gathered in front of the cabin. Tom came in from the privy, Charley from the dog run, Luke from the hemlocks, and Will from the ridge.

Mac sat against the front tire of the jeep. Amanda lay alongside, her head cradled in Mac's lap. Both were dirty with soot and grime. Both were hurt but alive. Red droplets streaked the front and back of Mac's t-shirt, welling from slits in the collar. Poorbaugh's knife had pierced the thick muscle between the neck and shoulder. There was nerve damage; Mac's right arm was drawn against his side. Although wounded, he was still able to give orders.

Charley tended their injuries while Tom secured the cabin and Luke and Will brought the vehicles in. On the way Luke stopped by the dog run and shot every dog.

Tom closed the shutters and barred the windows. He shut and barred the back door. The soot would just have to settle over everything inside. Mac didn't want Poorbaugh doubling back for the weapons, or releasing that pack of dogs. Tom looked for the shotgun, which he found under the stove. He unloaded it and smashed it over the stove. It had been one powerful gun. A full quarter of the privy had disintegrated in front of him as he ran toward it. He dove and Mac crashed inside. He could hear the fight and agonized until Mac yelled and emerged carrying Amanda. Then Poorbaugh's blackened face and yellow teeth appeared out of the dust, and then the bone-handled bowie. He thrust, he was actually grinning when he did it. Mac grimaced and ran clear. Tom started shooting. Wildly shooting. Just pointing and shooting. So did Charley and Luke. The trapper ducked into the dust and disappeared. Tom emptied his clip then emptied the two spares, praying that one slug would find the trapper, just one. Poorbaugh's appearance on the ridge was a chilling reminder that not all prayers are answered.

The cabin was a sieve of bullet holes. There was blood on the floor, on the woodshed door and on the laurel. Poorbaugh was hurt but still able, still dangerous. He could climb. He'd gone right by Will. Will must have froze up there.

———

Will was the last to come in. He stopped the one-ton near the jeep and unloaded the water cooler. Charley handed a full dipper to Mac who jerked when he took it and inadvertently spilled some on Amanda. She moaned and touched her head. "That's a good sign," said Charley.

Tom closed the front door of the cabin and approached Will. "Why didn't you shoot?" he asked.

Will stammered an honest reply. "I was so scared I was shaking. You guys were shooting at the cabin but I couldn't see anything. Then the laurel moved. Something coming my way. At first I thought it was a woodchuck, he was so low. I just stayed still. Then he stood up and Luke shot and he was gone."

Charley handed Will a drink. He spilled most of it.

"I saw the movement too," said Luke. "I could have shot earlier but thought it might be Will. Then Spike appeared. He couldn't have been more than twenty feet from you, Will."

"He was close. I could hear him talking."

"Talking?" asked Mac.

"Yeah, talking. He was talking to himself."

"What did he say?"

367

"Said he was going for the money on Caleb's Rock." Then Will lowered his voice, treating Amanda as if she was sleeping. "And he'd breed that girl another day."

"The bastard," said Tom.

"Must be Mort's money," observed Mac.

Charley took his own drink then refilled the dipper to pass is around again. "He's gonna hide out somewhere, then come back. We can't let him get away, Mac."

"He's gone."

"Yeah, but we know where he's goin'."

"What are you getting at, Charley?"

"Pick him off at Caleb's Rock. It's a long walk for him and he's hurt. We can drive to Mort's, take the switchbacks, and get there before he does.

"He's still got a straight line. It's roundabout for us."

"Poorbaugh's keep caches. I found one of Jesse's in a cave on Blackwolf. Had a blanket, gun, pocketknife, fishline, and some jerky. Spike scooted out without a gun. He'll hear the truck, think we're goin' for help. He'll think he has time, head for his hole, then the money. One of us will be waitin'."

"I can't climb those switchbacks in time, Charley."

"I wasn't thinkin' of you, Mac."

———

368

Charley insisted Tom take the Krag. Reloading it, Tom discovered the old veteran had made the long gun longer. He had fixed the bayonet.

"The pigsticker's a last resort," he warned. "Don't you let him get that close. And remember, that front sight is might fine."

They all expected an objection from Mac but it didn't come. Instead he told Will to drive the one-ton and reaffirmed Charley's warning. "If he finds you out, Tom, you run," he said.

"You run like hell," added Luke.

Tom nodded his assent. He took a last look at Amanda and shared a longer look with his brother. Mac sent him on his way wondering privately what his mother and Big Mike thought about letting Tom go.

Will started the rugged truck and was soon tearing down Jacob Miller's former ox-cart trail. The end of the rifle stuck out the passenger ride window, the blade shearing cleanly the branches that swished against it.

Nothing was said until they reached Mort's. The truck was slowing when Tom jumped out and started jogging up the junkyard road toward the switchbacks. Will stopped and called after him. "You mind what they said, Tom! You run if he gets close."

Will's concern was justified. Since they left the cabin Tom's strong-featured face had hardened to grim stone. He suspected Tom had made up his own mind about meeting Spike Poorbaugh.

Will's answer was a gesture. Tom raised the rifle and shook it. That meant he'd heard. It didn't mean he'd listen.

———

Tom's run up the switchbacks was a feat of youthful strength and resolve, a run fueled by anger. He kept images of those hurt by the trapper in his mind. He saw Delia in her blood-spattered clothes running to Mac. He saw Mac wince as he was stabbed while carrying Amanda. He saw Charley pulling up Amanda's shorts; Tom had never had a sister, never saw a girl in her underwear. He saw Mort circling dead and battered in the whirlpool and Charley's grief-stricken face at the funeral of his best friend. He saw Missy Morningstar and her confused twins at Jim's funeral. Their daddy didn't lay in that box. Where was daddy? She had asked him to sing and he tried and cried and barely got through it. He saw the sadness on Evie's face when he told her they didn't have the money to repair The Lady. And he recalled the savage hate on Spike Poorbaugh's face the day Mac killed his dog, and Spike's weighing the odds with Tom standing there with a rock. How much grief he would have saved had he thrown that rock!

Tom was eighteen, in peak condition and uncommonly big and smart and strong. When he reached Caleb's rock he was out of breath but not out of anger. He found a thick-trunked white oak that offered a clear view of the ledge and sat against it. He got his breath, recovered quickly. But he convinced himself he was tired of running. Yes sir, he was done running for the day.

———

In the cave on the north slope of Potash Spike Poorbaugh checked his wounds and rested. There were rustlings around him and he was concerned. He'd made noise before entering and lit a candle. You could light up a lot of cave with one candle. They didn't like fire, even a little one, and usually withdrew. But they were touchy today. They smelled blood. He'd rinse that off when the rain came. Also, it was nigh to evenin' and their time to hunt, but company showed up as they were leavin' and pissed them off. High caves like this one were snaky in the summer. Low caves, like the one behind the falls, weren't so bad.

He was beat up pretty good. His ear was split, his face cut, his cheekbone and collarbone broken. He's been bit and clawed and choked and clubbed and kicked. Like hand to hand in the trenches it was. In the trenches, though, Mac-Ewen would have finished the job. Damn him. He felt the throbbing lump on his collarbone and gritted his teeth, stifling a wince and a cry. No quick move or sharp sound in here! He didn't want to add snakebite to his troubles. He hurt some but his limbs all worked and his head had cleared. Snakebite would fog his thinkin' and make him sick. He couldn't afford a bite right now.

He reached for the package stored on the ledge overhead. He kept it wrapped in oilskin. He felt dry flesh first, indignant muscles rippling and cording. He cursed and squeezed and flung the snake aside. It struck the cave wall, slid to the floor, gathered in a crooked coil and started singing. Damn.

The rest chimed in. Liars! Not all were rattling. Others were sneaking about, flicking their tongues, seeking a hiding place to strike from without warning.

He knew their ways. He'd raided dens before, in August, when he was short of cash and the mama's were heavy with dollar-a-tail young and sluggish. They'd sing, sing, sing, from three directions, while one lurked silent in the fourth. Jesse claimed they were devilish smart and Songbird agreed, reading from her Bible where the first sin was committed by the devious snake. Songbird thought Eve wrongfully accused. First Woman did not commit First Sin and was not responsible for all that followed. First Sin was committed by the snake when he talked the woman into it.

He shook the package to make sure there weren't any clingers, put the bundle over his head to protect himself from droppers, and strode rapidly out of the cave. He kept to the middle which gave him five feet of clearance to a side. The biggest rattler in there was a six-foot yellow male so he was safe. From his coil the best he could strike was two-thirds of his length.

On a flat rock outside the den he untied the oilskin, revealing a wool blanket, a loaded Winchester, a Case pocketknife, more matches, a candle, and some venison jerky. The shells and matches and food were fresh; he restocked his

371

caches regularly. He rerolled the blanket, tied the roll around the small of his back, pocketed the matches and candle, and started eating the jerky. He would need energy for the hike to come.

From the opposite side of the ridge and below him came the sounds of a truck breaknecking down the dug road. Somebody from MacEwen's crew going for help. Get Doc Buckley to stitch him up and bring the fresh one around. MacEwen was Irish and had their luck. He'd swung sideways goin' out the door and the knife point missed his backbone. Damn him. Took his breeder and killed his dogs. He heard the shots and yelps on the way to the cave. Changed his plans some.

That truck was going for help to hunt him. They expected their hounds to run him down. Well, one of his caches held some poison. Now that his dogs were dead he could use it.

His attention turned to rustlings under the rock, the buzzing around him. They'd hunt him like these snakes were doin'. Find his scent. Track him. Kill him.

Fat chance. He'd wade the Longstar Branch to its source then cross Blackwolf to the Bear Wallow. There was a low cave near there, a catamount den Saul and Jesse cleaned out, that ran *under* Bear Mountain to the falls. Even if they tracked him that far none of those lillylivers would ever follow him into a cave. Only MacEwen, when he was able, or Bower in his prime.

There were plenty of provisions and a place to rest behind the falls. Noisy but you got used to it. He'd hole up and heal up and then cross the marsh and head northcountry to Kinzua.

But first he had to get that money. Wouldn't need it for travelin', but he would to buy silence and a woman at Kinzua. The tribe made allowances if you were on the run and had money. Had for Saul and Jesse.

———

The songbirds returned to their evening celebration. They had quieted down when Tom appeared. Once he got situated and still they turned up the music. When the music stopped meant the trapper was nearby.

Ain't no such thing as peace and quiet in the woods. Quiet ain't peace, it's danger.

This observation came from Charley Bower who got it from Jesse Porbaugh. The two teamed together in 1905 to track and kill an unbalanced boar bear which frequented Fallbrook's town dump and gradually, Fallbrook, and one day changed from a cute pest to a maneater. Jesse was a leathery old mountain man, Charley a young market hunter. Jesse led and Charley followed. That chase taught Charley a lot about the woods, bears...and Poorbaughs.

When Charley said don't get close to Spike Poorbaugh, he meant it.

But a righteous fury burned hot within Tom, the kind that incinerates fear. He would *not* run from this danger. This time *he* was the danger. He had a task to perform and the end justified the mean. He would give no quarter, take no prisoner, and torment if he could. Right or wrong, fair or foul, close or far, none of that mattered. He would kill Spike Poorbaugh!

Tom prayed for the music to end, for tranquility to begin, and it did. This time his prayer was answered. The woods grew still. The trapper was there. Somewhere.

The stillness was broken by the flapping of wings. A pair of doves burst out of the laurel and whistled down the switchbacks. They'd been flushed out of a stunted hemlock to Tom's right. Next to it stood a high hollow chestnut. Between Tom and the chestnut was a thick screen of tall laurel. Tom could see the upper half of that skeleton of tree, but not the lower. The top was home to a settled swarm of bees which now felt threatened and began sending squadrons out each woodpecker hole. The menace was thirty feet from them and the same number in yards from Tom, camouflaged by the laurel. The bees weaved and trailed between the high bony branches, irritated but not attack-mad like Tom.

373

Tom readied his own stinger, revolving the Krag's safety to OFF. He shouldered the gun and pointed it in the direction of the solitary rock oak that grew on the otherwise barren ledge. He and Mac had rested against that tree after losing Ebenezer and watched a winter storm roll in from the northwest. Today a summer one was blowing in from the same direction. And another one sat there, waiting for Poorbaugh. Once he passed that oak, he was fully exposed. Tom reasoned the trapper would view the valley before heading to his next covert, now he prayed for it.

From behind the screen Tom heard his quarry talking. Talking! Good. The crazy bastard had no idea he was walking into an ambush.

"Hello there bag of money. Wintered pretty good I see. I've come for you...Let's find out if they come for me."

God did answer avenger's prayers! Tom pressed his cheek to the stock, drew a belt-high bead on the oak tree.

Poorbaugh walked right into it, then, with careful steps, ventured out on the ledge.

The front bead left the tree and followed its target. It didn't waver. Poorbaugh carried a rifle in his left hand, a canvas bag in his right. A rolled blanket covered the small of his back. When he stopped, and he had to stop, and the bead split his torso vertically, then settled into the rear sight's vee, and a dark line formed parallel to that blanket...Tom would fire. He was twenty yards away now. The trapper was trapped.

———

When he was a boy he had no fear of heights. He would sit there on the point and look down on the hawks and eagles and dangle his bare feet over the world. Potash Mountain had been timbered and blackberry bushes grew as high as the saplings and laurel. His family'd go up here berryin' and he'd sneak off and sit and eat sweets from his pail and feel the wind tickle his toes. They'd notice he was gone and find him and threaten to switch him good. He didn't want to end up buried next to Blacksnake, did he? He'd plague them and lean way over and peer between his feet and say he didn't see no grave down there, just rocks and trees.

When it was safe Grandmother Songbird or Mother Hannah would switch him good. They feared that edge. Even Father Jesse feared the edge.

One day he dozed off and a bee stung him. He twisted and slipped over the edge. He held on by his arms and screamed, his feet churning for a purchase that wasn't there.

Father Jesse saved him, his cat's eyes wide with fear. He overcame that fear to save his son. He transmitted that fear too. That time Jesse switched him good. Then he switched Songbird and Hannah. Samuel was the last male Poorbaugh, the women ought to take better care of him.

He never lost his attraction for high places. But the edges made him dizzy and his loins tingle. He kept away from the edges.

He stopped ten feet short of the brink and looked northwest toward town and Bloss Mountain. From that direction trouble generally came. This evening was no exception – lights flashed throughout the northern half of Steam Valley. The whites from Bloss Mountain were lightning flashes. The reds below town were police cars. All were coming his way.

He then looked below him, to the places under the evening shadow of Caleb's Rock. It didn't have very long, that shadow. The storm or nightfall would soon snuff it. He expected the storm to get there first. Storms, when coming, always preceded the dark. There was no activity in Buttonwood but a set of red lights was getting close to the turnoff to Cole's. And MacEwen's truck was parked at Mort Fessler's.

The red lights were much closer than he'd expected. How'd they get here so fast?

His own thinkin' was bad! The whole crew didn't come to his cabin. MacEwen sent someone for help after he drove by with the girl! Then sent a man in that one-ton to lead the help in.

But it should be parked at the Longsdorf gate, not at Mort's. Why go to Mort's?

The switchbacks! Ambush!

The realization struck him the instant the bullet did.

His vest flap billowed and the impact propelled him to the edge. He flailed his arms, let go of the rifle and money. Both dropped over the side. He teetered and stayed. The shot echoed off Laurel and Blackwolf and Steam, then diminished, crackling back and forth down the hillsides fronting Packhorse Run.

Spike Poorbaugh stood on the point, trembling, purgatory one step away. He'd screamed for Jesse the last time. He screamed for Jesse again.

He heard the unmistakable snap of a bolt slamming a second shell home. He kept his back to the sound, expecting a second shot to ram him off the ledge. He closed his eyes. The shot didn't come.

Hope. A chance for survival. He reached across his stomach for the knife and something got in his way. He opened his eyes and looked. His vest smoldered and a mushroom of torn flesh protruded from his stomach. Flesh and...wool. The blanket tatters absorbed what it could then released a stream of blood.

Backshot. Gutshot maybe. Maybe not. Still standing. Still alive. He took a step backwards, giving him two steps from the edge. He pulled his knife and turned to face his adversary. He was unsteady. From the shock of the bullet or the gush of blood, he couldn't tell. There were ferns and herbs to staunch blood but he had to get off the ledge, get past...Donachy!

The big kid strode purposefully out of the laurel and past the rock oak. Had Bower's Cuban War gun with the bayonet fixed. He wasn't one bit scared of heights or him.

So the cat was going to play with his wounded mouse, was he? Well, maybe he'd get close.

He did.

Cocky kid! Why didn't that shale rock let loose under him? He looked into Donachy's eyes and saw the brutal determination of a revenge killer. Their gaze held. He felt then the torment of Blacksnake as he was backed off the point by the panther. The Bear Clan had failed to avenge Blacksnake and there was no one left to avenge him.

He would live! He would knock the gun aside with his left and slash high with his right. Then push Donachy off the point.

He glanced to his bowie to see if the cutting edge was inside and it was, but in that instant, the boy stuck him, run him through.

He couldn't get air!

With a grunt the boy lifted him and he squirmed and slashed vainly with the bowie. Then Donachy shook him. He dropped the bowie. There was searing wrenching pain and he couldn't breathe. Then he was lowered back to his feet and held up, impaled. Again their eyes met. The cat had finished with his prey. Donachy shoved the gun and him backward, then held firm. He felt himself slide off the blade and into space.

He turned face down and his eyes widened and his body sprayed blood as the rocks and trees rushed up at him. His horror lasted until impact. Only then did his spirit leave him.

Before the storm there came wailing. Wailing from the sirens in the valley, wailing from the woman keening over Bud Cole, and wailing from kindred spirits riding point on Brother Westwind. The spirits would wail forever.

Chapter 52 – Farewells

The valedictorian of the class of '55 leaned against the bus stop bench at Evie's. His duffel, his brother's actually, lay on the bench, absorbing a patch of morning dew. His pickup was parked by the store, the keys in the ignition. Joe would pick it up after work and use it until he and Carol agreed on a car.

This was the best place to wait. Evie didn't open 'til eight on Monday. And little Buttonwood awoke slow after school let out. He could be by himself, leave without fanfare. The stops at Fallbrook and the Turkey Ranch were too busy. He didn't want to be seen by a group right now, didn't want his apprehension to show, didn't want to be pointed out as the boy who shot that dreadful Spike Poorbaugh.

He'd done more than that and felt no regret. Still felt rage when he thought of the things the trapper had done. The coroner told Roby Tucker and Squire Hayes that it hadn't been a clean kill. The main puncture wound could not have come from the broken branch of a white oak. The boy knew more and done more than he was telling. One of the deputies reported seeing Charley Bower remove a bloody bayonet from the Krag.

The sheriff said it didn't matter. Providence determined that both vengeance and justice were served. Who were they to question Providence? There were some facts they didn't have to know. Tom saved the county the cost of a trial and the state a high electric bill. Poorbaugh deserved the death he got. Personally, he hoped it had been a slow one.

Tom wanted Poorbaugh to rot there, wedged in the tree with the bones of his dogs. The moneybag was found, intact, stuck in the branches of the second oak, and the rifle was found under the third. The knife was not found. The rifle lay broken on top of a pile of stones, supposedly the marker to the Indian boy's grave. They could cover Poorbaugh with the same stones, said Tom. The Indian was done with them.

The Squire said no.

The sheriff found Sedalia's Bible. In it she had listed the names of the Poorbaugh's and where they buried their dead. So they wrapped Samuel Poorbaugh in canvas, weighted him with a log chain, and buried him like a sailor at sea. In the bog. The Squire read from Sedalia's Bible. Tom thought it a waste of good tarp, chain, and scripture; but out of respect for the Squire, kept quiet. The Squire obviously carried his own secrets about Samuel "Spike" Poorbaugh and buried them with him in a quicksand grave.

Before the internment they dragged the bog and brought up the body of Jim Morningstar. Now the four that had died lay in their family plots. Tom prayed for three to rest peacefully.

———

A distant saw revved up then got down to business on the top of Blackwolf. Soon it was followed by another. Luke was falling. Joe was bucking. They were now a father-son team and for an instant Tom felt a twinge of envy. But it had been his decision to go. Luke was crew boss this week. Tom wondered if Joe would ever achieve his dad's skill in the woods.

Starting today Joe had two jobs. After logging all day he went to Raker's farm and Carol and the evening milking; the sequence, of course, determined by Carol. The Raker's had stuck a ring in Joe's nose but he didn't mind. He was getting paid and laid regular. Was there a better life for a high school graduate? They had set their wedding date for mid-July, seven weeks hence, after the first cutting of hay and before the county fair, and when Tom could return to sing at their wedding.

He'd sung a lot lately: Wednesday at Baccalaureate, Friday at graduation, Saturday at Mac and Julie's wedding, and yesterday for Aunt K's recital at the Brick Church. He figured he was done with solos for awhile.

Saturday the MacEwen's said their goodbyes. Sunday he said his. But Mac and Julie would only be gone a week. Tom wasn't sure how long he'd be.

Julie looked absolutely beautiful at her wedding. So flushed and happy. Hell, Mac looked flushed and happy. But Tom found his attention wandering to Nan, who stood near her sister, holding on to Danny. Tom envied Danny.

He watched a new friendship begin too. Missy Morningstar brought her twins. The girls were awful taken by the devil-may-care Will Pierce, all three of them.

And Charley Bower caught a stern rebuke from Aunt K, whose prized punch mysteriously acquired the bite of hard cider. Just followin' the path of Jesus, explained Charley, dipping a second glass for himself and a third for Reverend Klinger.

————

The tannery whistle blew and bounced from hill to hill, Fallbrook's towncrier announcing another day for Steam Valley. Seven o'clock and all is well! Shift break. If you aren't at the plant you should be going home from it. If you don't work there you're either rich or a fool. The world revolves around the sun and the factory and the factory is more predictable. You only toil eight hours at the factory. And there's always work. Days the sun don't show the whistle will still blow.

A nervous Squeaky started at the Tannery today. A desk job. A seven to three job. A good-paying job. Squeak's dad was Pemberton's barber. Lundy Barbano's position was still open; did he know of a young man good with figures? Harold Fabel, Sr. told him he sure did. The crafty old man knew Squeak was planning on business school, knew Squeak was sharp. Recommended he learn on the job instead a lot of useless theory. Tom bet Squeak would never get to college.

Pemberton kept things running after Bud Cole's death. Just as he had after the deaths of Reuben and Zebulon. Of the three, Benjamin had vexed him most, he said. Made him

380

old. Third generations sometimes have too much to prove. Benjamin had his faults, but he died protecting the fourth generation and he died brave. Zeb and Rube would be proud.

Pemberton recognized the union, sold the milk plant to the co-op, bought the Fall Brook Line, and chose the dynasty's successor – Delia Cole. He did this all in one month. He was in a hurry, he said. He wanted Delia to have a clean start; he wouldn't be around to pass the reins to Amanda.

The loafer's bench worried. Pemberton was talking dying and the town's two largest businesses, the bank and the tannery, were now run by women. Why the worry? said Pemberton. Those two firms were *started* by a woman.

Tom was there when Frank Sawyer relayed Pemberton's message to the Saturday night crowd. The reception was over. Mac and Julie were on their way to Niagara Falls. Tom sat there within the smoke and gossip and stories and felt the camaraderie one last time. He left at closing realizing the town's, and the valley's, legacy was not the Cole's but Lady Louisa's. A legacy that began with a farmer's daughter, a logger, and a pair of outlaws.

So things were different, but that was to be expected because change was the norm. Expected, not always accepted. He'd noticed a different attitude toward him now. The old familiarity was gone. He had been tainted by the violence against Spike Poorbaugh.

Word got out that he had made Spike Poorbaugh pay. He had a hardness in him, that Tom. Remember the game? He'd made Bud Cole pay too. Big Mike hadn't been that way. He was easy-going, gentle. Tom looked it but he wasn't. Must 'a got it from his mother's side; Mac could be hard, mighty hard, you know. Maybe they'd mellow, the half-brothers Donachy and MacEwen.

Maybe not, thought Tom.

————

A car southbound, slowed and turned up the lane to the schoolhouse. A late-model cream-colored car. Abigail.

She hadn't acknowledged him standing there. It was a tad foggy. She was probably too preoccupied with her own thoughts to notice.

She'd grown out of that some, the last six months especially. She'd gotten involved and accepted and made friendships that would last. Her kids loved her. Minded her too. The school board and Mr. Bates were pleased with that. They weren't always pleased with her spunk but recognized she was scrapping for her kids and her school. Danny said she was the best teacher he ever had and wondered why she wasn't at the wedding – Miss Whalen always went to the things her kids were in.

This was true. If there was a first communion, a scout or 4-H event, a sick kid, ... Abigail was there. She spent a lot of time with Amanda. Even talked Sully Thompson into an unscheduled and unauthorized bus trip to the hospital, a place only sick kids were allowed to go. Got herself in popular trouble which is best kind to get into. She helped Amanda, and Delia, through a very difficult time. She stopped in to see Mac, found Julie there, wished them well and bragged up Danny. Brightest kid she ever had, she said, and the handsomest. Whatever she meant to say to Mac remained unsaid. She got her contract renewed for the fifth grade at the new grade school. Aunt K said she turned it down.

Yesterday, while Tom was saying his goodbyes, she was saying hers. Their paths hadn't crossed. Until now.

Tom glanced at his watch. Ten minutes. Time for one last visit. He crossed 15 and started up the drive.

The globe lights came on. Through the drawn shades Tom could see her blurred figure make one final slow pass around her room. Her car was running. The back seat was crammed with suitcases and file boxes. She wasn't staying long.

Then the schoolbell rang. Then ran again. A displaced bat made an erratic circle around the schoolhouse then lit upside down under the eve of the porch roof. Through the wornout door whose screen always bowed toward recess came a frustrated "Oh, damn."

382

Tom mounted the porch steps and opened the door. The catch spring stretched and creaked and announced his presence.

Abigail stood on a tall stepladder placed under the bell-tower. She was wearing a tan cotton dress and brown pumps and the legs in between were very nice. She had the bellrope pulled tight and was sawing on it with a utility knife. Ike McFee's eighty-year-old rope was being cranky and difficult.

She looked down when the door opened, lost her concentration and hold, and the bell rang again.

Tom laughed. "Don't want anyone to sleep in, do you?"

She accepted his kidding with a warm smile. She was plainly glad to see him. "I've been ringing this thing for the past ten months," she said. "I guess one more day won't matter."

"Use some help?"

Abigail examined the little dent she'd made, sighed, and said, "Yes."

Tom helped her down, took the knife and climbed to where his waist was even with the top platform of the ladder. He slackened the rope, bent the uppermost section across the platform and pressed down hard with the knife. The rope separated cleanly.

Abigail, watching, said, "I should have thought of that."

Tom knotted the cut ends, coiled the freed section, and climbed down. He placed the knife on a nearby desk and handed Abigail her rope.

The first thing she did was smell it.

"Always smelled like hemp rope to me," he said.

"Smells like school to me. But to Evie it smells of pipe tobacco."

"Probably did once, then faded. But not for Evie. I don't think good memories ever fade."

"What smells do you remember, Tom?"

"Oh...My mom's hair. My dad's hands. Aunt K's sachet."

"Know what I remember, Tom?"

Tom looked at her closely and waited. Her blue eyes glistened.

"Mac's face after he shaves."

Here we go, thought Tom. He glanced down at his watch. Five minutes.

"I lost him, didn't I?"

Tom took his time. Weighed the impact of truth against tact and decided truth was best. He spoke gently. "You never had him, Abigail. Not really."

She bit her lip and turned away.

Tom admonished himself. He *was* hard sometimes.

She turned back. Smiled wanly. Closed her glistening eyes and smelled the rope again. She had long, delicate eyelashes. When she looked up she was composed. She handed him the rope. "Would you cut a length for me?"

Tom uncoiled a three-foot section, laid it over the desk, and again cut the rope cleanly. Cut into the desk too. Added to its inked and leaded and crayoned scars. Oh well, the school and everything in it was to be auctioned off soon. Replaced by a modern building and "modern" stuff. Twentieth century stuff.

Tom reknotted the cut ends and handed the two ropes to Abigail. She took them and thanked him. Then her gaze left and wandered around her room. "I'm going to miss this place," she said.

"Where are you headed?" he asked.

"My parents' beach house for the summer. Grad school in the fall. How about you?"

Just then a horn blared loud and insistent on 15. Tom opened a window blind to see a Greyhound idling along the curb.

"That bus!" he said, and tore out and off the screen door.

He shouted back to her. "Goodbye, Abigail Whalen!"

She answered. "Fare well, Tom Donachy."

He hadn't told her where he was going. She'd find out from Evie. She thought she knew. At his age and this time of year there was one predictable destination. College would have to wait for Tom Donachy.

The bus driver was patient. It was early and he was ahead of schedule. There was no one to complain. His only passenger was a seabound sailor who was asleep already. He'd ridden his bus before.

The driver recognized the signs. The bench with the lonely duffel. No rider in sight but obviously near. A young man saying a last goodbye. Then rushing aboard and taking mental pictures from a side window until he couldn't take anymore, memorizing for a lifetime permanent pictures of home.

A young man going off to soldier. Somewhere.

Epilogue – The General

Lycoming County, PA – May 1985

The sun broke slow over Steam Mountain, casting first rays on the high crag that was Caleb's rock and the solitary oak that grew from it. A man stood beside the gnarled oak, a great bear of a man, craggy like the cliff face and tough like the oak.

He surveyed a shared domain, for most of the wooded, fog-streaked expanse before him was deeded to the King's Arrow Timber Company. His, and his brother's, company.

A hen turkey made a plaintive call from Blackwolf swamp. She was immediately answered by a deep-voiced gobbler on Potash. His gobble echoed off the peaks and coursed the valley. She's mine, he was saying. I'm on my way.

But "she" was a camo-clad hunter, an expert with a call. It was spring gobbler season and the ardent suitor was headed into an ambush. Mac was low in the swamp and he was high on the ridge. Their boys were in between.

It seemed foolproof. One puffed-up exposed bird whose mind was on sex, versus four patient concealed hunters whose minds were on him.

But so far, they were the fools. That canny old gobbler had eluded them four days in a row. He was beginning to wonder if his brother really could talk turkey. Maybe that answering gobble was a laugh. Maybe he wasn't coming. Maybe they were his sport and not the other way around. And maybe they just weren't concentrating hard enough.

The General knew he wasn't.

He really hadn't come to hunt this week. He came to make a decision.

Caleb's Rock had changed little in thirty years. The point was sharper, the oak thicker, the laurel higher, and the dead chestnut hollower. Below him, the oaks and sumacs rustled with the wind that rose with the morning. Seemingly, they hadn't changed at all.

The oaks and sumacs were where the boys were.

It bothered him more than them...to be near the death-place of the Indian Boy and Spike Poorbaugh. In his final years Charley Bower suggested a connection between the two. Sometimes, the wind blows funny. The mountains are haunted and the haunts are related. Charley was very old and in a veterans home when he said it. His mind wandered and folks didn't pay his stories much mind.

Then last summer Luke and Hattie Ballard toured the Kinzua country. They got friendly with a Seneca guide who inquired where they were from. He'd heard of Steam Valley. Some of his tribe went there long ago – white name of Poorbaugh...

The rising sun and breeze dissipated the low-lying fog, and the pastelled view, as it appeared, revealed the most significant changes had occurred in the valley. Route 15 split into a four lane at Big Curve now, and that wisp of smoke to the east was breakfast cooking at the Turkey Ranch. The truck stop was an even busier place today, boasting a motel, convenience store and gas station.

In some respects the scenery was less severe than the fifties. Mort Fessler's junkyard and buildings were gone, replaced by Mac and Julie's sprawling ranch estate. And a mile south, on the exposed flank of the same foothill, The Lady and her pillars gleamed. Louisa's home had been restored by he and Nan, mostly Nan.

He had been away too much.

Too many crises at the Pentagon. Too many skirmishes abroad. And, in his career, two long wars. The cold one they won, the hot one they didn't.

Danny Spencer had been a prisoner in the hot war. That had been an agonizing wait for Julie and Mac. And true agony for the tortured navy flier. But Danny survived and recovered, and went from fighters to jetliners, married a stewardess, and made Julie one of the most beautiful grand-mothers in the world.

Nan said he needed to spend time at home. Be a father before he became a grandfather. Get close to his boy like

Mac got close to Danny. Their oldest would soon be leaving for college. You can't make up for lost time after they're lost, and Julie almost lost Danny. He was already a general. He only had room for two more stars. Refuse this promotion and stay home and work with your brother. Earn that King's Arrow profit check we've been banking for thirty years.

He objected at first. He was still young, the youngest general. He had impeccable credentials. He was West Point, a Ranger, a combat veteran. He was a natural leader, had education and experience, a combination in short supply in the military. His country needed him.

Nan's response was he'd done his share and more. The military did not need him now. His family did.

Up here, he felt it. A new calling. He'd brushed it off all week as one of those midlife yearnings that come with a change of pace and scenery. But the feeling persisted, grew stronger. The woods beckoned. The Big Woods beckoned.

Of course, the great trees of Bear Hollow were still there. What were a few decades to centuries-old trees? But these times weren't without their peril. There were harsh chemicals in the air and increased radiation from the sun. And new strains of insects that could defoliate the tallest and broadest and oldest of trees. The scientists told them the steam of Steam Valley was a shield against the threats in the sun and the air, but if they didn't eliminate the bugs, the shield would turn into a shroud.

Mac, the forester, struggled between the forces of nature and the forces of man. How could he protect the venerable, now vulnerable, trees? Was there a natural solution? A bug that eats the leaf-eating bugs? Or would he have to resort to an artificial solution, like spraying? What future ramifications could that have? Or was the best decision no decision?

Whatever course of action was taken, one thing was sure–this time they had the resources to combat the threat to the trees.

He wasn't sure where he'd fit in. Mac and Julie ran the company. Joe Ballard was woods boss, and a good one. They had room, they said. There was plenty to do. But they weren't the ones that had to slow down. He was. Mac and Luke, sixty-two and seventy-two, still teamed up to cut a load of logs or build a woods road. He and Joe should too. Joe could teach him a trick or two about falling a tree.

Joe was a single man now, had just finished paying off his daughter's college loans. Carol had had an affair with a big-talking farm equipment dealer and asked Joe for a divorce so she could marry the other man. Joe balked, said he'd stay for the kids, but it was Carol's farm and he had to go. Carol and her new husband then mortgaged the farm to expand the dealership. The venture failed, the farm failed, the second marriage failed, and the timber company bought the farm to save a place for Harry and Becky and Carol and Joe's kids. Carol wanted Joe to come back, but Joe only came to visit his kids.

Squeaky had stayed too. He married Sally Tate, raised five children, and assumed Pemberton's role at the tannery. But he wouldn't be staying much longer. Harold Fabel, Jr., CEO of Cole Enterprises and board chairman of Merchant's and Farmers Bank, was leaving the business world for the ministry. The tannery would be guided by Amanda Cole.

Poorbaugh's violence against her, and Danny's struggle as a POW, had profound impacts on Amanda. She withdrew and rebelled, eventually joined the counter-culture and feminist movements and wandered, just wandered. She kept in touch with Squeaky, who sent her money. She came home when Danny did. Danny left but Amanda stayed and later married her former classmate, Hank Broadwater. She kept her last name. This caused some consternation among the old-fashioned: Hank was Superintendent of Schools and Amanda president of the PTA.

Amanda's mother never remarried. After Squeaky took control of the tannery and while Amanda was God-knows-where, Delia traveled. Squeaky also sent her money. There were rumors of involvements and suitors but none ever followed her home. She spent more time at the mansion now, and had recently sold all the Cole land holdings to the timber company. She'd made the deal with Julie, and, like Julie, was a beautiful grandmother.

He recalled an observation made by Charley Bower years before. The nail keg boys were discussing age and pretty women. "You know you're gettin' older," said Charley, "when you start noticin' the mothers instead of the daughters." The general smiled. Charley had a salty way with truth. That transition was a gradual one. Right now he enjoyed noticing both...

The sun topped Steam Mountain and the purple shadow darkening the east flank of the valley shrunk past Buttonwood, and the school's belltower gleamed porcelain like The Lady.

It should. Joe had applied the same paint. Two resolute alumni, Nan Donachy and Julie MacEwen, had purchased and restored the school, converting it into a local library. The librarian was a pretty young woman, single, and employed by the timber company. Joe, who never took a book home in high school, had been doing an awful lot of reading lately. Carol said he was too old for that nonsense – why she was younger than their daughter Patty!

His buddies didn't think it was nonsense and doubted that the rugged Joe was too old.

The PTA was organizing a reunion of the classmates of the one-room school. One teacher was still living and she was coming. She was a Ph.D, a college president, author of books on reading, and also went by her own last name. Abigail Whalen had never married and kept in touch through Ruby Broadwater, current chairperson of the Fallbrook Ladies' Garden Club.

Ruby, earthy and gossipy as ever, said Abigail and Delia were waiting for Julie to tire of Mac, that handsome silver-haired devil. Just kidding, she'd add, but Nan knew better.

The years had been kind to Mac. He and Julie made the perfect team, in many ways fulfilling the legacies of Jacob Miller and Louisa Longsdorf. They had managed and invested well. They bought Fred Sheafer's mill and two other mills and thousands of acres of timberland. North American hardwoods were in great demand and would be for years to come. Synthetics couldn't take the place of wood. People drew comfort from wood.

Besides Danny, Mac and Julie had three children, two boys and a girl. The two oldest were grown and educated and careered and married. The youngest was standing watch under the Three Oaks right now.

He guessed the years had been kind to him too. Abigail wasn't the only Ph.D and Mac wasn't the only war hero. He had a beautiful, caring wife, four healthy children, and a demanding high-profile career. He had two houses, one in D.C. and one here, money in the bank, a vested pension, and a half-interest in an immensely profitable company with no debt. By the standards set by the fifties and the eighties he was a success.

So why was he here? Just what was success? It defied logic – to be so full and so empty at the same time.

Nan said they had two houses but only one home.

They had seen the world, but never found another place where they belonged. It hadn't mattered to him. He had his work, his career. Nan had *his* work, and *their* family. Consequently, the kids were closer to their mother. They confided in her. They conversed with him.

This week, he talked to his brother about it. There was a point where the brother's paths had diverged. As he had acquired a reserve, his brother had lost his. Mac's children, his grandchildren, his nieces and nephews, crawled all over him. What Mac had acquired was a grandfather's knack of getting to the heart of a matter, especially a family one. Count your blessings, he said, and get to know them.

Gather Nan and the kids and backpack into Bear Hollow, he added. He and Luke kept a trail open to the Boss Tree. You haven't sung in a long time, Tom. Strap on your guitar and leave that portable phone at home.

He leaned against the sturdy oak. It was true. He hadn't sung in a long time...

The sun rose full over Steam Mountain and the shadows and pastels of early morning waned away. He heard voices from the switchbacks and straightened and turned toward the sound. The sun glinted off ivory that flashed and moved with their excited voices. Had it not been for the reflection and the noise, he would not have been aware of the boys. Their green camo blended perfectly with the laurel.

Finally, they appeared. Two tall boys. His oldest and Mac's youngest. One blonde and green-eyed. The other blonde and hazel-eyed. Mac's boy took after him. His boy took after his mother, thank God.

The boys were named after their grandfathers. His boy Mike was carrying the object that had caught the sunbeam. As they drew closer, he saw what it was – a shed antler – the massive right antler of a mighty whitetail. Three feet long. Six high ivory-tipped tines.

Still hiding there…in the sumacs.

His son, whose gaze Nan said would soon be level with his father's, handed him the heavy antler. He did it easily – he was a strong boy.

"I knew you'd want this, Dad. Let's go back and find the other."

Their eyes met, and the General's misted, for they *were* the same level.

He took his son's gift and decided he would no longer be a general.

THE END

Coming Soon!

MY BROTHER METHUSELAH

The new novel by

ROD COCHRAN

Available from Infinity

This book is the first account of Jared of El, a roguish long-lived adventurer who wanders through the Old, New and Lost Testaments. The story source is Genesis 2-7, six chapters which describe First Earth, First Men and the Fall of First Men. The timeline spans 01 A.E. to 1656 A.E., the years After Eden to the Flood. During this time parts of First Earth become civilized. There is conflict between the Sethite Land of El and the Cainite Land of Nod.

Jared, born in 987 A.E., is the youngest brother of Methuselah, the seventh and last king of El and the longest-lived of the named antediluvian patriarchs (969 years). Their father was Enoch, the Holy Man, who did not die "because God took him away" (Genesis 5:24). Jared says Watchers (righteous angels) escorted Enoch to Eden where he walks with The Angel of the Lord. Jared, whose mother, a daughter of Eve, died having him and who was raised by his brother, thinks God can be harsh sometimes.

Enoch was also a prophet and burdened his sons with prophetic names. Jared means "Preserver of the Ages." Methuselah means "When he dies, It will come." Methuselah died the year of the Flood. These elements of the story are not made up.

First earth is a paradox – a wild, wonderful, advanced, primitive, depraved and violent place. Jared loves it, God does not. Jared and his gifted Sethite brethren build farms and cities and ships and pyramids, battle Cainites and giants and goatlegs and Nephilim. Myth springs from some ancient truth, the most ancient being the lost world recorded in Genesis 6, where the "Sons of God (fallen angels) went to the daughters of men and had children by them," where there were "Heroes of Old, men of renown." To my knowledge no modern writer has ever written of the antediluvian heroes and the mysterious race called the Nephilim. Could their exploits be detailed in The Wars of the Lord and The Book of Jasher? These books, long lost, are mentioned in Numbers, Joshua, and II Samuel. Could Jared have written or helped write them? Could they be discovered along with their long-lived author? My objective as Jared's "compiler" is to attract readers to their Bibles, for them discover a wild world that truly did happen. I pray their interest is piqued and they keep on reading...my books and their Bibles.

Author's Note: *My Brother Methuselah* was accepted for review by *The Writer's Edge*, a newsletter used by Christian publishers as a source of manuscripts.

To Order Bear Hollow from Infinity:

Fax: (610) 519-0261

Phone: Call toll free (877) 289-2665
          Local Phone (610) 520-2500

Postal Orders: Copy and mail this form to:
                          Infinity Publishing
                          519 West Lancaster Avenue
                          Haverford, PA 19041-1413

Email: Info@infinitypublishing.com
Website: www.buybooksontheweb.com

Name_____

Address_____

City_____ State_____Zip_____

Phone_____Fax_____

E-Mail_____

Payment: Check   Money Order   Credit Card
                                          Visa   Master Card

Card Number:_____

Name on Card:_____Exp. Date:_____

Cost: $21.95

Shipping & Handling: Include $4.50 for the first book, $1.00 for each
additional book (free shipping on orders of 20 or more!!)

Sales Tax: Please add 6% for books shipped to Pennsylvania addresses

Quantity discounts are available!

To customize books for your organization or company, contact Infinity
publishing at (610) 520-2500